UN

Before Dor's eye━━━━━━━━━━━━━med to appear, staring down at him.

"Where are you now?" Dor asked the vision.

The face frowned. "I am being held captive in a medieval castle in Mundania. I have no magic power here. You must bring me magic."

"But I can't do that," Dor protested. "Magic isn't something a person can carry, especially not into Mundania!"

"You must use the aisle to rescue me."

"What aisle?" Dor asked.

"The centaur aisle," Trent answered. Then his face vanished.

Dor had never heard of the centaur aisle or any other magic that could be taken to Mundania. But now he had to find it somehow—or be forever stuck with the fate that King Trent's vanishing had wished upon him.

Also by Piers Anthony
Published by Ballantine Books:

SPLIT INFINITY

BLUE ADEPT

Other Novels of Xanth

A SPELL FOR CHAMELEON

THE SOURCE OF MAGIC

CASTLE ROOGNA

CENTAUR AISLE

Piers Anthony

A Del Rey Book

BALLANTINE BOOKS • NEW YORK

The author thanks Jerome Brown for the notion of the "Spelling Bee" used in the first chapter, and the many other fans whose letters of encouragement have caused the Xanth trilogy to be expanded. May those who feel Xanth is sexist have pleasure in this novel, wherein Mundania is shown to be worse.

A Del Rey Book.
Published by Ballantine Books

Library of Congress Catalog Card Number: 81-67841

ISBN 0-345-29770-9

Manufactured in the United States of America

First Ballantine Books Edition: January 1982

Cover art by Michael Whelan

Contents

XANTH

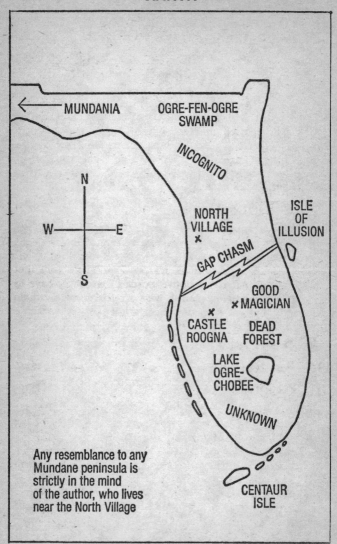

MUNDANIA ←

OGRE-FEN-OGRE
SWAMP

INCOGNITO

N
W   E
S

NORTH
VILLAGE
×

ISLE
OF
ILLUSION

GAP CHASM

GOOD
× MAGICIAN

×
CASTLE
ROOGNA

DEAD
FOREST

LAKE
OGRE-
CHOBEE

UNKNOWN

Any resemblance to any
Mundane peninsula is
strictly in the mind
of the author, who lives
near the North Village

CENTAUR
ISLE

Chapter 1. Spelling Bee

Dor was trying to write an essay, because the King had decreed that any future monarchs of Xanth should be literate. It was an awful chore. He knew how to read, but his imagination tended to go blank when challenged to produce an essay, and he had never mastered conventional spelling.

"The Land of Xanth," he muttered with deep disgust.

"What?" the table asked.

"The title of my awful old essay," Dor explained dispiritedly. "My tutor Cherie, on whom be a muted anonymous curse, assigned me a one-hundred-word essay telling all about Xanth. I don't think it's possible. There isn't that much to tell. After twenty-five words I'll probably have to start repeating. How can I ever stretch it to a whole hundred? I'm not even sure there are that many words in the language."

"Who wants to know about Xanth?" the table asked. "I'm bored already."

"I *know* you're a board. I guess Cherie, may a hundred curse-burrs tangle in her tail, wants to know."

"She must be pretty dumb."

Dor considered. "No, she's infernally smart. All centaurs are. That's why they're the historians and poets and tutors of Xanth. May all their high-IQ feet founder."

"How come they don't rule Xanth, then?"

"Well, most of them don't do magic, and only a Magician can rule Xanth. Brains have nothing to do with it—and neither do essays." Dor scowled at his blank paper.

"Only a Magician can rule any land," the table said smugly. "But what about you? You're a Magician, aren't you? Why aren't you King?"

"Well, I will be King, some day," Dor said defensively,

1

aware that he was talking with the table only to postpone a little longer the inevitable struggle with the essay. "When King Trent, uh, steps down. That's why I have to be educated, he says." He wished all kinds of maledictions on Cherie Centaur, but never on King Trent.

He resumed his morose stare at the paper, where he had now printed THU LANNED UV ZANTH. Somehow it didn't look right, though he was sure he had put the TH's in the right places.

Something tittered. Dor glanced up and discovered that the hanging picture of Queen Iris was smirking. That was one problem about working in Castle Roogna; he was always under the baleful eye of the Queen, whose principal business was snooping. With special effort, Dor refrained from sticking out his tongue at the picture.

Seeing herself observed, the Queen spoke, the mouth of the image moving. Her talent was illusion, and she could make the illusion of sound when she wanted to. "You may be a Magician, but you aren't a scholar. Obviously spelling is not your forte."

"Never claimed it was," Dor retorted. He did not know what the word "forte" meant—perhaps it was a kind of small castle—but whatever it meant, spelling was not there. He did not much like the Queen, and the feeling was mutual, but both of them were constrained by order of the King to be reasonably polite to one another. "Surely a woman of your extraordinary talents has more interesting things to do than peek at my stupid essay," he said. Then, grudgingly, he added: "Your Majesty."

"Indeed I do," the picture agreed, its background clouding. She had of course noted the pause before he gave her title; it was not technically an insult, but the message was clear enough. The cloud in the picture had become a veritable thunderstorm, with jags of lightning shooting out like sparks. She would get back at him somehow. "But you would never get your homework done if not supervised."

Dor grimaced into the surface of the table. She was right on target there!

Then he saw that ink had smeared all across his essay-paper, ruining it. With an angry grunt he picked it up—and the ink slid off, pooled on the surface of the table, bunched together, sprouted legs, and scurried away. It leaped off the table like a gross bug and puffed into momentary vapor. It had been an illusion. The Queen had gotten back at him already. She could be extraordinarily clever in ugly little ways. Dor could not admit being angry about being fooled—and that made him angrier than ever.

"I don't see why anyone has to be male to rule Xanth," the picture said. That was of course a chronic sore point with the Queen. She was a Sorceress fully as talented as any Magician, but by Xanth law/custom no woman could be King.

"I live in the Land of Xanth," Dor said slowly, voicing his essay as he wrote, ignoring the Queen with what he hoped was insulting politeness. "Which is distinct from Mundania in that there is magic in Xanth and none in Mundania." It was amazing how creative he became when there was a negative aspect to it. He had twenty-three words already!

Dor cracked an eyelid, sneaking a peek at the picture. It had reverted to neutral. Good; the Queen had tuned out. If she couldn't bug him with crawling illusions, she wasn't interested.

But now his inspiration dehydrated. He had an impossible one hundred whole words to do, six times his present total. Maybe five times; he was not particularly apt at higher mathematics either. Four more words, if he counted the title. A significant fraction of the way through, but only a fraction. What a dreary chore!

Irene wandered in. She was King Trent and Queen Iris's daughter, the palace brat, often a nuisance—but sometimes not. It griped Dor to admit it, but Irene was an extremely pretty girl, getting more so, and that exerted an increasing leverage upon him. It made fighting with her awkward. "Hi, Dor," she said, bouncing experimentally. "What are you doing?"

Dor, distracted momentarily by the bounce, lost track of the sharp response he had planned. "Oh, come on," he grumped. "You know your mother got tired of snooping on me, so she assigned you to do it instead."

Irene did not deny it. "Well, *some*body has to snoop on you, dummy. I'd rather be out playing with Zilch."

Zilch was a young sea cow that had been conjured for her fifteenth birthday. Irene had set her up in the moat and used her magic to promote the growth of sturdy wall-flowers to wall off a section of water, protecting Zilch from the moat-monsters while she grazed. Dor regarded Zilch as a great blubbery slob of an animal, but anything that distracted Irene was to some extent worthwhile. She took after her mother in certain annoying ways.

"Go ahead and play with the cow," Dor suggested disparagingly. "I won't tell."

"No, a Princess has to do her duty." Irene never spoke of duty unless it was something she wanted to do anyway. She picked up his essay-paper.

"Hey, give that back!" Dor protested, reaching for it.

"You heard him, snit!" the paper agreed. "Give me back!"

That only made Irene ornery. She backed away, hanging on to the paper, her eyes scanning the writing. Her bosom heaved with barely suppressed laughter. "Oh, say, this is something! I didn't think anybody could misspell 'Mundania' that badly!"

Dor leaped for her, his face hot, but she danced back again, putting the paper behind her. This was her notion of entertainment—teasing him, making him react one way or another. He tried to reach around her—and found himself embracing her, unintentionally.

Irene had always been a cute girl and socially precocious. In recent years nature had rushed to endow her generously, and this was quite evident at close range. Now she was a green-eyed, green-tint-haired—occurring naturally; she did not color her hair—buxom beauty. What was worse, she knew it, and constantly sought new ways to use it to her advantage. Today she was dressed in a green blouse and skirt that accentuated her figure and wore green slippers that enhanced her fine legs and feet. In short, she had prepared well for this encounter and had no intention of letting him write his essay in peace.

She took a deep breath, inflating herself against him. "I'll scream," she breathed in his ear, taunting him.

But Dor knew how to handle her. "I'll tickle," he breathed back.

"That's not fair!" For she could not scream realistically while giggling, and she was hyperticklish, perhaps because she thought it was fashionable for young ladies to be so.

She had heard somewhere that ticklishness made girls more appealing.

Irene's hand moved swiftly, trying to tuck the paper into her bosom, where she knew he wouldn't dare go for it. But Dor had encountered this ploy before, too, and he caught her wrist en route. He finally got his fingers on the essay-paper, for he was stronger than she, and she also deemed it unladylike to fight too hard. Image was almost as important to her as mischief. She let the paper go, but tried yet another ploy. She put her arms around him. "I'll kiss."

But he was ready even for that. Her kisses could change to bites without notice, depending on her mercurial mood. She was not to be trusted, though in truth the close struggle had whetted his appetite for some such diversion. She was scoring on him better than she knew. "Your mother's watching."

Irene turned him loose instantly. She was a constant tease; but in her mother's presence she always behaved angelically. Dor wasn't sure why this was so, but suspected that the Queen's desire to see Irene become Queen after her had something to do with it. Irene didn't want to oblige her mother any more than she wanted to oblige anyone else, and expressing overt interest in Dor would constitute a compromising attitude. The Queen resented Dor because he was a full Magician while her daughter was not, but she was not about to let him make anyone else's daughter Queen. Irene, ironically, did want to be Queen, but also wanted to spite her mother, so she always tried to make it seem that Dor was chasing her while she resisted. The various facets of this cynical game became complex on occasion.

Dor himself wasn't sure how he felt about it all. Four years ago, when he was twelve, he had gone on an extraordinary adventure into Xanth's past and had occupied the body of a grown, muscular, and highly coordinated barbarian. He had learned something about the ways of men and women. Since he had had an opportunity to play with adult equipment before getting there himself, he had an inkling that the little games Irene played were more chancy than she knew. So he stayed somewhat clear, rejecting her teasing advances, though this was not always easy. Sometimes he had strange, wicked dreams, wherein he called one of her bluffs, and it wasn't exactly a bluff, and then the hand of an anonymous censor blotted out a scene of impending fascination.

"Dumbo!" Irene exclaimed irately, staring at the still picture on the wall. "My mother isn't watching us!"

"Got you off my case, though, didn't it?" Dor said smugly. "You want to make like Millie the Ghost, and you don't have the stuff." That was a double-barreled insult, for Millie—who had stopped being a ghost before Dor was born, but retained the identification—was gifted with magical sex appeal, which she had used to snare one of the few Magicians of Xanth, the somber Zombie Master. Dor himself had helped bring that Magician back to life for her, and now they had three-year-old twins. So Dor was suggesting to Irene that she lacked sex appeal and womanliness, the very things she was so assiduously striving for. But it was a hard charge to make stick, because Irene was really not far off the mark. If he ever forgot she was the palace brat, he would be in trouble, for what hidden censor would blot out a dream-turned-real? Irene could be awfully nice when she tried. Or maybe it was when she stopped trying; he wasn't sure.

"Well, you better get that dumb essay done, or Cherie Centaur will step on you," Irene said, putting on a new mood. "I'll help you spell the words if you want."

Dor didn't trust that either. "I'd better struggle through on my own."

"You'll flunk. Cherie doesn't put up with your kind of ignorance."

"I know," he agreed glumly. The centaur was a harsh taskmistress—which was of course why she had been given the job. Had her mate Chester done the tutoring, Dor would have learned much about archery, swordplay, and bare-knuckle boxing, but his spelling would have sunk to amazing new depths. King Trent had a sure hand in delegating authority.

"I know what!" Irene exclaimed. "You need a spelling bee!"

"A what?"

"I'll fetch one," she said eagerly. Now she was in her helpful guise, and this was especially hard to resist, since he did need help. "They are attracted by letter plants. Let me get one from my collection." She was off in a swirl of sweet scent; it seemed she had started wearing perfume.

Dor, by dint of phenomenal effort, squeezed out another sentence. "Everyone in Xanth has his one magic talent; no two are the same," he said as he wrote. Thirteen more words. What a deadly chore!

"That's not true," the table said. "My talent is talking. Lots of things talk."

"You're not a person, you're a thing," Dor informed it brusquely. "Talking isn't your talent, it's mine. I make inanimate things talk."

"Awww . . ." the table said sullenly.

Irene breezed back in with a seed from her collection and an earth-filled flowerpot. "Here it is." In a moment she had the seed planted—it was in the shape of the letter L—and had given it the magic command: "Grow." It sprouted and grew at a rate nature could not duplicate. For that was her talent—the green thumb. She could grow a giant acorn tree from a tiny seed in minutes, when she concentrated, or cause an existing plant to swell into monstrous proportions. Because she could not transform a plant into a totally different creature, as could her father, or give animation to lifeless things, as Dor and the Zombie Master could, she was deemed to be less than a Sorceress, and this had been her lifelong annoyance. But what she could do, she could do well, and that was to grow plants.

The letter plant sent its main stalk up the breadth of a hand. Then it branched and flowered, each blossom in the form of a letter of the alphabet, all the letters haphazardly represented. The flowers emitted a faint, odd odor a bit like ink and a bit like musty old tomes.

Sure enough, a big bee in a checkered furry jacket arrived to service the plant. It buzzed from letter to letter, harvesting each and tucking it into little baskets on its six legs. In a few minutes it had collected them all and was ready to fly away.

But Irene had closed the door and all the windows. "That was my letter plant," she informed the bee. "You'll have to pay for those letters."

"BBBBBB," the bee buzzed angrily, but acceded. It knew the rules. Soon she had it spelling for Dor. All he had to do was say a word, and the bee would lay down its flower-letters to spell it out. There was nothing a spelling bee couldn't spell.

"All right, I've done my good deed for the day," Irene said. "I'm going out and swim with Zilch. Don't let the bee out until you've finished your essay, and don't tell my mother I stopped bugging you, and check with me when you're done."

"Why should I check with you?" he demanded. "You're not my tutor!"

"Because I have to be able to say I nagged you until you got your stupid homework done, idiot," she said sensibly. "Once you clear with me, we're both safe for the day. Got it straight now, knothead?"

Essentially, she was proffering a deal; she would leave him alone if he didn't turn her in for doing it. It behooved him to acquiesce. "Straight, green-nose," he agreed.

"And watch that bee," she warned as she slipped out the door. "It's got to spell each word right, but it won't tell you if you have the wrong word." The bee zoomed for the aperture, but she closed it quickly behind her.

"All right, spelling bee," Dor said. "I don't enjoy this any more than you do. The faster we get through, the faster we both get out of here."

The bee was not satisfied, but buzzed with resignation. It was accustomed to honoring rules, for there were no rules more finicky and senseless than those for spelling words.

Dor read aloud his first two sentences, pausing after every word to get the spelling. He did not trust the bee, but knew it was incapable of misspelling a word, however much it might wish to, to spite him.

"Some can conjure things," he continued slowly, "and others can make a hole, or illusions, or can soar through the air. But in Mundania no one does magic, so it's very dull. There are not any dragons there. Instead there are bear and horse and a great many other monsters."

He stopped to count the words. All the way up to eighty-two! Only eight more to go—no, more than that; his fingers had run out. Twenty-eight to go. But he had already covered the subject. What now?

Well, maybe some specifics. "Our ruler is King Trent, who has reigned for seventeen years. He transforms people into other creatures." There were another seventeen words, bringing the total to—say, it was ninety-nine words! He must have miscalculated before. One more word and he'd be done!

But what one word would finish it? He couldn't think of one. Finally he made a special effort and squeezed out another whole sentence: "No one gets chased here; we fare in peace." But that was nine more words—eight more than he needed. It really hurt him to waste energy like that!

Sigh. There was no help for it. He would have to use the words, now that he had ground them out. He wrote them down as the bee spelled them, pronouncing each carefully so the bee would get it right. He was sure the bee had little or no sense of continuity; it merely spelled on an individual basis.

In a fit of foolish generosity, he fired off four more valuable words: "My tale is done." That made the essay one hundred and twelve words. Cherie Centaur should give him a top grade for that!

"Okay, spelling bee," he said. "You've done your part. You're free, with your letters." He opened the window and the bee buzzed out with a happy "BBBBBB!"

"Now I need to deliver it to my beloved female tutor, may fleas gnaw her coat," he said to himself. "How can I do that without her catching me for more homework?" For he knew, as all students did, that the basic purpose of instruction was not so much to teach young people good things as to fill up all their time unpleasantly. Adults had the notion that juveniles needed to suffer. Only when they had suffered enough to wipe out most of their naturally joyous spirits and innocence were they staid enough to be considered mature. An adult was essentially a broken-down child.

"Are you asking me?" the floor asked.

Inanimate things seldom had much wit, which was why he hadn't asked any for help in his spelling. "No, I'm just talking to myself."

"Good. Then I don't have to tell you to get a paper wasp."

"I couldn't catch a paper wasp anyway. I'd get stung."

"You wouldn't have to catch it. It's trapped under me. The fool blundered in during the night and can't find the way out; it's dark down there."

This was a positive break. "Tell it I'll take it safely out if it'll deliver one paper for me."

There was a mumble as the floor conversed with the wasp. Then the floor spoke to Dor again. "It's a fair sting, it says."

"Very well. Tell it where there's a crack big enough to let it through to this room."

Soon the wasp appeared. It was large, with a narrow waist and fine reddish-brown color: an attractive female of her species, marred only by shreds of dust on her wings. "WWWWWW?" she buzzed, making the dust fly off so that she was completely pretty again.

Dor gave her the paper and opened the window again. "Take this to the lady centaur Cherie. After that you're on your own."

She perched momentarily on the sill, holding the paper. "WWWWWW?" she asked again.

Dor did not understand wasp language, and his friend Grundy the Golem, who did, was not around. But he had a fair notion what the wasp was thinking of. "No, I wouldn't advise trying to sting Cherie. She can crack her tail about like a whip, and she never misses a fly." Or the seat of someone's pants, he added mentally, when someone was foolish enough to backtalk about an assignment. Dor had learned the hard way.

The wasp carried the paper out the window with a satisfied hum. Dor knew it would deliver; like the spelling bee, it had to be true to its nature. A paper wasp could not mishandle a paper.

Dor went out to report to Irene. He found her on the south side of the castle in a bathing suit, swimming with a contented sea cow and feeding the cow handfuls of sea oats she was magically growing on the bank. Zilch mooed when she saw Dor, alerting Irene.

"Hi, Dor—come in swimming!" Irene called.

"In the moat with the monsters?" he retorted.

"I grew a row of blackjack oaks across it to buttress the wallflowers," she said. "The monsters can't pass."

Dor looked. Sure enough, a moat-monster was pacing the line, staying just clear of the blackjacks. It nudged too close at one point and got tagged by a well-swung blackjack. There was no passing those trees!

Still, Dor decided to stay clear. He didn't trust what Zilch might have done in the water. "I meant the monsters on this side," he said. "I just came to report that the paper is finished and off to the tutor."

"Monsters on this side!" Irene repeated, glancing down at herself. "Sic him, Weedles!"

A tendril reached out of the water and caught his ankle. Another one of her playful plants! "Cut that out!" Dor cried, windmilling as the vine yanked at his leg. It was no good; he lost his balance and fell into the moat with a great splash.

"Ho, ho, ho!" the water laughed. "Guess that doused your fire!" Dor struck at the surface furiously with his fist, but it did no good. Like it or not, he was swimming in all his clothes.

"Hey, I just thought of something," Irene called. "That spelling bee—did you define the words for it?"

"No, of course not," Dor spluttered, trying to scramble out of the water but getting tangled in the tendrils of the plant that had pulled him in. Pride prevented him from asking Irene for help, though one word from her would tame the plant.

She saw the need, however. "Easy, Weedles," she said, and the plant eased off. Then she returned to her subject. "There may be trouble. If you used any homonyms—"

"No, I couldn't have. I never heard of them." Weedles was no longer attacking, but each time Dor tried to swim to the bank, the plant moved to intercept him. He had antagonized Irene by his monsters crack, and she was getting back at him mercilessly. She was like her mother in that respect. Sometimes Dor felt the world would be better off if the entire species of female were abolished.

"Different words that sound the same, dunce!" she said with maidenly arrogance. "Different spellings. The spelling bee isn't that smart; if you don't tell it exactly which word—"

"Different spellings?" he asked, experiencing a premonitory chill.

"Like wood and would," she said, showing off her vocabulary in the annoying way girls had. "Wood-tree, would-could. Or isle and aisle, meaning a bit of land in a lake or a cleared space between objects. No connection between the two except they happen to sound the same. Did you use any of those?"

Dor concentrated on the essay, already half forgotten. "I think I mentioned a bear. You know, the fantastic Mundane monster."

"It'll come out bare-naked!" she exclaimed, laughing. "That bee may not be smart, but it wasn't happy about having to work for its letters. Oh, are you ever in trouble, Dor! Wait'll Cherie Centaur reads that paper!"

"Oh, forget it!" he snapped, disgruntled. How many homonyms had he used?

"Bear, bare!" she cried, swimming close and tugging at his clothing. The material, not intended for water, tore readily, exposing half his chest.

"Bare, bare, bare!" he retorted furiously, hooking two fingers into the top of her suit and ripping it down. This material, too, came apart with surprising ease, showing that her body was fully as developed as suggested by the contours of her clothing. Her mother the Queen often made herself pretty through illusion; Irene needed no such enhancement.

"Eeeeek!" she screamed enthusiastically. "I'll get *you!*" And she ripped more of his clothing off, not stopping at his shirt. Dor retaliated, his anger mitigated by his intrigue with the flashes of her that showed between splashes. In a moment they were both thoroughly bare and laughing. It was as if they had done in anger something they had not dared to do by agreement, but had nevertheless wanted to do.

At this point Cherie Centaur trotted up. She had the forepart of a remarkably full-figured woman, and the rearpart of a beautiful horse. It was said that Mundania was the land of beautiful women and fast horses, or maybe vice versa on the adjectives; Xanth was the land where the two were one. Cherie's brown human hair trailed back to rest against her brown equine coat, with her lovely tail matching. She wore no clothing, as centaurs did not believe in such affectations, and she was old, despite her appearance, of Dor's father's generation. Such things made her far less interesting than Irene. "About this paper, Dor—" Cherie began.

Dor and Irene froze in place, both suddenly conscious of their condition. They were naked, half embraced in the water. Weedles was idly playing with fragments of their clothing. This was definitely not proper behavior, and was bound to be misunderstood.

But Cherie was intent on the paper. She shook her head, so that her hair fell down along her breasts—a mannerism that signaled something serious. "If you can interrupt your sexplay a moment," she said, "I would like to review the spelling in this essay." Centaurs did not really care what human beings did with each other in the water; to them, such interaction was natural. But if Cherie reported it to the Queen—

"Uh, well—" Dor said, wishing he could sink under the water.

"But before I go into detailed analysis, let's obtain another opinion." Cherie held the paper down so Irene could see it.

Irene was fully as embarrassed by her condition as Dor was about his. She exhaled to decrease her buoyancy and lower herself in the water, but in a moment she was gasping and had to breathe again—which caused her to rise once more, especially since her most prominent attributes tended to float anyway. But as her eyes scanned the paper, her mood changed. "Oh, no!" she exclaimed. "What a disaster!" she chortled. "You've outdone yourself this time, Dor!" she tittered. "Oh, this is the worst that ever was!" she cried gleefully.

"What's so funny?" the water asked, and its curiosity was echoed by the rocks, sand, and other inanimate things within range of Dor's talent.

Cherie disapproved of magic in centaurs—she was of the old-fashioned, conservative school that considered magic obscene in the civilized species of Xanth—but appreciated its uses in human beings. "I will read the essay to you, attempting to present the words as they are spelled," she said. She did—and somehow the new meanings came through even though the actual pronunciation of the words had not changed. Dor quailed; it was even worse than he had feared.

THE LAND OF XANTH
buy door

Eye live inn the Land of Xanth, witch is dis-
stinked from Mundania inn that their is magic inn
Xanth and nun inn Mundania. Every won inn
Xanth has his own magic talent; know to are the
same. Sum khan conjure things, and others khan
make a whole ore illusions ore khan sore threw the
heir. Butt inn Mundania know won does magic,
sew its very dull. They're are knot any dragons
their. Instead their are bare and hoarse and a grate
many other monsters. Hour ruler is King Trent,
whoo has rained four seventeen years. He transforms people two other creatures. Know won gets
chaste hear; oui fair inn piece. My tail is dun.

By the end of it Irene was in tears from helpless laughter, the sea cow was bellowing bovine mirth, the water,
beach, and stones were chortling, the blackjack oaks were
zapping each other on the branches, and the moat-monsters
were guffawing. Even Cherie Centaur was barely control-
ling a rebellious smirk. Dor was the only one who was unable to appreciate the excruciatingly funny nature of it; he
wished he could tunnel through the bottom of the earth.

"O doesn't that beet awl!" Irene gasped. "Lets go two
Mundania and sea a hoarse bare ore whatever!" And the
creatures and landscape relapsed into a cacophony of fresh
laughter. The stones themselves were squeezing out helpless tears of hilarity.

Cherie controlled her levity enough to form a proper
frown. "Now I think you had better report to the King,
Dor."

Oh, no! How much trouble could he get into in one afternoon? He'd be lucky if King Trent didn't transform him
into a slug and drop him back in the moat. As if flunking
his essay wasn't bad enough, getting caught naked with the
King's daughter—

Dor wrapped his tatters of clothing about his midsection
and scrambled out of the water. He would simply have to
go and take his medicine.

He stopped off at home to get quickly into fresh clothing. He hoped his mother would be elsewhere, but she

was cleaning house. Fortunately, she was in her nymph state, looking like a lovely doll, though in fact she was in the vicinity of forty. There was no one prettier than Chameleon when she was up, and no one uglier when she was down. But her intelligence varied inversely, so right now she was quite stupid. Thus she lacked the wit to inquire why he was wearing his clothing tied about his middle, sopping wet, while the objects in his path sniggered. But she was sensitive to the water. "Don't drip on the floor, dear," she warned.

"I'll be dry in a moment," he called reassuringly. "I was swimming with Irene."

"That's nice," she said.

Soon he was on his way to the King, who always interviewed him in the library. Dor's heart was beating as he hurried up the stairs. Cherie Centaur must have shown King Trent the paper before she came for Dor; maybe the King didn't know about the disaster in the moat.

King Trent was awaiting him. The King was a solid, graying, handsome man nearing sixty. When he died, Dor would probably assume the crown of Xanth. Somehow he was not eager for the post.

"Hello, Dor," the King said, shaking his hand warmly, as he always did. "You look fresh and clean today."

Because of the episode in the moat. That was one way to take a bath! Was the King teasing him? No, that was not Trent's way. "Yes, sir," Dor said uncomfortably.

"I have serious news for you."

Dor fidgeted. "Yes, sir. I'm sorry."

Trent smiled. "Oh, it has nothing to do with that essay. The truth is, I was none too apt in spelling in my own youth. That sort of thing is mastered in time." His face turned grave, and Dor quailed, knowing it had to be the other thing that perturbed the King.

Dor considered offering an explanation, but realized it would sound too much like an excuse. Kings and potential Kings, he understood, did not excuse themselves; it was bad for the image. So he waited in dreading silence.

"Please, Dor, be at ease," the King said. "This is important."

"It was an accident!" Dor blurted, his guilt overriding his resolve. It was so difficult to be Kingly!

"Are you by chance referring to that fall into the moat?"

Confirmation was as bad as suspicion! "Yes, sir." Dor realized that anything more he said could only put the blame on Irene, and that wouldn't be wise.

"Funniest splash I've seen in years!" King Trent said, smiling gravely. "I saw it all from the embrasure. She pulled you in, of course, and then tore into your clothes. This is ever the way of the distaff."

"You're not angry?"

"Dor, I trust you. You tend to come to grief in minor particulars, but you are generally sound in the major ones. And I have to admit my daughter is a provocative brat at times. But mainly, it is good to get into mischief while you're still young enough to profit from the experience. Once you are King, you are unlikely to have that luxury."

"Then that's not why you summoned me?" Dor asked, relieved.

"If I had the time and privacy, I would be splashing in that moat, too." Then the King's smile faded as he turned to business. "Dor, the Queen and I are making an official trip to Mundania. The excursion is scheduled to last one week. We have to go through a black body of water, up a great river, up to a beleaguered Kingdom in the mountains surrounded by hostile A's, B's, and K's. Normal trade has been largely cut off; they can't get out—or so my scout informs me. They have sent a message of welcome for our offer of trade. But the details remain obscure; I will have to work them out personally. I am the only one in authority here who has had sufficient experience in Mundania to cope. It is a small beginning, a cautious one—but if we establish a limited, viable, continuing trade with a section of Mundania, it will prove well worthwhile, if only for the experience. So we're investing this time now, while there is no crisis in Xanth. You will have to be King in that period of my absence, and rain—ah, reign over Xanth."

This caught Dor completely by surprise. "Me? King?"

"Commencing one week from today. I thought it best to give you warning."

"But I can't be King! I don't know anything about—"

"I would say this is an excellent time to learn, Dor. The Kingdom is at peace, and you are well regarded, and there are two other Magicians available to advise you." He winked solemnly. "The Queen offered to remain here to advise you, but I insisted I wanted the pleasure of her companionship myself. It is essential that you be prepared, in case the duty should come on you suddenly."

Despite his shock at this abrupt onset of responsibility, Dor appreciated the logic. If the Queen remained in Xanth, she would run the whole show and Dor would get no experience. The two remaining Magicians, Humfrey and the Zombie Master, would not interfere at all; neither participated voluntarily in the routine matters of Xanth. So Dor would have a free hand—which was exactly what King Trent wanted.

But the other reference—the duty coming on him suddenly? Was this a suggestion that something was amiss with King Trent? Dor was appalled at the thought. "But it'll be a long time before—I mean—"

"Do not be unduly concerned," King Trent said, comprehending Dor's poorly expressed notion, as he always did. "I am not yet sixty; I daresay you will be thirty before the onus falls on you. I remain in good health. But we must always be ready for the unexpected. Now is there anything you will need to prepare yourself?"

"Uh—" Dor remained numbed. "Can it be secret?"

"Kingship is hardly secret, Dor."

"I mean—does everyone have to know you're gone? From Xanth, I mean. If they thought you were near, that it was just a trial run—"

King Trent frowned. "You do not feel up to it?"

"Yes, sir. I don't."

The King sighed. "Dor, I am disappointed but not surprised. I believe you underestimate yourself, but you are young yet, and it is not my purpose to cause you unnecessary difficulties. We shall announce that the Queen and I are taking a week's vacation—a working vacation—and are allowing you to practice your future craft. I do not believe that is too great a deviation from the truth. We shall be working, and for me a visit to Mundania is a vacation. The Queen has never been there; it will be a novel experience for her. But you will know, privately, that we shall not be available to help you if there is any problem. Only the Council of Elders and the other Magicians will know where I am."

Dor's knees felt weak. "Thank you, sir. I'll try not to mess up."

"Do try that. See that you do not fall into the moat," King Trent said, smiling. "And don't let my daughter boss you around; it ill befits a King." He shook his head. "Hasn't she become a vixen, though? When you pulled her suit down—"

"Uh—" Dor said, blushing. He had hoped they were safely beyond this subject.

"She certainly asked for it! The Queen and I are entirely too lenient with her. I had to threaten to turn Iris into a cactus to keep her from interfering. And I proved correct; you two worked it out satisfactorily to yourselves."

Actually, Cherie Centaur had interrupted the struggle; otherwise there was no guessing where it might have led. For one of the few times in his life, Dor was thankful, in retrospect, for Cherie's intervention. Perhaps the King knew that, too.

"Uh, thanks, I mean, yes, sir," Dor agreed weakly. This was almost too much understanding; the Queen would certainly have dealt with him more harshly than this. Yet he knew the King had not been joking about the cactus; easygoing as he seemed, he tolerated absolutely no insubordination from anyone—which was of course one of his prime qualities of Kingship.

Unfortunately, Dor's own talent was not that forceful. He could not transform those who opposed him. If he gave an order, and someone refused to obey, what would he do? He had no idea.

"At any rate, you will work it out," King Trent said. "I am depending on you to carry through despite whatever hazards my daughter interposes."

"Yes, sir," Dor agreed without enthusiasm. "Do you really have to go?"

"We do have to go, Dor. I feel this can be an excellent opportunity for continuing trade. Mundania has vast and largely unexploited resources that would do us a great deal of good, while we have magic abilities that could help them equivalently. To date, our trade with Mundania has been sporadic, owing to difficulties of communication. We require a reliable, private connection. But we must exercise extreme caution, for we do not want the Mundanes invading Xanth again. So we are deliberately dealing with a small Kingdom, one unlikely to be able to mount such an offensive, should it ever choose to."

Dor could appreciate that. Xanth had a long history of being invaded by waves of Mundanes, until preventive measures had been taken. Actually, there was no firm route from Mundania to Xanth; Mundanian time seemed to be different, so that contacts were haphazard. Any Xanth citizen, in contrast, could go to Mundania merely by stepping beyond the region of magic. If he kept close track of his route, he could theoretically find his way back. That was academic, however; no one wanted to leave Xanth, for he would leave his magic talent behind.

No, Dor had to qualify that thought. His mother Chameleon had once sought to leave Xanth, before she met his father Bink, to eliminate her changes of phase. Also, the Gorgon had spent some years in Mundania, where her face did not turn people to stone. Perhaps there had been others. But that was a strategy of desperation. Xanth was so obviously the best place to be that very few would leave it voluntarily.

"Uh, suppose you get lost, Your Majesty?" Dor asked worriedly.

"You forget, Dor, I have been to Mundania before. I know the route."

"But Mundania changes! You can't go back to where you were!"

"Probably true. Certainly I would not take the Queen to the site of my first marriage." The King was silent a moment, and Dor knew this was a secret side of him he preferred not to discuss. King Trent had had a wife and child in Mundania, but they had died, so he had returned to Xanth and become King. Had his family lived, Trent would never have come back to Xanth. "But I believe I can manage."

Yet Dor was nervous. "Mundania is a dangerous place, with bears and horses and things."

"So your essay advised me. I do not pretend this trip is entirely without risk, Dor, but I believe the potential benefits make the risk worthwhile. I am an excellent swordsman and did have twenty years to perfect survival techniques, based on other things than magic. But I must confess that I do miss Mundania somewhat; perhaps that is the underlying motive for this excursion." The King pondered again, then broached a new aspect. "More tricky is the nature of the interface. You see, when we step through to Mundania, we may find ourselves at any point in its history. Until very recently, we could not select the point; this much has been chance. The Queen believes she has found a way to alleviate this problem. That is one reason I must negotiate a trade agreement personally. I can trust no one else to handle the vagaries of the transition. We may fail to reach our target Kingdom, or may reach it and return empty-handed; in that case I will have no one to blame except myself."

"But if you don't know where you'll arrive in Mundania, how do you know there's an opportunity? I mean, you might land somewhere else entirely."

"As I said, I do have a hint. I believe the time is now propitious to enter Mundania's medieval age, and the Queen has studied the matter and believes she can, as it were, fine-tune our entry to match the particular place-time our scout scouted. This spot should have copious natural resources like wood and cloth that we can work by magic into carvings and clothing they can't match. Perhaps something else will offer. Perhaps nothing. I believe a week will suffice to explore the situation. We can not afford to stand still; we must keep working to improve our situation. Magic is not enough to keep Xanth prosperous; the land also requires alert administration."

"I guess so," Dor agreed. But it seemed to him he would never be able to do the job King Trent was doing. Xanth was indeed doing well now, and the improvement had been steady from the time of Trent's ascension to power. The Kingdom was well disciplined and well ordered; even the dragons no longer dared to maraud where men had staked their territory. Dor had a morbid fear that at such time as he, Dor, became King, the golden age would deteriorate. "I wish you well in Mundania, sir."

"I know you do, Dor," King Trent said affably. "I ask you to bear in mind this before all else—honesty."

"Honesty?"

"When you are in doubt, honesty is generally the best course. Whatever may happen, you will not have cause for shame if you adhere scrupulously to that."

"I'll remember," Dor said. "Honesty."

"Honesty," King Trent repeated with peculiar emphasis. "That's it."

Chapter 2. King Dor

In an instant, it seemed, the dread day came. Dor found himself huddled on the throne, feeling terribly alone. King Trent and Queen Iris had announced their vacation and disappeared into a cloud. When the cloud dissipated, they were gone; Iris' power of illusion had made them invisible. She had always liked dramatic entrances and exits.

Dor gritted his teeth and got into it. Actually, the business of governing was mostly routine. There was a trained palace staff, quite competent, whose members Dor had always known; they did whatever he asked and answered any questions he had. But they did not make important decisions—and Dor discovered that *every* decision, no matter how minor, seemed vitally important to the people it concerned. So he let the routine handle itself and concentrated on those areas that demanded the decision of the King, hoping his voluminous royal robe would conceal any tremor of his knees.

The first case concerned two peasants who had a difference about a plantation of light bulbs. Each claimed to be entitled to the brightest bulbs of the current crop. Dor questioned their wooden belt buckles and got the straight story, while both peasants stood amazed at this magic. Dor did this deliberately so they could see that he was, indeed, a Magician; they respected that caliber of magic and would be more likely to pay attention to him now.

Peasant A had farmed the field for many years with
indifferent success; it belonged to him. Peasant B had been
hired to help this season—and the field had brightened into
the best crop in years, so that it never saw darkness. To
whom, then, did the first choice of bulbs belong?

Dor saw that some diplomacy was called for here. He
could of course make an arbitrary decision, but that would
surely leave one party unsatisfied. That could lead to future trouble. He didn't want any of his decisions coming
back to haunt King Trent in future months. "Peasant B
obviously has the special touch that made this crop of bulbs
glow so well," he said. "So he should be given his choice of
the best, as many as he wants. After all, without him the
crop would not be worth much." Peasant B looked pleased.
"However, Peasant A does own the field. He can hire
whomever he wants next year, so he can get to keep more
of his crop." Peasant A nodded grim agreement. "Of
course," Dor continued blithely, "Peasant A won't have
much of a crop, and Peasant B won't have a job. The bulbs
won't grow elsewhere, and won't brighten as well for anyone else, so both peasants will lose. Too bad. It would have
been so simple to share the best bulbs equally, taking turns
selecting each bulb, sharing the profit of the joint effort,
and setting up for an even better future season . . ." Dor
shrugged sadly.

The two peasants looked at each other, a notion dawning. Wasn't it, after all, more important to share many future harvests than run off with the best of only one?
Maybe they could work this out themselves.

They departed, discussing the prospects with animation.
Dor relaxed, his muscles unknotting. Had he done it the
right way? He knew he could not make everyone happy in
every case, but he did want to come as close as possible.

Dor woke next morning to discover a ghost standing beside the royal bed. It was Doreen, the kitchen maid. There
had been half a dozen recognizable ghosts on the premises,
each with his or her sad story, but most were close-
mouthed about their living pasts. Dor had always liked Doreen because of the coincidence of names—Dor, Doreen—
though apart from that they had little in common. Maybe
he had been named after her, since she was a friend of
Millie the Ghost, who had been his nursemaid during his

early years. No one had seen fit to tell him, and the local furniture didn't know. There were many moderate little mysteries like that around this castle; it was part of its atmosphere. At any rate, Doreen was middle-aged and portly and often snappish, not having much to do with the living. Thus it was a surprise to find her here. "What can I do for you, Doreen?" he asked.

"Sir, Your Majesty King Dor," she said diffidently. "We just only merely wondered—I mean, maybe just possibly— since you're the Royal Monarch now, temporarily, for a while—"

Dor smiled. Doreen always found it hard to pinpoint the point. "Out with it, blithe spirit."

"Well, we, you know we haven't really quite seen very much of Millie since she passed on—"

To the ghosts, Millie's return to life was passing on. She had been one of their number for several centuries, and now was mortal again. "You miss her?"

"Yes, certainly, in a way we do, Your Majesty. She used to come see us every day, right after she, you know, but since she got herself in the matrimonial way she hasn't— she—"

Millie had married the Zombie Master and gone to share the castle now possessed by Good Magician Humfrey. It had been the Zombie Master's castle, eight hundred years before. "You'd like to see her again," Dor finished.

"Yes, sir, Your Majesty. You were her friend in life, and now that you're in the way of being the Royal King—"

"She hardly needs the King's approval to visit her old companions." Dor smiled. "Not that such approval would ever be withheld, but even if it were, how could anyone stop a ghost from going anywhere?"

"Oh, sir, *we* can't go anywhere!" Doreen protested. "We are forever bound by the site of our cruel demise, until our, you might say, to put it politely, our onuses are abated."

"Well, if you'd tell me your onuses, maybe I could help," Dor suggested.

It was the first time he had ever seen a ghost blush. "Oh, no, no, n-never!" she stammered.

Evidently he had struck a sensitive area. "Well, Millie can certainly come to see you."

"But she never, she doesn't, she won't seem to come,"

Doreen wailed. "We have heard, had information, we believe she became a mother—"

"Of twins," Dor agreed. "A boy and a girl. It was bound to happen, considering her talent."

Prudish Doreen let that pass. "So of course, naturally she's busy. But if the King suggested, intimated, asked her to visit—"

Dor smiled. "Millie was my governess for a dozen years. I had a crush on her. She never took orders from me; it was the other way around. Nobody who knows me takes me seriously." As he spoke, Dor feared he had just said something significant and damaging or damning; he would have to think about that in private.

"But now that you're King—" Doreen said, not debating his point.

Dor smiled again. "Very well. I will invite Millie and her family here for a visit so you can meet the children. I can't guarantee they'll come, but I will extend the invitation."

"Oh, thank you, Your Majesty, sir!" Doreen faded gratefully out.

Dor shook his head. He hadn't realized the ghosts liked children. But of course one of them was a child, Button, so that could account for it. Millie's babies were only three years old, while Button was six—but of course in time the twins would grow to his age, while the ghost would not change. He had been six for six hundred years. Children were children. Dor had not met Millie's twins himself; a visit should be interesting. He wondered whether Millie retained her talent of sex appeal, now that she was happily married. Did any wife keep up with that sort of thing? He feared that by the time he found out, it would be too late.

Later that day, perhaps by no coincidence, Dor was approached by a zombie. The decrepit creatures normally remained comfortably buried in their graveyard near the castle, but any threat to the castle would bring them charging gruesomely forth. This one dropped stinking clods of earth and goo as it walked, and its face was a mass of pus and rot, but somehow it managed to talk. "Yhoor Mhajustee—" it pleaded loathsomely, spitting out a decayed tooth.

Dor had known the zombies well in his day, including zombie animals and a zombie ogre named Egor, so they no longer repulsed him as badly as they might have done.

"Yes?" he said politely. The best way to deal with a zombie was to give it what it wanted, since it could not be killed or discouraged. Theoretically, it was possible to dismember one and bury the pieces separately, but that was hardly worth the trouble and still was not guaranteed effective. Besides, zombies were all right, in their place.

"Ohur Massssterr—"

Dor caught on. "You have not seen the Zombie Master in some time. I will ask him to visit here so you can get together and rehash old times. Must be many a graveyard you've patronized with him. I can't promise he'll come—he does like his privacy—but I'll make the effort."

"Thaaanks," the zombie whistled, losing part of its moldy tongue.

"Uh, remember—he has a family now. Two little children. You might find them scooping sand out of graves, playing with stray bones—"

But the zombie didn't seem concerned. The maggots squirmed alertly in its sunken eyes as it turned to depart. Maybe it was fun to have children play with one's bones.

Meanwhile, the daily chores continued. Another case concerned a sea monster invading a river and terrorizing the fish there, which caused a slack harvest. Dor had to travel there and make the ground in the vicinity rumble as if shaken by the passage of a giant. The inanimate objects went to it with a will; they liked conspiring to frighten a monster. And the sea monster, none too smart and not really looking for trouble, decided it was more at home in the deep sea, innocently gobbling down shipwrecked sailors and flashing at voyeuristic Mundane investigators of the supernatural. It made a "You'll be sorry when you don't have C. Monster to kick around any more!" honk and departed.

Again Dor relaxed weakly. This device would not work against a smart monster; he had been lucky. He was highly conscious of the potential for some colossal foulup, and felt it was only a matter of time before it occurred. He knew he didn't have any special talent for governing.

At night he had nightmares, not the usual kind wherein black female Mundane-type horses chased him, but the worse kind wherein he thought he was awake and made some disastrous decision and all Xanth went up in magic

flames, was overrun by wiggle-worms, or, worst of all, lost
its magic and became like drear Mundania. All somehow
his fault. He had heard it said that the head that wore the
crown was uneasy. In truth, not only was that crown wearing a blister into his scalp, making him quite uneasy; that
head was terrified by the responsibility of governing
Xanth.

Another day there was a serious theft in a northern village. Dor had himself conjured there; naturally Castle
Roogna had a resident conjurer. The problem village was
in central Xanth, near the Incognito territory largely unexplored by man, where dragons remained unchastened, and
that made Dor nervous. There were many devastating
monsters in Xanth; but as a class, the dragons were the
worst because there were many varieties and sizes of them,
and their numbers were large. But actually, it turned out to
be a pleasant region, with most of the modern magic con-
veniences like soda-water springs and scented soapstones
for laundry. This was fur-harvesting country, and this year
there had been a fine harvest from the local stand of ever-
green fur trees. The green furs had been seasoning in the
sun and curing in the moon and sparkling in the stars, until
one morning they were gone without trace.

Dor questioned the platform on which the furs had been
piled, and learned that a contingent from another village
had sneaked in and stolen them. This was one time his
magic talent was superior to that of King Trent—the gath-
ering of information. He then arranged to have the furs
conjured back. No action was taken against the other village; those people would know their deed had been discovered, and would probably lie low for some time.

Through all this Irene was a constant nag. She resented
Dor's ascension to the throne, though she knew it was temporary, and she kept hoping he would foul up. "My father
could have done it better," she muttered darkly when Dor
solved a problem and was hardly mollified when he agreed.
"You should have punished that thieving village." And Dor
wondered whether he had in fact been wishy-washy there,
taking the expedient route instead of the proper one. Yet
what could he do, except whatever seemed best at the time
of decision? The crushing responsibility for error made him

painstakingly cautious. Only experience, he suspected, could provide the necessary confidence to make excellent decisions under pressure. And that was exactly what King Trent, in his own experienced wisdom, had arranged for Dor to obtain here.

Dor, to his surprise, did not quite foul up. But the variety of problems he encountered strained his ingenuity, and the foreboding grew that his luck had to turn. He counted the passing days, praying that no serious problem would arise before King Trent returned. Maybe when Dor was Trent's age he'd be competent to run a kingdom full-time; right now it was such nervous business it was driving him to distraction.

Irene, at length perceiving this, flipflopped in girlish fashion and started offering support. "After all," she said consolingly, "it's not forever, even though it seems like it. Only two more days before the danger's over. Then we can all faint with relief." Dor appreciated the support, though he might have preferred a less pointed summation of his inadequacy.

He made it. The day of King Trent's return came, to Dor's immense relief and Irene's mixed gratification and subdued dismay. She wanted her father back, but had expected Dor to make more of a mess of things. Dor had escaped more or less unscratched, which she felt was not quite fair.

Both of them dressed carefully and made sure the Castle Roogna grounds were clean. They were ready to greet the returning royalty in proper style.

The expectant hours passed, but the King and Queen did not appear. Dor quelled his nervousness; of course it took time to travel, especially if a quantity of Mundane trade goods was being moved. Irene joined Dor for a lunch of number noodles and milk shakes; they tried to divert themselves by spelling words with numbers, but the milk kept shaking so violently that nothing held together. That fitted their mood.

"Where *are* they?" Irene demanded as the afternoon wore on. She was really getting worried. Now that she had a genuine concern, so that she wasn't concentrating her energy to embarrass Dor, she manifested as the infernally pretty girl she could be. Even the green tint of her hair was attractive; it did match her eyes, and after all, there was nothing wrong with plants.

"Probably they had stuff to carry, so had to go slow," Dor said, not for the first time. But a qualm was gnawing at him. He cuffed it away, but it kept returning, as was the nature of its kind.

Irene did not argue, but the green was spreading to her face, and that was less pretty.

Evening came, and night, without Trent and Iris's return. Now Irene turned to Dor in genuine apprehension. "Oh, Dor, I'm scared! What's happened to them?"

He could bluff neither her nor himself. He put his arm about her shoulders. "I don't know. I'm scared, too."

She clung to him for a moment, all soft and sweet in her anxiety. Then she drew away and ran to her own apartment. "I don't want you to see me cry," she explained as she disappeared.

Dor was touched. If only she could be like that when things were going well! There was a good deal more to her than mischief and sexual suggestion, if she ever let it show.

He retired and slept uneasily. The real nightmares came this time, not the sleek and rather pretty equines he had sometimes befriended, but huge, nebulous, misshapen creatures with gleaming white eyes and glinting teeth; he had to shake himself violently awake to make them leave. He used the royal chambers, for he was King now—but since his week was over, he felt more than ever like an imposter. He stared morosely at the dark hoofprints on the floor, knowing the mares were waiting only for him to sleep again. He was defenseless; he had geared himself emotionally for relief when the week expired, and now that relief had been negated. If the King and Queen did not return today, what would he do?

They did not return. Dor continued to settle differences and solve problems in the Kingly routine; what else could he do? But a restlessness was growing in the palace, and his own dread intensified as each hour dragged by. Everyone knew King Trent's vacation had been scheduled for one week. Why hadn't he returned?

In the evening Irene approached Dor privately. There was no mischief about her now. She was conservatively garbed in a voluminous green robe, and her hair was in disorder, as if overrun by weeds. Her eyes were preternaturally bright, as if she had been crying more than was good for her and had used vanishing cream to make the signs of it disappear. "Something's happened," she said. "I know it. We must go check on them."

"We can't do that," Dor said miserably.

"Can't? That concept is not in my lexicon." She had grown so used to using fancy words, she now did it even when distracted. Dor hoped he never deteriorated to that extent. "I can do anything I want, except—"

"Except rule Xanth," Dor said. "And find your parents."

"Where are they?" she demanded.

She didn't know, of course. She had not been part of the secret. He saw no way to avoid telling her now, for she was, after all, King Trent's daughter, and the situation had become serious. She did have the right to know. "In Mundania."

"Mundania!" she cried, horrified.

"A trade mission," he explained quickly. "To make a deal so Xanth can benefit. For progress."

"Oh, this is twice as awful as I feared. Oh, woe! Mundania! The awfullest of places! They can't do magic there! They're helpless!"

That was an exaggeration, but she was prone to it when excited. Neither Trent nor Iris was helpless in nonmagical terms. The King was an expert swordsman, and the Queen had a wonderfully devious mind. "Remember, he spent twenty years there, before he was King. He knows his way around."

"But he didn't come back!"

Dor could not refute that. "I don't know what to do," he confessed.

"We'll have to go find them," she said. "Don't tell me no again." And there was such a glint in her bright eyes that Dor dared not defy her.

Actually, it seemed so simple. Anything was better than the present doubt. "All right. But I'll have to tell the Council of Elders." For the Elders were responsible for the Kingdom during the absence of the King. They took care of routine administrative chores and had to select a new

King if anything happened to the old one. They had chosen Trent, back when the prior monarch, the Storm King, had died. Dor's grandfather Roland was a leading Elder.

"First thing in the morning," she said, her gaze daring him to demur.

"First thing in the morning," he agreed. She had forced this action upon him, but he was glad for the decision.

"Shall I stay with you tonight? I saw the hoofprints."

Dor considered. The surest way to banish nightmares was to have compatible company while sleeping. But Irene was too pretty now and too accommodating; if he kissed her this night, she wouldn't bite. That made him cautious. Once Good Magician Humfrey had suggested to him that it might be more manly to decline a woman's offer than to accept it; Dor had not quite understood that suggestion, but now he had a better inkling of its meaning. "No," he said regretfully. "I fear the nightmares, but I fear you more."

"Gee," she said, pleased. Then she kissed him without biting and left in her swirl of perfume.

Dor sat for some time, wishing Irene were that way all the time. No tantrums, no artful flashes of torso, no pretended misunderstandings, just a sincere and fairly mature caring. But of course her niceness came only in phases, always wiped out by other phases.

His decision had one beneficial effect: the nightmares foraged elsewhere that night, letting him sleep in peace.

"Cover for me," he told Irene in the morning. "I would rather people didn't know where I am, except for the conjurer."

"Certainly," she agreed. If people knew he was consulting privately with an Elder, they would know something was wrong.

He went to see his grandfather Roland, who lived in the North Village, several days' walk beyond the Gap Chasm. Kings of Xanth had once resided here, before Trent restored Castle Roogna. He marched up the neat walk and knocked on the humble door.

"Oh, grandfather!" Dor cried the moment the strong old man appeared. "Something has happened to King Trent, and I must go look for him."

"Impossible," Roland said sternly. "The King may not

leave Castle Roogna for more than a day without appointing another Magician as successor. At the moment there are no other Magicians who would assume the crown, so you must remain there until Trent returns. That is the law of Xanth."

"But King Trent and Queen Iris went to Mundania!"

"Mundania!" Roland was as surprised as Irene had been. "No wonder he did not consult with us! We would never have permitted that."

So there had been method in the manner King Trent had set Dor up for this practice week. Trent had bypassed the Council of Elders! But that was not Dor's immediate concern. "I'm not fit to govern, grandfather. I'm too young. I've got to get King Trent back!"

"Absolutely not! I am only one member of the Council, but I know their reaction. You must remain here until Trent returns."

"But then how can I rescue him?"

"From Mundania? You can't. He will have to extricate himself from whatever situation he is in, assuming he lives."

"He lives!" Dor repeated emphatically. He had to believe that! The alternative was unthinkable. "But I don't know how long I can keep governing Xanth. The people know I'm not really King. They think King Trent is nearby, just giving me more practice. They won't obey me much longer."

"Perhaps you should get help," Roland suggested. "I disapprove on principle of deception, but I think it best in this case that the people not know the gravity of the situation. Perhaps it is not grave at all; Trent may return in good order at any time. Meanwhile, the Kingdom need not be governed solely by one young man."

"I could get help, I guess," Dor said uncertainly. "But what about King Trent?"

"He must return by himself—or fail to. None of us can locate him in Mundania, let alone help him. This is the obvious consequence of his neglect in obtaining the prior advice of the Council of Elders. We must simply wait. He is a resourceful man who will surely prevail if that is humanly possible."

With that Dor had to be satisfied. He was King, but he

could not go against the Elders. He realized now that this was not merely a matter of law or custom, but of common sense. Any situation in Mundania that was too much for King Trent to handle would be several times too much for Dor.

Irene was more positive than he had expected, when he gave her the news on his return. "Of course the Elders would say that. They're old and conservative. And right, I guess. We'll just have to make do until my father gets back."

Dor didn't quite trust her change of heart, but knew better than to inquire. "Who can we get to help?" He knew it would be impossible to exclude Irene from any such activity. King Trent was, after all, her father, the one person to whom her loyalty was unfailing.

"Oh, all the kids. Chet, Smash, Grundy—"

"To run a Kingdom?" he asked dubiously.

"Would you rather leave it to the Elders?"

She had a point. "I hope the situation doesn't last long," he said.

"You certainly don't hope it more than I do!" she agreed, and he knew that was straight from her heart.

Irene went off to locate the people mentioned so that Dor would not arouse suspicion by doing it himself. The first she found was Grundy the Golem. Grundy was older than the others and different in several respects. He had been created as a golem, animated wood and clay and string, and later converted to full-person status. He was only a handspan tall, and spoke all the languages of all living things—which was the useful talent for which he had been created. Grundy could certainly help in solving the routine problems of Xanth. But he tended to speak too often and intemporately. In other words, he was mouthy. That could be trouble.

"Now this is a secret," Dor explained. "King Trent is lost in Mundania, and I must run the Kingdom until he returns."

"Xanth is in trouble!" Grundy exclaimed.

"That's why I need your help. I don't know how much longer I'll have to be King, and I don't want things to get out of control. You generally have good information—"

"I snoop a lot," Grundy agreed. "Very well; I'll snoop

for you. First thing I have to tell you is that the whole
palace is sniggering about a certain essay someone wrote
for a certain female tutor—"

"That news I can dispense with," Dor said.

"Then there's the gossip about how a certain girl went
swimming in her birthday suit, which suit seems to have
stretched some since her birth, along with—"

"That, too," Dor said, smiling. "I'm sure you comprehend my needs."

"What's in it for me?"

"Your head."

"He's King, all right," the golem muttered. One of the
walls chuckled.

Irene brought in Chet. He was a centaur a little older
than Dor, but he seemed younger because centaurs matured more slowly. He was Cherie's son, which meant he
was highly educated but very cautious about showing any
magic talent. For a long time centaurs had believed they
lacked magical talents, because most creatures of Xanth either *had* magic or *were* magic. Modern information had
dissipated such superstitions. Chet did have a magic talent;
he could make large things small. It was a perfectly decent
ability, and many people had fine miniatures he had reduced for them, but it had one drawback; he could not
reverse the process. His father was Chester Centaur, which
meant Chet tended to be ornery when challenged, and was
unhandsome in his human portion. When he reached his
full stature, which would not be for some years yet, he
would be a pretty solid animal. Dor, despite the maledictions he heaped on the race of centaurs while sweating over
one of Cherie's assignments, did like Chet, and had always
gotten along with him.

Dor explained the situation. "Certainly I will help," Chet
said. He always spoke in an educated manner, partly because he was unconscionably smart, but mostly because his
mother insisted. Technically, Cherie was Chet's dam, but
Dor refrained from using that term for fear Cherie would
perceive the "n" he mentally added to it. Dor had sympathy for Chet; it was probably almost as hard being Cherie's
son as it was trying to be King. Chet would not dare misspell any words. "But I am uncertain how I might assist."

"I've just barely figured out decent answers to the problems I've already dealt with," Dor said earnestly. "I'm bound to foul up before long. I need good advice."

"Then you should apply to my mother. Her advice is irrefutable."

"I know. That's *too* authoritative."

Chet smiled. "I suspect I understand." That was as close as he would come to criticizing his dam.

Later in the day Irene managed to bring in Smash. He was the offspring of Crunch the Ogre, and also not yet at full growth—but he was already about twice Dor's mass and strong in proportion. Like all ogres, he was ugly and not smart; his smile would spook a gargoyle, and he could barely pronounce most words, let alone spell them. That quality endeared him to Dor. But the ogre's association with human beings had made him more intelligible and sociable than others of his kind, and he was loyal to his friends. Dor had been his friend for years.

Dor approached this meeting diplomatically. "Smash, I need your help."

The gross mouth cracked open like caked mud in a dehydrated pond. "Sure me help! Who me pulp to kelp?"

"No one, yet," Dor said quickly. Again like all ogres, Smash was prone to rhymes and violence. "But if you could sort of stay within call, in case someone tries to pulp *me*—"

"Pulp me? Who he?"

Dor realized he had presented too convoluted a thought. "When I yell, you come help. Okay?"

"Help whelp!" Smash agreed, finally getting it straight.

Dor's choice of helpers proved fortuitous. Because they were all his peers and friends, they understood his situation better than adults would have and kept his confidences. It was a kind of game—run this Kingdom as if King Trent were merely dallying out of sight, watching them, grading them. It was important not to foul up.

A basilisk wandered into a village, terrorizing the people, because its stare caused them to turn to stone. Dor wasn't sure he could scare it away as he had the sea monster, though it was surely a stupid creature, for basilisks had exceedingly ornery personalities. He couldn't have a boulder conjured to squish it, for King Trent decreed the basilisk to be an endangered species. This was an alien concept the King had brought with him from Mundania—the notion that rare creatures, however horrible, should be protected. Dor did not quite understand this, but he was trying to preserve the Kingdom for Trent's return, so did it Trent's way. He needed some harmless way to persuade the creature to leave human villages alone—and he couldn't even talk its language.

But Grundy the Golem could. Grundy used a helmet and periscope—that was a magic device that bent vision around a corner—to look indirectly at the little monster, and told it about the most baleful she-bask he had ever heard of, who was lurking somewhere in the Dead Forest southeast of Castle Roogna. Since the one Grundy addressed happened to be a cockatrice, the notion of such a henatrice appealed to it. It was no lie; there was a palace guard named Crombie who had the ability to point to things and he had pointed toward that forest when asked where the most baleful female basilisk resided. Of course, sex was mostly illusion among basilisks, since each was generated from the egg of a rooster laid in a dungheap under the Dog Star and hatched by a toad. That was why this was an endangered species, since very few roosters laid eggs in dungheaps under the Dog Star—they tended to get confused and do it under the Cat Star—and most toads had little patience with the seven years it normally required to hatch the egg. But like human beings, the basilisks pursued such illusions avidly. So this cock-bask took off in all haste—i.e., a fast snail's pace—for the Dead Forest, where the lonesome hen basked, and the problem had been solved.

Then there was an altercation in the Barracks—the village set up by the old soldiers of Trent's erstwhile Mundane army, dismantled when he came to power. Each had a farmstead, and many had Mundane wives imported to balance the sexual ratio. They could not do magic, but their children had talents, just like the real citizens of Xanth. The old soldiers entertained themselves by setting up a war-games spectacular, using wooden swords and engaging in complex maneuvers. King Trent allowed this sort of exercise, so long as no one was hurt; soldiers unable to stifle their murderous propensities were issued genuine bayonets from bayonet plants cultured for the purpose and were assigned to dragon-hunting duty. They went after those dragons who insisted on raiding human settlements. This tended to eliminate some of the dragons and most of the violent soldiers. It all worked out. But this time there was a difference of opinion concerning a score made by the Red team on the Green team.

The Reds had set up a catapult and fired off a puffball that puffed into lovely smoke at the apex of its flight. In the games, soldiers were not permitted to hurl actual rocks or other dangerous things at each other, to their frustration. The Reds claimed a direct score on the Greens' headquarters tent, wiping out the Green Bean and his Floozie of the Day. The Greens insisted that the Reds' aim had been off, so that they had not, after all, puffed Bean and Floozie. Since the Floozie was the brains of the outfit, this was a significant distinction. The Reds countered that they had surveyed in the positions of their catapult and the target tent, allowed for windage, humidity, air pressure, and stray magic, double-checked the azimuth, elevation, and charge with their Red Pepper and his Doll of the Day, and fired off the mock-shot in excellent faith. The victory should be theirs.

Dor had no idea how to verify the accuracy of the shot. But Chet Centaur did. Lower, middle, and higher math had been pounded into his skull by the flick of a horsewhip at his tail. He reviewed all the figures of the survey, including the Floozie and Doll figures, spoke with the military· experts about corrected azimuths and trigonometric functions—which made Dor nervous; it wasn't nice to talk dirty in public—and concluded that the shot had been off-target by seven point three lengths of the Red Pepper's left foot. Presented with formal protests, he engaged in a brief debate in which obscure mathematical spells radiated like little whirlpools and nebulae from his head to clash with those of the Reds. A purple tangent spun into a yellow vector, breaking it in two; an orange cosine ground up a dangling cube root. The Red surveyors, impressed by Chet's competence, conceded the point. However, since the target tent had been twelve Pepper-foots in diameter, it was recognized that the probability of a glancing strike was high, even with due margin for error. The Greens were adjudged to have lost the services of the Floozie, and therefore to be at a serious disadvantage in the engagement. The maneuvers resumed, and Chet returned to Castle Roogna, problem solved.

Then a huge old rock-maple tree fell across one of the magic paths leading to Castle Roogna. This was a well-traveled path, and it was not safe to leave it, for beyond its protection the nickelpedes lurked. No one would risk setting foot into a nickelpede nest, for the vicious little creatures, five times the size and ferocity of centipedes, would instantly gouge out nickels of flesh. The tree had to be cleared—but the rock was far too heavy for any ordinary person to move.

Smash the Ogre took a hammer, marched down the path, and blasted away at the fallen trunk. He was as yet a child ogre, not more than half again as tall as Dor, so possessed of only a fraction of his eventual strength, but an ogre was an ogre at any age. The hammer clanged resoundingly, the welkin rang, the stone cracked asunder, dust flew up in clouds that formed a small dust storm wherein dust devils played, and fragments of maple shot out like shrapnel. Soon the little ogre had hewn a path-sized section through the trunk, so that people could pass again. The job had been simple enough for him, though as an adult, he would not have needed the hammer. He would merely have picked up the whole trunk and heaved it far away.

So it went. Another week passed—and still King Trent and Queen Iris did not return. Irene's nervousness was contagious. "You've got to *do* something, Dor!" she screamed, and several ornamental plants in the vicinity swelled up and burst, responding to her frustration.

"The Elders won't let me go after him," he said, as nervous as she.

"You do something right now, Dor, or I'll make your life completely miserable!"

Dor quailed anew. This was no empty bluff. She could make him miserable on her good days; how bad would it be when she really tried? "I'll consult with Crombie," he said.

"What good will that do?" she demanded. "My father is in Mundania; Crombie can't point out his location beyond the realm of magic."

"I have a feeble notion," Dor said.

When Crombie arrived, Dor put it to him: how about

pointing out something that would help them locate King Trent? Crombie could point to anything, even an idea; if there were some device or some person with special information—

Crombie closed his eyes, spun about, flung out one arm, and pointed south.

Dor was almost afraid to believe it. "There really is something that will help?"

"I never point wrong," Crombie said with certainty. He was a stout, graying soldier of the old school, who had a wife named Jewel who lived in the nether caves of Xanth, and a daughter named Tandy of whom no one knew anything. Jewel had been a nymph of the rock; it was her job to salt the earth with all the diamonds, emeralds, sapphires, rubies, opals, spinels, and other gemstones that prospectors were destined eventually to find. She was said to be a lovely, sweet, and tolerant woman now, satisfied to see Crombie on those irregular occasions when he got around to visiting her. Dor understood that Jewel had once loved his father Bink, or vice versa—that had never been made quite clear—but that Crombie had captured her heart with a wish-spell. Love had transformed her from nymph to woman; that process, too, was not quite within Dor's comprehension. What was the distinction between a nymph and a girl like Irene? "Sometimes people interpret it wrong, but the point is always right," Crombie finished.

"Uh, do you have any idea how far it is?"

"Can't really tell, but pretty far, I think. I could triangulate for you, maybe." He went to another room of the castle and tried again. The point remained due south. "Too far to get a proper fix. Down beyond Lake Ogre-Chobee, I'd say."

Dor knew about that lake; it had been part of the geography Cherie Centaur had drilled into him. A tribe of friends lived beneath it, who hurled curses at anyone who bothered them; they had driven off most of the ogres who had once resided on its shores. A number of those displaced ogres had migrated north, settling in the Ogre-fen-Ogre Fen; woe betide the curse-fiend who tried to follow them there! He didn't want to go to that lake; anything that could drive away a tribe of ogres was certainly too much for him to handle.

"But you're sure it will help us?" Dor asked nervously. "Not curse us?"

"You hard of hearing, Your Majesty? I said so before." Crombie was a friend of Dor's father and of King Trent; he did not put up with much nonsense from youngsters who had not even existed when he was sowing his wild oats. All he sowed now were tame oats; Jewel saw to that.

"*How* will it help us?" Irene asked.

"How should I know?" Crombie demanded. He was also a woman hater; this was another aspect of his personality whose consistency eluded Dor. How could a tamely married man hate women? Evidently Irene had changed, in Crombie's eyes, from child to woman; indeed, there was something in the way the old soldier looked at her now that made Irene tend to fade back. She played little games of suggestion with a harmless person like Dor, but lost her nerve when confronted by a real man, albeit an old one like Crombie. "I don't define policy; I only point the way."

"Yes, of course, and we do appreciate it," Dor said diplomatically. "Uh, while you're here—would you point out the direction of any special thing I should be taking care of while I'm King?"

"Why not?" Crombie whirled again—and pointed south again.

"Ha!" Dor exclaimed. "I hoped that would be the case. I'm supposed to go find whatever it is that will help us locate King Trent."

Irene's eyes lighted. "Sometimes you border on genius!" she breathed, gratified at this chance to search for her parents.

"Of course I do," Crombie agreed, though the remark had not been directed at him. He marched off on his rounds, guarding the castle.

Dor promptly visited Elder Roland again, this time having Irene conjured along with him. She had never before been to the North Village, and found it quaint. "What's that funny-looking tree in the center court?" she inquired.

"That's Justin Tree," Dor replied, surprised she didn't know about it. "Your father transformed him to that form from a man, about forty years ago, before he went to Mundania the first time."

She was taken aback. "Why didn't he transform him back, once he was King?"

"Justin likes being a tree," Dor explained. "He has become a sort of symbol to the North Village. People bring him fresh water and dirt and fertilizer when he wants them, and couples embrace in his shade."

"Oh, let's try that!" she said.

Was she serious? Dor decided not to risk it. "We're here on business, rescuing your father. We don't want to delay."

"Of course," she agreed instantly. They hurried on to Roland's house, where Dor's grandmother Bianca let them in, surprised at Dor's return.

"Grandfather," Dor said when Roland appeared. "I have to make a trip south, according to Crombie. He points out a duty I have there, way down beyond Lake Ogre-Chobee. So the Elders can't say no to that, can they?"

Roland frowned. "We can try, Your Majesty." He glanced at Irene. "Would this relate to the absence of Magician Trent?"

"*King* Trent!" Irene snapped.

Roland smiled indulgently. "We Elders are just as concerned about this matter as you are," he said. He spoke firmly and softly; no one would know from his demeanor that he had the magic power to freeze any person in his tracks. "We are eager to ascertain Trent's present state. But we can not allow our present King—that's you, Dor—to risk himself foolishly. I'm afraid a long trip, particularly to the vicinity of Ogre-Chobee, is out of the question at this time."

"But it's a matter I'm supposed to attend to!" Dor protested. "And it's not exactly the lake; it's south of it. So I don't have to go near the fiends. If a King doesn't do what he's supposed to do, he's not fit to be King!"

"One could wish King Trent had kept that more firmly in mind," Roland said, and Irene flushed. "Yet at times there are conflicts of duty. Part of the art of governing is the choosing of the best route through seeming conflicts. You have done well so far, Dor; I think you'll be a good King. You must not act irresponsibly now."

"King Trent said much the same," Dor said, remembering. "Just before he left, he told me that when I was in doubt, to concentrate on honesty."

"That is certainly true. How strange that he did not do the honest thing himself, and consult with the Elders before he departed."

That was bothering Dor increasingly, and he could see that Irene was fit to explode. She hated denigration of her father—yet Roland's pique seemed justified. Had King Trent had some deeper motive than mere trade with Mundania? Had he, incredibly, actually planned not to return? "I'd like just to go to bed and hide my head under the blanket," Dor said.

"That is no longer a luxury you can afford. I think the nightmares would seek you out."

"They already have," Dor agreed ruefully. "The castle maids are complaining about the hoofprints in the rugs."

"I would like to verify your findings, if I may," Roland said.

There was a break while Dor arranged to have Crombie conjured to the North Village. Grandmother Bianca served pinwheel cookies she had harvested from her pinwheel bush. Irene begged a pinwheel seed from her; Irene had a collection of seeds she could grow into useful plants.

"My, how you've grown!" Bianca said, observing Irene.

Irene dropped her cookie—but then had it back unbroken. Bianca's magic talent was the replay; she could make time drop back a few seconds, so that some recent error could be harmlessly corrected. "Thank you," Irene murmured, recovering.

Crombie arrived. "I would like to verify your findings, if I may," Roland repeated to the soldier. Dor noted how the old man was polite to everyone; somehow that made Roland seem magnified in the eyes of others. "Will you point out to me, please, the greatest present threat to the Kingdom of Xanth?"

Crombie obligingly went through his act again—and pointed south again. "That is what I suspected," Roland said. "It seems something is developing in that region that you do indeed have to attend to, Dor. But this is a serious matter, no pleasure excursion."

"What can I do?" Dor asked plaintively. The horror of King Trent's unexplained absence was closing in on him, threatening to overwhelm his tenuous equilibrium.

"You can get some good advice."

Dor considered. "You mean Good Magician Humfrey?"

"I do. He can tell you which course is best, and if you must make this trip, he can serve in your stead as King."

"I don't think he'll agree to that," Dor said.

"I'm sure he won't," Irene agreed.

"There must be a Magician on the throne of Xanth. Ask Humfrey to arrange it, should he approve your excursion."

That was putting the Good Magician on the spot! "I will." Dor looked around, trying to organize himself. "I'd better get started. It's a long walk."

"You're the King, Dor. You don't have to walk there any more than you had to walk here. Have yourself conjured there."

"Oh. Yes. I forgot." Dor felt quite foolish.

"But first get the rest of us safely back to Castle Roogna," Irene told him, nibbling on another cookie. "I don't want to have to cross over the Gap Chasm on the invisible bridge and have the Gap Dragon looking up my skirt." She held the cookie up by the pin while she chewed around the wheel, delicately.

Chapter 3. Wedding Spell

Dor did not arrive inside Magician Humfrey's castle. He found himself standing just outside the moat. Something had gone wrong!

No, he realized. He had been conjured correctly—but the Good Magician, who didn't like intrusions, had placed a barrier-spell in the way, to divert anyone to this place outside. Humfrey didn't like to talk to anyone who didn't get into the castle the hard way. Of course he wasn't supposed to make the King run the gauntlet—but obviously the old wizard was not paying attention at the moment. Dor should have called him on a magic mirror; he hadn't thought of it, in his eagerness to get going. Which meant he deserved what he had gotten—the consequence of his own lack of planning.

Of course, he could probably yell loud enough to attract the attention of someone inside the castle so he could get admitted without trouble. But Dor had a slightly ornery streak. He had made a mistake; he wanted to work his way out of it himself. Rather, into it. He had forced his way into this castle once, four years ago; he should be able to do it now. That would prove he could recover his own fumbles—the way a King should.

He took a good look at the castle environs. The moat was not clear and sparkling as it had been the last time he was here; it was dull and noisome. The shape of the castle wall was now curved and slanted back, like a steep conical mountain. It was supremely unimpressive—and therefore suspect.

Dor squatted and dipped a finger in the water. It came up festooned with slime. He sniffed it. Ugh! Yet there was a certain familiarity about it he could not quite place. Where had he smelled that smell before?

One thing was certain: he was not about to wade or swim through that water without first ascertaining exactly what lurked in it. Magician Humfrey's castle defenses were intended to balk and discourage, rather than to destroy— but they were always formidable enough. Generally it took courage and ingenuity to navigate the several hazards. There would be something in the moat a good deal more unpleasant than slime.

Nothing showed. The dingy green gook covered the whole surface, unbroken by any other horror. Dor was not encouraged.

"Water, are there any living creatures lurking in your depths?" he inquired.

"None at all," the water replied, its voice slurred by the goop. Yet there was a tittery overtone; it seemed to find something funny in the question.

"Any inanimate traps?"

"None." Now little ripples of mirth tripped across the glutinous surface.

"What's so funny?" Dor demanded.

The water made little elongated splashes, like dribbles of spoiled mucus. "You'll find out."

The trouble with the inanimate was that it had very shallow notions of humor and responsibility. But it could usually be coaxed or cowed. Dor picked up a rock and hefted it menacingly. "Tell me what you know," he said to the water, "or I'll strike you with this stone."

"Don't do that!" the water cried, cowed. "I'll squeal! I'll spill everything I know, which isn't much."

"Ugh!" the rock said at the same time. "Don't throw me in that feculent sludge!"

Dor remembered how he had played the Magician's own defenses against each other, last time. There had been a warning sign, TRESPASSERS WILL BE PERSECUTED—and sure enough, when he trespassed he had been presented with a button with the word TRESPASSER on one side, and PERSECUTED on the other. The living-history tome that had recorded the episode had suffered a typo, rendering PERSECUTED into PROSECUTED for the sign, but not for the button, spoiling the effect of these quite different words. These things happened; few people seemed to know the distinction, and Dor's spelling had not been good enough to correct it. But this time there was no sign. He had to generate his own persecution. "Get on with it," he told the water, still holding the rock.

"It's a zombie," the water said. "A zombie sea serpent."

Now Dor understood. Zombies were dead, so it was true there were no living creatures in the moat. But zombies were animate, so there were no inanimate traps either. It made sudden sense—for Dor remembered belatedly that the Zombie Master was still here. When the Zombie Master appeared in the present Xanth, there had been a problem, since Good Magician Humfrey now occupied the castle the Zombie Master had used eight hundred years ago. The one had the claim of prior tenancy, the other the claim of present possession. Neither wanted trouble. So the two Magicians had agreed to share the premises until something better was offered. Evidently the Zombie Master had found nothing better. Naturally he helped out with the castle defenses; he was not any more sociable than Humfrey was.

As it happened, Dor had had experience with zombies. Some of his best friends had been zombies. He still was not too keen on the way they smelled, or on the way they dropped clods of dank glop and maggots wherever they went, but they were not bad creatures in their place. More important, they were hardly smarter than the inanimate objects Dor's magic animated, because their brains were literally rotten. He was confident he could fool a zombie.

"There should be a boat around here," he said to the rock. "Where is it?"

"Over there, chump," the rock said. "Now will you let me go?"

Dor saw the boat. Satisfied, he let the rock go. It dropped with a satisfied thunk to the ground and remained there in blissful repose. Rocks were basically lazy; they hardly ever did anything on their own.

He went to the boat. It was a dingy canoe with a battered double paddle—exactly what he needed. Dor walked away.

"Hey, aren't you going to use me?" the canoe demanded. Objects weren't supposed to talk unless Dor willed it, but they tended to get sloppy about the rules.

"No. I'm going to fetch my friend the zombie."

"Oh, sure. We see lots of that kind here. They make good fertilizer."

When Dor was out of sight of the castle, he stopped and stooped to grub in the dirt. He smeared dirt on his face and arms and over his royal robes. Naturally he should have changed to more suitable clothing for this trip, but of course that was part of his overall carelessness. He had not planned ahead at all.

Next, he found a sharp stone and used it to rip into the cloth of the robe. "Ooooh, ouch!" the robe groaned. "What did I ever do to *you* that you should slay me thus?" But the sharp stone only chuckled. It liked ripping off clothing.

Before long, Dor was a tattered figure of a man. He scooped several double handfuls of dirt into a fold of his robe and walked back to the castle. As he approached the moat, he shuffled in the manner of a zombie and dropped small clods to the ground.

He got into the canoe. "Oooooh," he groaned soulfully. "I hope I can make it home before I go all to pieces." And he used the paddle to push off into the scum of the moat. He was deliberately clumsy, though in truth he was not

well experienced with canoes and would have been awkward anyway. The water slurped and sucked as the paddle
dipped into the ooze.

Now there was a stirring as the zombie sea monster
moved. The slime parted and the huge, mottled, decaying
head lifted clear of the viscous surface. Globules of slush
dangled and dripped, plopping sickly into the water. The
huge, sloppy mouth peeled open, revealing scores of loose
brownish teeth set in a jaw almost stripped of flesh.

"Hi, friend!" Dor called windily. "Can you direct me to
my Master?" As he spoke he slipped forth a moist clod of
dirt, so that it looked as if his lip were falling off.

The monster hesitated. Its grotesque head swung close to
inspect Dor. Its left eyeball came loose, dangling by a
gleaming string. "Sooo?" the zombie inquired, its breath redolent of spoiled Limberger.

Dor waved his arms, losing some more earth. One choice
clod struck the monster on the nose with a dank squish. He
was sorry he hadn't been able to find anything really pu-
trid, like a maggoty rat corpse, but that was the luck of the
game. "Whe-eere?" he demanded, every bit as stupid as a
zombie. The big advantage to playing stupid was that it
didn't take much intelligence. He knocked at his right ear
and let fall another clod, as if a piece of his brain had been
dislodged.

At last the serpent caught on. "Theeere," it breathed,
spraying out several loose fragments of teeth and bone with
the effort. Its snout seemed to be afflicted with advanced
gangrene, and the remaining teeth were crumbling around
their caries.

"Thaaanks," Dor replied, dropping another clod into the
water. He took up the paddle again and scraped on toward the castle. "Hope I don't fall apart before I get
there."

He had won the first round. The sea serpent was in poor
condition, as most zombies were, but could have capsized
the boat and drowned Dor in slime without difficulty. Had
its brain been a better grade of pudding, it might have done
just that. But zombies did not attack their own kind; that
was too messy. Even the completeness of Dor's own body,
conspicuously healthy under the tatters and dirt, did not

count too much against him; fresh zombies were complete. It took time for most of the flesh to fall off.

He docked at the inner edge of the moat, where the castle wall emerged at its steep angle. Now Dor splashed a hole in the slime and cleared a section of halfway clean water he could wash in. His zombie ploy was over; he didn't want to enter the castle in this condition. The rents in his robe could not be repaired, but at least he would look human.

He got out of the canoe, but found it hard to stand on the sloping wall. The surface was not brick or stone, as he had supposed, but glass—solid, translucent, seamless, cold hard glass. A mountain of glass.

Glass. Now he grasped the nature of the second challenge. The slope became steeper near the top, until the wall was almost vertical. How could he scale that?

Dor tried. He placed each foot carefully and found that he could stand and walk, slowly. He had to remain straight upright, for the moment he leaned into the mountain, as was his natural inclination, his feet began to skid. He could quickly get dumped into the awful moat if he let his feet slide out from under him. Fortunately, there was no wind; he could stand erect and step slowly up.

He noticed, however, a small cloud in the sky. As he watched, it seemed to extend rapidly. Oops—that surely meant rain, which would wash him out. That was surely no coincidence; probably the touch of his foot on the glass had summoned the storm. He had to hike to the top of the mountain before the cloud arrived. Well, the distance was not far. With care and good foot-friction, he could probably make it.

Then something came galloping around the mountain. It had four legs, a tail, and a funny horned head. But its chief oddity—

It was heading right for Dor, those horns lowered. The creature was no taller than he, and the horns were small and blunt, but the body was far more massive. Dor had to jump to get out of its way—and lost his footing and slid down to the brink of the water before stopping, his nose barely clear of the slime.

He stabilized himself while the zombie sea serpent

watched with a certain aloof amusement. Dor wiped a dangle of goo from his nose. "What was that?"

"The Sidehill Hoofer," the glass responded.

"Something funny about that creature. The legs—"

"Oh, sure," the glass said. "The two left legs are shorter than the two rights. That's so she can charge around the mountain in comfort. It's natural selection; lots of the better mountains have them."

Shorter left legs—so the Hoofer could stay level while running on a slope. It did make a certain kind of sense. "How come I never heard of this creature before?" Dor demanded.

"Probably because your education has been neglected."

"I was tutored by a centaur!" Dor said defensively.

"The centaur surely told you of the Sidehill Hoofer," the glass agreed. "But did you listen? Education is only as good as the mind of the student."

"What are you implying?" Dor demanded.

"I rather thought you were too dense to grasp the implication," the glass said with smug condescension.

"You're a mountain of glass!" Dor said irately. "How bright can you be?"

"Thought you'd never ask. I'm the brightest thing on the horizon." And a beam of sunlight slanted down, avoiding the looming cloud, causing the mountain to glow brilliantly.

Dor had walked into that one! With the lifetime experience he had had, he still fell into the trap of arguing with the inanimate. He changed the subject. "Is the Hoofer dangerous?"

"Not if you have the wit to stay out of her way."

"I've got to climb to the top of this slope."

"Extraordinary fortune," the glass said brightly.

"What?"

The glass sighed. "I keep forgetting that animate creatures can not match my brilliance. Recognizing your handicap, I shall translate: Lots of luck."

"Oh, thank you," Dor said sarcastically.

"That's irony," the glass said.

"Irony—not glassy?"

"Spare me your feeble efforts at repartee. If you do not get moving before that cloud arrives, you will be washed right into the sea."

"That's an exaggeration," Dor grumped, starting back up the slope.

"That is hyperbole." The glass began humming a tinkly little tune.

Dor made better progress than before. He was getting the hang of it. He had to put his feet down flat and softly and will himself not to skid. But the Sidehill Hoofer came charging around the cone again, spooking him with a loud "Moooo!" and Dor slid down the slope again. He was no more partial to this bovine than he had been to Irene's sea cow.

The cloud was definitely closer, and playful little gusts of wind emanated from it. "Oh, get lost!" Dor told it.

"Fat chance!" it blew back, ruffling his hair with an aggravating intimacy.

Dor went up the slope a third time, by dint of incautious effort getting beyond the slight gouge in the mountain worn by the Hoofer's pounding hooves. The glass hummed louder and finally broke into song: "She'll be coming 'round the mountain when she comes."

Sure enough, the Sidehill Hoofer came galumphing around again, spied Dor, and corrected course slightly to charge straight at him. Her uneven legs pounded evenly on the incline, so that her two short horns were dead-level as they bore on him. Blunt those horns might be, but they were formidable enough in this situation.

Oh, no! It was no accident that brought this creature around so inconveniently; she was trying to prevent him from passing. Naturally this was the third barrier to his entry into the castle.

Dor jumped out of the way and slid down to the brink again, disgruntled. The Hoofer thundered by, disappearing around the curve.

Dor wiped another dribble of slime off his nose. He wasn't making much progress! This was annoying, because he had passed his first challenge without difficulty and faced only two comparatively simple and harmless ones— to avoid the Hoofer and scale the slippery slope. Either alone was feasible; together they baffled him. Now he had perhaps ten minutes to accomplish both before the ornery raincloud wiped him out. Already the forward edge of the cloud had cut off the sunbeam.

Dor didn't like leaning on his magic talent too much, but decided that pride was a foolish baggage at this point. He had to get inside the castle any way he could and get Good Magician Humfrey's advice—for the good of Xanth.

"Glass, since you're so bright—tell me how I can get past the Hoofer and up your slope before the cloud strikes."

"Don't tell him!" the cloud thundered.

"Well, I'm not so bright any more, now that I'm in your shadow," the glass demurred. This was true; the sparkle was gone, and the mountain was a somber dark mass, like the quiet depths of an ocean.

"But you remember the answer," Dor said. "Give."

"Take!" the storm blew.

"I've got to tell him," the glass said dolefully. "Though I'd much rather watch him fall on his as—"

"Watch your language!" Dor snapped.

"—inine posterior again and dip his nose in the gunk. But he's a Magician and I'm only silicon." The glass sighed. "Very well. Cogitate and masticate on—"

"What?"

"Give me strength to survive the monumental idiocy of the animate," the glass prayed obnoxiously. The cloud had let a gleam of sunlight through, making it bright again. "Think and chew on this: who can most readily mount the slope?"

"The Sidehill Hoofer," Dor said. "But that's no help. *I'm* the one who—"

"Think and chew," the glass repeated with emphasis.

That reminded Dor of the way King Trent had stressed the importance of honesty, and that annoyed Dor. This mountain was no King! What business did it have making oblique allusions, as if Dor were a dunce who needed special handling? "Look, glass—I asked you a direct question—"

"An indirect question, technically. My response reflects your approach. But surely you realize that I am under interdiction by another Magician."

Dor didn't know what "interdiction" meant, but could guess. Humfrey had told the mountain not to blab the secret. But the cloud was looming close and large and dense with water, and he was impatient. "Hey, I insist that you tell me—"

"That is of course the answer."

Dor paused. This too-bright object was making a fool of him. He reviewed his words. *Hey, I insist that you tell me*—how was that the answer? Yet it seemed it was.

"You'll never get it," the glass said disparagingly.

"Hey, now—" Dor started angrily.

"There you go again."

Hey, now?

Suddenly Dor got it. Hey—spelled H A Y. "Hay—now!" he cried. It was a homonym.

The zombie sea serpent, taking that for an order, swam across the moat and reached out to take a clumsy bite of dry grass from the outer bank. It brought this back to Dor.

"Thank you, serpent," Dor said, accepting the armful. He shook out the residual slime and dottle, and several more of the monster's teeth bounced on the glass. Zombies had an inexhaustible supply of fragments of themselves to drop; it was part of their nature.

He started up the slope yet again, but this time he wanted to meet the Hoofer. He stood there with his hay, facing her.

The creature came 'round the mountain—and paused as she sighted him. Her ears perked forward and her tongue ran over her lips.

"That's right, you beautiful bovine," Dor said. "This hay is for you. Think and chew—to chew on while you think. I noticed that there isn't much forage along your beat. You must use a lot of energy, pounding around, and work up quite an appetite. Surely you could use a lunch break before the rain spoils everything."

The Hoofer's eyes became larger. They were beautiful and soulful. Her square nose quivered as she sniffed in the odor of the fresh hay. Her pink tongue ran around her muzzle again. She was certainly hungry.

"Of course, if I set it down, it'll just slide down the slope and into the moat," Dor said reasonably. "I guess you could fish it out, but slime-coated hay doesn't taste very good, does it?" As he spoke, a stronger gust of wind from the eager storm swirled through, tugging at the hay and

wafting a few strands down to the goo of the moat. The
Hoofer fidgeted with alarm.

"Tell you what I'll do," Dor said. "I'll just get on your
back and carry the hay, and feed it to you while you walk.
That way you'll be able to eat it all, without losing a wisp,
and no one can accuse you of being derelict in your duty.
You'll be covering your beat all the time."

"Mmmooo," the Hoofer agreed, salivating. She might
not be bright, but she knew a good deal when she smelled
it.

Dor approached, gave her a good mouthful of hay, then
scrambled onto her back from the uphill side. His left foot
dragged, while his right foot dangled well above the surface
of the glass, but he was sitting level. He leaned forward
and extended his left hand to present another morsel of
hay.

The Hoofer took it and chewed blissfully, walking forward. When she finished masticating that—Dor realized he
had learned a new word, though he would never be able to
spell it—he gave her more, again left-handedly. She had to
turn her head left to take it, and her travel veered slightly
that way, uphill.

They continued in this manner for a full circuit of the
mountain. Sure enough, they were higher on the slope than
they had been. His constant presentation of hay on the upward side caused the Hoofer to spiral upward. That was
where he wanted to go.

The storm was almost upon them. *It* had not been
fooled! Dor leaned forward, squeezing with his knees, and
the Hoofer unconsciously speeded up. The second circuit of
the mountain was much faster, because of the accelerated
pace and the narrower diameter at this elevation, and the
third was faster yet. But Dor's luck, already overextended,
was running out. His supply of hay, he saw, would not last
until the top—and the rain would catch them anyway.

He made a bold try to turn liabilities into assets. "I'm
running out of hay—and the storm is coming," he told the
Hoofer. "You'd better set me down before it gets slippery;
no sense having my weight burden you."

She hesitated, thinking this through. Dor helped the
process. "Anywhere will do. You don't have to take me all

the way to the base of the mountain. Maybe there at the top, where I'll be out of your way; it's certainly closer."

That made good cow-sense to her. She trotted in a rapidly tightening spiral to the pinnacle, unbothered by the nearly vertical slope, where Dor stepped off. "Thanks, Hoofer," he said. "You do have pretty eyes." His experience with Irene had impressed upon him the advantage of complimenting females; they all were vain about their appearance.

Pleased, the Hoofer began spiraling down. At that point, the storm struck. The cloud crashed into the pinnacle; the cloud substance tore asunder and water sluiced out of the rent. Rain pelted down, converting the glass surface instantly to something like slick ice. Wind buffeted him, whistling past the needle-pointed apex of the mountain that had wounded the cloud, making dire screams.

Dor's feet slipped out, and he had to fling his arms around the narrow spire to keep from sliding rapidly down. The Hoofer had trouble, too; she braced all four feet—but still skidded grandly downward, until the lessening pitch of the slope enabled her to achieve stability. Then she ducked her head, flipped her tail over her nose, and went to sleep standing. The storm could not really hurt her. She had nowhere to go anyway. She was secure as long as she never tried to face the other way. He knew that when the rain abated, the Sidehill Hoofer would be contentedly chewing her cud.

So Dor had made it to the top, conquering the last of the hurdles. Only—what was he to do now? The mountain peaked smoothly, and there was no entrance. Had he gone through all this to reach the wrong spot? If so, he had outsmarted himself.

The water sluicing from the cloud was cold. His tattered clothing was soaked through, and his fingers were turning numb. Soon he would lose his grip and slide down, probably plunking all the way into the gook of the moat. That was a fate almost worse than freezing!

"There *must* be a way in from here!" he gasped.

"Of course there is, dumbbell," the spire replied. "You're not nearly as sharp as I am! Why else did you scheme your way up here? To wash off your grimy body? I trust I'm not being too pointed."

Why else indeed! He had just assumed this was the correct route, because it was the most difficult one. "Okay, brilliant glass—your mind has more of a cutting edge than mine. Where is it?"

"Now I don't have to tell you that," the glass said, chortling. "Any idiot, even one as dull as you, could figure that out for himself."

"I'm not just any idiot!" Dor cried, the discomfort of the rain and chill giving him a terrible temper.

"You certainly aren't! You're a prize idiot."

"Thank you," Dor said, mollified. Then he realized that he was being as gullible as the average inanimate. Furious, Dor bashed his forehead against the glass—and something clicked. Oops—had he cracked his skull?

No, he had only a mild bruise. Something else had made the noise. He nudged the surface again and got another click.

Oho! He hit the glass a third time—and suddenly the top of the mountain sprang open, a cap whose catch had been released. It hung down one side on stout hinges, and inside was the start of a spiral staircase. Victory at last!

"That's using your head," the glass remarked.

Dor scrambled into the hole. He entered headfirst, then wrestled himself around to get his feet on the steps. Then he hauled the pointed cap of the mountain up and over, at last closing off the blast of the rain. "Curses!" the cloud stormed as he shut it out.

He emerged into Humfrey's crowded study. There were battered leather-bound tomes of spells, magic mirrors, papers, and a general litter of indecipherable artifacts. Amidst it all, almost lost in the shuffle, stood Good Magician Humfrey.

Humfrey was small, almost tiny, and grossly wrinkled. His head and feet were almost as large as those of a goblin, and most of his hair had gone the way of his youth. Dor had no idea how old he was and was afraid to ask; Humfrey was an almost ageless institution. He was the Magician of Information; everything that needed to be known in Xanth, he knew—and he would answer any question for the payment of one year's service by the asker. It was amazing how many people and creatures were not discouraged by that exorbitant fee; it seemed information was the most precious thing there was.

"About time you got here," the little man grumped, not even noticing Dor's condition. "There's a problem in Centaur Isle you'll have to attend to. A new Magician has developed."

This was news indeed! New Magicians appeared in Xanth at the rate of about one per generation; Dor had been the last one born. "Who is he? What talent does he have?"

"He seems to be a centaur."

"A centaur! But most of them don't believe in magic!"

"They're very intelligent," Humfrey agreed.

Since centaurs did have magic talents—those who admitted it—there was no reason why there could not be a centaur Magician, Dor realized. But the complications were horrendous. Only a Magician could govern Xanth; suppose one day there were no human Magician, only a centaur one? Would the human people accept a centaur King? Could a centaur King even govern his own kind? Dor doubted that Cherie Centaur would take orders from any magic-working centaur; she had very strict notions about obscenity, and that was the ultimate. "You didn't tell me his talent."

"I don't know his talent!" Humfrey snapped. "I've been burning the midnight magic and cracking mirrors trying to ascertain it—but there seems to be nothing he does."

"Then how can he be a Magician?"

"That is for you to find out!" Obviously the Good Magician was not at all pleased to admit his inability to ascertain the facts in this case. "We can't have an unidentified Magician-caliber talent running loose; it might be dangerous."

Dangerous? Something connected. "Uh—would Centaur Isle be to the south?"

"Southern tip of Xanth. Where else would it be?"

Dor didn't want to admit that he had neglected that part of his geography. Cherie had made nonhuman history and social studies optional, since Dor was human; therefore he hadn't studied them. He had learned about the ogre migration only because Smash had been curious. His friend Chet lived in a village not far north of the Gap Chasm, in easy galloping range of Castle Roogna via one of the magic bridges. Of course Dor knew that there were other colonies of centaurs; they were scattered around Xanth just as the human settlements were. He just hadn't paid attention to the specific sites. "Crombie the soldier pointed out the greatest threat to Xanth there. Also a job I need to attend to. And a way to get help to rescue King Trent. So it all seems to fit."

"Of course it fits. Everything in Xanth makes sense, for those with the wit to fathom it. You're going to Centaur Isle. Why else did you come here?"

"I thought it was for advice."

"Oh, that. The Elders' face-saving device. Very well. Gather your juvenile friends. You'll be traveling incognito; no conjuring or other royal affectations. You can't roust out this hidden Magician if he knows you're coming. So the trip will take a week or so—"

"A week! The Elders won't let me be away more than a day!"

"Ridiculous! They made no trouble about King Trent going to Mundania for a week, did they?"

"Because they didn't know," Dor said. "He didn't tell them."

"Of course he told them! He consulted with me, and for the sake of necessary privacy I agreed to consult with the Elders and let him know if they raised any objections—and they didn't."

"But my grandfather Roland says he was never told," Dor insisted. "The truth is, he is somewhat annoyed."

"I told him myself. Here, verify it with the mirror." He gestured to a magic mirror on the wall. Its surface was finely crazed; evidently this was one of the ones that had suffered in the course of Humfrey's recent investigation of the centaur Magician.

"When did Magician Humfrey tell Elder Roland about King Trent's trip to Mundania?" Dor asked it carefully. One had to specify things exactly, for mirrors' actual depth was much less than their apparent depth, and they were not smart at all despite their ability to answer questions. "Garbage in, garbage out," King Trent had once remarked cryptically, apparently meaning that a stupid question was likely to get a stupid answer.

The tail of a centaur appeared in the marred surface. Dor knew that meant NO. "It says you didn't," he said.

"Well, maybe I forgot," Humfrey muttered. "I'm too busy to keep up with every trifling detail." And the front of the centaur appeared—a fetching young female.

No wonder there had been no protest from the Elders! Humfrey, distracted by other things, had never gotten around to informing them. King Trent, believing the Magician's silence meant approval from the Elders, had departed as planned. Trent had not intentionally deceived them. That gratified Dor; it had been difficult to think of the King as practicing deliberate deception. Trent had meant his words about honesty.

"I believe the Elders will veto my trip," Dor said. "Especially after—"

"The Elders can go—"

"Humfrey!" a voice called warningly from the doorway. "Don't you dare use such language on this day. You've already cracked one mirror that way!"

So that was how the mirror had suffered! Humfrey had uttered too caustic a word when balked on news of the new Magician.

Dor looked to the voice. It came from the nothingness that was the face of the Gorgon, an absolutely voluptuous, statuesque, shapely, and buxom figure of a lovely woman whose face no one could look at. Humfrey had put a temporary spell on it, ten or fifteen years ago, to protect society from the Gorgon's involuntary magic while he worked out a better way to solve the problem. It seemed he had never gotten around to that solution either. He was known to be a bit absent-minded.

Humfrey's brow wrinkled as if bothered by a pink mosquito. "What's special about this day?"

She seemed to smile. At least, the little serpents that were her hair writhed in a more harmonious manner. "It will come to you in due course, Magician. Now you get into your suit. The good one that you haven't used for the past century or so. Make the moth unball it for you." Her facelessness turned to Dor. "Come with me, Your Majesty."

Perplexed, Dor followed her out of the room. "Uh, am I intruding or something?"

She laughed, sending jiggles through her flesh. Dor squinted, to prevent his eyeballs from popping. "Hardly! You have to perform the ceremony."

Dor's bafflement intensified. "Ceremony?"

She turned and leaned toward him. It embarrassed him to look into her empty head, so he glanced down—and found himself peering through the awesome crevice of her burgeoning cleavage. Dor closed his eyes, blushing.

"The ceremony of marriage," the Gorgon murmured. "Didn't you get the word?"

"I guess not," Dor said. "A lot of words seem to get mislaid around here."

"True, true. But you arrived on schedule anyway, so it's all right. Only the King of Xanth can make it properly binding on that old curmudgeon. It has taken me a good many years to land him, and I mean to have that knot tied chokingly tight."

"But I've never—I know nothing about—" Dor opened his eyes again, and goggled at the mountains and valley of her bosom, and at the empty face, and retreated hastily back into darkness. Too little and too much, in such proximity!

"Do not be alarmed," the Gorgon said. "The sight of me will not petrify you."

That was what she thought. It occurred to him that it was not merely the Gorgon's face that turned a man to stone. Other parts of her could do it to other parts of him. But he forced his eyes open and up, from the fullness to the emptiness, meeting her invisible gaze. "Uh, when does it happen?"

"Not long after the nuptials," she said. "It will be a matter of pride with me to handle it without recourse to any potency spell."

Dor found himself blushing ferociously. "The—I meant the ceremony."

She pinched his cheek gently with her thumb and forefinger. "I know you did, Dor. You are so delightfully pristine. Irene will have quite a time abating your naïveté."

So his future, too, had been mapped out by a woman—and it seemed all other women knew it. No doubt there was a female conspiracy that continued from generation to generation. He could only be thankful that Irene had neither the experience nor the body of the Gorgon. Quite. Yet.

They emerged into what appeared to be a bedroom. "You'll have to change out of those soaking things," the Gorgon said. "Really, you young people should be more careful. Were you playing tag with a bayonet plant? Let me just get these tatters off you—"

"No!" Dor cried, though he was shivering in the wet and ragged robe.

She laughed again, her bosom vibrating. "I understand. You are such a darling boy! I'll send in the Zombie Master. You must be ready in half an hour; it's all scheduled." She turned and swept out, leaving Dor relieved, bemused, and guiltily disappointed. A woman like that could play a man like a musical instrument!

In a moment the gaunt but halfway handsome Zombie Master arrived. He shook hands formally with Dor. "I will never forget what I owe you, Magician," he said.

"You paid off any debt when you made Millie the Ghost happy," Dor said, gratified. He had been instrumental in getting the Zombie Master here, knowing Millie loved him; but Dor himself had profited greatly from the experience. He had, in a very real sense, learned how to be a man. Of course, it seemed that he had forgotten much of that in the ensuing years—the Gorgon had certainly set him in his place!—but he was sure the memory would help him.

"That debt can never be paid," the Zombie Master said gravely.

Dor was not inclined to argue. He was glad he had helped this Magician and Millie to get together. He remembered that he had promised to invite them both to visit Castle Roogna so that the ghosts and zombies could renew acquaintance.

"Uh—" Dor began, trying to figure out how to phrase the invitation.

The Zombie Master produced an elegant suit of clothing tailored to Dor's size, and set about getting him changed and arranged. "Now we must review the ceremony," he said. He brought out a book. "Millie and I will organize most of it; we have been through this foolishness before. You just read this service when I give the signal."

Dor opened the book. The title page advised him that this text contained a sample service for the unification of Age-Old Magicians and Voluptuous Young Maidens. Evidently the Gorgon had crafted this one herself. The service was plain enough; Dor's lines were written in black, the groom's in blue, the bride's in pink.

Do you, Good Magician Humfrey, take this lovely creature to be your bride, to love and cherish as long as you shall live? Well, it did make sense; the chances of him outliving her were remote. But this sort of contract made Dor nervous.

Dor looked up. "It seems simple enough, I guess. Uh, if we have a moment—"

"Oh, we have two or three moments, but not four," the Zombie Master assured him, almost smiling.

Dor broke into a full smile. This Magician had been cadaverously gaunt and sober when Dor had first known him; now he was better fleshed and better tempered. Marriage had evidently been good for him. "I promised the ghosts and zombies of Castle Roogna that your family would visit soon. I know you don't like to mix with ordinary people too much, but if you could see your way clear to—"

The Magician frowned. "I did profess a deep debt to you. I suppose if you insist—"

"Only if you want to go," Dor said quickly. "These creatures—it wouldn't be the same if it wasn't voluntary."

"I will consider. I daresay my wife will have a sentiment."

On cue, Millie appeared. She was as lovely as ever, despite her eight hundred and thirty-odd years of age. She was less voluptuous than the Gorgon, but still did have her talent. Dor became uncomfortable again; he had once had a crush on Millie. "Of course we shall go," Millie said. "We'll be glad to, won't we, Jonathan?"

The Zombie Master could only acquiesce solemnly. The decision had been made.

"It's time," Millie said. "The bride and groom are ready."

"The bride, perhaps," the Zombie Master said wryly. "I suspect I will have to coerce the groom." He turned to Dor. "You go down to the main chamber; the wedding guests are assembling now. They will take their places when you appear."

"Uh, sure," Dor agreed. He took the book and made his way down a winding stair. The castle layout differed from what it had been the last time he was here, but that was only to be expected. The outside defenses changed constantly, so it made sense that the inner schematic followed.

But when he reached the main chamber, Dor stood amazed. It was a grand and somber cathedral, seemingly larger than the whole of the castle, with stately columns and ornate arches supporting the domed glass ceiling. At one end was a dais whose floor appeared to be solid silver. It was surrounded by huge stained-glass windows, evidently another inner aspect of the exterior glass mountain. A jeweled chandelier supported the sun, which was a brilliantly golden ball, borrowed for this occasion. Dor had always wondered what happened to the sun when clouds blocked it off; perhaps now he knew. What would happen if they didn't finish the ceremony before the storm outside abated and the sun needed to be returned?

The guests were even more spectacular. There were hundreds of them, of all types. Some were human, some humanoid, and most were monsters. Dor spied a griffin, a dragon, a small sphinx, several merfolk in a tub of sea water, a manticora, a number of elves, goblins, harpies, and sprites; a score of nickelpedes, a swarm of fruitflies, and a needle cactus. The far door was dwarfed by its guardian—Crunch the Ogre, Smash's father, as horrendous a figure of a monster as anyone cared to imagine.

"What is this?" Dor asked, astonished.

"All the creatures who ever obtained answers from the Good Magician, or interacted significantly with him during the past century," the nearest window explained.

"But—but why?"

A grotesque bespectacled demon detached himself from conversation with a nymph. "Your Majesty, I am Beauregard, of the Nether Contingent. We are assembled here, in peace, not because we necessarily love the Good Magician, but because not one of us would pass up the chance to see him finally get impressed into bondage himself—and to the most fearsome creature known to magic. Come; you must take your place." And the demon guided Dor down the

center aisle toward the dais, past as diversified an assortment of creatures as Dor had ever encountered. One he
thought he recognized—Grundy the Golem, somehow spir-
ited here for the unique occasion. How had all these creatures gotten past the castle defenses? No one had been
around when Dor himself had braved them.

"Oh, you must be King Dor!" someone cried. Dor turned
to discover a handsome woman whose gown was bedecked
with a fantastic array of gems.

"You must be Jewel!" he exclaimed, as a diamond in her
hair almost blinded him. It was the size of his fist, and cut
in what seemed like a million facets. "The one with the
barrel of gems—Crombie's wife."

"How did you ever guess?" she agreed, flashing sapphires, garnets, and giant opals. "You favor your father,
Dor. So good of you to come in his stead."

Dor remembered that this woman had loved his father.
Perhaps that explained why Bink wasn't here; a meeting,
even after all these years, could be awkward. "Uh, I guess
so. Nice to meet you, Jewel."

"I'm sorry my daughter Tandy couldn't meet you,"
Jewel said. "It would be so nice—" She broke off, and
again Dor suspected he understood why. Jewel had loved
Bink; Dor was Bink's son; Tandy was Jewel's daughter. It
was almost as if Dor and Tandy were related. But how
could that be said?

Jewel pressed a stone into his hand. "I was going to give
this to Bink, but I think you deserve it. You will always
have light."

Dor glanced down at the gift. It shone like a miniature
sun, almost too bright to gaze at directly. It was a midnight
sunstone, the rarest of all gems. "Uh, thanks," he said
lamely. He didn't know how to deal with this sort of thing.
He tucked the gem into a pocket and rejoined Beauregard,
who was urging him on. As he reached the dais and
mounted it, the hubbub diminished. The ceremony was incipient.

The music started, the familiar theme played only at
nuptials. It gave Dor stage fright. He had never officiated
at an affair like this before; the opportunities for blunder-
ing seemed limitless. The assembled creatures became abso-

lutely quiet, waiting expectantly for the dread denouement.
The Good Magician Humfrey was finally going to get his!

There was a scuffle to the side. The groom appeared in
a dark suit that looked slightly motheaten; perhaps the
guardian moth had not balled it properly. He was somewhat disheveled, and obliquely compelled by the Zombie
Master. "I survived it; so can you!" the best man whispered, audible throughout the chamber. Somewhere in the
Stygian depth of the audience, a monster chuckled. The
expression on Humfrey's face suggested that he was in serious doubt about survival. More members of the audience
grinned, showing assorted canine teeth; they liked this.

The music got louder. Dor glanced across and saw that
the organist was a small tangle tree, its tentacles writhing
expertly over the keys. No wonder there was a certain predatory intensity to the music!

The Zombie Master, dourly handsome in his funereal-
tailed suit, straightened Humfrey's details, actually brushing him off with a little whisk broom. Then he put Humfrey in a kind of armlock and marched him forward. The
music surged vengefully.

One demon in the front row twitched its tail and leaned
toward another. "A creature doesn't know what happiness
is," he said, "until he gets married."

"And then it's too late!" half a dozen others responded
from the next row back. There was a smattering of applause.

Magician Humfrey quailed, but the best man's grip was
as firm as death itself. At least he had not brought his
zombies to this ceremony! The presence of the walking
dead would have been too much even for such a wedding.

Now the music swelled to sublime urgency, and the
bridal procession appeared. First came Millie the Ghost,
radiant in her maid-of-honor gown, her sex appeal making
the monsters drool. Dor had somehow thought that an unmarried person was supposed to fill this office, but of
course Millie had been unmarried for eight centuries, so it
must be all right.

Then the bride herself stepped out—and if the Gorgon
had seemed buxom before, she was amazing now. She wore
a veil that shrouded the nothingness of her face, so that

there was no way to tell by looking that she was not simply a ravishingly voluptuous woman. Nevertheless, few creatures looked directly at her, wary of her inherent power. Not even the boldest dragon or tangle tree would care to stare the Gorgon in the face.

Behind her trooped two cherubs, a tiny boy and girl. Dor thought at first they were elves, but realized they were children—the three-year-old twins that Millie and the Zombie Master had generated. They certainly looked cute as they carried the trailing end of the bride's long train. Dor wondered whether these angelic tots had manifested their magic talents yet. Sometimes a talent showed at birth, as had Dor's own; sometimes it never showed, as had Dor's father's—though he knew his father did have some sort of magic that King Trent himself respected. Most talents were in between, showing up in the course of childhood, some major, some minor.

Slowly the Gorgon swept forward, in the renewed hush of dread and expectation. Dor saw with a small start that she had donned dark glasses, a Mundane import, so that even her eyes behind the gauzy veil seemed real.

Now at last Humfrey and the Gorgon stood together. She was taller than he—but everyone was taller than Humfrey, so it didn't matter. The music faded to the deceptive calm of the center of a storm.

The Zombie Master nodded to Dor. It was time for the King to read the service, finally tying the knot.

Dor opened the book with trembling fingers. Now he was glad that Cherie Centaur had drilled him well in reading; he had the text to lean on, so that his blank mind couldn't betray him. All he had to do was read the words and follow the directions and everything would be all right. He knew that Good Magician Humfrey really did want to marry the Gorgon; it was just the ceremony that put him off, as it did all men. Weddings were for women and their mothers. Dor would navigate this additional Kingly chore and doubtless be better off for the experience. But his knees still felt like limp noodles. Why did experience have to be so difficult?

He found the place and began to read. "We are gathered here to hogtie this poor idiot—"

There was a stir in the audience. The weeping matrons

paused in mid-tear, while males of every type smirked. Dor blinked. Had he read that right? Yes, there it was, printed quite clearly. He might have trouble spelling, but he could read well enough. "To this conniving wench—"

The demons sniggered. A snake stuck its head out over the Gorgon's veil and hissed. Something was definitely wrong.

"But it says right here," Dor protested, tapping the book with one forefinger. "The gride and broom shall—"

There was a raucous creaking sound that cut through the chamber. Then the Zombie Master's whisk broom flew out of his pocket and hovered before Dor.

Astonished, Dor asked it: "What are you doing here?"

"I'm the broom," it replied. "You invoked the gride and broom, didn't you?"

"What's a gride?"

"You heard it. Awful noise."

So a gride was an awful noise. Dor's vocabulary was expanding rapidly today! "That was supposed to be a bride and groom," Dor said. "Get back where you belong."

"Awww. I thought I was going to get married." But the broom flew back to the pocket.

Now Millie spoke. "Lacuna!" she said.

One of the children jumped. It was the little girl, Millie's daughter.

"Did you change the print?" Millie demanded.

Now Dor caught on. The child's talent—changing printed text! No wonder the service was fouled up!

The Zombie Master grimaced. "Kids will be kids," he said dourly. "We should have used zombies to carry the train, but Millie wouldn't have it. Let's try it again."

Zombies to attend the bride! Dor had to agree with Millie, privately; the stench and rot of the grave did not belong in a ceremony like this.

"Lacuna, put the text back the way it was," Millie said severely.

"Awww," the child said, exactly the way the whisk broom had.

Dor lifted the book. But now there was an eye in the middle of the page. It winked at him. "What now?" he asked.

"Eh?" the book asked. An ear sprouted beside the eye.

"Hiatus!" Millie snapped, and the little boy jumped. "Stop that right now!"

"Awww." But the eye and ear shrank and disappeared, leaving the book clear. Now Dor knew the nature and talent of the other twin.

He read the text carefully before reading it aloud. It was titled *A Manual of Simple Burial*. He frowned at Lacuna, and the print reverted to the proper text: *A Manual of Sample Wedding Services*.

This time he got most of the way through the service without disruption, ignoring ears and noses that sprouted from unlikely surfaces. At one point an entire face appeared on the sun-ball, but no one else was looking at it, so there was no disturbance.

"Do you, Good Magician Humfrey," he concluded, "take this luscious, faceless female Gorgon to be your—" He hesitated, for the text now read *ball and chain*. Some interpolation was necessary. "Your lawfully wedded wife, to have and to hold, to squeeze till she—uh, in health and sickness, for the few measly years you hang on before you croak—uh, until you both become rotten zombies—uh, until death do you part?" He was losing track of the real text.

The Good Magician considered. "Well, there are positive and negative aspects—"

The Zombie Master elbowed him. "Stick to the format," he muttered.

Humfrey looked rebellious, but finally got it out. "I suppose so."

Dor turned to the Gorgon. "And do you, you petrifying creature, take this gnarled old gnome—uh—" The mischievous text had caught him again. A monster in the audience guffawed. "Take Good Magician Humfrey—"

"I do!" she said.

Dor checked his text. Close enough, he decided. "Uh, the manacles—" Oh, no!

Gravely the Zombie Master brought forth the ring. An eye opened on its edge. The Zombie Master frowned at Hiatus, and the eye disappeared. He gave the ring to Humfrey.

The Gorgon lifted her fair hand. A snakelet hissed. "Hey, I don't want to go on that finger!" the ring protested. "It's dangerous!"

"Would you rather be fed to the zombie sea serpent?" Dor snapped at it. The ring was silent. Humfrey fumbled it onto the Gorgon's finger. Naturally he got the wrong finger, but she corrected him gently.

Dor returned to the manual. "I now pronounce you gnome and monst—uh, by the authority vested in me as King of Thieves—uh, of Xanth, I now pronounce you Magician and Wife." Feeling weak with relief at having gotten this far through despite the treacherous text, Dor read the final words. "You may now miss the gride." There was the awful banshee noise. "Uh, goose the tide." There was a sloppy swish, as of water reacting to an indignity. "Uh—"

The Gorgon took hold of Humfrey, threw back her veil, and kissed him soundly. There was applause from the audience, and a mournful hoot from the distance. The sea monster was signaling its sorrow over the Good Magician's loss of innocence.

Millie was furious. "When I catch you, Hi and Lacky—" But the little imps were already beating a retreat.

The wedding party adjourned to the reception area, where refreshments were served. There was a scream. Millie looked and paled, for a moment resembling her ghostly state. "Jonathan! You didn't!"

"Well, somebody had to serve the cake and punch," the Zombie Master said defensively. "Everyone else was busy, and we couldn't ask the guests."

Dor peered. Sure enough, zombies in tuxedos and formal gowns were serving the delicacies. Gobbets of rot were mixing with the cake, and yellowish drool was dripping in the punch. The appetite of the guests seemed to be diminishing.

The assembled monsters, noting that Humfrey had not been turned to stone despite being petrified, were now eager to kiss the bride. They were in no hurry to raid the refreshments. A long line formed.

Millie caught Dor's elbow. "That was very good, Your Majesty. I understand that my husband is to substitute for you during your journey to Centaur Isle."

"He is?" But immediately the beauty and simplicity of it came clear. "He's a Magician! He would do just fine! But I know he doesn't like to indulge in politics."

"Well, since we are going there for a visit anyway, to see the zombies and ghosts, it's not really political."

Dor realized that Millie had really helped him out. Only she could have persuaded the Zombie Master to take the office of King even temporarily. "Uh, thanks. I think the ghosts will like the twins."

She smiled. "The walls will have ears."

That was Hi's talent. "They sure will!"

"Let's go join the monsters," she said, taking his arm. Her touch still sent a rippling thrill through him, perhaps not just because of her magic talent. "How is Irene? I understand she will one day do with you what we women have always done with Magicians."

"Did it ever occur to any of you scheming conspirators that I might have other plans?" Dor asked, nettled despite the effect she had on him. Perhaps he was reacting in order to counter his illicit liking for her. She certainly didn't seem like eight hundred years old!

"No, that never occurred to any of us," she said. "Do you think you have a chance to escape?"

"I doubt it," he said. "But first we have to deal with this mysterious Magician of Centaur Isle. And I hope King Trent comes back soon."

"I hope so, too," Millie said. "And Queen Iris. She was the one who helped bring me back to life. She and your father. I'm forever grateful to them. And to you, too, Dor, for returning Jonathan to me."

She always referred to the Zombie Master by his given name. "I was glad to do it," Dor said.

Then a mishmash of creatures closed in on them, and Dor gave himself up to socializing, perforce. Everyone had a word for the King. Dor wasn't good at this; in fact, he felt almost as awkward as Good Magician Humfrey looked. What was it really like, getting married?

"You'll find out!" the book he still carried said, chuckling evilly.

Chapter 4. Hungry Dune

They had surveyed prospective routes and decided to travel down the coast of Xanth. Dor's father Bink had once traveled into the south-center region, down to the great interior Lake Ogre-Chobee, where the curse-fiends lived, and he recommended against that route. Dragons, chasms, nickelpedes, and other horrors abounded, and there was a massive growth of brambles that made passing difficult, as well as a region of magic-dust that could be hazardous to one's mental health.

On the other hand, the open sea was little better. There the huge sea monsters ruled, preying on everything available. If dragons ruled the wilderness land, serpents ruled the deep water. Where the magic ambience of Xanth faded, the Mundane monsters commenced, and these were worse yet. Dor knew them only through his inattentive geography studies—toothy alligators, white sharks, and blue whales. He didn't want any part of those!

But the coastal shallows excluded the larger sea creatures and the solid-land monsters. Chances were that with a strong youth like the ogre Smash along, they could move safely through this region without raising too much commotion. Had that not been the case, the Elders would never have permitted this excursion, regardless of the need. As it was, they insisted that Dor take along some preventive magic from the Royal Arsenal—a magic sword, a flying carpet, and an escape hoop. Irene carried a selected bag of seeds that she could use to grow particular plants at need— fruits, nuts, and vegetables for the food, and watermelons and milkweed if they had no safe supply of liquid.

They used a magic boat that would sail itself swiftly and quietly down any channel that was deep enough, yet was light enough to be portaged across sand bars. The craft was indefatigable; all they had to do was guide it, and in one full day and night it would bring them to Centaur Isle. This would certainly be faster and easier than walking. Chet, whose geographic education had not been neglected, had a clear notion of the coastal outline and would steer the boat past the treacherous shoals and deeps. Everything was as routine as the nervous Elders could make it.

They started in midmorning from the beach nearest Castle Roogna that had been cleared of monsters. The day was clear, the sea calm. Here there was a brief bay between the mainland and a long chain of barrier islands, the most secure of all waters, theoretically. This trip should not only be safe, but also dull. Of course nothing in Xanth could be taken for granted.

For an hour they traveled south along the bay channel. Dor grew tired of watching the passing islands, but remained too keyed up to rest. After all, it was a centaur Magician they were going to spy out—something never before known in Xanth, unless one counted Herman the Hermit Centaur, who hadn't really been a Magician, just a strongly talented individual who related to the Will-o'-Wisps.

Smash, too, was restive; he was a creature of physical action, and this free ride irked him. Dor would have challenged him to a game of tic-tac-toe, an amusement he had learned from the child of one of the soldier settlers, but knew he would win every game; ogres were not much on intellect.

Grundy the Golem entertained himself by chatting with passing fish and sea creatures. It was amazing, the gossip he came up with. A sneaky sawfish was cutting in on the time of the damselfish of a hammerhead, and the hammerhead was getting suspicious. Pretty soon he would pound the teeth out of the sawfish. A sea squirt was shoring himself up with the flow from an undersea fresh-water spring, getting tipsy on the rare liquid. A certain little oyster was getting out of bed at midnight and gambling with the sand dollars; he was building up quite an alluvial deposit at the central bank of sand. But when his folks found out, he would be gamboling to a different tune.

Irene, meanwhile, struck up a dialogue with the centaur.

"You're so intelligent, Chet. How is it that your magic is so, well, simple?"

"No one is blessed with the selection of his personal talent," Chet said philosophically. He was lying in the middle of the boat, so as to keep the center of gravity low, and seemed comfortable enough. "We centaurs less than most, since only recently has our magic been recognized. My mother—"

"I know. Cherie thinks magic is obscene."

"Oh, she is broad-minded about its presence in lesser creatures."

"Like human beings?" Irene asked dangerously.

"No need to be sensitive about it. We do not discriminate against your kind, and your magic does to a considerable extent compensate."

"How come we rule Xanth, then?" she demanded. Dor found himself getting interested; this was better than fish gossip anyway.

"There is some question whether humans are actually dominant in Xanth," Chet said. "The dragons of the northern reaches might have a different opinion. At any rate, we centaurs permit you humans your foibles. If you wish to point to one of your number and say, 'That individual rules Xanth,' we have no objection so long as that person doesn't interfere with important things."

"What's so important?"

"You would not be in a position to understand the nuances of centaur society."

Irene bridled. "Oh, yeah? Tell me a nuance."

"I'm afraid that is privileged information."

Dor knew Chet was asking for trouble. Already, stray wild seeds in Irene's vicinity were popping open and sending out shoots and roots, a sure sign of her ire. But like many girls, she concealed it well. "Yet humans have the best magic."

"Certainly—if you value magic."

"What would you centaurs say if my father started changing you into fruitflies?"

"Fruit neat," Smash said, overhearing. "Let's eat!"

"Don't be a dunce," Grundy said. "It's two hours yet till lunch."

"Here, I'll start a breadfruit plant," Irene said. "You can

watch it grow." She picked a seed from her collection and set it in one of the earth-filled pots she had brought along. "Grow," she commanded, and the seed sprouted. The ogre watched its growth avidly, waiting for it to mature and produce the first succulent loaf of bread.

"King Trent would not do anything as irresponsible as that," Chet said, picking up on the question. "We centaurs have generally gotten along well with him."

"Because he can destroy you. You'd *better* get along!"

"Not so. We centaurs are archers. No one can get close enough to harm us unless we permit him. We get along because we choose to."

Irene adroitly changed the subject. "You never told me how you felt about your own magic. All your brains, but all you can do is shrink rocks."

"Well, it does relate. I render a stone into a calx. A calx is a small stone, a pebble used for calculating. Such calculus can grow complex, and it has important ramifications. So I feel my magic talent contributes—"

"Monster coming," Grundy announced. "A little fish told me."

"There aren't supposed to be monsters in these waters," Dor objected.

Grundy consulted with the fish. "It's a sea dragon. It heard the commotion of our passage, so it's coming in to investigate. The channel's deep enough for it here."

"We'd better get out of the channel, then," Dor said.

"This is not the best place," Chet objected.

"No place is best to get eaten, dummy!" Irene snapped. "We can't handle a water dragon. We'll have to get out of its way. Shallow water is all we need."

"There are groupies in these shallows," Chet said. "Not a threat, so long as we sail beyond their depth, but not fun to encounter. If we can get farther down before diverging—"

But now they saw the head of the dragon to the south, gliding above the water. Its neck cut a wake; the monster was traveling fast. It was far too big for them to fight.

Smash, however, was game. Ogres were too stupid to know fear. He stood, making the craft rock crazily. "For me's to squeeze!" he said, gesturing with his meathooks.

"All you could do is gouge out handfuls of scales," Irene

said. "Meanwhile, it would be chomping the rest of us. You know an ogre has to have firm footing on land to tackle a dragon of any type."

Without further argument, Chet swerved toward the mainland beach. But almost immediately the sand began to writhe. "Oh, no!" Dor exclaimed. "A sand dune has taken over that beach. We can't go there."

"Agreed," Chet said. "That dune wasn't on my map. It must have moved in the past few days." He swerved back the other way.

That was the problem about Xanth; very little was permanent. In the course of a day, the validity of a given map could be compromised; in a week it could be destroyed. That was one reason so much of Xanth remained unexplored. It had been traveled, but the details were not fixed.

The dune, noting their departure, reared up in a great sandy hump, its most typical form. Had they been so foolish as to step on that beach, it would have rolled right over them, buried them, and consumed them at leisure.

But now the water dragon was much closer. They cut across its path uncomfortably close and approached the island's inner shore. The dragon halted, turning its body to pursue them—but in a moment its nether loops ran aground in the shallows, and it halted. Jets of steam plumed from its nostrils; it was frustrated.

A flipper slapped at the side of the boat. "It's a groupie," Grundy cried. "Knock it off!"

Smash reached out a gnarled mitt to grasp the flipper and haul the thing up in the air. The creature was a fattish fish with large, soft extremities.

"That's a groupie?" Irene asked. "What's so bad about it?"

The fish curled about, got its flippers on the ogre's arm, and drew itself up. Its wide mouth touched Smash's arm in a seeming kiss.

"Don't let it do that!" Chet warned. "It's trying to siphon out your soul."

The ogre understood that. He flung the groupie far over the water, where it landed with a splash.

But now several more were slapping at the boat, trying to scramble inside. Irene shrieked. "Just knock them away," Chet said. "They can't take your soul unless you let them. But they'll keep trying."

"They're coming in all over!" Dor cried. "How can we get away from them?"

Chet smiled grimly. "We can move into the deep channel. Groupies are shallow creatures; they don't stir deep waters."

"But the dragon's waiting there!"

"Of course. Dragons eat groupies. That's why groupies don't venture there."

"Dragons also eat people," Irene protested.

"That might be considered a disadvantage," the centaur agreed. "If you have a better solution, I am amenable to it."

Irene opened her bag of seeds and peered in. "I have watercress. That might help."

"Try it!" Dor exclaimed, sweeping three sets of flippers off the side of the boat. "They're overwhelming us!"

"That is the manner of the species," Chet agreed, sweeping several more off. "They come not single spy, but in battalions."

She picked out a tiny seed. "Grow!" she commanded, and dropped it in the water. The others paused momentarily in their labors to watch. How could such a little seed abate such a pressing menace?

Almost immediately there was a kind of writhing and bubbling where the seed had disappeared. Tiny tendrils writhed outward like wriggling worms. Bubbles rose and popped effervescently. "Cress!" the mass hissed as it expanded.

The groupies hesitated, taken aback by this phenomenon. Then they pounced on it, sucking in mouthfuls.

"They're eating it up!" Dor said.

"Yes," Irene agreed, smiling.

In moments the groupies began swelling up like balloons. The cress had not stopped growing or gassing, and was now inflating the fish. Soon the groupies rose out of the water, impossibly distended, and floated through the air. The dragon snapped at those who drifted within its range.

"Good job, I must admit," Chet said, and Irene flushed with satisfaction. Dor experienced a twinge of jealousy and a twinge of guilt for that feeling. There was nothing be-

tween Chet and Irene, of course; they were of two different species. Not that that necessarily meant much, in
Xanth. New composites were constantly emerging, and the
chimera was evidently descended from three or four other
species. Irene merely argued with Chet to try to bolster her
own image and was flattered when the centaur bolstered it
for her. And if there were something between them, why
should he, Dor, care? But he did care.

They could not return to the main channel, for the
dragon paced them alertly. It knew it had them boxed.
Chet steered cautiously south, searching out the deepest
subchannels of the bay, avoiding anything suspicious. But
the island they were skirting was coming to an end; soon
they would be upon the ocean channel the water dragon
had entered by. How could they cross that while the
dragon lurked?

Chet halted the boat and stared ahead. The dragon took
a stance in mid-channel, due south, and stared back. It
knew they had to pass here. Slowly, deliberately, it ran its
long floppy tongue over its gleaming chops.

"What now?" Dor asked. He was King; he should be
leader, but his mind was blank.

"I believe we shall have to wait until nightfall," Chet
said.

"But we're supposed to make the trip in a day and
night!" Irene protested. "That'll waste half the day!"

"Better waste time than life, green-nose," Grundy remarked.

"Listen, stringbrain—" she retorted. These two had
never gotten along well together.

"We'd better wait," Dor said reluctantly. "Then we can
sneak by the dragon while it's sleeping and be safely on our
way."

"How soundly do dragons sleep?" Irene asked suspi-
ciously.

"Not deeply," Chet said. "They merely snooze with their
nostrils just above the water. But it will be better if there is
fog."

"Much better," Irene agreed weakly.

"Meanwhile, we would do well to sleep in the daytime,"
Chet said. "We will need to post one of our number as a

guard, to be sure the boat doesn't drift. He can sleep at night, while the others are active."

"What do you mean, *he?*" Irene demanded. "There's too much sexism in Xanth. You think a girl can't guard?"

Chet shrugged with his foresection and flicked his handsome tail about negligently. "I spoke generically, of course. There is no sexual discrimination among centaurs."

"That's what you think," Grundy put in. "Who's the boss in your family—Chester or Cherie? Does she let him do anything he wants?"

"Well, my mother *is* strong-willed," Chet admitted.

"I'll bet the fillies run the whole show at Centaur Isle," Grundy said. "Same as they do at Castle Roogna."

"Ha. Ha. Ha." Irene said, pouting.

"You may guard if you wish," Chet said.

"You think I won't? Well, I will. Give me that paddle." She grabbed the emergency paddle, which would now be needed to keep the boat from drifting.

The others settled down comfortably, using pads and buoyant cushions. Chet's equine portion was admirably suited for lying down, but his human portion was more awkward. He leaned against the side of the boat, head against looped arms.

"Say—how will I sleep when we're nudging past that dragon?" Irene asked. "My sleeping turn will come then."

There was a stifled chuckle from Grundy's direction. "Guess one sexist brought that on herself. Just don't snore too loud when we're passing under its tail. Might scare it into—"

She hurled a cushion at the golem, then settled resolutely into her guard position, watching the dragon.

Dor tried to sleep, but found himself too wound up. After a while he sat upright. "It's no use; maybe I'll sleep tomorrow," he said.

Irene was pleased to have his company. She sat crosslegged opposite him, and Dor tried not to be aware that in that position her green skirt did not fully cover her legs. She had excellent ones; in that limited respect she had already matched the Gorgon. Dor liked legs; in fact, he liked anything he wasn't supposed to see.

She sprouted a buttercup plant while Dor plucked a loaf from the breadfruit, and they feasted on fresh bread and butter in silence. The dragon watched, and finally, mischievously, Dor rolled some bread into a compact wad and threw it at the monster. The dragon caught it neatly and gulped it down. Maybe it wasn't such a bad monster; maybe Grundy could talk to it and arrange for safe passage.

No—such a predator could not be trusted. If the dragon wanted to let them pass, it would go away. Better strategy would be to keep it awake and alert all day, so that it would be tired at night.

"Do you think this new centaur Magician will try to take over Xanth?" Irene asked quietly when it seemed the others were asleep.

Dor could appreciate her concern. Chet, who was a friend, was arrogant enough about centaur-human relations; what would be the attitude of a grown centaur with the power of a Magician? Of course the Magician would not be grown right now; it must be new-birthed. But in time it could become adult, and then it could be an ornery creature, like Chet's sire Chester, but without Chester's redeeming qualities. Dor knew that some centaurs did not like human beings; those tended to stay well clear of Castle Roogna. But Centaur Isle was well clear, and that was where this menace was. "We're on our way to investigate this matter," he reminded her. "There is help for King Trent there, too, according to Crombie's pointing. Maybe we just need to figure out how to turn this situation positive instead of negative."

She shifted her position slightly, unconsciously showing a little more of her legs, including a tantalizing flash of inner thigh. "You *are* going to try to help my father, aren't you?"

"Of course I'm going to try!" Dor said indignantly, hoping that if there was any flush on his face, she would assume it was because of his reaction to her words, rather than her flesh. Dor had in the past seen some quite lovely nymphs in quite scanty attire—but nymphs didn't really count. They were *all* well formed and scantily attired, so were not remarkable. Irene was a real girl, and that type ranged from lovely to ugly—in fact, his mother Chameleon covered that range in the course of each month—and Irene did not normally display a great deal of her body at a time.

Thus each glimpse, beyond a certain perimeter, was special. But more special when the display was unintentional.

"I know if my father doesn't come back, you'll stay King."

"I'm not ready to stay King. In twenty years, maybe, I'll be able to handle it. Right now I just want King Trent back. He's your father; I think he's my friend."

"What about my mother?"

Dor grimaced. "Even Queen Iris," he said. "I'd rather face a lifelike illusion of a dragon than the real thing."

"You know, I never had any real privacy till she left," Irene said. "She was always watching me, always telling on me. I hardly dared even to think for myself, because I was afraid she'd slip one of her illusions into my mind and snitch on me. I used to wish something would happen to her—not anything bad, just something to get her out of my hair for a while. Only now that it has—"

"You didn't really want her gone," Dor said. "Not like this."

"Not like this," she agreed. "She's a bitch, but she is my mother. Now I can do anything I want—and I don't know what I want." She shifted position again. This time the hem of her skirt dropped to cover more of her legs. It was almost as if her reference to privacy from her mother's snooping around her mind had brought about privacy from Dor's surreptitious snooping around her body. "Except to have them back again."

Dor found he liked Irene much better this way. Perhaps her prior sharpness of tongue, back when her parents had been in Xanth, had been because of that constant feeling of being watched. Anything real might have been demeaned or ridiculed, so she never expressed anything real. "You know, I've had the opposite problem. I have privacy—but no one around me does. Because there's not much anybody does that I can't find out about. All I have to do is ask their furniture, or their clothing. So they avoid me, and I can't blame them. That's why I've found it easier to have friends like Smash. He wears nothing but his hair, and he thinks furniture is for bonfires, and he has no embarrassing secrets anyway."

"That's right!" she said. "I have no more privacy with

you than I do with my mother. How come I don't feel threatened with you?"

"Because I'm harmless," Dor said with a wry chuckle. "Not by choice; it's just the way I am. The Gorgon says you have me all wrapped up anyway."

She smiled—a genuine, warm smile he liked a lot. "She snitched. She would. She naturally sees all men as creatures to be dazzled and petrified. Good Magician Humfrey never had a chance. But I don't know if I even want you. That way, I mean. My mother figures I've got to marry you so I can be Queen—but that's her desire, not necessarily mine. I mean, why would I want to grow up just like her, with no real power and a lot of time on my hands? Why make my own daughter as miserable as she made me?"

"Maybe you will have a son," Dor offered. This was an intriguing new avenue of exploration.

"You're right. You're harmless. You don't know a thing." She finished her bread and tossed the crumbs on the water. They floated about, forming evanescent picture patterns before drifting away.

Somehow the afternoon had passed; the sun was dropping into the water beyond the barrier island. There was a distant sizzle as it touched the liquid, and a cloud of steam; then it was extinguished.

The others woke and ate. Then Chet guided the boat to the island shore. "Anything dangerous to people here?" Dor asked it.

"Only boredom," the island replied. "Nothing interesting ever happens here, except maybe a seasonal storm or two."

That was what they wanted: a dull locale. They took turns leaving the boat in order to attend to sanitary needs. Irene also took time to grow a forgetme flower.

As the darkness closed, Dor reviewed the situation. "We're going to sneak by that dragon in the night. Irene will harvest some forgetme flowers to discourage memory of our passage; that way the reactions of fish in the area will not betray us. But that won't help us if the dragon sees us or hears us or smells us directly. We don't have any sight- or sound-blanking plants; we didn't anticipate this particular squeeze. So we must go extremely carefully."

"I wish I were string and clay again," Grundy said. "Then I couldn't be killed."

"Now we do have some other resources," Dor said. "The magic sword will make any person expert the moment he takes it in his hand. It won't help much against a pouncing dragon, but any lesser creature will be balked. If we get in serious trouble, we can climb through the escape hoop. The problem with that is that it leads to the permanent storage vat of the Brain Coral, deep under the earth, and the Coral doesn't like to release creatures. It happens to be my friend, but I'd rather not strain that friendship unless absolutely necessary. And there is the flying carpet—but that can only take one person at a time, plus Grundy. I think it could support Smash, but not Chet, so that's not ideal."

"I wouldn't fit through the hoop either," Chet said.

"Yes. So you, Chet, are the most vulnerable one in this situation, because of your mass. So we need to plan for another defense." Dor paused, for Irene was looking at him strangely. "What's the matter?"

"You're glowing," she said.

Startled, Dor checked himself. Light was streaming from one of his pockets. "Oh—that's the midnight sunstone Jewel gave me so I'll always have light. I had forgotten about it."

"We don't want light at the moment," she pointed out. "Wrap it up." She handed him a piece of cloth.

Dor wrapped the gem carefully, until its glow was so muted as to be inconsequential, and put it back in his pocket. "Now," he continued. "Irene has some seeds that will grow devastating plants—she really is Magician level, regardless of what the Elders say—but most of those plants would be as dangerous to us as to the enemy. We'd have to plant and run."

"Any that would block off the water so the dragon couldn't pursue?" Chet asked.

"Oh, yes," Irene said, glowing at Dor's compliment about her talent. "The kraken weed—"

"I see what Dor means," the centaur said quickly. "I don't want to be swimming in the same ocean with a kraken!"

"Or I could start a stunflower on the island here, but it would be likely to stun us, too." She considered. "Aha! I do have some popcorn. That's harmless, but it makes an awful racket. That might distract the dragon for a while."

"Grow me some of that," Chet said. "I'll throw it behind me if I have to swim."

"Only one problem," she said. "I can't grow that at night. It's a dayplant."

"I could unwrap the sunstone," Dor offered.

"That's too small, I think. We'd need a lot of light, radiating all about, not gleaming from tiny facets."

"What can you grow naturally at night?" Chet asked grimly.

"Well, hypno-gourds do well; they generate their own light, inside. But you wouldn't want to look in the peephole, because—"

"Because I'd be instantly hypnotized," Chet finished. "Grow me one anyway; it might help."

"As you wish," she agreed dubiously. She leaned over the side of the boat to drop a seed on the shore. "Grow," she murmured.

"Now if there is trouble," Dor said, "you, Irene, get on the flying carpet. You can drop a kraken seed near the dragon, while the rest of us use the hoop or swim for it. But we'll do our best to escape the notice of the dragon. Then we can proceed south without further trouble."

There was no objection. They waited until the hypno-gourd had fruited, producing one fine specimen. Chet wrapped it in cloth and tucked it in the boat. The craft started moving, nudging silently south toward the channel while the occupants hardly dared breathe. Chet guided it in an eastward curve, to intersect the main channel first, so that he could avoid the monster that was presumably waiting due south. In this silent darkness, they could not see it any more than it could see them.

But the dragon had outsmarted them. It had placed a sunfish in this channel that operated on a similar principle to the sunstone, but it was thousands of times as large. When they came near, the fish suddenly glowed like the sun itself, blindingly. The rounded fin projected above the surface of the water, and its light turned night to day.

"Oh, no!" Dor cried. He had so carefully wrapped his sunstone—and now this was infinitely worse.

There was a gleeful honk from the dragon. They saw its

eyes glowing as it forged toward them. Water dragons did not have internal fire; the eyes were merely reflecting the blaze of the sunfish.

"Plant the kraken!" Dor cried.

"No!" Chet countered. "We can make it to the mainland shallows!"

Sure enough, the boat glided smoothly across the channel before the dragon arrived. The monster was silhouetted before the sunfish, writhing in frustration. It had planned so well, and just missed victory. It honked. "Curses!" Grundy translated. "Foiled again!"

"What about the sand dune?" Irene asked worriedly.

"They are usually quiescent by night," Chet said.

"But this isn't night any more," she reminded him, her voice taking on a pink tinge of hysteria.

Indeed, the dark mound was rippling, sending a strand of itself toward the water. The sand had enough mass, and the water was so shallow, that it was possible for the dune to fill it in. The ravenous shoreline was coming toward them.

"If we retreat from the dune, we'll come within reach of the dragon," Chet said.

"Feed goon to dune," Smash suggested.

"Goon? Do you mean the dragon?" Dor asked. The ogre nodded.

"Say, yes!" Irene said. "Talk to the dune, Dor. Tell it we'll lure the dragon within its range if it lets us go."

Dor considered. "I don't know. I'd hate to send any creature to such a fate—and I'm not sure the dune can be trusted."

"Well, string it out as long as you can. Once the dune tackles the dragon, it won't have time to worry about small fry like us."

Dor eyed the surging dune on one side, the chop-slurping dragon on the other, and noted how the region between them was diminishing. "Try reasoning with the dragon first," he told Grundy.

The golem emitted a series of honks, grunts, whistles, and tooth-gnashings. It was amazing how versatile he was with sounds—but of course this was his magic. In a moment the dragon lunged forward, trying to catch the entire boat in its huge jaws, but falling short. The water washed up in a small tsunami. "I asked it if it wouldn't like to let a nice group of people on the King's business like us go on in peace," Grundy said. "It replied—"

"We can see what it replied," Dor said. "Very well; we'll go the other route." He faced the shore and called: "Hey, dune!"

Thus hailed, the dune was touched by Dor's magic. "You calling me, tidbit?"

"I want to make a deal with you."

"Ha! You're going to be consumed anyway. What kind of deal can you offer?"

"This whole boatload is a small morsel for the likes of you. But we might arrange for you to get a real meal, if you let us go in peace."

"I don't eat, really," the dune said. "I preserve. I clean and secure the bones of assorted creatures so that they can be admired millennia hence. My treasures are called fossils."

So this monster, like so many of its ilk, thought itself a benefactor to Xanth. Was there any creature or thing, no matter how awful, that didn't rationalize its existence and actions in similar fashion? But Dor wasn't here to argue with it. "Wouldn't you rather fossilize a dragon than a sniveling little collection of scraps like us?"

"Oh, I don't know. Snivelers are common, but so are dragons. Size is not as important for the fossil record as quality and completeness."

"Well, do you have a water dragon in your record yet?"

"No, most of them fall to my cousin the deepsea muck, just as most birds are harvested by my other cousin, the tarpit. I would dearly like to have a specimen like that."

"We offer you that water dragon there," Dor said. "All you need to do is make a channel deep enough for the dragon to pass. Then we'll lure it in—and then you can close the channel and secure your specimen for fossilization."

"Say, that would work!" the dune agreed. "It's a deal."

"Start your channel, then. We'll sail down it first, leading the dragon. Make sure you let us go, though."

"Sure. You go, the dragon stays."

"I don't trust this," Irene muttered.

"Neither do I," Dor agreed. "But we're in a bind. Chet, can you apply your calculus?"

"The smallest of stones can be considered calculi," Chet said. "That is to say, sand. Now sand has certain properties . . ." He trailed off, then brightened. "You have sea-grass seed?" he asked Irene.

"Lots of it. But I don't see how—" Then her eyes glowed. "Oh, I *do* see! Yes, I'll be ready, Chet!"

The sand began to hump itself into twin mounds, opening a narrow channel of water between them. Chet guided the boat directly down that channel. The dragon, perceiving their seeming escape, honked wrathfully and gnashed its teeth.

"Express hope the dragon doesn't realize how deep this channel is," Dor told Grundy. "In dragon talk."

Grundy smiled grimly. "I know my business!" He emitted dragon noises.

Immediately the dragon explored the end of the channel, plunging its head into it. With a glad honk it writhed on into the inviting passage.

Soon the dragon was close on their wake. Its entire body was now within the separation in the dune. "Now—close it up!" Dor cried to the dune.

The dune did so. Suddenly the channel was narrowing and disappearing as sand heaped into it. Too late the dragon realized its peril; it tried to turn, to retreat, but the way out was blocked. It honked and thrashed, but was in deep trouble in shallow water.

However, the channel ahead of the boat was also filling in. "Hey, let us out!" Dor cried.

"Why should I let perfectly good fossil material go?" the dune asked reasonably. "This way I've got both you and the dragon. It's the haul of the century!"

"But you promised!" Dor said plaintively. "We made a deal!"

"Promises and deals aren't worth the breath it takes to utter them—and I don't even breathe."

"I knew it," Chet said. "Betrayal."

"Do your stuff, Irene," Dor said.

Irene brought out two handfuls of seeds. "Grow!" she yelled, scattering them widely. On either side the grass

sprouted rapidly, sending its deep roots into the sand, grabbing, holding.

"Hey!" the dune yelled, much as Dor had, as it tripped
over itself where the grass anchored it.

"You reneged on our agreement," Dor called back.
"Now you pay the penalty." For the sand in this region was
no longer able to move; the grass had converted it to ordinary ground.

Enraged, the dune made one final effort. It humped up
horrendously in the region beyond the growing grass, then
rolled forward with such impetus that it spilled into the
channel, filling it.

"It's swamping the boat!" Dor cried. "Abandon ship!"

"Some gratitude!" the boat complained. "I carry you loyally all over Xanth, risking my keel, and the moment
things get rough, you abandon me!"

The boat had a case, but they couldn't afford to argue it.
Heedless of its objection, they all piled out as the sand
piled in. They ran across the remaining section of grass-
anchorage while the boat disappeared into the dune. The
sand was unable to follow them here; its limit had been
reached, and already the blades of grass were creeping up
through the new mound, nailing it down. The main body of
the dune had to retreat and concentrate on the thrashing
dragon that bid fair to escape by coiling out of the vanished channel and writhing back toward the sea.

The party stood at the edge of the bay. "We lost our
boat," Irene said. "And the flying carpet, and escape hoop,
and food."

"And my bow and arrows," Chet said mournfully. "All I
salvaged was the gourd. We played it too close; those monsters are stronger and smarter than we thought. We learn
from experience."

Dor was silent. He was the nominal leader of this party;
the responsibility was his. If he could not manage a single
trip south without disaster, how could he hope to handle
the situation when he got to Centaur Isle? How could he
handle the job of being King, if it came to that?

But they couldn't remain here long, whether in thought
or in despair. Already the natives of the region were becoming aware of them. Carnivorous grass picked up where
the freshly planted sea grass left off, and the former was

sending its hungry shoots toward them. Vines trembled, bright droplets of sap-saliva oozing from their surfaces. There was a buzzing of wings; something airborne would soon show up.

But now at last the sunfish dimmed out, and night returned; the day creatures retreated in confusion, and the night creatures stirred. "If there's one thing worse than day in the wilderness," Irene said, shivering, "it's night. What do we do now?"

Dor wished he had an answer.

"Your plants have saved us once," Chet told her. "Do you have another plant that could protect us or transport us?"

"Let me see." In the dark she put her hand in her bag of seeds and felt around. "Mostly food plants, and special effects . . . a beerbarrel tree—how did that get in here? . . . water locust . . . bulrush—"

"Bulrushes!" Chet said. "Aren't those the reeds that are always in a hurry?"

"They rush everywhere," she agreed.

"Suppose we wove them into a boat or raft—could we control its motion?"

"Yes, I suppose, if you put a ring in the craft's nose. But—"

"Let's do it," the centaur said. "Anything will be better than waiting here for whatever is creeping up on us."

"I'll start the bulrushes growing," she agreed. "We can weave them before they're mature. But you'll have to find a ring before we can finish."

"Dor and Grundy—please question your contacts and see if you can locate a ring," the centaur said.

They started in, Dor questioning the nonliving, Grundy the living. Neither could find a ring in the vicinity. The weaving of the growing bulrushes proceeded apace; it seemed Chet and Irene were familiar with the technique and worked well together. But already the rushes were thrashing about, trying to free themselves to travel. The mass of the mat-raft was burgeoning; soon it would be too strong to restrain.

"Bring ring," Smash said.

"We're trying to!" Dor snapped, clinging to a corner of the struggling mat. The thing was hideously strong.

"Germ worm," the ogre said insistently. His huge hairy paw pushed something at Dor. The object seemed to be a loop of fur.

A loop? "A ring!" Dor exclaimed. "Where did you get it?"

"Me grow on toe," Smash explained. "Which itch."

"You grew the ring on your toe—and it itched?" Dor was having trouble assimilating this.

"Let me check," Grundy said. He made a funny sizzle, talking with something, then laughed. "You know what that is? A ringworm!"

"A ringworm!" Dor cried in dismay, dropping the hideous thing.

"If it's a ring, we need it," Chet said. "Before this mat gets away."

Chagrined, Dor felt on the ground and picked up the ringworm. He passed it gingerly to the centaur. "Here."

Chet wove it into the nose of the craft, then jerked several long hairs from his beautiful tail and twined them into a string that he passed through the ring. Suddenly the bulrush craft settled down. "The nose is sensitive," Chet explained. "The ring makes it hurt when jerked, so even this powerful entity can be controlled."

"Some come!" Smash warned.

Rather than wait to discover what it was that could make an ogre nervous, the others hastened to lead the now-docile bulrush boat to the water. Once it was floating, they boarded carefully and pushed off from the shore. The craft was not watertight, but the individual rushes were buoyant, so the whole business floated.

Something growled in the dark on the shore—a deep, low, throbbing, powerful, and ugly sound. Then, frustrated, it moved away, the ground shuddering. A blast of odor passed them, dank and choking. No one inquired what it might be.

Now Chet gave the bulrushes some play. The raft surged forward, churning up a faintly phosphorescent wake. Wind rushed past their faces.

"Can you see where we're going?" Irene asked, her voice thin.

"No," Chet said. "But the bulrushes travel best in open

water. They won't run aground or crash into any monsters."

"You trust them more than I do," she said. "And I grew
them."

"Elementary calculation of vegetable nature," the centaur said.

"May I lean against your side?" she asked. "I didn't
sleep today, and your coat is so soft—"

"Go ahead," Chet said graciously. He was lying down
again, as the woven fabric of the raft could not support his
weight afoot. The rushes had swelled in the water, and Dor
had succeeded in bailing it out; they were no longer sitting
in sea water. Dor had not slept either, but he didn't feel
like leaning against Chet's furry side.

The stars moved by. Dor lay on his back and determined
the direction of travel of the raft by the stars' apparent
travel. It wasn't even; the bulrushes were maneuvering to
find the course along which they could rush most freely.
They did seem to know where they were going, and that
sufficed for now.

Gradually the constellations appeared, patterns in the
sky, formations of stars that shifted from randomness to
the suggestion of significance. There seemed to be pictures
shaping, representations of creatures and objects and notions. Some resembled faces; he thought he saw King Trent
peering down at him, giving him a straight, intelligent look.

Where are you now? Dor asked wordlessly.

The face frowned. *I am being held captive in a medieval
Mundane castle,* it said. *I have no magic power here. You
must bring me magic.*

But I can't do that! Dor protested. *Magic isn't something
a person can carry, especially not into Mundania!*

You must use the aisle to rescue me.

What aisle? Dor asked, excited.

The centaur aisle, Trent answered.

Then a waft of ocean spray struck Dor's face, and he
woke. The stellar face was gone; it had been a dream.

Yet the message remained with him. Center Isle? His
spelling disability made him uncertain, now, of the meaning. How could he use an island to seek King Trent? The
center of what? If it was centaur, did that mean Chet had
something essential to do with it? If it was an aisle, an aisle

between what and what? If this were really a message, a prophecy, how could he apply it? If it were merely a random dream or vision, a construct of his overtired and meandering mind, he should ignore it. But such things were seldom random in Xanth.

Troubled, Dor drifted to sleep again. What he had experienced could not have been a nightmare, for it hadn't scared him, and of course the mares could not run across the water. Maybe it would return and clarify itself.

But the dream did not repeat, and he could not evoke it by looking at the stars. Clouds had sifted across the night sky.

Chapter 5. Girding Loins

Dor woke again as dawn came. The sun had somehow gotten around to the east, where the land was, and dried off so that it could shine again. Dor wondered what perilous route it employed. Maybe it had a tunnel to roll along. If it ever figured out a way to get down without taking a dunking in the ocean, it would really have it made! Maybe he should suggest that to it sometime. After all, some mornings the sun was up several hours before drying out enough to shine with full brilliance; obviously some nights were worse than others. But he would not make the suggestion right now; he didn't want the sun heading off to explore new routes, leaving Xanth dark for days at a time. Dor needed the light to see his way to Centaur Isle. Jewel's midnight sunstone was not enough.

Centaur Isle—was that where he was supposed to find King Trent? No, the centaurs wouldn't imprison the King, and anyway, Trent was in Mundania. But maybe something at Centaur Isle related. If only he could figure out how!

Dor sat up. "Where are we now, Chet?" he inquired.

There was no answer. The centaur had fallen asleep, too, Irene in repose against his side. Smash and Grundy snored at the rear of the raft.

Everyone had slept! No one was guiding the craft or watching the course! The bulrushes had rushed wherever they wanted to go, which could be anywhere!

The raft was in the middle of the ocean. Bare sea lay on all sides. It was sheer luck that no sea monster had spied them and gobbled them down while they slept. In fact, there was one now!

But as the monster forged hungrily toward the craft, Dor saw that the velocity of the rushes was such that the serpent could not overtake the craft. They were safe because of their speed. Since they were heading south, they should be near Centaur Isle now.

No, that did not necessarily follow. Dor had done better in Cherie's logic classes than in spelling. He always looked for alternatives to the obvious. The craft could have been doing loops all night, or traveling north, and then turned south coincidentally as dawn came. They could be anywhere at all.

"Where are we?" Dor asked the nearest water.

"Longitude 83, Latitude 26, or vise versa," the water said. "I always confuse parallels with meridians."

"That doesn't tell me anything!" Dor snapped.

"It tells *me*, though," Chet said, waking. "We are well out to sea, but also well on the way to our destination. We should be there tonight."

"But suppose a monster catches us way out here in the sea?" Irene asked, also waking. "I'd rather be near land."

Chet shrugged. "We can veer in to land. Meanwhile, why don't you grow us some food and fresh-water plants so we can eat and drink?"

"And a parasol plant, to shield us from the sun," she said. "And a privacy hedge, for you-know."

She got on it. Soon they were drinking scented water from a pitcher plant and eating bunlike masses from puff-ball plants. The new hedge closed off the rear of the craft, where the expended pitchers were used for another purpose. Several parasols shaded them nicely. It was all becoming quite comfortable.

The bulrush craft, responsive to Chet's tug on the string

tied to the ring in its nose, veered toward the east, where the distant land was supposed to be.

Smash the Ogre sniffed the air and peered about. Then he pointed. "Me see the form of a mean ol' storm," he announced.

Oh, no! Dor spied the roiling clouds coming up over the southern horizon. Smash's keen ogre senses had detected it first, but in moments it was all too readily apparent to them all.

"We're in trouble," Grundy said. "I'll see what I can do."

"What can you do?" Irene asked witheringly. "Are you going to wave your tiny little dumb hand and conjure us all instantly to safety?"

Grundy ignored her. He spoke to the ocean in whatever language its creatures used. In a moment he said: "I think I have it. The fish are taking word to an eclectic eel."

"A what?" Irene demanded. "Do you mean one of those shocking creatures?"

"An eclectic eel, dummy. It chooses things from all over. It does nothing original; it puts it all together in bits and pieces that others have made."

"How can something like that possibly help us?"

"Better ask it *why* it will help us."

"All right, woodenhead. Why?"

"Because I promised it half your seeds."

"Half my seeds!" she exploded. "You can't do that!"

"If I don't, the storm will send us all to the depths."

"He's right, Irene," Chet said. "We're over a barrel, figuratively speaking."

"I'll put the confounded golem in a barrel and glue the cork in!" she cried. "A barrel of white-hot sneeze-pepper! He has no right to promise *my* property."

"Okay," Grundy said. "Tell the eel no. Give it a shock."

A narrow snout poked out of the roughening water. A cold gust of wind ruffled Irene's hair and flattened her clothing against her body, making her look extraordinarily pretty. The sky darkened.

"It says, figuratively speaking, your figure isn't bad," Grundy reported with a smirk.

This incongruous compliment put her off her pace. It was hard to tell off someone who made a remark like that.

"Oh, all right," she said, sulking. "Half the seeds. But I choose which half."

"Well, toss them in, stupid," Grundy said, clinging to the side of the craft as it pitched in the swells.

"But they'll sprout!"

"That's the idea. Make them all grow. Use your magic. The eclectic eel demands payment in advance."

Irene looked rebellious, but the first drop of rain struck her on the nose and she decided to carry through. "This will come out of your string hide, golem," she muttered. She tossed the seeds into the heaving water one by one, invoking each in turn. "Grow, like a golem's ego. Grow, like Grundy's swelled head. Grow, like the vengeance I owe the twerp . . ."

Strange things developed in the water. Pink-leaved turnips sprouted, turning in place, and tan tomatoes, and yellow cabbages and blue beets. Snap beans snapped merrily and artichokes choked. Then the flowers started, as she came to another section of her supply. White blossoms sprang up in great clusters, decorating the entire ocean near the raft. Then they moved away in herds, making faint *baa-aa-aas*.

"What's that?" Grundy asked.

"Phlox, ninny," Irene said.

Oh, flocks, Dor thought. Of course. The white sheep of flowers.

Firecracker flowers popped redly, tiger lilies snarled, honeybells tinkled, and bleeding hearts stained the water with their sad life essence. Irises that Irene's mother had given her flowered prettily in blue and purple. Gladiolas stretched up happily; begonias bloomed and departed even before they could be ordered to begone. Periwinkles opened their orbs to wink; crocuses parted their white lips to utter scandalous imprecations.

Grundy leaned over the edge of the raft to sniff some pretty multicolored little flowers that were vining upward. Then something happened. "Hey!" he cried suddenly, outraged, wiping golden moisture off his head. "What did they do that for?"

Irene glanced across. "Dummy," she said with satisfaction, "what do you expect sweet peas to do? You better stay away from the pansies."

On Dor's side there was an especially rapid development, the red, orange, and white flowers bursting forth almost before the buds formed. "My, these are in a hurry," he commented.

"They're impatiens," Irene explained.

The display finished off with a dazzling emergence of golden balls—marigolds. "That's half. Take it or leave it," Irene said.

"The eel takes it," Grundy said, still shaking pea out of his hair. "Now the eclectic eel will lead us through the storm to shore, in its fashion."

"About time," Chet said. "Everyone hang on. We have a rough sail coming."

The eel wriggled forward. The craft followed. The storm struck with its moist fury. "What do you have against us?" Dor asked it as the wind tore at his body.

"Nothing personal," it blew back. "It's my job to clear the seas of riffraff. Can't have flotsam and jetsam cluttering up the surface, after all."

"I don't know those people," Dor said. The raft was rocking and twisting as it followed the elusive eel, but they were somehow avoiding the worst of the violence.

A piece of planking floated by. "I'm flotsam," it said. "I'm part of the ship that wrecked here last month, still floating."

A barrel floated by on the other side, the battered trunk of a harvested jellybarrel tree. "I'm jetsam," it blew from its bung. "I was thrown overboard to lighten the ship."

"Nice to know you both," Dor said politely.

"The eel uses them for markers," Grundy said. "It uses anything it finds."

"Where's the riffraff?" Irene asked. "If the storm is here to clear it from the seas, there should be some to clear."

"I'm the raf'," the raft explained. "You must be the rif'." And it chuckled.

Now the rain pelted down full-strength. All of them were soaked in an instant. "Bail! Bail!" Chet screamed thinly through the wind.

Dor grabbed his bucket—actually, it was a bouquet Irene had grown, which his spelling had fouled up so that its nature had completely changed—and scooped out water.

Smash the Ogre worked similarly on the other side, using a pitcher. By dint of colossal effort they managed to stay marginally ahead of the rain that poured in.

"Get low!" Grundy cried through the weather. "Don't let her roll over!"

"She's not rolling," Irene said. "A raft can't—"

Then the craft pitched horribly and started to turn over. Irene threw herself flat in the bottom of the center depression, joining Dor and Smash. The raft listed sickeningly to right, then to left, first throwing Irene bodily into Dor, then hurling him into her. She was marvelously soft.

"What are you doing?" Dor cried as his wind was almost knocked from him despite his soft landings.

"I'm yawing," the raft said.

"Seems more like a roll to me," Chet grumbled from the rear.

Irene fetched up against Dor again, hip to hip and nose to nose. "Dear, we've got to stop meeting this way," she gasped, attempting to smile.

In other circumstances Dor would have appreciated the meetings more. Irene was padded in appropriate places, so that the shocks of contact were pleasantly cushioned. But at the moment he was afraid for his life and hers. Meanwhile, she looked as if she were getting seasick.

The craft lurched forward and down, as if sliding over a waterfall. Dor's own gorge rose. "Now what are you doing?" he heaved.

"I'm pitching," the raft responded.

"We're out of the water!" Chet cried. His head remained higher despite his prone position. "There's something beneath us! That's why we're rolling so much!"

"That's the behemoth," Grundy said.

"The what?" Dor asked.

"The behemoth. A huge wallowing creature that floats about doing nothing. The eclectic eel led us up to it, to help weather the storm."

Irene unglued herself from Dor, and all of them crawled cautiously up and looked over the edge of the raft. The storm continued, but now it beat on the glistening blubbery back of the tremendous animal. The craft's perch seemed insecure because of the way it rolled and slid on the slick surface, but the enormous bulk of the monster provided security from the heaving ocean.

"But I thought behemoths were fresh-water creatures," Dor said. "My father encountered one below Lake Ogre-Chobee, he said."

"Of course he did. I was there," Grundy said supercil-iously. "Behemoths are where you find them. They're too big to worry about what kind of water it is."

"The eel just happened to find this creature and led us to it?" Chet asked. He also looked somewhat seasick.

"That's the eclectic way," Grundy agreed. "To use any-thing handy."

"Aw, you cheated," the storm howled. "I can't sink that tub." A whirling eye focused on Dor. "That's twice you have escaped me, man-thing. But we shall meet again." Disgruntled, it blew itself away to the west.

So that had been the same storm he had encountered at Good Magician Humfrey's castle. It certainly traveled about!

The behemoth, discovering that its pleasant shower had abated, exhaled a dusty cloud of gas and descended to the depths. There was no point in staying on the surface when the storm didn't want to play any more. The raft was left floating in a calming sea.

Now that he was no longer in danger of drowning, Dor almost regretted the passing of the storm. Irene was a good deal more comfortable to brace against than the reeds of the raft. But he knew he was foolish always to be most interested in what he couldn't have, instead of being satis-fied with what he did have.

A monster showed on the horizon. "Get this thing mov-ing!" Irene cried, alarmed. "We aren't out of the weather yet!"

"Follow the eel!" Grundy warned.

"But the eel's headed straight for the monster!" Chet protested.

"That must be the way, then." But even Grundy looked doubtful.

They forged toward the monster. It was revealed now as extremely long and flat, as if a sea serpent had been squeezed under a rolling boulder. "What is it?" Dor asked, amazed.

"A ribbonfish, dolt," Grundy said.

"How can that help us?" For the storm had taken up more of the day than it had seemed to; the sun was now at zenith, and they remained far from shore.

"All I know is the eel agreed to get us to land by night-fall," Grundy said.

They forged on. But now the pace was slowing; the bul-rushes were losing their power. Dor realized that some of the material of the boat was dead now; that was why it had been able to speak to him, since his power related only to the inanimate. Soon the rushes would become inert, strand-ing the craft in mid-sea. They had no paddle; that had been lost with the first boat.

The ribbonfish brought its preposterously flat head down as the bulrush craft sputtered close. Then the head dipped into the water and slid beneath them. In a moment it emerged behind them, and the neck came up under the boat, heaving it right out of the water.

"Oh, no!" Irene screamed as they were carried high into the air. She flung her arms about Dor in terror. Again, he wished this could have happened when he wasn't terrified himself.

But the body of the ribbonfish was slightly concave; the raft remained centered, not falling off. As the head ele-vated to an appalling height, the boat began to slide down along the body, which was slick with moisture. They watched, horrified, as the craft tilted forward, then accel-erated down the creature's neck. Irene screamed again and clung smotheringly to Dor as their bodies turned weight-less.

Down they zoomed. But the ribbonfish was undulating, so that a new hump kept forming just behind them while a new dip formed ahead of them. They zoomed at frighten-ing velocity along the creature, never getting down to the water.

"We're traveling toward land," Dor said, awed. "The monster's moving us there!"

"That's how it gets its jollies," Grundy said. "Scooping up things and sliding them along its length. The eel just made use of this for our benefit."

Perceiving that they were not, after all, in danger, Irene

regained confidence. "Let go of me!" she snapped at Dor, as if he had been the one doing the grabbing.

The ribbonfish seemed interminably long; the raft slid and slid. Then Dor realized that the monster's head had looked down under the water and come up to follow its tail; the creature was running them through again. The land was coming closer.

At last the land arrived. The ribbonfish tired of the game and dumped them off with a jarring splash. The rushes had just enough power left to propel them to the beach; then they expired, and the raft began to sink.

The sun was well down toward the horizon, racing to cut off their day before they could travel anywhere further. Soon the golden orb would be quenched again. "From here we go by foot, I think," Chet remarked. "We will not achieve Centaur Isle this day."

"We can get closer, though," Dor said. "I've had enough of boats for now anyway." The others agreed.

First they paused to forage for some food. Wild fruitcakes were ripe and a water chestnut provided potable water; Irene did not have to expend any of her diminished store of seeds. In fact, she found a few new ones here.

Suddenly something jumped from behind a tree and charged directly at Dor. He whipped out his magic sword without thinking—and the creature stopped short, spun about, and ran away. It was all hair and legs and glower.

"What was that?" Dor asked, shaking.

"That's a jump-at-a-body," the nearest stone said.

"What's a jump-at-a-body?" Irene asked.

"I don't have to answer *you*," the stone retorted. "You can't take me for granite."

"Answer her," Dor told it.

"Awww, okay. It's what you just saw."

"That's not much help," Irene said.

"You aren't much yourself, doll," it said. "I've seen a better complexion on mottled serpentine."

Bedraggled and disheveled from the ocean run, Irene was hardly at her best. But her vanity had been pricked. "I can choke you with weeds, mineral."

"Yeah, greenie? Just try it!"

"Weeds—grow!" she directed, pointing to the rock. Immediately the weeds around it sprouted vigorously.

"Weed's the best that ever was!" the weeds exclaimed.
Startled, Dor looked closely, for his talent did not extend to
living things. He found that some sand caught in the plants
had actually done the talking.

"Oh, for schist sake!" the rock said. "She's doing it!"

"Tell me what a jump-at-a-body is," Irene insisted.

The rock was almost hidden by vegetation. "All right, all
right, doll! Just clear these junky plants out of my face."

"Stop growing," Irene told the weeds, and they stopped
with a frustrated rustle. She tramped them down around
the rock.

"You do have pretty legs," the rock said. "And that's not
all."

Irene, straddling the rock, leaped away. "Just answer my
question."

"They just jump out and scare people and run away,"
the rock said. "They're harmless. They came across from
Mundania not long ago, when the Mundanes stopped believing in them, and don't have the courage to do anything
bad."

"Thank you," Irene said, gratified by her victory over
the ornery stone.

"I think the grass needs more tramping down," the rock
suggested.

"Not while I'm wearing a skirt."

"Awww . . ."

They finished their repast and trekked on south. Very
little remained of the day, but they wanted to find a decent
place to camp for the night. Dor questioned other rocks to
make sure nothing dangerous remained in the vicinity; this
did seem to be a safe island. Perhaps their luck had turned,
and they would reach their destination without further ill
event.

But as dusk closed, they came to the southern border of
the island. There was a narrow channel separating it from
the next island in the chain.

"Maybe we'd better camp here for the night," Dor said.
"This island seems safe; we don't know what's on the next
one."

"Also, I'm tired," Irene said.

They settled in for the night, protected by a palisade
formed of asparagus spears grown for the occasion. The

jump-at-a-bodies kept charging the stockade and fleeing it harmlessly.

Chet and Smash, being the most massive individuals, lay at the outside edges of the small enclosure. Grundy needed so little room he didn't matter. Dor and Irene were squeezed into the center. But now she had room enough and time to settle herself without quite touching him. Ah, well.

"You know, that rock was right," Dor said. "You do have nice legs. And that's not all."

"Go to sleep," she said, not displeased.

In the morning a large roundish object floated in the channel. Dor didn't like the look of it. They would have to swim past it to reach the next island. "Is it animal or plant?" he asked.

"No plant," Irene said. She had a feel for this sort of thing, since it related to her magic.

"I'll talk to it," Grundy said. His talent applied to anything living. He made a complex series of whistles and almost inaudible grunts. Much of his communication was opaque to others, since some animals and most plants used inhuman mechanisms. In a moment he announced: "It's a sea nettle. A plantlike animal. This channel is its territory, and it will sting to death anyone who intrudes."

"How fast can it swim?" Irene asked.

"Fast enough," Grundy said. "It doesn't look like much, but it can certainly perform. We could separate, crossing in two parties; that way it could only get half of us, maybe."

"Perhaps you had better leave the thinking to those better equipped for it," Chet said.

"We have to get it out of there or nullify it," Dor said. "I'll try to lead it away, using my talent."

"Meanwhile, I'll start my stunflower," Irene said.

"Thanks for the vote of confidence." But Dor couldn't blame her; he had had success before in tricking monsters with his talent, but it depended on the nature and intelligence of the monster. He hadn't tried it on the water dragon, knowing that effort would be wasted. This sea nettle was a largely unknown quantity. It certainly didn't look smart.

He concentrated on the water near the nettle. "Can you

do imitations?" he asked it. The inanimate often thought it had talent of this nature, and the less talent it had, the more vain it was about it. Once, years ago, he had caused water to imitate his own voice, leading a triton a merry chase.

"No," the water said.

Oh. "Well, repeat after me: 'Sea nettle, you are a big blob of blubber.' "

"Huh?" the water asked.

He *would* have to encounter a stupid quantity of water! Some water was volatile in its wit, with cleverness flowing freely; some just lay there in puddles. "Blob of blubber!" he repeated.

"You're another!" the water retorted.

"Now say it to the sea nettle."

"You're another!" the water said to the sea nettle.

The others of Dor's party smiled. Irene's plant was growing nicely.

"No!" Dor snapped, his temper shortening. "Blob of blubber."

"No blob of blubber!" the water snapped.

The sea nettle's spines wiggled. "It says thank you," Grundy reported.

This was hopeless. In bad temper, Dor desisted.

"The flower is almost ready," Irene said. "It's a bit like the Gorgon; it can't stun you if you don't look at it. So we'd better all line up with our backs to it—and don't look back. There'll be no returning this way; once a plant like this matures, I can't stop it."

They lined up. Dor heard the rustle of rapidly expanding leaves behind him. This was nervous business!

"It's blossoming," Grundy said. "It's beginning to feel its power. Oh, it's a bad one!"

"Sure it's a bad one," Irene agreed. "I picked the best seed. Start wading into the channel. The flower will strike before we reach the sea nettle, and we want the nettle's attention directed this way."

They waded out. Dor suddenly realized how constrictive his clothing would be in the water. He didn't want anything hampering him as he swam by the nettle. He started removing his apparel. Irene, apparently struck by the same thought, quickly pulled off her skirt and blouse.

"Dor's right," Grundy remarked. He was riding Chet's back. "You do have nice legs. And that's not all."

"If your gaze should stray too far from forward," Irene said evenly, "it could encounter the ambience of the stunflower."

Grundy's gaze snapped forward. So did Chet's, Smash's, and Dor's. But Dor was sure there was a grim smirk on Irene's face. At times she was very like her mother.

"Hey, the flower's bursting loose!" Grundy cried. "I can tell by what it says; it has a bold self-image. What a head on that thing!"

Indeed, Dor could feel a kind of heat on his bare back. The power of the flower was now being exerted.

But the sea nettle seemed unaffected. It quivered, moving toward them. Its headpart was gilled like a toadstool all around. Driblets of drool formed on its surface.

"The nettle says it will sting us all so hard—oooh, that's obscene!" Grundy said. "Let me see if I can render a properly effective translation—"

"Keep moving," Irene said. "The flower's incipient."

"Now the flower's singing its song of conquest," Grundy reported, and broke into the song: "I'm the one flower, I'm the STUNflower!"

At the word "stun" there was a burst of radiation that blistered their backs. Dor and the others fell forward into the channel, letting the water cool their burning flesh.

The sea nettle, facing the flower, stiffened. Its surface glazed. The drool crystallized. The antennae faded and turned brittle. It had been stunned.

They swam by the nettle. There was no reaction from the monster. Dor saw its mass extending down into the depths of the channel with huge stinging tentacles. That thing certainly could have destroyed them all, had it remained animate.

They completed their swim in good order, Chet and Grundy in the lead, then Dor, Smash, and finally Irene. He knew she could swim well enough; she was staying back so the others would not view her nakedness. She wasn't actually all that shy about it; it was mainly her sense of propriety, developing apace with her body, and her instinct for preserving the value of what she had by keeping it reasonably scarce. It was working nicely; Dor was now several times as curious about her body as he would have been had he seen it freely. But he dared not look; the stunning radiation of the stunflower still beat upon the back of his head.

They found the shallows and trampled out of the water. "Keep going until shaded from the flower," Irene called. "Don't look back, whatever you do!"

Dor needed no warning. He felt the heat of stun travel down his back, buttocks, and legs as he emerged from the water. What a monster Irene had unleashed! But it had done its job, when his own talent had failed; it had gotten them safely across the channel and past the sea nettle.

They found a tangle of purple-green bushes and maneuvered to put them between their bodies and the stunflower. Now Dor could put his clothing back on; he had kept it mostly dry by carrying it clenched in his teeth, the magic sword strapped to his body.

"You have nice legs, too," Irene said behind him, making him jump. "And that's not all."

Dor found himself blushing. Well, he had it coming to him. Irene was already dressed; girls could change clothing very quickly when they wanted to.

They moved on south, but it was a long time before Dor lost his nervousness about looking back. That stunflower . . .

Chet halted. "What's this?" he asked.

The others looked. There was a flat wooden sign set in the ground. On it was neatly printed NO LAW FOR THE LOIN.

It was obvious that no one quite understood this message, but no one wanted to speculate on its meaning. At last Dor asked the sign: "Is there any threat to us nearby?"

"No," the sign said.

They went on, each musing his private musings. They had come to this island naked; could that relate? But obviously that sign had been there long before their coming. Could it be a misspelling? he wondered. But his own spelling was so poor, he hesitated to draw that conclusion.

Now they came to a densely wooded marsh. The trees were small but closely set; Dor and Irene could squeeze between them, but Smash could not, and it was out of the question for Chet.

"Me make a lake," Smash said, readying his huge hamfist. With the trees gone, this would be a more or less open body of murky water.

"No, let's see if we can find a way through," Dor said. "King Trent never liked to have wilderness areas wantonly destroyed, for some reason. And if we make a big commotion, it could attract whatever monsters there are."

They skirted the thicket and soon came across another sign: THE LOIN WALKS WHERE IT WILL. Near it was a neat, dry path through the forest, elevated slightly above the swamp.

"Any danger here?" Dor inquired.

"Not much," the sign said.

They used the path. As they penetrated the thicket, there were rustlings in the trees and slurpings in the muck below. "What's that noise?" Dor asked, but received no answer. This forest was so dense there was nothing inanimate in it; the water was covered with green growth, and the path itself was formed of living roots.

"I'll try," Grundy said. He spoke in tree language, and after a moment reported: "They are cog rats and skug worms; nothing to worry about as long as you don't turn your back on them."

The rustlings and slurpings became louder. "But they are all around us!" Irene protested. "How can we avoid turning our backs?"

"We can face in all directions," Chet said. "I'll go forward; Grundy can ride me facing backward. The rest of you can look to either side."

They did so, Smash on the left, Dor and Irene on the right. The noises stayed just out of sight. "But let's get on out of this place!" Irene said.

"I wonder how the loin makes out, since this seems to be its path," Dor said.

As if in answer to his question, they came upon another sign: THE LOIN IS LORD OF THE JUNGLE. Obviously the cog rats and skug worms didn't dare bother the loin.

"I am getting more curious about this thing," Irene said. "Does it hunt, does it eat, does it play with others of its kind? What *is* it?"

Dor wondered, too, but still hesitated to state his conjectures. Suppose it wasn't a misspelling? How, then, would it hunt, eat, and play?

They hurried on and finally emerged from the thicket—only to encounter another sign. THE LOIN SHALL LIE WITH THE LAMB.

"What's a lamb?" Irene asked.

"A Mundane creature," Chet said. "Said to be harmless, soft, and cuddly, but stupid."

"That's the kind the loin would like," she muttered darkly.

Still no one openly expressed conjectures about the nature of this creature. They traveled on down to the southern tip of this long island. The entire coastline of Xanth, Chet explained, was bordered by barrier reefs that had developed into island chains; this was as good and safe a route as they could ask for, since they no longer had a boat. There should be very few large predators on the islands, since there was insufficient hunting area for them, and the sea creatures could not quite reach the interiors of the isles. But no part of Xanth was wholly safe. All of them were ready to depart this Isle of the Loin.

As they came to the beach, they encountered yet another sign: A PRIDE OF LOINS. And a roaring erupted behind them, back along the path in the thicket. Something was coming—and who could doubt what it was?

"Do we want to meet a pride of loins?" Chet asked rhetorically.

"But do we want to swim through that?" Grundy asked.

They looked. A fleet of tiger sharks had sailed in while Dor's party stood on the beach. Each had a sailfin and the head of a tiger. They crowded in as close to the shore as they could reach, snarling hungry welcome.

"I think we're between the dragon and the dune again," Grundy said.

"I can stop the tiger sharks," Irene said. "I have a kraken seaweed seed."

"And I still have the hypno-gourd; that should stop a loin," Chet said. "Assuming it's a case of misspelling. There is a Mundane monster like the front half of a tiger shark, called a—"

"But there must be several loins in a pride," Grundy said. "Unless it's just one loin standing mighty proud."

"Me fight the fright," Smash said.

"A pride might contain twenty individuals," Chet said.

"You might occupy half a dozen, Smash—but the remaining dozen or so would have opportunity to eat up the rest of us. If that is what they do."

"But we don't know there are that many," Irene protested uncertainly.

"We've got to get out of here!" Grundy cried. "Oh, I never worried about my flesh when I was a real golem!"

"Maybe you weren't as obnoxious then," Irene suggested. "Besides which, you didn't *have* any flesh then."

But the only way to go was along the beach—and the tiger sharks paced them in the water. "We can't escape either menace this way," Irene said. "I'm planting my kraken." She tossed a seed into the water. "Grow, weed!"

Chet held forward the hypno-gourd that he had retained through all their mishaps, one palm covering the peephole. "I'll show this to the first loin, regardless."

Smash joined him. "Me reckon the secon'," he said, his hamfists at the ready. "An' nerd the third."

"You're the Magician," Grundy told Dor. "Do something."

Dor made a wild attempt. "Anything—is there any way out of here?"

"Thought you'd never ask," the sand at his feet said. "Of course there's a way out."

"You know a way?" Dor asked, gratified.

"No."

"For goodness' sake!" Irene exclaimed. "What an idiot!"

"You'd be stupid, too," the sand retorted, "if your brains were fragmented mineral."

"I was referring to *him!*" she said, indicating Dor. "To think they call him a Magician! All he can do is play ventriloquist with junk like you."

"That's telling him," the sand agreed. "That's a real load of sand in his eyes."

"Why did you say there was a way out if you don't know it?" Dor demanded.

"Because my neighbor the bone knows it."

Dor spotted the bone and addressed it. "What's the way out?"

"The tunnel, idiot," the bone said.

The sound of the pride of loins was looming louder. The

tiger sharks were snarling as the growing kraken weed menaced them. "Where's the tunnel?" Dor asked.

"Right behind you, at the shore," the bone said. "I sealed it off, took three steps, and fell prey to the loins."

"I don't see it," Dor said.

"Of course not; the high tide washes sand over it. Last week someone goosed the tide and it dumped a lot more sand. I'm the only one who can locate the tunnel now."

Dor picked up the bone. It resembled the thighbone of a man. "Locate the tunnel for me."

"Right there, where the water laps. Scrape the sand away." It angled slightly in his hand, pointing.

Dor scraped, and soon uncovered a boulder. "This seals it?" he asked.

"Yes," the bone said. "I hid my pirate treasure under the next island and tunneled here so no one would know. But the loins—"

"Hey, Smash," Dor called. "We have a boulder for you to move."

"Oh, I wouldn't," the bone cautioned. "That's delicately placed so the thieves can't force it. The tunnel will collapse."

"Well, how do we get in, then?"

"You have to use a sky hook to lift the boulder out without jarring the sides."

"We don't have a sky hook!" Dor exclaimed angrily.

"Of course you don't. That was my talent, when I was alive. No one but me could safely remove that boulder. I had everything figured, except the loin."

As the bone spoke, the kraken weed, having driven back the tiger sharks, was questing toward the shore. Soon it would be more of a menace to them than the tiger sharks had been.

"Any progress?" Chet asked. "I do not want to rush you, but I calculate we have thirty seconds before the loins, whatever they are, burst out of the forest."

"Chet!" Dor exclaimed. "Make this boulder into a pebble! But don't jar anything."

The centaur touched the boulder, and immediately it shrank. Soon it was a pebble that fell into the hole beneath it. The passage was open.

"Jump in!" Dor cried.

Irene was startled. "Who, me?"

"Close enough," Grundy said. "Want to stand there and show off your legs to the loins?"

Irene jumped in. "Say, this is neat!" she called from below, her voice echoing hollowly. "Let me just grow something to illuminate it—"

"You next," Dor said to Chet. "Try not to shake the tunnel; it's not secure." Chet jumped in with surprising delicacy, Grundy with him.

"Okay, Smash," Dor said.

"No go," the ogre said, bracing to face the land menace. "Me join the loin." And he slammed one huge fist into a hammy palm with a sound like a crack of thunder.

Smash wanted to guard the rear. Probably that was best. Otherwise the loins might pursue them into the tunnel. "Stand next to the opening," Dor said. "When you're ready, jump in and follow us. Don't wait too long. Soon the kraken will reach here; that will stop the loins, I think. Don't tangle with the kraken; we need it to stand guard after you rejoin us."

The ogre nodded. The bellow of the loins became loud. Dor jumped in the hole.

He found himself in a man-sized passage, leading south, under the channel. The light from the entrance faded rapidly. But Irene had thoughtfully planted starflowers along the way, and their pinpoint lights marked the progress of the tunnel. Dor paused to unwrap his midnight sunstone; its beam helped considerably.

As Dor walked, he heard the approach of the pride of loins outside. Smash made a grunt of surprise. Then there was the sound of contact. "What's going on?" Dor cried, worried.

"The ogre just threw a dandyloin to the kraken," the pebble in the mouth of the tunnel said. "Now he's facing up to their leader, Sir Loin Stake. He's tough and juicy."

"Smash, come on!" Dor cried. "Don't push your luck!"

The ogre's reply was muffled. All Dor heard was ". . . luck!"

"Oooo, what you said!" the pebble exclaimed. "Wash out your mouth with soapstone!"

In a moment Smash came lumbering down the tunnel, head bowed to clear the ceiling. A string of kraken weed was strewn across his hairy shoulder. Evidently he had held off the loins until the kraken took over the vicinity. "Horde explored, adored the gourd," he announced, cracking a smile like a smoking cleft in a lightning-struck tree. Those who believed ogres had no sense of humor were obviously mistaken; Smash could laugh with the best, provided the joke was suitably fundamental.

"What did the loins look like?" Dor asked, overcome by morbid curiosity.

Smash paused, considering, then uttered one of his rare nonrhyming utterances. "Ho ho ho ho ho!" he bellowed—and the fragile tunnel began to crumble around them. Rocks dislodged from the ceiling and the walls oozed moisture.

Dor and the ogre fled that section. Dor was no longer very curious about the nature of the loins; he just wanted to get out of this tunnel alive. They were below the ocean; they could be crushed inexorably if the tunnel support collapsed. A partial collapse, leading to a substantial leak, would flood the tunnel. Even an ogre could not be expected to hold up an ocean.

They caught up to the others. There was no crash behind them; the tunnel had not collapsed. Yet.

"This place makes me nervous," Irene said.

"No way out but forward," Chet said. "Quickly."

The passage seemed interminable, but it did trend south. It must have been quite a job for the pirate to excavate this, even with his sky hook to help haul out the refuse. How ironic that the loin should be his downfall, after he had finished the tunnel! They hurried onward and downward, becoming more nervous as the depth deepened. To heighten their apprehension, the bottom of the tunnel became clammy, then slick. A thin stream of water was flowing in it—and soon it was clear that this water was increasing.

Had the ogre's laugh triggered a leak, after all? If so, they were doomed. Dor was afraid even to mention the possibility.

"The tide!" Chet said. "The tide is coming in—and high tide covers the entrance. This passage is filling with water!"

"Oh, good!" Dor said, relieved.

Four pairs of eyes focused on him, perplexed.

"Uh, I was afraid the tunnel was collapsing," Dor said lamely. "The tide—that's not so bad."

"In the sense that a slow demise is better than a fast one," the centaur said.

Dor thought about that. His apprehension became galloping dread. How could they escape this? "How much longer is this tunnel?" Dor asked.

"You're halfway through," the tunnel said. "But you'll have trouble getting past the cave-in ahead."

"Cave-in!" Irene squealed. She tended to panic in a crisis.

"Oh, sure," the tunnel said. "No way around."

In a moment, with the water ankle-deep and rising, they encountered it—a mass of rubble that sealed the passage.

"Me bash this trash," Smash said helpfully.

"Um, wait," Dor cautioned. "We don't want to bring the whole ocean in on us in one swoop. Maybe if Chet reduces the pieces to pebbles, while Smash supports the ceiling—"

"Still won't hold," Chet said. "The dynamics are wrong. We need an arch."

"Me shape escape," Smash offered. He started to fashion an arch from stray chunks of stone. But more chunks rolled down to splash in the deepening water as he took each one.

"Maybe I can stabilize it," Irene said. She found a seed and dropped it in the water. "Grow."

The plant tried, but there was not enough light. Dor shone his sunstone on it; then the plant prospered. That was all it needed; Jewel's gift was proving useful!

Soon there was a leafy kudzu taking form. Tendrils dug into the sand; vines enclosed the rocks, and green leaves covered the wall of the tunnel. Now Smash could not readily dislodge the stones he needed to complete his arch without hurting the plant.

"I believe we can make it without the arch," Chet said. "The plant has secured the debris." He touched a stone, reducing it to a pebble, then touched others. Soon the tunnel was restored, the passage clear to the end.

But the delay had been costly. The water was now knee-deep. They splashed onward.

Fortunately, they were at the nadir. As they marched up

the far slope, the water's depth diminished. But they knew this was a temporary respite; before long the entire tunnel would be filled.

Now they came to the end of it—a chamber in which there stood a simple wooden table whose objects were covered by a cloth.

They stood around it, for the moment hesitant. "I don't know what treasure can help us now," Dor said, and whipped off the cloth.

The pirate's treasure was revealed: a pile of Mundane gold coins—they had to be Mundane, since Xanth did not use coinage—a keg of diamonds, and a tiny sealed jar.

"Too bad," Irene said. "Nothing useful. And this is the end of the tunnel; the pirate must have filled it in as he went, up to this point, so there would be only the one way in. I'll have to plant a big tuber and hope it runs a strong tube to the surface, and that there is no water above us here. The tuber isn't watertight. If that fails, Smash can try to bash a hole in the ceiling, and Chet can shrink the boulders as they fall. We just may get out alive."

Dor was relieved. At least Irene wasn't collapsing in hysterics. She did have some backbone when it was needed.

Grundy was on the table, struggling with the cap of the jar. "If gold is precious, and gems are precious, maybe this is the most precious of all."

But when the cap came off, the content of the jar was revealed as simple salve.

"This is your treasure?" Dor asked the bone.

"Oh, yes, it's the preciousest treasure of all," the bone assured him.

"In what way?"

"Well, I don't know. But the fellow I pirated it from fought literally to the death to retain it. He bribed me with the gold, hid the diamonds, and refused to part with the salve at all. He died without telling me what it was for. I tried it on wounds and burns, but it did nothing. Maybe if I'd known its nature, I could have used it to destroy the loins."

Dor found he had little sympathy for the pirate, who had died as he had lived, ignominiously. But the salve intrigued him increasingly, and not merely because he was now standing knee-deep in water. "Salve, what is your property?" he asked.

"I am a magic condiment that enables people to walk on smoke and vapor," it replied proudly. "Merely smear me on the bottoms of your feet or boots, and you can tread any trail in the sky you can see. Of course, the effect only lasts a day at a time; I get scuffed off, you know. But repeated applications—"

"Thank you," Dor cut in. "That is very fine magic indeed. But can you help us get out of this tunnel?"

"No. I make mist seem solid, not rock seem misty. You need another salve for that."

"If I had known your property," the bone said wistfully, "I could have escaped the loins. If only I had—"

"Serves you right, you infernal pirate," the salve said. "You got exactly what you deserved. I hope you loined your lesson."

"Listen, greasepot—" the bone retorted.

"Enough," Dor said. "If neither of you have any suggestions to get us out of here, keep quiet."

"I am suspicious of this," Chet said. "The pirate took this treasure, but never lived to enjoy it. Ask it if there is a curse associated."

"Is there, salve?" Dor asked, surprised by the notion.

"Oh, sure," the salve said. "Didn't I tell you?"

"You did not," Dor said. How much mischief had Chet's alertness saved them? "What is it?"

"Whoever uses me will perform some dastardly deed before the next full moon," the salve said proudly. "The pirate did."

"But I never used you!" the bone protested. "I never knew your power!"

"You put me on your wounds. That was a misuse—but it counted. Those wounds could have walked on clouds. Then you killed your partner and took all the treasure for yourself."

"That was a dastardly deed indeed!" Irene agreed. "You certainly deserved your fate."

"Yeah, he was pur-loined," Grundy said.

The bone did not argue.

"Oops," Chet said. He reached down and ripped something from his foreleg, just under the rising waterline. It was a tentacle from the kraken.

"I was afraid of that," Irene said. "That weed is way beyond my control. It won't stop growing if I tell it to."

Dor drew his sword. "I'll cut off any more tentacles," he said. "They can't come at me too thickly here at the end of the tunnel. Go ahead and start your tuber, Irene."

She dipped into her seedbag. "Oh-oh. That seed must've fallen out somewhere along the way. It's not here."

They had had a violent trip on the raft; the seed could have worked loose anywhere. "Chet and Smash," Dor said without pause, "go ahead and make us a way out of here, if you can. Irene, if you have another stabilization plant—"

She checked. "That I have."

They got busy. Dor faced back down the dark tunnel as the water rose to thigh level, spearing at the dark liquid with his sword, shining the sunstone here and there. The sounds of the ogre's work grew loud. "Water, tell me when a tentacle's coming," he directed. But there was so much crashing behind him as Smash pulverized the rock of the ceiling that he could not hear the warnings of the water. A tentacle caught his ankle and jerked him off his feet. He choked on water as another tentacle caught his sword arm. The kraken had him—and he couldn't call for help!

"What's going on here?" Grundy demanded. "Are you going swimming while the rest of us work?" Then the go-lem realized that Dor was in trouble. "Hey, why didn't you say something? Don't you know the kraken's got you?"

The kraken seaweed certainly had him! The tentacles were dragging him back down the tunnel, half drowning.

"Well, somebody's got to do something!" Grundy said, as though bothered by an annoying detail. "Here, kraken—want a cookie?" He held out a gold coin, which seemed to weigh almost as much as he did.

A tentacle snatched the coin away, but in a moment discovered it to be inedible and dropped it.

Grundy grabbed a handful of diamonds. "Try this rock candy," he suggested. The tentacle wrapped around the gems—and got sliced by their sharp edges. Ichor welled into the water as the tentacle thrashed in pain.

"Now there's a notion," Grundy said. He swam to where Dor was still being dragged along, and sliced with another diamond, cutting into the tentacles. They let go, stung, though the golem was only able to scratch them, and Dor finally gasped his way back to his feet, waist-deep in coloring water.

"I have to go help the others," Grundy said. "Yell if you get in more trouble."

Dor fished in the water and recovered his magic sword and the shining sunstone. He was more than disheveled and disgruntled. He had had to be bailed out by a creature no taller than the span of his hand. Some hero he was!

But the others had had better success. A hole now opened upward, and daylight glinted down. "Come on, Dor!" Grundy called. "We're getting out of here at last!"

Dor crammed coins and diamonds into one pocket with the sunstone, and the jar of salve into another. Smash and Chet were already scrambling out the top, having had to mount the new passage as they extended it. The centaur was actually pretty good at this sort of climbing because he had six extremities; four or five were firmly braced in crevices while one or two were searching for new holds. Grundy had no trouble; his small weight allowed him to scramble freely. Only Dor and Irene remained below.

"Hurry up, slowpoke!" she called. "I can't wait forever!"

"Start up first," he called. "I'm stashing the treasure."

"Oh, no!" she retorted. "You just want to see up my skirt!"

"If I do, that's my profit," he said. "I don't want this hole collapsing on you." For, indeed, gravel and rocks were falling down as Chet's efforts dislodged them. The whole situation seemed precarious, despite the effort of the plant Irene had grown to help stabilize the wall.

"There is that," she agreed nervously. She started to climb, while Dor completed his stashing.

The kraken's tentacles, given respite from the attacks of sword and diamond, quested forward again. The water was now chest-high on Dor, providing the weed ample play. "There's one!" the water said, and Dor stabbed into the murky fluid. He was rewarded by a jerk on his sword that indicated he had speared something that flinched away. For a creature as bloodthirsty as the kraken, it certainly was finicky about pinpricks!

"There's another!" the water cried, enjoying this game.

Dor stabbed again. But it was hard to do much damage, despite the magic skill the sword gave him, since he couldn't slash effectively through water. Stabbing only hurt the tentacles without doing serious damage. Also, the weed was learning to take evasive action. It wasn't very smart, but it did learn a certain minimum under the constant prodding of pain.

Dor started to climb, at last. But to do this he had to put away his sword, and that gave the tentacles a better chance at him. Also, the gold was very solid for its size and weighed him down. As he drew himself out of the water, a tentacle wrapped around his right knee and dragged him down again.

Dor's grip slipped, and he fell back into the water. Now three more tentacles wrapped themselves around his legs and waist. That kraken had succeeded in infiltrating this tunnel far more thoroughly than Dor had thought possible! The weed must be an enormous monster now, since this must be only a fraction of its activity.

Dor clenched his teeth, knowing that no one else could help him if he got dragged under this time, and drew his sword again. He set the edge carefully against a tentacle and sawed. The magically sharp edge sliced through the tender flesh of the kraken, cutting off the extremity. The tentacle couldn't flinch away because it was wrapped around Dor; its own greed anchored it. Dor repeated the process with the other tentacles until he was free in a milky, viscous pool of kraken blood. Then he sheathed the sword again and climbed.

"Hey, Dor—what's keeping you?" Irene called from halfway up.

"I'm on my way," he answered, glancing up. But as he did, several larger chunks of rock became dislodged, perhaps by the sound of their voices, and rattled down. Dor stood chest-deep in the water, shielding his head with his arms.

"Are you all right?" she called.

"Just stop yelling!" he yelled. "It's collapsing the passage!" And he shielded his head again from the falling rocks. This was hellish!

"Oh," she said faintly, and was quiet.

Another tentacle had taken hold during this distraction.

The weed was getting bolder despite its losses. Dor sliced it away, then once more began his climb. But now ichor from the monster was on his hands, making his hold treacherous. He tried to rinse off his hands, but the stuff was all through the water. With his extra weight, he could not make it.

Dor stood there, fending off tentacles, while Irene scrambled to the surface. "What am I going to do?" he asked, frustrated.

"Ditch the coins, idiot," the wall said.

"But I might need them," Dor protested, unwilling to give up the treasure.

"Men are such fools about us," a coin said from his pocket. "This fool will die for us—and we have no value in Xanth."

It did make Dor wonder. Why was he burdening himself with this junk? Wealth that was meaningless, and a magic salve that was cursed. He could not answer—yet neither could he relinquish the treasure. Just as the-kraken was losing tentacles by anchoring them to his body, he was in danger of losing his life by anchoring it to wealth—and he was no smarter about it than was the weed.

Then a tentacle dangled down from above. Dor shied away; had the weed found another avenue of attack? He whipped up his sword; in air it was far more effective. "You can't nab me that way, greedy-weedy!" he said.

"Hey, watch your language," the tentacle protested. "I'm a rope."

Dor was startled. "Rope? What for?"

"To pull you up, dumbbell," it said. "What do you think a rescue rope is for?"

A rescue rope! "Are you anchored?"

"Of course I'm anchored!" it said indignantly. "Think I don't know my business? Tie me about you and I'll rescue you from this foul hole."

Dor did so, and soon he was on his way, treasure and all. "Aw, you lucked out," the coin in his pocket said.

"What do you care?"

"Wealth destroys men. It is our rite of passage: destroy a man. We were about to destroy you, and you escaped through no merit of your own."

"Well, I'm taking you with me, so you'll have another chance."

"There is that," the coin agreed, brightening.

Soon Dor emerged from the hole. Chet and Smash were hauling on the rope, drawing him up, while Grundy called directions so that no snag occurred. "What were you doing down there?" Irene demanded. "I thought you'd never come up!"

"I had some trouble with the kraken," Dor said, showing off a fragment of tentacle that remained hooked to his leg.

It was now latening afternoon. "Any danger here?" Dor asked the ground.

"There's a nest of wyverns on the south beach of this island," the ground replied. "But they hunt only by day. It's quite a nest, though."

"So if we camp here at the north end we'll be safe?"

"Should be," the ground agreed grudgingly.

"If the wyverns hunt by day, maybe we should trek on past them tonight," Irene said.

Smash smiled. "We make trek, me wring neck," he said, his brute mitts suggesting what he would do to an unfortunate wyvern. The ogre seemed larger now, taller and more massive than he had been, and Dor realized that he probably *was* larger; ogres put on growth rapidly in their teen years.

But Dor was too tired to do it. "I've got to rest," he said.

Irene was unexpectedly solicitous. "Of course you do. You stood rearguard, fighting off the kraken, while we escaped. I'll bet you wouldn't have made it out at all if Chet hadn't found that vine-rope."

Dor didn't want to admit that the weight of the gold had prevented him from climbing as he should have done. "Guess I just got tired," he said.

"The fool insisted on bringing us gold coins along," the coin blabbed loudly from his pocket.

Irene frowned. "You brought the coins? We don't need them, and they're awful heavy."

Dor sat down heavily on the beach, the coins jangling. "I know."

"What about the diamonds?"

"Them, too," he said, patting the other pocket, though he wasn't sure which pocket he had put them in.

"I do like diamonds," she said. "I regard them as friends." She helped him get his jacket off, then his wet shirt. He had avoided the Kingly robes for this trip, but his garden-variety clothing seemed hardly better now. "Dor! Your arms are all scraped!"

"That's the work of the kraken," Grundy said matter-of-factly. "It hooked his limbs and dragged him under. I had to carve it with diamonds to make it let go."

"You didn't tell me it was that bad!" she exclaimed to Dor. "Krakens are dangerous up close!"

"You were busy making the escape," Dor said. Now the abrasions on his arms and legs were stinging.

"Get the rest of this clothing off!" she said, working at it herself. "Grundy, go find some healing elixir; we forgot to bring any, but a number of plants manufacture it."

Grundy went into the forest. "Any of you plants have healing juice?" he called.

Dor was now too tired to resist. Irene tugged at his trousers. Then she paused. "Oh, my—I forgot about that," she said.

"What?" Dor asked, not sure how embarrassed he should be.

"I'm certainly glad you brought that along!" she said. "Hey, Chet—look at this!"

The centaur came over and looked. "The salve!" he said. "Yes, that could be quite useful."

Dor relaxed. For a moment he had thought—but of course she had been talking about the salve.

Soon Irene had him stripped. "Your skin's abraded all over!" she scolded. "It's a wonder you didn't faint down there!"

"Guess I'll do it now," Dor said, and did.

Chapter 6. Silver Lining

Dor woke fairly well refreshed. Evidently Grundy had located a suitable balm, for the scraped skin was largely healed. His head was pillowed on something soft; after a moment he realized it was Irene's lap. Irene was asleep with her back against an ash tree, and a fine coating of ashes now powdered her hair. She was lovely in that unconscious pose.

He seemed to be wearing new clothing, too. They must have located a flannel plant, or maybe Irene had grown one from seed. As he considered that, he heard a faint bleat in the distance and was sure; newly shorn flannel plants did protest for a while. He decided not to dwell on how she might have measured or fitted him for the clothing she had made. Obviously she was not entirely naïve about such things. In fact, Irene was shaping up as a pretty competent girl.

Dor sat up. Immediately Irene woke. "Well, someone had to keep you from thrashing about in the sand until you healed," she said, embarrassed.

He had liked her better without the explanation. "Thank you. I'm better now."

Chet and Smash had gathered red and blue berries from colorberry bushes and tapped a winekeg tree for liquid. They got pleasantly high on breakfast while they discussed the exigencies of the day. "I don't think we had better try to walk by that wyverns' nest," Chet said. "But our most feasible alternative carries a penalty."

"The curse," Grundy said.

"Beware the air," Smash agreed.

Dor scratched his head. "What are you talking about?"

"The salve," Chet explained. "To walk on clouds."

"I don't want to perform some dastardly deed," Irene

said. "But I don't want to get chewed up by wyverns either."

Now a shape loomed on the ocean horizon. "What's that?" Dor asked the sea.

"A big sea serpent," the water answered. "She comes by here every morning to clean off the beaches."

Now Dor noticed how clean this beach was. The sand gleamed as whitely as bone.

"I think our decision has just been made for us," Chet said. "Let's risk the curse and walk the vapors."

"But the clouds are way out of reach," Irene protested.

"Light a fire," Grundy said. "We can walk up the smoke."

"That ought to work," Chet agreed.

Hurriedly they gathered dry wood from the interior of the island while Irene grew a flame-vine. Soon the vine was blazing, and they set the wood about it, forming a bonfire. Several fine bons puffed into the sky, looking like burning bones; then smoke billowed up, roiling its way slantwise to the west. It seemed thick enough; but was it high enough?

The sea monster was looming close, attracted by the fire. "Let's move it!" Grundy cried. "Where's the salve?"

Dor produced the salve, and the golem smeared it on his little feet. Then he made a running leap for the smoke—and flipped over and rolled on the ground. "Lift me up to the top of it," he cried, unhurt. "I need to get it firmly under me, I think."

Smash lifted him up. Yes, the ogre was definitely taller than he had been at the start of their trip.

Now the golem found his footing. "Hey—it's hot!" he cried, dancing. He ran up the column—but the smoke was moving, making his footing uncertain, and in a moment he stumbled, fell—and plummeted through the smoke toward the ground.

Smash caught him before he struck. The golem disappeared entirely inside the ogre's brute hand. "Small fall," Smash commented.

"How about putting it on his hands, too?" Irene asked.

Dor did so, dabbing it on the golem with the tip of his little finger. They put Grundy up again. This time when the golem stumbled, he was able to catch himself by grabbing handfuls of smoke. "Come on up," he cried. "The vapor's fine!"

The sea monster was almost upon them. The others put salve on their hands and feet and scrambled onto the smoke. Chet, with four feet, balanced on the shifting surface fairly handily, but Smash, Irene, and Dor had trouble. Finally they scrambled on hands and feet, getting from the hot lower smoke to the cooler higher smoke. This was less dense, but the footing remained adequate.

The surface was spongy, to Dor's sensation, like a soft balloon that was constantly changing its shape. The smoke seemed solid to their soles and palms, but it remained gaseous in nature, with its own whorls and eddies. They could not stand still on it. Dor had to keep shifting his weight to maintain balance. It was a challenge—and became fun.

Now the sea monster arrived. She sniffed the beach, then followed her nose up to the smoke and the creatures on it. The wind was extending the smoke on an almost level course at this elevation, not quite beyond reach of the monster. The creature spied Irene up there, did a double take, then snapped at the girl—who screamed and jumped off the smoke.

For an instant Dor saw her there in midair, as if she were frozen, her shriek descending with her. He knew he could not reach her or help her. The fool girl!

Then a loop of rope snagged her and drew her back to the smoke. Chet had saved his rope, the one used to draw Dor up from the hole, and now had used it to rescue Irene from her folly. Dor's heart dropped back into place.

The sea monster, deprived of her morsel, emitted an angry honk and lunged again. But this time Irene had the wit to scramble away, and the huge snout bit into the smoke and passed through it harmlessly. The teeth made an audible clash as they closed on nothing.

However, the passage of the monster's head through the smoke disturbed the column, and Dor and Smash were caught on the side nearer the fire. They could not rejoin the others until the column mended itself.

Now the monster concentrated on the two of them, since they were closest to the ground. They could not move off the smoke, so she had a good shot at them. Her huge ugly snout oriented on Dor and lunged forward.

Dor had had enough of monsters. He danced aside and whipped out his magic sword. The weapon moved dazzlingly in his hand, slicing through the soft tissue of the monster's left nostril. The creature honked with pain and rage.

"Oooo, that's not ladylike!" Grundy called from upsmoke.

"Depends on the lady," Irene remarked.

Now the sea monster opened her ponderous and mottled jaws and advanced agape. Dor had to retreat, for the mouth was too big for him to handle; it could take him in with one chomp. The monsters of the ocean grew larger than those of the lakes!

But, stepping back, he stumbled over a fresh roil of smoke and sat down hard—on nothing solid. His seat passed right through, and he had to snatch madly with both hands to save himself. He was caught as if in a tub, supported only by his feet and hands.

The monster hissed in glee and moved in to take him in, bottom-first. But Smash stepped into her mouth, hamfists bashing into the giant teeth with loud clashing sounds, knocking chips from them. Startled, the monster paused, mouth still open. The ogre stomped on her tongue and jumped back to the smoke.

By the time Dor had regained his feet, the monster had retreated, and Smash was bellowing some rhyming imprecation at her. But the monster was not one of the shy little creatures of the inland lakes that gobbled careless swimmers; she was a denizen of the larger puddle. She had been balked, not defeated; she was really angry now.

The monster honked. "I have not yet begun to bite!" Grundy translated. She cast about for some better way to get at the smokeborne morsels—and spied the fire on the beach.

The monster was not stupid for her kind. The tiny wheels rotated almost visibly in her huge ugly head as she contemplated the blaze. Then she dropped her head down, gathered herself, and with her flippers swept a huge wash of water onto the beach.

The fire hissed and sent up a violent protest of steam, then ignominiously capitulated and died. The smoke stopped billowing up.

Dor and his friends were left standing on dissipating smoke. Soon they would be left with no visible means of support.

The remaining cloud of smoke coalesced somewhat as it shrank. Dor and Smash rejoined the other three. Now all were balancing on a diffusing mass; soon they would fall into the ocean, where the sea monster slavered eagerly.

"Well, *do* something!" Irene screamed at Dor.

Dor's performance under pressure had been spotty. Now his brain percolated more efficiently. "We must make more smoke," he said. "Irene, do you have any more flammable plants in your bag?"

"Just some torchflowers," she replied. "I lost so many good seeds to the eclectic eel! But where can I grow them? They need solid ground."

"Smear magic salve on the roots," Dor told her. "Let a torch grow in this smoke."

Her mouth opened in a cute O of surprise. "That just might work!" She took out a seed, smeared it in the salve Dor held out, and ordered it to grow.

It worked. The torch developed and matured, guttering into flame and smoke. The wind carried the smoke west in a thin, dark brown stream.

Irene looked at it with dismay. "I expected it to spread out more. It will take a balancing act to walk on that!"

"In addition to which," Chet said, "the smoke in which the torch is rooted is rapidly dwindling. When it falls into the ocean—"

"We'll have to root it in its own smoke," Dor said. "Then it will never fall."

"Can't," she protested. "The smoke won't curl down, and anyway it's always moving; the thing would go into a tailspin."

"It also smacks of paradox," Chet said. "This is a problematical concept when magic is involved; nevertheless—"

"Better do *something*," Grundy warned. "That sea monster's waiting open-mouthed beneath this cloud."

"Have you another torch-seed?" Dor asked.

"Yes, one more," Irene said. "But I don't see—"

"Grow it in smoke from this one. Then we'll play leapfrog."

"Are you sure that makes sense?"

"No."

She proceeded. Soon the second torch was blazing, rooted in the smoke of the first, and its own trail of smoke ran above and parallel to the first. "But we still can't balance on those thin lines," Chet said.

"Yes, we can. Put one foot on each."

Dubiously, Chet tried it. It worked; he was able to brace against the two columns, careful not to fall between them, and walk slowly forward. Irene followed, more awkwardly, for the twin columns were at slightly different elevations and varied in separation.

There was a honking chuckle from below. Irene colored. "That monster is looking up my skirt!" she exclaimed, furious.

"Don't worry," Grundy said. "It's a female monster."

"You can be sure your legs are the first it will chomp if it gets the chance," Dor snapped. He had little patience with her vanity at this moment.

Smash went out on the columns next, balancing easily; the ogre was not nearly as clumsy as he looked.

"Go on, Grundy," Dor said. "I'll move the first torch."

"How can you move it?" the golem demanded. "You can't balance on one column."

"I'll manage somehow," Dor said, though this was a complication he hadn't worked out. Once the first torch was moved, there would be no smoke from it for him to walk on.

"You're so busy trying to be a hero, you're going to wind up monster food," Grundy said. "Where is Xanth, if you go the way of King Trent?"

"I don't know," Dor admitted. "Maybe the Zombie Master will discover he likes politics after all."

"That dourpuss? Ha!"

"But those torches have to be moved."

"*I'll* move them," Grundy said. "I'm small enough to walk on one column. You go ahead."

Dor hesitated, but saw no better alternative. "Very well. But be careful."

Dor straddled the two columns. This felt more precarious than it had looked, but was far better than dropping to the water and monster below. When he had progressed a fair distance, he braced himself and looked back.

Grundy was laboring at the first torch. But the thing was about as big as the golem, and was firmly rooted in the remaining cloud of smoke from the erstwhile beach fire; the tiny man could not get it loose. The sea monster, perceiving the problem, was bracing herself for one good snap at the whole situation.

"Grundy, get out of there!" Dor cried. "Leave the torch!"

Too late. The monster's head launched forward as her flippers thrust the body out of the water. Grundy cried out with terror and leaped straight up as the snout intersected the cloud.

The monster's teeth closed on the torch—and the golem landed on the massive snout. The saucer-eyes peered crosseyed at Grundy, who was no bigger than a mote that might irritate one of those orbs, while smoke from the torch drifted from the great nostrils. The effect was anomalous, since no sea monster had natural fire. Fire was the perquisite of dragons.

Then the sea monster's body sank back into the ocean. Grundy scrambled up along the wispy trail of smoke from the nostrils and managed to recover his perch on the original smoke cloud. But the torch was gone.

"Run up the other column!" Dor shouted. "Save yourself!"

For a moment Grundy stood looking down at the monster. "I blew it," he said. "I ruined it all."

"We'll figure out something!" Dor cried, realizing that everything could fall apart right here if every person did not keep scrambling. "Get over here now."

Numbly the golem obeyed, walking along the widening but thinning column. Dor saw that their problems were still mounting, for the smoke that supported the second torch was now dissipating. Soon the second column, too, would be lost.

"Chet!" Dor called. "Smear salve on your rope and hook it over one smoke column. Tie yourself to the ends and grab the others!"

"You have the salve," the centaur reminded him.

"Catch it!" Dor cried. He hefted the small jar in his right hand, made a mental prayer to the guiding spirit of Xanth, and hurled the jar toward the centaur.

The tiny missile arched through the air. Had his aim been good? At first its course seemed too high; then it seemed to drop too rapidly; then it became clear the missile was off to the side. He had indeed missed; the jar was passing well beyond Chet's reach. Dor, too, had blown his chance.

Then Chet's rope flung out, and the loop closed neatly about the jar. The centaur, expert in the manner of his kind, had lassoed it. Dor's relief was so great he almost sat down—which would have been suicidal.

"But this rope's not long enough," Chet said, analyzing the job he had to do with it.

"Have Irene grow it longer," Dor called.

"I can only grow live plants," she protested.

"Those vine-ropes live a long time," Dor replied. "They can root after months of separation from their parent-plants, even when they look dead. Try it." But as he spoke, he remembered that the rope had spoken to him when it came for him down the hole. That meant that it was indeed dead.

Dubiously, Irene tried it. "Grow," she called.

They all waited tensely. Then the rope grew. One end of it had been dormant; it must have been the other end that had been dead. Once more Dor's relief was overwhelming. They were skirting about as close to the brink of disaster as they could without falling in.

Once the rope started, it grew beautifully. Not only did it lengthen, it branched, becoming a full-fledged rope-vine. Soon Chet had enough to weave into a large basket. He smeared magic salve all over it and suspended it from the smoke column. Chet himself got into it, and Irene joined him, then Smash. It was a big basket, and strong; it had to be, to support both centaur and ogre. The two massive creatures clapped each other's hands together in victory; they liked each other.

Now the second torch lost footing and started to fall. Dor charged back along the two columns, dived down, reached out, and grabbed it. But his balance on one column was precarious. He windmilled his arms, but could not quite regain equilibrium.

Then another loop of rope flung out. Dor was caught under the arms just as he slipped off the column.

Chet hauled him in as he fell, so that he described an arc toward the water. The sea monster pursued him eagerly. Dor's feet barely brushed the waves; then he swung up on the far side of the arc.

"Sword!" Grundy cried, perched on smoke far above.

Dazedly, Dor transferred the torch to his left hand and drew his sword. Now he swung back toward the grinning head of the monster.

Chet heaved, lifting Dor up a body length. As a result, instead of swinging into the opening mouth, he smacked into the upper lip, just below the flaring nostrils. Dor shoved his feet forward, mashing that lip against the upper teeth. Then he stabbed forward with the sword, spearing the tender left nostril. "How's that feel, garlic-snoot?" he asked.

The snoot blasted out an angry gale of breath that was indeed redolent of garlic and worse. Creatures with the most objectionable qualities were often the ones with the most sensitive feelings about them. Dor was blown back out over the ocean, still rising as Chet hauled him up.

But now the smoke supporting the rope and basket was dissipating. Soon they would all fall—and the monster was well aware of this fact. All the pinpricks and taps on teeth and snout she had suffered would be avenged. She hung back for the moment, avoiding Dor's sword, awaiting the inevitable with hungry eagerness.

"The smoke!" Grundy cried.

Dor realized that the torch he held was pouring its smoke up slantingly. The breeze had diminished, allowing a steeper angle. "Yes! Use this smoke to support the rope!" he ordered.

Chet, catching on, rocked the rope-basket and set it swinging. As the smoke angled up, the basket swung across to intersect it. But that caused Dor to swing also, moving his torch and its smoke.

"Grow a beanpole!" he told Irene.

"Gotcha," Irene said. Soon another seed was sprouting: a bean in the form of a pole. Smash wedged this into the basket and bent it down so that Dor could reach the far tip. Dor grabbed it and hung on. Now the pole held him at an angle below the basket. Chet and Smash managed to rotate the whole contraption so that Dor was upwind from them.

The smoke poured up and across, passing just under the basket, buoying it up, each wrinkle in the smoke snagging on the woven vines. The rising smoke simply carried the basket up with it.

The sea monster caught on that the situation had changed. It charged forward, snapping at Dor—but Dor was now just out of its reach. Slowly and uncertainly the whole party slid upward, buoyed by the smoke from the torch. The arrangement seemed too fantastic and tenuous to operate even with magic, but somehow it did.

The sea monster, seeing her hard-won meal escape, vented one terrible honk of outrage that caused the smoke to waver. This shook their entire apparatus. The sound reverberated about the welkin, startling pink, green, and blue birds from their island perches and sending sea urchins fleeing in childish tears.

"I can't even translate that," Grundy said, awed.

The honk had one other effect. It attracted the attention of the nest of wyverns. The empty nest flew up, a huge mass of sticks and vines and feathers and scales and bones. "What's this noise?" it demanded.

Oh, no! Dor's talent had to be responsible for this. He had been under such pressure, his magic was manifesting erratically. "The sea monster did it!" he cried, truthfully enough.

"That animated worm?" the nest demanded. "I'll teach it to disturb my repose. I'll squish it!" And it flew fiercely toward the monster.

The sea monster, justifiably astonished, ducked her head and dived under the water. Xanth was the place of many incredible things, but this was beyond incredibility. The nest, pursuing the monster, landed with a great splash, became waterlogged, and sank. "I'm all washed up!" it wailed desparingly as it disappeared.

Dor and the others stared. They had never imagined an event like this. "But where are the wyverns?" Chet asked.

"Probably out hunting," Grundy answered. "We'd better be well away from here when they return and find their nest gone."

They had by this devious route made their escape from the sea monster. As time passed, they left the monster far below. Dor began to relax again—and his torch guttered

out. These plants did not burn forever, and this one had
expended all its smoke.

"Smoke alert!" Dor cried, waving the defunct torch.
They were now so high in the air that a fall would be disastrous even without an angry monster below.

"So close to the clouds!" Chet lamented, pointing to a
looming cloudbank. They had almost made it.

"Grow the rope some more," Grundy said. "Make it
reach up to those clouds."

Irene complied. A new vine grew up, anchored in the
basket. It penetrated the lowest cloud.

"But it has no salve," Chet said. "It can't hold on there."

"Give me the salve," Grundy said. "I'll climb up there."

He did so. Nimbly he mounted the rope-vine. In moments he disappeared into the cloud, a blob of salve stuck
to his back.

The supportive smoke column dissipated. The basket
sagged, and Dor swung about below it, horrified. But it
descended only a little; the rope-vine had been successfully
anchored in the cloud, and they were safe.

There was no way the rest of them could climb that
rope, though. They had to wait suspended until a vagary of
the weather caused a new layer of clouds to form beneath
them, hiding the ocean. The new clouds were traveling
south, in contrast to the westward-moving higher ones.

When the positioning was right, they stepped out and
trod the billowy white masses, jumping over the occasional
gaps, until they were safely ensconced in a large cloudbank. In due course this cleared away from the higher
clouds, letting the sky open. The winds at different levels
of the sky were traveling in different directions, carrying
their burdens with them; this wind was bearing south.
Since the basket was firmly anchored to the higher cloudbank, they had to unload it quickly so they would not lose
their remaining possessions. They watched it depart with
mixed emotions; it had served them well.

They sprouted a grapefruit tree and ate the grapes as
they ripened. It was sunny and warm here atop the clouds;
since this wind was carrying them south, there was no need
for the travelers to walk. Their difficult journey had become an easy one.

"Only one thing bothers me," Chet murmured. "When we reach Centaur Isle—how do we get down?"

"Maybe we'll think of something by then," Dor said. He was tired again, mentally as well as physically; he was unable to concentrate on a problem of the future right now, however critical that problem might be.

They smeared salve on their bodies so they could lie down and rest. The cloud surface was resilient and cool, and the travelers were tired; soon they were sleeping.

Dor dreamed pleasantly of exploring in a friendly forest; the action was inconsequential, but the feeling was wonderful. He had half expected more nightmares, but realized they could not reach him up here in the sky. Not unless they got hold of some magic salve for their hooves.

Then in his dream he looked into a deep, dark pool of water, and in its reflection saw the face of King Trent. "Remember the Isle," the King told him. "It is the only way you can reach me. We need your help, Dor."

Dor woke abruptly, to find Irene staring into his face. "For a moment you almost looked like—" she said, perplexed.

"Your father," he finished. "Don't worry; it's only his message, I guess. I must use the Isle to find him."

"How do you spell that?"

Dor scratched his head. "I don't know. I thought—but I'm not sure. Island. Does aisle make sense?"

"A I S L E?" she spelled. "Not much."

"I guess I'm not any better at visions than I am at adventure," he said with resignation.

Her expression changed, becoming softer. "Dor, I just wanted to tell you—you were great with the smoke and everything."

"Me?" he asked, unbelieving. "I barely scrambled through! You and Chet and Grundy did all the—"

"You guided us," she said. "Every time there was a crisis and we froze or fouled up, you called out an order and that got us moving again. You were a leader, Dor. You had what it took when we really had to have it. I guess you don't know it yourself, but you *are* a leader, Dor. You'll make a decent King, some day."

"I don't want to be King!" he protested.

She leaned down and kissed him on the lips. "I just had to tell you. That's all."

Dor lay there after she moved away, his emotions mixed. The kiss had been excruciatingly sweet, but the words sweeter yet. He tried to review the recent action, to fathom where he might have been heroic, but it was all a nightmare jumble, despite the absence of the nightmares. He had simply done what had to be done on the spur of the moment, sometimes on the very jagged edge of the moment, and had been lucky.

He didn't like depending on luck. It was not to be trusted. Even now, some horrendous unluck could be pursuing them. He almost thought he heard it through the cloudbank, a kind of leathery swishing in the air—

Then a minor kind of hell broke loose. The head of a dragon poked through the cloud, uttering a raucous scream.

Suddenly the entire party was awake and on its feet. "The wyverns!" Chet cried. "The ones whose nest we swamped! They have found us!"

There was no question of avoiding trouble. The wyverns attacked the moment they appeared. In this first contact, it was every person for himself.

Dor's magic sword flashed in his hand, stabbing expertly at the vulnerable spots of the wyvern nearest him. The wyvern was a small dragon, with a barbed tail and only two legs, but it was agile and vicious. The sword went unerringly for the beast's heart, but glanced off the scales of its breast. The dragon was past in a moment; it was flying, while Dor was stationary, and contact was fleeting.

There were a number of the wyverns, and they were expert flyers. Smash was standing his own, as one ogre was more than a match for a dragon of this size, but Chet had to gallop and dodge madly to avoid trouble. He whirled his lasso, trying to snare the wyvern, but so far without success.

Irene was in the most trouble. Dor charged across to her. "Grow a plant!" he cried. "I'll protect you!"

A wyvern oriented on them and zoomed in, its narrow lance of fire shooting out ahead. Cloud evaporated in the path of the flame, leaving a trench; they had to scramble aside. "Some protection!" Irene snorted. Her complexion was turning green; she was afraid.

But Dor's magic sword slashed with the uncanny accuracy inherent in it and lopped off the tip of a dragon's wing. The wyvern squawked in pain and rage and wobbled, partly out of control, and finally disappeared into the cloud. There were sputtering sounds and a trail of smoke fusing with the cloud vapor where the dragon went down.

It was a strange business, with Dor's party standing on the puffy white surface, the dragons passing through it as if it were vapor—which of course it was. The dragons had the advantage of maneuverability and concealment, while the people had the leverage of a firm anchorage. But Dor knew the wyverns could undercut the people's footing by burning out the clouds beneath them; all the dragons needed to do was think of it. Fortunately, wyverns were not very smart; their brains were small, since any expendable weight was sacrificed in the interest of better flight, and what brains they had were kept too hot by the fire to function well. Wyverns were designed for fighting, not thinking.

Irene was growing a plant; evidently she had saved some salve for it. It was a tangler, as fearsome a growth as the kraken seaweed, but one that operated on solid land—or cloud. In moments it was big enough to be a threat to all in its vicinity. "Try to get the tree between you and the dragon," Irene advised, stepping back from the vegetable monster.

Dor did so. When the next wyvern came at him, he scooted around behind the tangler. The dragon, hardly expecting to encounter such a plant in the clouds, did a double take and banked off. But the tangler shot out a tentacle and hooked a wing. It drew the wyvern in, wrapping more tentacles about it, like a spider with a fly.

The dragon screamed, biting and clawing at the plant, but the tangler was too strong for it. The other wyverns heeded the call. They zoomed in toward the tangler. Chet lassoed one as it passed him; the dragon turned ferociously on him, biting into his shoulder, then went on to the plant. Three wyverns swooped at the tangler, jetting their fires at it. There was a loud hissing; foul-smelling steam expanded outward. But a tentacle caught a second dragon and drew it in. No one tangled with a tangler without risk!

"We'd better get out of here," Irene said. "Whoever wins this battle will be after us next."

Dor agreed. He called to Grundy and Smash, and they went to join Chet.

The centaur was in trouble. Bright red blood streamed down his left side, and his arm hung uselessly. "Leave me," he said. "I am now a liability."

"We're all liabilities," Dor said. "Irene, grow some more healing plants."

"I don't have any," she said. "We have to get down to ground and find one; then I can make it grow."

"We can't get down," Chet said. "Not until night, when perhaps fog will form in the lower reaches, and we can walk down that."

"You'll bleed to death by night!" Dor protested. He took off his shirt, the new one Irene had made for him. "I'll try to bandage your wound. Then—we'll see."

"Here, I'll do it," Irene said. "You men aren't any good at this sort of thing. Dor, you question the cloud about a fast way down."

Dor agreed. While she worked on the centaur, he interrogated the cloud they stood on. "Where are we, in relation to the land of Xanth?"

"We have drifted south of the land," the cloud reported.

"South of the land! What about Centaur Isle?"

"South of that, too," the cloud said smugly.

"We've got to get back there!"

"Sorry, I'm going on south. You should have disembarked an hour ago. You must talk to the wind; if it changed—"

Dor knew it was useless to talk to the wind; he had tried that as a child. The wind always went where it wanted and did what it pleased without much regard for the preferences of others. "How can we get down to earth in a hurry?"

"Jump off me. I'm tired of your weight anyway. You'll make a big splash when you get there."

"I mean safely!" It was pointless to get mad at the inanimate, but Dor was doing it.

"What do you need for safely?"

"A tilting ramp of clouds, going to solid land."

"No, none of that here. Closest we have is a storm working up to the east. Its turbulence reaches down to the water."

Dor looked east and saw a looming thunderhead. It looked familiar. He was about to have his third brush with that particular storm. "That will have to do."

"You'll be sor-ree!" the cloud sang. "Those T-heads are mean ones, and that one has a grudge against you. I'm a cumulus humilis myself, the most humble of fleecy clouds, but that one—"

"Enough," Dor said shortly. He was already nervous enough about their situation. The storm had evidently exercised and worked up new vaporous muscle for this occasion. This would be bad—but what choice did they have? They had to get Chet down to land—and to Centaur Isle—quickly.

The party hurried across the cloud surface toward the storm. The thunderhead loomed larger and uglier as they approached; its huge damp vortex eyes glared at them, and its nose dangled downward in the form of a whirling cone. New muscle indeed! But the slanting sunlight caught the fringe, turning it bright silver on the near side.

"A silver lining!" Irene exclaimed. "I'd like to have some of that!"

"Maybe you can catch some on the way down," Dor said gruffly. She had criticized him for saving the gold, after all; now she wanted silver.

A wyvern detached itself from the battle with the tangler and winged toward them. "Look out behind; enemy at six o'clock!" Grundy cried.

Dor turned, wearily drawing his sword. But this dragon was no longer looking for trouble. It was flying weakly, seeming dazed. Before it reached them it sank down under the cloud surface and disappeared. "The tangler must have squeezed it," Grundy said.

"The tangler looks none too healthy itself," Irene pointed out. She was probably the only person in Xanth who would have sympathy for such a growth. Dor looked back; sure enough, the tentacles were wilting. "That was quite a fight!" she concluded.

"But if the tangler is on its last roots," Dor asked, "why

did the wyvern fly away from it? It's not like any dragon to quit a fight unfinished."

They had no answer. Then, ahead of them, the wyvern pumped itself above the cloud again, struggling to clear the thunderstorm ahead. But it failed; it could not attain sufficient elevation. It blundered on into the storm.

The storm grabbed the dragon, tossed it about, and caught it in the whirling cone. The wyvern rotated around and around, scales flying out, and got sucked into the impenetrable center of the cloud.

"I hate to see a storm feeding," Grundy muttered.

"That thing's worse than the tangler!" Irene breathed. "It gobbled that dragon just like that!"

"We must try to avoid that cone," Dor said. "There's a lot of vapor outside it; if we can climb down that, near the silver lining—"

"My hooves are sinking in the cloud," Chet said, alarmed.

Now they found that the same was happening to all their feet. The formerly bouncy surface had become mucky. "What's happening?" Irene demanded, her tone rising warningly toward hysteria.

"What's happening?" Dor asked the cloud.

"Your salve is losing its effect, dolt," the thunderhead gusted, sounding blurred.

The salve did have a time limit of a day or so. Quickly they applied more. That helped—but still the cloud surface was tacky. "I don't like this," Grundy said. "Maybe our old salve was wearing off, but the new application isn't much better. I wonder if there's any connection with the wilting tangler and the fleeing wyvern?"

"That's it!" Chet exclaimed, wincing as his own animation shot pain through his shoulder. "We're drifting out of the ambience of magic! That's why magic things are in trouble!"

"That has to be it!" Dor agreed, dismayed. "The clouds are south of Xanth—and beyond Xanth the magic fades. We're on the verge of Mundania!"

For a moment they were silent, shocked. The worst had befallen them.

"We'll fall through the cloud!" Irene cried. "We'll fall into the sea! The horrible Mundane sea!"

"Let's run north," Grundy urged. "Back into magic!"

"We'll only come to the edge of the cloud and fall off," Irene wailed. "Dor, *do* something!"

How he hated to be put on the spot like that! But he already knew his course. "The storm," he said. "We've got to go through it, getting down, before we're out of magic."

"But that storm hates us!"

"That storm will have problems of its own as the magic fades," Dor said.

They ran toward the thunderhead, who glared at them and tried to organize for a devastating strike. But it was indeed losing cohesion as the magic diminished, and could not concentrate properly on them. As they stepped onto its swirling satellite vapors, their feet sank right through, as if the surface were slush. The magic was certainly fading, and very little time remained before they lost all support and plummeted.

Yet as they encountered the silver lining, Dor realized there was an unanticipated benefit here. This slow sinking caused by the loss of effect of the salve was allowing them to descend in moderate fashion, and just might bring them safely to ground. They didn't have to depend on the ambience of the storm.

They caught hold of each other's hands, so that no one would be lost as the thickening winds buffeted them. Smash put one arm around Chet's barrel, holding him firm despite the centaur's useless arm. They sank into the swirling fog, feeling it about them like stew. Dor was afraid he would be smothered, but found he could breathe well enough. There was no salve on his mouth; cloud was mere vapor to his head.

"All that silver lining," Irene said. "And I can't have any of it!"

The swirl of wind grew stronger. They were thrown about by the buffets and drawn into the central vortex— but it now had only a fraction of its former strength and could not fling them about as it had the wyvern. They spiraled down through it as the magic continued to dissipate. Dor hung on to the others, hoping the magic would hold out long enough to enable them to land softly. But if they splashed into deep water—

After an interminably brief descent, they did indeed

splash into deep water. The rain pelted down on them and monstrous waves surged around them. Dor had to let go of the hands he held, in order to swim and let the others swim. He held his breath, stroked for the surface of the current wave and, when his head broke into the troubled air, he cried, "Help! Spread the word!"

Did any magic remain? Yes—a trifle. "Help!" the wave echoed faintly. "Help!" the next wave repeated. "Help! Help! Help!" the other waves chorused.

A raft appeared. "Someone's drowning!" a voice cried. "Where are you?"

"Here!" Dor gasped. "Five of us—" Then a cruel wash of water smacked into his face, and he was choking. After that, all his waning energies were taken trying to stay afloat in the turbulence, and he was not quite succeeding.

Then strong hands caught him and hauled him onto a broad wooden raft. "The others!" Dor gasped. "Four others—"

"We've got them, King Dor," his rescuer said. "Water-logged but safe."

"Chet—my friend the centaur—he's wounded—needs healing elixir—"

The rescuer smiled. "He has it, of course. Do you suppose we would neglect our own?"

Dor's vision cleared enough to take in the full nature of his rescuer. It was an adult centaur! "We—we made it—"

"Welcome to the waters of the coast of Centaur Isle, Your Majesty."

"But—" Dor spluttered. "You aren't supposed to know who I am!"

"The Good Magician Humfrey ascertained that you were in trouble and would require assistance when you touched water. The Zombie Master asked us to establish a watch for you in this locale. You are a most important person in your own land, King Dor! It is fortunate we honored their request; we do not ordinarily put to sea during a funnel-storm."

"Oh." Dor was abashed. "Uh, did they tell you what my mission was?"

"Only that you were traveling the Land of Xanth and making a survey of the magic therein. Is there something else we should know?"

"Uh, no, thanks," Dor said. At least that much had been salvaged. The centaurs would not have taken kindly to the notion of a Magician among them—a centaur Magician. Dor did not like deceit, but felt this much was necessary.

Irene appeared, soaked through, bedraggled, and unkempt, but still quite pretty. Somehow she always seemed prettiest to him when she was messed up; perhaps it was because then the artifice was gone. "I guess you did it again, Dor," she said, taking his hand. "You got us down alive."

"But you didn't get your silver lining," he reminded her.

She laughed. "Some other time! After the way that storm treated us, I don't want any of its substance anyway."

Then the centaurs led them into the dry cabin of the raft. Irene continued to hold his hand, and that pleased Dor.

Chapter 7. Dastardly Deed

It was dark by the time the centaurs' raft reached port. Chet was taken to a vet for treatment, as the wyvern's bite seemed to be resisting the healing elixir. Dor and his companions were given a good meal of blues and oranges and greens and conducted to a handsome stable for the night. It commanded a fine view of a succulent pasture, was adequately ventilated, and was well stocked with a water trough, hay, and a block of salt.

They stared at the accommodations for a moment; then Smash stepped inside. "Say, hay!" he exclaimed, and plunked himself down into it with a crash that shook the building.

"Good idea," Grundy said, and did likewise, only the shaking of the building was somewhat less. After another moment, Dor and Irene settled down, too. The hay was comfortable and sweetly scented, conducive to relaxation and thoughts of pleasant outdoors. Irene held Dor's hand, and they slept well.

In the morning a stately elder centaur male entered the stable. He seemed oddly diffident. "I am Gerome, the Elder of the Isle. King Dor, I am here to apologize for the error. You were not supposed to be bedded here."

Dor got hastily to his feet, brushing hay off his crumpled clothing while Irene straightened out her skirt and brushed brown hay out of her green hair. "Elder, we're so glad to be rescued from the ocean, and fed and housed, that these accommodations seem wonderful. We'll be happy to complete our business and go home; this was never intended as an official occasion. The stable was just fine."

The centaur relaxed. "You are gracious, Your Majesty. We maintain assorted types of housing for assorted types of guests. I fear a glitch got into the program; we try to fence them out, but they keep sneaking in."

"They infest Castle Roogna also," Dor said. "We catch them in humane glitch traps and deport them to the far forests, but they breed faster than we can catch them."

"Come," the centaur said. "We have attire and food for you." He paused. "One other thing. Some of our number attended the Good Magician's wedding. They report you performed splendidly in trying circumstances. Magician Humfrey had intended to give you an item; it seems the distractions of the occasion caused it to slip his mind." The centaur almost smiled.

"He does tend to be forgetful," Dor said, remembering the lapse about notifying the human Elders about King Trent's excursion to Mundania.

"Accordingly, the Gorgon asked one of our representatives to convey the item to you here." Gerome held out a small object.

Dor accepted it. "Thank you, Elder. Uh, what is it?"

"I believe it is a magic compass. Note that the indicator points directly to you—the one Magician on the Isle."

Dor studied the compass. It was a disk within which a needle of light showed. "This isn't pointing to me."

Gerome looked. "Why, so it isn't. But I'm sure it was until a moment ago; that is how I was certain it had reached its proper destination. Perhaps I misunderstood its application; it may have pointed to you only to guide us to you. Certainly it assisted our search for you yesterday afternoon."

"That must be it!" Dor agreed. The Good Magician might have anticipated the problem with the storm and sent down the one thing that would bring help to him unerringly. Humfrey was funny that way, doing things anachronistically. Dor tucked the compass in a pocket with the diamonds and sunstone and changed the subject. "Chet— how is he doing this morning?"

Gerome frowned. "I regret to report that he is not fully recovered. Apparently he was bitten near the fringe of magic—"

"He was," Dor agreed.

"And a Mundane infection got in. This is resistive to magic healing. Perhaps, on the other hand, it was merely the delay in applying the elixir. We can not be certain. Odd things do happen at the fringe of magic. He is in no danger of demise, but I fear it will be some time before his arm is again at full strength."

"Maybe we can help him back at Castle Roogna," Dor said, uncomfortable. "He is our friend; without him, we could not have made it down here. I feel responsible—"

"He must not indulge in any further violence until he recovers completely," Gerome said gravely. "It is not at all wise to take a magic-resistive illness lightly. Come—he awaits you at breakfast."

On the way there, Gerome insisted they pause at the centaur clothier. Dor was outfitted with bright new trousers, shirt, and jacket, all intricately woven and comfortable. Irene got a dress set that set her off quite fetchingly, though it was not her normal shade of green. Even Smash and Grundy got handsome jackets. The ogre had never worn clothing before, but his jacket was so nice he accepted it with pride.

"This material," Irene said. "There's something magic about it."

Gerome smiled. "As you know, we centaurs frown on personal magic talents. But we do work with magic. The apparel is woven by our artisans from iron curtain thread, and is strongly resistant to penetration by foreign objects. We use it for vests during combat, to minimize injuries."

"But this must be very precious stuff!" Dor said.

"Your welfare is important to us, Your Majesty. Had you and Chet been wearing this clothing, the wyvern's teeth would not have penetrated his shoulder."

Dor appreciated the rationale. It would be a big embarrassment to the centaurs if anything happened to the temporary King of Xanth or his friends during their stay here. "Thank you very much."

They entered a larger room, whose tall ceiling was supported by ornate white columns. Huge windows let in the slanting morning sunlight, lending a pleasant warmth and brilliance. On an enormous banquet table in the center were goblets of striped sardonyx and white alabaster, doubly pretty in the sun. The plates were of green jadeite. "A King's ransom," Irene whispered. "I think they trotted out the royal crockery for you, Dor."

"I wish they hadn't," he whispered back. "Suppose something gets broken?"

"Keep an eye on Smash," she said. That made Dor more nervous than ever. How would the ogre handle the delicate tableware?

They were given high chairs, for the table was too tall for them. Several more centaurs joined them, male and female, introduced as the other Elders of the Isle. They stood at the table; centaurs had no way to use chairs, and the table was crafted to their height.

The food was excellent. Dor had been halfway fearful that it would be whole oats and cracked corn with silage on the side, but the glitch of the stable-housing was not repeated. There was a course of yellow cornmeal mush, from cornmeal bushes, and fine chocolate milk from cocoa-nuts. For sweetening there was an unusual delicacy called honey, said to be manufactured by a rare species of bees imported from Mundania. Dor had encountered sneeze-bees and the spelling bee, but it was odd indeed to think of honey-bees!

Smash, to Dor's surprise and relief, turned out to be a connoisseur of delicate stone. His kind, he informed them happily in rhyme, had developed their power by smashing and shaping different kinds of minerals. They could not turn out goblets as nice as these, but did produce pretty fair marble and granite blocks for walls and buildings.

"Indeed," Gerome agreed. "Some fine cornerstones here

were traded from ogres. Those corners stand up to anything."

Smash tossed down another couple mugs of milk,
pleased. Few other creatures recognized the artistic propensities of ogres.

Chet was there, looking somewhat wan and eating very
little, which showed that his injury was paining him somewhat. There was nothing Dor could do except politely ignore it, as his friend obviously wanted no attention drawn
to his weakness. Chet would not be traveling with them
again for some time.

After the meal they were treated to a guided tour of the
Isle. Dor was conscious of King Trent's reference to isle or
aisle in the vision. If it were the only way Dor could reach
him, he must be alert for the mechanism. Somewhere here,
perhaps, was the key he needed.

The outside streets were broad, paved with packed dirt
suitable for hooves, and were banked on the curves for
greatest galloping comfort. At intervals were low wooden
props that the centaurs could use to knock the dottle from
their feet. The buildings were mixed; some were stables,
while others were more like human residences.

"I see you are perplexed by our premises," Gerome said.
"Our architecture derives from our origin; in due course
you shall see our historical museum, where this will be
made clear."

During their walk, Dor surreptitiously looked at the
magic compass Good Magician Humfrey had sent him. He
had believed he had figured out its application. "Compass—do you point to the nearest and strongest Magician
who is not actually using you?" he asked.

"Sure," the compass replied. "Any fool knows that."

So it was now pointing to the centaur Magician. Once
Dor got free of these formalities, he would follow that needle to the object of his quest.

They stopped at the extensive metalworking section of
town. Here were blacksmiths and silversmiths and copper-
smiths, fashioning the strange shoes that important centaurs
used, and the unusual instruments they employed for eating, and the beautiful pots they cooked with. "*They* had no
trouble harvesting plenty of silver linings," Irene commented enviously.

"Ah—you appreciate a silver lining?" Gerome inquired. He showed the way to another craftshop, where hundreds of silver linings were being fashioned as the fringes of jackets and such. "This is for you." And the centaur gave her a fresh fur with a fine silver lining sewn in, which gleamed with the splendor of sunlight after storm.

"Ooooh," Irene breathed, melting into it. "It's soft as cloud!" Dor had to admit, privately, that the decorative apparel did enhance her appearance.

One centaur was working with a new Mundane import, a strong light metal called aluminum. "King Trent's encouragement of trade with Mundania has benefited us," Gerome remarked. "We have no natural aluminum in Xanth. But the supply is erratic, because we never seem to be able to trade with the same aspect of Mundania twice in succession. If that problem could be ameliorated, it would be a great new day for commerce."

"He's working on it," Irene said. But she had to stop there; they had agreed not to spread the word about King Trent's situation.

They saw the weaving section, where great looms integrated the threads garnered from assorted sources. The centaurs were expert spinners and weavers, and their products varied from silkenly fine cloth to heavy ruglike mats. Dor was amazed; it had never occurred to him that the products of blanket trees could be duplicated artificially. How wonderful it would be to be able to make anything one needed, instead of having to wait for a plant to grow it!

Another section was devoted to weapons. Centaurs were superlative bowmen and spearmen, and here the fine bows and spears were fashioned, along with swords, clubs, and ropes. A subsection was devoted to armor, which included woven metal clothing as well as helmets, greaves, and gauntlets. Smash tried on a huge gauntlet and flexed it into a massive fist. "Me see?" he inquired hopefully.

"By all means," Gerome said. "There is a boulder of quartz we mean to grind into sand. Practice on it."

Smash marched to the boulder, lifted his fist high, and smashed it down upon the boulder. There was a crack of sound like thunder, and a cloud of dust and sand erupted from the point of contact, enveloping him. When it settled, they saw the ogre standing knee-deep in a mound of sand, a blissful smile cracking his ugly face. "Love glove," he grunted, reluctantly removing it. Wisps of smoke rose from its fingertips.

"Then it is yours, together with its mate," Gerome said. "You have saved us much labor, reducing that boulder so efficiently."

Smash was thrilled with the gift, but Dor was silent. He knew ogres were strong, but Smash was not yet grown. The metal gauntlet must have enhanced his power by protecting his hand. As an adult, Smash would be a truly formidable creature, with almost too much power. That could get him exiled from the vicinity of Castle Roogna. But more than that, Dor was disquieted by something more subtle. The centaurs were evidently giving choice gifts to each member of Dor's party—fine protective clothing, plus whatever else offered, such as Irene's silver lining and Smash's gauntlets. This might be a fine gesture of friendship—but Dor distrusted such largesse. What was the purpose in it? King Trent had warned him once to beware strangers bearing gifts. Did the centaurs suspect Dor's mission, and were they trying to affect the manner he pursued it? Why? He had no ready answer.

They viewed the centaur communal kitchen, where foodstuffs from a wide area were cleaned and prepared. Obviously the centaurs ate very well. In fact, in most respects they seemed to be more advanced and to have more creature comforts than the human folk of the Castle Roogna area. Dor found this unsettling; he had somehow expected to find Centaur Isle inhabited by a few primitives galloping around and fighting each other with clubs. Now that he was here, Centaur Isle seemed more like the center of culture, while Castle Roogna appeared to be the hinterland.

The power of magic was surely weaker here near the fringe, which helped explain why most centaurs seemed to lack talents, while those farther toward the center of Xanth were showing them. How was it, then, that these deficient centaurs were doing so well? It was almost as if the lack of magic was an advantage, causing them to develop other skills that in the end brought more success than the magic would have. This was nonsense, of course; but as he viewed the things of the Isle, he almost believed it. Suppose, just suppose, that there *was* a correlation between success and the lack of magic. Did it then follow that Mundania, the land completely devoid of music, was likely to become a better place to live than Xanth?

That brought a puff of laughter. He had followed his thought to its logical extremity and found it ludicrous. Therefore the thought was false. It was ridiculous on the face of it to think of drear Mundania as a better place than Xanth!

The others were looking askance at him because of his pointless laughter. "Uh, just a chain of thought that snapped in a funny place," Dor explained. Then, fearing that wasn't enough to alleviate their curiosity, he changed the subject. "Uh, if I may inquire—since you centaurs seem to be so well organized here—certainly better than we humans are—how is it that you accept human government? You don't seem to need us, and if it ever came to war, you could destroy us."

"Dor!" Irene protested. "What a thing to say!"

"You are too modest, Your Majesty," Gerome said, smiling. "There are several compelling reasons. First, we are not interested in empire; we prefer to leave decisions of state to others, while we forward our arts, crafts, skills, and satisfaction. Since you humans seem to like the tedious process of government, we gladly leave it to you, much as we leave the shaping of granite stones to the ogres and the collection of diamonds to the dragons. It is far simpler to acquire what we need through trade."

"Well, I suppose so," Dor agreed dubiously.

"Second, you humans have one phenomenal asset that we generally lack," Gerome continued, evidently embarked on a favorite subject. "You can do magic. We utilize magic, but generally cannot perform it ourselves, nor would we wish to. We prefer to borrow it as a tool. Can you imagine one of us prevailing over King Trent in an altercation? He would convert us all to inchworms!"

"If he could get close enough," Dor said. He remembered that this matter had been discussed before; Chet had pointed out how the centaurs' skill with the bow and arrow nullified Trent's magic. Was there an answer to that? Dor would much prefer to believe that magic was the supreme force in Xanth.

"Who can govern from a distance?" Gerome inquired

rhetorically. "Armies in the field are one thing; governing people is another. King Trent's magic enables him to govern, as does your own. Even your lesser talents are far beyond our capacities."

Was the centaur now gifting him with flattery? "But centaurs can do magic!" Dor protested. "Our friend Chet—"

"Please," Gerome said. "You humans perform natural functions, too, but we do not speak publicly of such things, in deference to your particular sensitivities. It is a fact that we centaurs were not aware of any personal magic talents through most of our history, and even now suspect manifestations are an aberration. So we have never considered personal magic as being available for our use and would prefer that no further mention of this be made."

"Uh, sure," Dor agreed awkwardly. It seemed the other centaurs were just as sensitive and unreasonable about this as Dor's tutor Cherie was. Humans were indeed finicky about certain natural functions, as the centaur Elder had reminded him, while centaurs were not; while humans were not finicky about the notion of personal magic the way the centaurs were. Probably one attitude made as much nonsense as the other.

But how would the citizens of Centaur Isle react to the news that a full Magician of their species was among them? Eventually Dor would have to tell them. This mission could be awkward indeed!

"Third, we honor an understanding dating from the dawn of our species," Gerome continued, leaving the distasteful subject of magic behind like a clod of manure. "We shall not indulge in politics, and will never compete with our human brethren for power. So even if we desired empire and had the ability to acquire it, we would not do so. We would never renege on that binding commitment." And the centaur looked so serious that Dor dared not pursue the matter further.

At last they came to the historical museum. This was an impressive edifice of red brick, several stories high, with small windows and a forbidding external aspect. But it was quite interesting inside, being crowded with all manner of artifacts. There were samples of all the centaurs' products, going back decade by decade to before the First Wave of

human conquest. Dor could see how the earlier items were
cruder; the craftsmen were still improving their skills.
Everything was identified by neat plaques providing dates,
places, and details of manufacture. The centaurs had a
keen sense of history!

During the tour, Dor had continued to sneak glances at
the magic compass. He was gratified to see that it pointed
toward the museum; maybe the Magician was here!

"And this is our keeper of records," Gerome said, intro-
ducing a middle-aged, bespectacled centaur. "He knows
where all the bodies are hidden. Arnolde the Archivist."

"Precisely," Arnolde agreed dourly, peering over his
glasses. The demon Beauregard was the only other creature
Dor had seen wearing such devices. "So nice to encounter
you and your party, King Dor. Now if you will excuse me,
I have a new shipment of artifacts to catalogue." He retreated to his cubby, where objects and papers were piled
high.

"Arnolde is dedicated to his profession," Gerome explained. "He's quite intelligent, even by our standards, but
not sociable. I doubt there is very much about Xanth natural history he doesn't know. Recently he has been picking
up items from the fringe of magic; he made one trip to an
island to the south that may have taken him entirely out of
magic, though he denies this. Prior to the time King Trent
dropped the shield that enclosed Xanth, such expeditions
were impossible."

Dor remembered the shield, for his tutor had drilled him
on it. Cherie Centaur was particularly strong on social history. The Waves of human conquerors had become so bad
that one King of Xanth had finally put a stop to further
invasion by setting up a magic shield that killed any living
thing that passed through it. But that had also kept the
inhabitants of Xanth in. The Mundanes, it seemed, came to
believe that Xanth did not exist at all and that magic was
impossible, since none of it leaked out any more. There
had, it seemed, been many recorded cases of magic that
Mundanes had witnessed or experienced; all these were
now written off as superstition. Perhaps that was the Mundanes' way of reconciling themselves to the loss of something as wonderful as enchantment, to pretend it did not
exist and never had existed.

But Xanth had suffered, too. In time it had become apparent that mankind in Xanth needed those periodic infusions of new blood, however violently they came, for without the Waves there was a steady attrition of pure human beings. First, people developed magic talents; later generations became magic themselves, either mating with animals to form various composite species like harpies or fauns or merfolk, or simply evolving into gnomes or giants or nymphs. So King Trent had lowered the shield and brought in a number of settlers from Mundania, with the understanding that these new people would be drawn on as warriors to repel any future violent invasion that might come. So far there had been none—but the Waves had been a pattern of centuries, not of decades, so that meant little. Immigration was an uncertain business, as it was far easier to go from Xanth to Mundania than the other way around, at least for individual people. But the human situation in Xanth did seem to be improving now. Dor could appreciate how an intelligent, inquisitive centaur would be eager to begin cataloguing the wonders of Mundania, which long had been a great mystery. It was still hard to accept the notion that here was a region where magic was inoperative, and where people survived.

They moved on down the narrow hall. Dor checked the compass again—and found that it pointed directly toward Arnolde the Archivist.

Could he be the centaur Magician, the threat to the welfare of Xanth, the important business Dor had to attend to? That didn't seem to make much sense. For one thing, Arnolde showed no sign of magic ability. For another, he was hardly the type to threaten the existing order; he was dedicated to recording it. For yet another, he was a settled, middle-aged person, of a species that lived longer than man. Magic talents might not be discovered early, but the evidence was that they existed from birth on. Why should this talent become an issue now, perhaps a century into Arnolde's life? So it must be a mistake; Dor's target had to be a young centaur, perhaps a newborn one.

Yet as Dor moved about the building, only half listening to the presentation, the compass pointed unerringly toward Arnolde's cubby.

Maybe Arnolde was married, Dor thought with exasperated inspiration. Maybe he had a baby centaur, hidden there among the papers. The compass could be pointing to the foal, not to Arnolde. Yes, that made sense.

"If you don't get that glazed look off your face, the Elder will notice," Irene murmured, jolting Dor's attention.

After that he concentrated and managed to assimilate more of the material. After all, there was nothing he could do about the Magician at the moment.

At length they completed the tour. "Is there anything else you would like to see, King Dor?" Gerome inquired.

"No, thank you, Elder," Dor replied. "I think I've seen enough."

"Shall we arrange to transport your party back to your capital? We can contact your conjurer."

This was awkward. Dor had to complete his investigation of the centaur Magician, so he was not ready to leave this Isle. But it was obvious that his mission and discovery would not be well received here. He could not simply tell the centaur Elders the situation and beg their assistance; to them that would be obscenity, and their warm hospitality would abruptly chill. A person's concept of obscenity was not subject to reasonable discussion, for of course the concepts of obscenity and reason were contradictory.

In fact, that might be the root of the centaurs' accommodation and generosity. Maybe they suspected his mission, so were keeping him reined at all times, in the guise of hospitality. How could he decline to go home promptly, after they had seemingly catered to his needs so conscientiously? They wanted him off the Isle, and he had little chance to balk their wish.

"Uh, could I talk with Chet before I decide anything?" Dor asked.

"Of course. He is your friend." Again Gerome was the soul of accommodation. That made Dor more nervous, ironically. He was almost sure, now, that he was being managed.

"And my other friends," Dor added. "We need to decide things together."

It was arranged. In the afternoon the five got together in a lovely little garden site of guaranteed privacy. "You all know our mission," Dor said. "It is to locate a centaur Magician and identify his talent—and perhaps bring him back to Castle Roogna. But the centaurs don't much like magic in themselves; to them it's obscene. They react to it somewhat the way we do to—well, like people looking up Irene's skirt."

"Don't start on that!" she said, coloring slightly. "I think the whole world has been looking up my skirt recently!"

"Your fault for having good legs," Grundy said. She kicked at him, but the golem scooted away. Dor noted that she hadn't tried very hard to tag Grundy; she was not really as displeased as she indicated.

"I happen to be in a position to understand both views," Chet said. His left arm was now in a sling, and he wore a packing of anti-pain potions. His outlook seemed improved, but not his immediate physical condition. "I admit that both centaur and human foibles are foolish. Centaurs do have magic talents and should be proud to display them, and Irene does have excellent limbs for her kind and should be proud to display them. And that's not all—"

"All *right*!" Irene snapped, her color deepening. "Point made. We can't go blabbing our mission to everyone on Centaur Isle. They just wouldn't understand."

"Yes," Dor said, glad to have this confirmation of his own analysis of the situation. "So now I need some group input. You see, I believe I have located the centaur Magician. It has to be the offspring of Arnolde the Archivist."

"Arnolde?" Chet asked. "I know of him. He's been at his job for fifty years; my mother speaks of him. He's a bachelor. He has no offspring. He's more interested in figures of the numerical persuasion than in figures of fillies."

"No offspring? Then it must be Arnolde himself," Dor said. "The magic compass points directly to him. I don't know how it is possible, since I'm sure no such Magician was known in Xanth before, but I don't believe Good Magician Humfrey would give me a bad signal on this."

"What's his talent?" Irene asked.

"I don't know. I didn't have a chance to find out."

"I could ask around," Grundy offered. "If there are any plants or animals around his stall, they should know."

"I can ask around myself," Dor said. "There are bound to be inanimate objects around his stall. That's not the problem. The Elders are ready to ship us home now, and I have no suitable pretext to stay. Even one night might be enough. But what do I tell them without lying or alienating them? King Trent told me that when in doubt, honesty is the best policy, but in this case I'm in doubt even about honesty."

"Again I perceive both sides," Chet said. "Honesty *is* best—except perhaps in this case. My kind can become exceedingly ornery when faced with an incompatible concept. While I would not wish to imply any criticism of my sire—"

The others knew what he meant. Chester Centaur's way to handle something he didn't like was to pick it up in a chokehold and shake the stuffing from it. The centaurs of Centaur Isle were more civilized, but just as ornery underneath.

"Tell them your business is unfinished and you need another day," Irene suggested. "That's the literal truth."

"That, simplistic as it sounds, is an excellent answer," Chet said. "Then go out at night and spy out Arnolde's talent. Have Grundy scout the route first, so you don't arouse suspicion. That way you can complete the mission without giving offense and go home tomorrow."

"But suppose we need to take him with us? A full Magician should come to Castle Roogna."

"No problem at all," Chet said. "I can tell you right now he won't come, and no Magician can be compelled. There's hardly a thing that could dislodge the archivist from his accustomed rounds."

"Knowing his talent should be enough," Irene said. "Our own Council of Elders can decide what to do about it, once they have the information."

Dor was relieved. "Yes, of course. Tonight, then. The rest of you can sleep."

"Fat chance," Irene said, and Smash grunted agreement. "We're in this mess together. You're certain to foul it up by yourself."

"I appreciate your vote of confidence, as always," Dor said wryly. But he also appreciated their support. He was afraid he would indeed foul it up by himself, but hadn't wanted to ask them to participate in what might be a nasty business.

That night they put their plot into execution. Grundy went out first, his tiny dark body concealed by the darkness. There was no trouble, and soon all of them left their comfortable human-style beds—Chet excepted, as he was separately housed and could not readily leave his stall unobserved—and moved into the moonlit evening. They had no difficulty seeing, because the moon was nearing full and gave plenty of light.

They found the museum without trouble. Dor had assumed it would be closed for the night, but to his dismay it was lighted. "Who is in there?" he asked the ground.

"Arnolde the Archivist," the ground replied. "You have to be pretty stupid not to know he's been working late all week, cataloguing those new Mundane artifacts, though what he finds so interesting about such junk—"

"What's his magic talent?"

"His what?" the ground asked, bewildered.

"You know of no magic associated with him?" Dor asked, surprised. Normally people were very free about what they did around only inanimate things, and it was hard to avoid the inanimate. That was what made Dor's own talent so insidious; the complete privacy people thought they had became complete disclosure in his presence. He tried not to pry into what did not rightly concern him, but most people, including his own parents, normally stayed clear of him, without making any issue of it. The people who had traveled with him were different, for their separate reasons; when he thought about it, he appreciated it immensely. Even Irene, who professed to value her privacy, was not truly uncomfortable in Dor's presence. She really didn't have to make any great play for him; gratitude would haul him into her orbit any time she wished. He knew she was accustomed to lack of privacy because of the way her mother was, but still found it easier to get along with her than with other girls. Others got unduly upset when their clothing started telling Dor their secrets.

Dor glanced at the large round moon again. It was amazing how that orb stimulated his thoughts along such lines!

Meanwhile, the ground had answered: "None at all. Centaurs don't do magic."

Dor sighed. "I guess we'll have to go in and brace him directly."

They went in. Arnolde had artifacts spread out all over a

main table and was attaching tags to them and making notes. There were fragments of stone and crockery and rusted metal. "I wish the archaeologists would get these classified sooner," he grumbled. "This table is not available by day, so I have to tag them at night." Then he did a startled double take. "What are you doing here? The guest tour is over."

Dor considered making a bald statement of purpose and decided against it. He needed to get to know the centaur a little better before broaching so delicate a subject. "I have an important matter to discuss with you. A, uh, private matter. So I didn't bring it up during the tour."

Arnolde shrugged. "I have no inkling what the King of Xanth would want with me. Just keep your hands off the artifacts, and I will listen to what you have to impart. Mundane items are difficult to come by."

"I'm sure they are," Dor agreed. "We came here by air, riding the clouds, and almost went beyond the limit of magic. We were lucky we didn't fall. Mundania is no place for the creatures of Xanth."

"Oh?" the centaur said without much interest. "Did you see the southern island?"

"No. We weren't that far south. We came down in sight of Centaur Isle."

"There should have been plenty of magic. My raft was powered by a propulsion spell, and it never failed. I was needlessly concerned; evidently that island was Mundane historically, but is now magic." The centaur's hands were busy affixing each tag neatly and making careful entries in a ledger. He evidently liked his work, tedious as it seemed, and was conscientious.

"I think we were north of it, but we certainly had trouble," Dor said. "But there was a storm; that could have disrupted the magic."

"Quite possible," Arnolde agreed. "Storms do seem to affect it."

The centaur seemed sociable enough, now that they were not taking him away from his beloved work. But Dor still did not feel easy. "Uh, the Elder Gerome mentioned a— some kind of pact the centaurs made with my kind, back at the beginning. Do you have artifacts from that time?"

"Indeed I do," Arnolde said, growing animated. "Bones,

arrowheads, the hilt of an iron sword—the record is fragmentary, but documents the legend. The full truth may never be known, sadly, but we do have a fair notion."

"Uh, if you're interested—I'm a Magician. I make things talk. If you'd like to question one of those old artifacts—"

Now Arnolde grew excited. "I had not thought of that! Magic is all right for you, of course. You're only human. I pride myself on being reasonably realistic. Yes, I would like to question an artifact. Are you familiar with the legend of centaur origin?"

"No, not really," Dor said, growing interested himself. "It would help me if I did know it; then I could ask the artifact more specific questions."

"Back CBP 1800—that's Circa Before Present one thousand, eight hundred years," the archivist intoned reverently, "the first man and first horse—you are aware of the nature of that animal? Front of a sea horse merged with the rear of a centaur—"

"Yes, like a nightmare, only in the day," Dor said.

"Exactly. These two, the first of each kind we know of, reached Xanth from Mundania. Xanth was already magic then; its magic seems to have existed for many thousands of years. The plants were already well evolved—you do know what I mean by evolution?"

"How nickelpedes developed from centipedes."

"Um, yes. The way individual species change with the times. Ah, yes, the King always has a centaur tutor, so you would have been exposed to such material. Back then the dragons dominated the land—one might term it the Age of Reptiles—and there were no human hybrids and no dwarves, trolls, goblins, or elves. This man saw that the land was good. He was able and clever enough to stay clear of the more predatory plants and to balk the dragons; he was a warrior, with a bow, sword, spear, club, and the ability to use them, and a valiant spirit.

"But though he found Xanth delightful, he was lonely. He had, it seemed, fled his home tribe—we like to think he was an honorable man who had run afoul of an evil King—such things do happen in Mundania, we understand—and could not safely return there. Indeed, in time a detachment of other warriors came after him, intent on his murder. There is an opacity about the manner Mundanes may enter Xanth; normally people from the same Mundane subsociety may enter Xanth only if they are grouped together, not separately, but it seems these ones were, after all, able to follow—I don't pretend to understand this, but perhaps it is a mere distortion of the legend—at any rate, they were less able than he and fell prey to the natural hazards of Xanth. All but two of them died—and these two, severely wounded, survived only because this first good man—we call him Alpha, for what reason the record does not divulge—rescued them from peril and put healing balm on their wounds. After that they declined to attack him any more; they owed life-debts to him, and swore friendship instead. There was a kind of honor in those days, and we have maintained it since.

"Now they were three men, with three fine mares they had salvaged. None of them could leave Xanth, for news of their betrayal had somehow spread, and enemies lurked just beyond the realm of magic. Or perhaps the Mundane culture had somehow become alien, one variant of the legend has reference to their attempt to return, and discovery of Babel—that they could no longer speak the language or comprehend the culture of the Mundanians. One of them had been a mercenary, a paid soldier, who it seemed spoke a different Mundanian dialect, but he spoke the same language as the others when they met in Xanth. We know this is a property of the magic of Xanth; all cultures and languages become one, including the written language; there is no language barrier between creatures of the same species. For whatever reason—I might wish that the legend was absolutely firm and clear, but must deal with a story line that fragments into mutually incompatible aspects, each of which has elements that are necessary to the continuation of the whole—a most intriguing riddle!—the three men and their mounts were safe, as long as they remained within the realm of magic they had come to understand and use so well—but they longed for the companionship of women of their kind. They wished to colonize the land, but could only live on it.

"Then, exploring deep in new territory, they came upon a spring on a lovely offshore island, and all three drank deeply and watered their horses. They did not know it was a spring of love that would compel instant love with the first creature of the opposite sex spied after drinking. And so it happened that each man, in that critical moment, saw first his good mare—and each mare saw her master. And so it was that the species of the centaur began. This is another of the perplexing distinctions between Xanth and Mundania; in the latter Kingdom representatives of different species are unable to interbreed to produce offspring, while in Xanth it is a matter of course, though normally individuals are most attracted to their own species. The offspring of these unions, perceiving that their parents differed from themselves and that the masters were human beings who were possessed of the greater part of the intellect while the mares possessed the greater part of the strength, learned to respect each species for its special properties. The men taught their offspring all the skills they knew so well, both mental and physical, and commanded in return the right to govern this land of Xanth. In time the mares died, after foaling many times, and eventually the men died, too, leaving only the continuing species of centaur on the island. But the tradition remained, and when, centuries later, other men came, and women, too, the centaurs accorded them the dominance of the Kingdom. So it continues to the present day."

"That's beautiful," Irene said. "Now I know why you centaurs have always supported us, even when our kind was unworthy, and why you served as our mentors. You have been more consistent than we have been."

"We have the advantage of cultural continuity. Yet it is a legend," Arnolde reminded her. "We believe it, but we have no detailed proof."

"Bring me an artifact," Dor said, moved by the story. He had no desire to mate with a creature of another species, but could not deny that love matches of many types existed in Xanth. The harpies, the merfolk, the manticora, the werewolves and vampire-bats—all had obvious human and animal lineage, and there were also many combinations of different animals, like the chimera and griffin. It would be unthinkable to deny the validity of these mixed species; Xanth would not be the same at all without them. "I'll get you the proof."

But now the centaur hesitated. "I thought I wanted the proof—but now I am afraid it would be other than the legend. There might be ugly elements in lieu of the beautiful ones. Perhaps our ancestors were not nice creatures. I sheer away; for the first time I discover a limit to my eagerness for knowledge. Perhaps it is best that the legend remain unchallenged."

"Perhaps it is," Dor agreed. Now at last he felt the time had come to express his real concern. "Since centaurs derive from men, and men have magic talents—"

"Oh, I suppose some centaurs do have some magic," Arnolde said in the manner of an open-minded person skirting a close-minded issue. "But it has no bearing on our society. We leave the magic, like the governing, to you humans."

"But some centaurs do—even Magician level—"

"Oh, you mean Herman the Hermit Centaur," Arnolde said. "The one who could summon the Will-o'-Wisps. He was wronged, I think; he used his power to save Xanth from the ravage of wiggles, and gave his life in that effort, eighteen years ago. But of course, though some magic has perforce been accepted recently in our society, if another centaur Magician appeared, he, too, would be outcast. We centaurs have a deep cultural aversion to obscenity."

Dor found his task increasingly unpleasant. He knew Cherie Centaur considered magic in her species to be obscene, though her mate Chester, Chet's father, had a magical talent. Cherie had adjusted to that situation with extraordinary difficulty. "There is one, though."

"A centaur Magician?" Arnolde's brow wrinkled over his spectacles. "Are you certain?"

"Almost certain. We have had a number of portents at Castle Roogna and elsewhere."

"I pity that centaur. Who is it?"

Now Dor was unable to answer.

Arnolde looked at him, the import dawning. "Surely you do not mean to imply—you believe it is I?" At Dor's miserable nod, the centaur laughed uncertainly. "That's impossible. What magic do you think I have?"

"I don't know," Dor said.

"Then how can you make such a preposterous allegation?" The centaur's tail was swishing nervously.

Dor produced the compass. "Have you seen one of these?"

Arnolde took the compass. "Yes, this is a magic compass. It is pointing at you, since you are a Magician."

"But when I hold it, it points to you."

"I can not believe that!" Arnolde protested. "Here, take it back, and stand by that mirror so I can see its face."

Dor did as bid, and Arnolde saw the needle pointing to himself. His face turned a shade of gray. "But it can not be! I can not be a Magician! It would mean the end of my career! I have no magic."

"It doesn't make sense to me," Dor agreed. "But Good Magician Humfrey's alarms point to a Magician on Centaur Isle; that's what brought me here."

"Yes, our Elders feared you had some such mischief in mind," Arnolde agreed, staring at the compass. Then, abruptly, he moved. "No!" he cried, and galloped from the room.

"What now?" Irene asked.

"We follow," Dor said. "We've got to find out what his talent is—and convince him. We can't leave the job half done."

"Somehow I'm losing my taste for this job," she muttered.

Dor felt the same. Going after an anonymous Magician was one thing; tormenting a dedicated archivist was another. But they were caught in the situation.

They followed. The centaur, though hardly in his prime, easily outdistanced them. But Dor had no trouble picking up the trail, for all he had to do was ask the surrounding terrain. The path led south to the ocean.

"He took his raft with the magic motor," Irene said. "We'll have to take another. He must be going to that Mundane island."

They pre-empted another raft, after Dor had questioned several to locate one with a suitable propulsion-spell. Dor hoped this would not be construed as theft; he had every intention of returning the raft, but had to catch up with Arnolde and talk to him before the centaur did something more foolish than merely fleeing.

The storm had long since passed, and the sea was glassy calm in the bright moonlight. The centaur's raft was not in sight, but the water reported its passage. "He's going for the formerly Mundane island," Grundy said. "Good thing it is magic now, since we're magical creatures."

"Did you suffer when the magic faded near the storm?" Irene asked.

"No, I felt the same—scared," Grundy admitted. "How about you, Smash?"

"This freak feel weak," the ogre said.

"In the knees," Irene said. "We all did."

"She's knees please me's," Smash agreed.

Irene's face ran a peculiar gamut from anger to embarrassment. She decided the ogre was not trying to tease her. He really wasn't that smart. "Thank you, Smash. Your own knees are like the boles on twisted ironwood trunks."

The ogre went into a small bellow of delight that churned up waves behind them and shoved the raft forward at a faster pace. She had found the right compliment.

The spell propelled them swiftly, and soon the island came into sight. Then progress slowed. "Something's the matter," Dor said. "We're hanging up on something."

But there was nothing; the raft was free in the water, unbothered by waves or sea creatures. It continued to slow, until it was hardly moving at all.

"We would get one with a defective go-spell," Irene complained.

"What's the matter with you?" Dor asked it.

"I—ugnh—" the raft whispered hoarsely, then was silent.

"The magic!" Irene cried. "We're beyond the magic! Just as we were during the storm!"

"Let's check this out," Dor said, worried. At least they were not in danger of falling from a cloud, this time! "Irene, grow a plant."

She took a bottleneck seed. "Grow," she ordered.

The seed began to sprout, hesitated, then fell limp.

"Is there anything you can talk to, Grundy?" Dor asked.

The golem spied some kelp in the water. He made strange sounds at it. There was no response.

"Smash, try a feat of strength," Dor said.

The ogre picked up one of his feet. "Uh, no," Dor said quickly. "I mean do something strong. Stand on one finger, or squeeze juice from a log."

Smash put one paw on the end of one of the raft's log-supports. He squeezed. Nothing happened. "Me unprepared, me awful scared," he said.

Dor brought out his midnight sunstone. Now it possessed only the faintest internal glimmer—and in a moment that, too, faded out.

"So that answers two questions," Dor said, trying to sound confident, though, in fact, he was deeply alarmed. "First, we are passing out of the region of magic; the propulsion-spell is defunct. I can't talk to the inanimate, and Irene can't grow plants magically. Second, it's only our magic that fades, not our bodies. Grundy can't translate the talk of other creatures, and Smash has lost his superhuman strength—but both are alive and healthy. Irene's plants won't grow, but she—" He paused, looking at her. "What happened to your hair?"

"Hair?" She took a strand and pulled it before her face. "Eeek, it's faded!"

"Aw, just the green's gone," Grundy said. "Looks better this way."

Irene, stunned, did not even try to kick at him. She, like Dor, had never realized that her hair tint was magical in nature.

"So Mundania doesn't hurt us," Dor continued quickly. "It just inconveniences us. We'll simply have to paddle the rest of the way to the island."

They checked the raft's supplies. The centaurs were a practical species; the raft was equipped with several paddles and a pole. Dor and Irene took the former and Smash the latter, and Grundy steadied the tiller. It was hard work, but they resumed progress toward the island.

"How did Arnolde ever get so far ahead alone?" Irene gasped. "He would have had an awful time paddling and steering."

Finally they reached the beach. There was Arnolde's raft, drawn up just out of the water. "He moved it along, all right," Grundy remarked. "He must be stronger than he looks."

"This is a fairly small island," Dor said. "He can't be far away. We'll corner him. Smash, you stand guard by the rafts and bellow if he comes back here; the rest of us will try to run him down."

They spread out and crossed the island. It had a distinctly Mundanian aspect; there was green grass growing that did not grab at their feet, and leafy trees that merely stood in place and rustled only in the wind. The sand was fine without being sugar, and the only vines they saw made no attempt to writhe toward them. How could the centaur have mistaken this for a spot within the realm of magic?

They discovered Arnolde at his refuge—a neat excavation exposing Mundane artifacts: the scholar's place of personal identification. Apparently he was more than a mere compiler or recorder of information; he did some field work, too.

Arnolde saw them. He had a magic lantern that illuminated the area as the moon sank into the sea. "No, I realize I can not flee the situation," he said sadly. "The truth is the truth, whatever it is, and I am dedicated to the truth. But I can not believe what you say. Never in my life have I evinced the slightest degree of magic talent, and I certainly have none now. Perhaps some of the magic of the artifacts with which I associate has rubbed off on me, giving the illusion of—"

"How can you use a magic lantern here in Mundania?" Irene asked.

"This is not Mundania," Arnolde said. "I told you that before. The limits of magic appear to have extended, reaching out far enough to include this island recently."

"But our magic ceased," Dor said. "We had to paddle here."

"Impossible. My raft spelled forward without intermission, and there is no storm to disrupt the magic ambience. Try your talent now, King Dor; I'll warrant you will discover it operative as always."

"Speak, ground," Dor said, wondering what would happen.

"Okay, chump," the ground answered. "What's on your slow mind?"

Dor exchanged glances with Irene and Grundy, astonished—and saw that Irene's hair in the light of the lantern was green again. "It's back!" he said. "The magic's back! Yet I don't see how—"

Irene threw down a seed. "Grow!" she ordered.

A plant sprouted, rising rapidly into a lively raspberry bush. "Brrrppp!" the plant sounded, making obscene sounds at them all.

"Is this really a magic island?" Grundy asked the nearest

tree, translating into its language. The tree made a rustling response. "It says it is—now!" he reported.

Dor brought out the sunstone again. It was shining brightly.

"How could the magic return so quickly?" Irene asked. "My father always said the limit of magic was pretty constant; in fact, he wasn't sure it varied at all."

"The magic never left this island," Arnolde said. "You must have passed through a flux, an aberration, perhaps after all a lingering consequence of yesterday's storm."

"Maybe so," Dor agreed. "Magic is funny stuff. Ours certainly failed—for a while."

The centaur had a bright idea. "Maybe the magic compass was affected by a similar flux and thrown out of kilter, so it pointed to the wrong person."

Doubt nagged Dor. "I guess that's possible. Something's certainly wrong. If that's so, I must apologize for causing you such grief. It did seem strange to me that you should so suddenly manifest as a Magician when such power remains with a person from birth to death."

"Yes indeed!" Arnolde agreed enthusiastically. "An error in the instrument—that is certainly the most facile explanation. Of course I could not manifest as a Magician, after ninety years of pristine nonmagic."

So they had guessed correctly about one thing: the centaur was close to a century old. "I guess we might as well go back now," Dor said. "We had to borrow a raft to follow you, and its owner will be upset if it stays out too long."

"Feel no concern," Arnolde said, growing almost affable in his relief. "The rafts are communal property, available to anyone at need. However, there would be concern if one were lost or damaged."

They walked back across the island, the magic lantern brightening the vicinity steadily. As they neared the two rafts they saw Smash. He was holding a rock in both hands, squeezing as hard as he could, a grimace of concentration and disgust making his face even uglier than usual.

Suddenly the rock began to compress. "At length, my strength!" the ogre exclaimed as the stone crumbled into sand.

"You could never have done it, you big boob, if the magic hadn't come back," the sand grumbled.

"The magic returned—just now?" Dor asked, something percolating in the back of his mind.

"Sure," the sand said. "You should have seen this musclebrained brute straining. I thought I had him beat. Then the magic came back just as you did, more's the pity."

"The magic—came with us?" Dor asked.

"Are you dimwitted or merely stupid, nitbrain?" the sand asked with a gravelly edge. "I just said that."

"When was the magic here before?" Dor asked.

"Only a little while ago. Horserear here can tell you; he was here when it happened."

"You mean this is normally a Mundane island?"

"Sure, it's always been Mundane, except when ol' hoofleg's around."

"I think we're on to something," Grundy said.

Arnolde looked stricken. "But—but how can—this is preposterous!"

"We owe it to you and ourselves to verify this, one way or another," Dor said. "If the power of magic travels with you—"

"Oh, horrible!" the centaur moaned. "It must not be!"

"Let's take another walk around the island." Dor said. "Grundy, you go with Arnolde and talk to the plants and creatures you encounter; ask them how long magic has been here. The rest of us will spread out and wait for Arnolde to approach. If our magic fades out during his absence, and returns when he comes near—"

Grudgingly the centaur cooperated. He set out on a trot around the island, pretty spry for his age, the golem perching on his back.

No sooner were they on their way than Dor's magic ceased. His sunstone no longer shone, and he could no longer talk to the inanimate. It was evident that Irene and Smash were similarly discommoded.

In a few minutes the circuit was complete. They compared notes. "The magic was with us all along," Grundy reported. "But all the plants and shellfish said it had come only when we were there."

"When he go, me not rhyme," Smash said angrily. "Not even worth a dime."

That was extreme distress for the ogre. Dor had not realized that his rhyming was magic-related. Maybe frustration had flustered him—or maybe magic had shaped the lives of the creatures of Xanth far more than had been supposed. Irene's hair, Smash's rhymes . . .

"My potted petunia would not grow at all," Irene said. "But when the centaur came near, it grew and got roaring drunk."

"And my talent operated only when Arnolde was near," Dor said. "So my talent seems to be dependent on his presence here, as with the rest of you. Since I am a full Magician, what does that make him?"

"A Magician's Magician," Irene said. "A catalyst for magic."

"But I never performed any magic in my life!" Arnolde protested, still somewhat in shock. "Never!"

"You don't perform it, you promote it," Dor said. "You represent an island of magic, an extension of Xanth into Mundania. Wherever you go, magic is there. This is certainly a Magician's talent."

"How could that be true, when there was no indication of it in all my prior life? I can not have changed!"

But now Dor had an answer. "You left Xanth only recently, you said. You came to this Mundane island for research. Good Magician Humfrey's magic indicators never oriented on you before because you are completely camouflaged in Xanth proper; you are like a section of mist in the middle of a cloud. But when you left Xanth, your power manifested, triggering the alarms. Once the indicators had oriented on you, they continued to point you out; maybe your presence makes magic slightly more effective, since Centaur Isle is near the fringe of magic. It's like a bug on a distant leaf; once you know exactly where it is, you can see it. But you can't locate it when it sits still and you don't even know it exists."

Arnolde's shoulders slumped and his coat seemed to lose luster. He was an appaloosa centaur, with white spots on his brown flank, a natural blanket that made him quite handsome. Now the spots were fading out. "I fear you are correct. My associates always considered this to be a Mundane island; I thought them mistaken. But oh, what havoc this wreaks on my career! The profession of a lifetime ruined! I can never return to the museum."

"Do the other centaurs have to know?" Grundy asked.

"I may be contaminated by obscene magic," Arnolde said gravely. "But it is beneath me to prevaricate."

Dor considered the attitude of the various centaurs he had known. He realized Arnolde was right. The archivist could not conceal the truth, and the other centaurs would not tolerate a centaur Magician in their society. They had exiled Herman the Hermit in the past generation, then termed him a hero after he was dead. Some reward!

Dor's quest had gained him nothing and had destroyed the livelihood and pride of a decent centaur. He felt responsible; he had never wanted to hurt anyone this way.

The moon had been descending into the ocean. Now, just before it got soaked, it seemed to have swelled. Great and round and greenish, its cheese was tantalizingly close. Dor gazed at it, pondering its maplike surface. Could a column of smoke lead all the way up to the moon, and could they use the salve some day to—

Then he suffered an awful realization. "The curse!" he cried.

The centaur glanced dourly at him. "You have certainly cursed me, King Dor."

"The magic salve we used to tread the clouds—it had a curse attached. Whoever used it would do some dastardly deed before the next full moon. This is our deed; we have forced you out of your satisfied existence and made you into something you abhor. The curse made us do it."

"Such curses are a readily avoidable nuisance," the centaur remarked. "All that is required is an elementary curse-counterspell. There are dozens in our archives; we don't even file them carefully. Ironic that this ignorance on your part should have such a serious consequence for me."

"Do something, Dor," Irene said.

"What is there to be done?" Arnolde asked disconsolately. "I am rendered at one fell stroke into an exile."

But Dor, cudgeling his brain under pressure, had a sudden explosion of genius. "You take magic with you anywhere you go," he said. "Right into Mundania. This relates in all the three ways we were warned. It is certainly a matter I must attend to, for the existence of any new Magician in Xanth is the King's business. It also could pose a threat to Xanth, for if you go out into Mundania on your own, taking that magic with you, bad people could capture you and somehow use your magic for evil. But most important, somewhere in Mundania is someone we fear is trapped or in trouble, who perhaps needs this magic to escape. Now if I were to take you into Mundania proper—"

"We could rescue my father!" Irene exclaimed, jumping up and down and clapping her hands in the manner of her kind. She bounced phenomenally, so that even the centaur paused to look, as if regretting his species and his age. "Oh, Dor, I could kiss you!" And without waiting for his reaction, she grabbed him and kissed him with joyful savagery on the mouth. In that moment of hyperanimation she became very special, radiant and compelling in the best sort of way; but by the time he realized it, she was already away and talking to the centaur.

"Arnolde, if you have to be exiled anyway, you might as well come with us. We don't care about your magic—not negatively, I mean—we all of us have talents. And think of the artifacts you can collect deep in Mundania; you can start your own museum. And if you help rescue my father, King Trent—"

The centaur was visibly wavering. Obviously he did not like the notion of exile, but could not return to his job on Centaur Isle. "And the centaurs around Castle Roogna are used to magic," Irene continued apace. "Chester Centaur plays a magic silver flute, and his uncle was Herman the Hermit. He would be glad for your company, and—"

"I believe I have little alternative," Arnolde said heavily.

"You will help us? Oh, thank you!" Irene cried, and she flung her arms about the centaur's forepart and kissed him, too. Arnolde was visibly startled, but not entirely displeased; his white spots wavered. Dor suffered a wash of jealousy, thinking of the legend of the origin of the centaurs. Kisses between different species were not necessarily innocent, as that legend showed. But it seemed Irene had convinced the centaur Magician to help, and that was certainly worthwhile.

Then Dor remembered another complication. "We can't just leave for Mundania. The Council of Elders would never permit it."

"How can they prevent it?" Irene asked, glancing meaningfully at him.

"But we must at least tell them—"

"Chet can tell them. He has to go home anyway."

Dor tried to dissemble. "I don't know——"

Then Irene focused her stare on him full-force, daring him to attempt to balk her; she was extremely pretty in her challenge, and Dor knew their course was set. She intended to rescue her father, no matter what.

Chapter 8. Mundane Mystery

They sailed the two rafts back to Centaur Isle that night. In the process they discovered that Arnolde's ambience of magic extended farthest toward the front, perhaps fifteen paces, and half that distance to the rear. It was least potent to the sides, going hardly beyond the centaur's reach. It was, in fact, less an isle of magic than an aisle, always preceding the centaur's march. Thus the second raft was able to precede Arnolde's raft comfortably, or to follow it closely, but not to travel beside it. They had verified that the hard way, having the magic propulsion fail, until Arnolde turned to face them.

Once they re-entered the main magic of Xanth, Arnolde's power was submerged. It seemed to make no difference how close he was or which way he faced; there was no enhancement of enchantment near him. But of course they had no way to measure the intensity of magic in his vicinity accurately.

Grundy sneaked in to wake Chet and explain the situation, while Arnolde researched in his old tomes for the best and swiftest route to Mundania. He reported that there was the tunnel the sun used to return from the ocean east to its position of rising, drying out and recharging along the way. This tunnel would be suitable by day, when the sun wasn't using it; they could trot right along it.

"But that would take us west," Irene protested. "My father left Xanth to the north."

Dor had to agree. "The standard route to Mundania is across the northwest isthmus. We must go there and hope to pick up traces of his passage. We can't use the sun's tunnel. But it's a long way to the isthmus, and I don't think we want to make another trip like the one down the coast; we might never get there. Are there any other good notions?"

"Well, tomorrow is destined to have intermittent showers," Arnolde said. "There should be a rainbow. There is a spell in the archives for traveling the rainbow. It is very fast, for rainbows do not endure long. There is some risk—"

"Speed is what we need," Dor said, remembering his dream-visions, where there had been a sensation of urgency. "I think King Trent is in trouble and needs to be rescued soon. Maybe not in the next day, but I don't think we can afford to wait a month."

"There is also the problem of mounting the rainbow," Arnolde said. Now that he had accepted the distasteful notion of his own magic, his mind was relating to the situation very readily. Perhaps it was because he was trained in the handling of information and knew how to organize it. "Part of the rainbow's magic, as you know, is that it appears equally distant from all observers, with its two ends touching the ground equally far from them, north and south. We must ascend to its top, then slide down quickly before it fades."

"The salve!" Grundy said. "We can mount smoke to a cloud, and run across the cloud to the top of the rainbow, if we start early, before the rainbow forms."

"You just don't understand," the centaur said. "It will seem just as far from us when we board the cloud. Catching a rainbow is one of the hardest things to do."

"I can see why," Dor muttered. "How can we catch one if it always retreats?"

"Excise the eyes," Smash suggested, covering his own gross orbs with his gauntleted mitts.

"Of course the monster is right," Arnolde said, not looking at Smash, whom he seemed to find objectionable. "That is the obvious solution."

It was hardly obvious to Dor. "How can covering our eyes get us to the rainbow?"

"It can hardly appear distant if you don't look at it," Arnolde said.

"Yes, but—"

"I get it," Grundy said. "We spot it, then close our eyes and go to where we saw it, and it can't get away because we aren't looking at it. Simple."

"But somebody has to look at it, or it isn't there," Irene protested. "Is it?"

"Chet can look at it," Grundy said. "He's not going on it anyway."

Dor distrusted this, but the others seemed satisfied. "Let's get some sleep tonight and see what happens tomorrow," he said, hoping it all made sense.

They slept late, but that was all right because the intermittent rain wasn't due until midmorning. Arnolde dutifully acquainted the centaur Elders with his situation; as expected, they encouraged him to depart the Isle forever at his very earliest convenience, without directly referring to the reason for his loss of status in their community. A Magician was not wanted here; they could not be comfortable with him. They would let it be known that Arnolde was retiring for reasons of health, so as to preserve his reputation, and they would arrange to break in a new archivist. No one would know his shame. To facilitate his prompt departure they provided him with a useful assortment of spells and counterspells for his journey, and wished him well.

"The hypocrites!" Irene exclaimed. "For fifty years Arnolde serves them well, and now, suddenly, just because—"

"I said you would not comprehend the nuances of centaur society," Chet reminded her, though he did not look comfortable himself.

Irene shut up rebelliously. Dor liked her better for her feeling, however. It was time to leave Centaur Isle, and not just because they had a new mission.

The intermittent clouds formed and made ready to shower. Dor set up a smudge pot and got a column of smudge angling up to intersect the cloud level. They applied the salve to their feet and hands, invoked the curse-counterspells Arnolde distributed, and marched up the column. Arnolde adjusted to this odd climb remarkably well for his age; he had evidently kept himself in traveling shape by making archaeological field trips.

For a moment they paused to turn back to face Chet, who was standing on the beach, watching for the rainbow. Dor found himself choking up, and could only wave. "I hope to see you again, cousin," Arnolde called. Chet was not related to him; what he referred to was the unity of their magic talents. "And meet your sire." And Chet smiled, appreciating the thought.

When they reached the cloud layer, they donned blindfolds. "Clouds," Dor said, "tell us where the best path to the top of the rainbow is. Don't let any of us step too near the edge of you."

"What rainbow?" the nearest cloud asked.

"The one that is about to form, that my friend Chet Centaur will see from the ground."

"Oh, *that* rainbow. It isn't here yet. It hasn't finished its business on the eastern coast of Xanth."

"Well, guide us to where it's going to be."

"Why don't you open your eyes and see it for yourself?" the canny cloud asked. The inanimate was often perverse, and the many folds and convolutions of clouds made them smarter than average.

"Just guide us," Dor said.

"Awww." But the cloud had to do it.

There was a popping sound behind them, down on the ground. "That's the popcorn I gave Chet," Irene said. "I told him to set it off when he saw the rainbow. Now that rainbow is fixed in place, as long as he looks at it and we don't; we must be almost upon it."

"Are we?" Dor asked the cloud.

"Yeah," the cloud conceded grudgingly. "It's right ahead, though it has no head. That's cumulus humor."

"Rainbow!" Dor called. "Sing out if you hear me!"

Back came the rainbow's song: "Tra-la-la-fol-de-rol!" It sounded beautiful and multicolored.

They hurried over to it. Once they felt its smooth surface projecting above the cloud and climbed upon it, they removed their blindfolds; the rainbow could no longer work its deceptive magic.

The rainbow was fully as lovely as it sounded. Bands of red and yellow, blue and green, extended lengthwise, and sandwiched between them, where ground observers couldn't see them, were the secret riches of the welkin: bands of polka-dot, plaid, and checkerboard. Some internal bands were translucent, and some blazed with colors seldom imagined by man, like fortissimo, charm, phon, and torque. It would have been easy to become lost in their wonders, and Irene seemed inclined to do just that, but the rainbow would not remain here long. It seemed rainbows had tight schedules, and this one was due for a showing somewhere in Mundania in half an hour. Some magic, it seemed, did extend to Mundania; Dor wondered briefly whether the Mundanes would have the same trouble actually catching up to a rainbow, or whether there it would stay firmly in place regardless how the viewers moved.

Arnolde brought out his rainbow-travel spell, which was sealed in a paper packet. He tore it open—and abruptly they began to slide.

The speed was phenomenal. They zoomed past the clouds, then down into the faintly rainy region below, plunging horrendously toward the sea to the north.

Below them was the Land of Xanth, a long peninsula girt by thin islands along the coastlines. Across the center of it was the jagged chasm of the Gap that separated the northern half of Xanth from the southern. It appeared on no maps because no one remembered it, but this was no map. It was reality, as viewed from the rainbow. There were a number of lakes, such as Ogre-Chobee in the south, but no sign of the human settlements Dor knew were there. Man had simply not made much of an impression on Xanth, physically.

"Fun begun!" Smash cried joyfully.

"Eeek—my skirt!" Irene squealed as the mischievous gusts whipped it up, displaying her legs to the whole world. Dor wondered why she insisted on wearing a skirt despite such constant inconveniences; pants of some kind would have solved the problems decisively. Then it occurred to him that she might not want that particular problem solved. She was well aware that her legs were the finest features of a generally excellent body and perhaps was not averse to letting the world know it also. If she constantly protested any inadvertent exposures that occurred, how could anyone blame her for showing herself off? She had a pretty good system going.

Dor and Grundy and Arnolde, less sanguine about violence than the ogre and less modest (?) than Irene, hung on to the sliding arc of the rainbow and stared ahead and down with increasing misgiving. How were they to stop, once the end came? The descent was drawing close at an alarming velocity. The northern shoreline of Xanth loomed rapidly larger, the curlicues of beaches magnifying. The ocean in this region seemed oddly reddish; Dor hoped that wasn't from the blood of prior travelers of the rainbow. Of course it wasn't; how could he think such a thought?

Then the travel-spell reversed, and they slid rapidly slower until, as they reached the water at the end of the rainbow, they were moving at no more than a running pace. They plunged into the crimson water and swam for the shore to the north. The color was not blood; it was translucently thin, up close. Dor was relieved.

Now that he could no longer see it from the air, Dor remembered other details of Xanth. The length of it was north-south, with the narrowest portion near where his grandfather Elder Roland's village was, in the middle north on the western side. At the top, Xanth extended west, linking to Mundania by the isthmus they were headed for—and somehow Mundania beyond that isthmus seemed huge, much larger than Xanth. Dor decided that must be a misimpression; surely Mundania was about the same size as Xanth, or somewhat smaller. How could a region of so little importance be larger, especially without magic?

Now they came to the shallows and waded through the dark red water to the beach. That crimson bothered him, as the color intensified near the tideline; how could the normally blue water change color here, in the Mundane quadrant? What magic could affect it here, where no magic existed?

"Maybe some color leaked from the rainbow," Irene said, following his thought.

Well, maybe. Of course there was the centaur aisle of magic now, so that wherever they were was no longer strictly Mundane. Yet the red water extended well beyond the area of temporary enchantment. It seemed to be a regular feature of the region.

They gathered on the beach, dripping pink water. Grundy and Smash didn't mind, but Dor felt uncomfortable, and Irene's blouse and skirt were plastered to her body. "I'm not walking around this way, and I'm not taking off my clothes," she expostulated. She felt in her seedbag, which she had refilled at Centaur Isle, and brought out a purple seed. It seemed the bag was waterproof, for the seed was dry. "Grow," she ordered it as she dropped it on the sand.

The thing sprouted into a heliotrope. Clusters of small purple flowers burst open aromatically. Warm dry air wafted outward. This plant did not really travel toward the sun; it emulated the sun's heat, dehydrating things in the vicinity. Soon their clothing was dry again. Even Smash and Grundy appreciated this, since both now wore the special jackets given them by the centaurs. Smash also shook out his gauntlets and dried them, and Irene spread her silver-lined fur out nearby.

"Do we know where we go from here?" Irene asked once she had her skirt and blouse properly fluffed out.

"Did King Trent pass this way?" Dor inquired of the landscape.

"When?" the beach-sand asked.

"Within the past month."

"I don't think so."

They moved a short distance north, and Dor tried again. Again the response was negative. As the day wore into afternoon and on into evening, they completed their traverse of the isthmus—without positive result. The land had not seen the King.

"Maybe the Queen still had an illusion of invisibility enchantment," Grundy suggested. "So nothing could see them."

"Her illusion wouldn't work here in Mundania, dummy," Irene retorted. She was still miffed at the golem because of the way Grundy had caused her to lose half her seeds to the eclectic eel. She carried a little grudge a long time.

"I am not properly conversant with King Trent's excursion," Arnolde said. "Perhaps he departed Xanth by another route."

"But I know he came this way!" Irene said.

"You didn't even know he was leaving Xanth," Grundy reminded her. "You thought he was inside Xanth on vacation."

She shrugged that off as irrelevant. "But this is the only route out of Xanth!" Her voice was starting its hysterical tremor.

"Unless he went by sea," Dor said.

"Yes, he could have done that," she agreed quickly. "But he would have come ashore somewhere. My mother gets seasick when she's in a boat too long. All we have to do is walk along the beach and ask the stones and plants."

"And watch for Mundane monsters," Grundy said, still needling her. "So they can't look up your—"

"I am inclined to doubt that countermagical species will present very much of a problem," Arnolde said in his scholarly manner.

"What he know, he hoofed schmoe?" Smash demanded.

"Evidently more than you, you moronic oaf," the centaur snapped back. "I have been studying Mundania somewhat, recently, garnering information from immigrants, and by most reports most Mundane plants and animals are comparatively shy. Of course there is a certain margin for error, as in all phenomena."

"What dray, he say?" Smash asked, perplexed by the centaur's vocabulary.

"Dray!" Arnolde repeated, freshly affronted. "A dray is a low cart, not a creature, you ignorant monster. I shall thank you to address me by my proper appellation."

"What's the poop from the goop?" Smash asked.

Dor stifled a laugh, turning it into a choking cough. In this hour of frustration, tempers were fraying, and they could not afford to have things get too negative.

Grundy opened his big mouth, but Dor managed to cover it in time. The golem could only aggravate the situation with his natural penchant for insults.

It was Irene who retained enough poise to alleviate the crisis. "You just don't understand a person of education, Smash. He says the Mundane monsters won't dare bother us while you're on guard."

"Oh. So," the ogre said, mollified.

"Ignorant troglodyte," the centaur muttered.

That set it off again. "Me know he get the place of

Chet!" Smash said angrily, forming his gauntlets into horrendous fists.

So that was the root of the ogre's ire! He felt Arnolde had usurped the position of his younger centaur friend. "No, that's not so," Dor started, seeking some way to alleviate his resentment. If their party started fracturing now, before they were fairly clear of Xanth, what would happen once they got deep into Mundania?

"And he called you a caveman, Smash," Grundy put in helpfully.

"Compliments no good; me head like wood," the ogre growled, evidently meaning that he refused to be swayed by soft talk.

"Indubitably," Arnolde agreed.

Dor decided to leave it at that; a more perfect understanding between ogre and centaur would only exacerbate things.

They walked along the beach. Sure enough, nothing attacked them. The trees were strange oval-leafed things with brownish, inert bark and no tentacles. Small birds flitted among the branches, and gray animals scurried along the ground.

Arnolde had brought along a tome of natural history, and he consulted it eagerly as each thing turned up. "An oak tree!" he exclaimed. "Probably the root stock of the silver oak, the blackjack oak, the turkey oak, and the acorn trees!"

"But there's no silver, blackjacks, or acorns," Grundy protested.

"Or turkeys," Irene added.

"Certainly there are, in rudimentary forms," the centaur said. "Observe a certain silvery aspect to some leaves, and the typical shape of others, primitively suggestive of other, eventual divergencies. And I suspect there are also acorns, in season. The deficiency of magic prevents proper manifestation, but to the trained perception—"

"Maybe so," the golem agreed, shrugging. This was evidently more than he cared to know about oak trees.

Dor continued to query the objects along the beach, and the water of the sea, but with negative results. All denied seeing King Trent or Queen Iris.

"This is ridiculous!" Irene expostulated. "I *know* he came this way!"

Arnolde stroked his chin thoughtfully. "There does appear to be a significant discontinuity."

"Something doesn't fit," Grundy agreed.

As the sun set, they made camp high on the beach. Rather than post watches, they decided to trust in magic. Dor told the sand in their vicinity to make an exclamation if anything dangerous or obnoxious intruded, and the sand promised to do so. Irene grew a blanket bush for their beds and set a chokecherry hedge around them for additional protection. They ate beefsteak tomatoes that they butchered and roasted on flame-vines, and drank the product of wine-and-rain lilies.

"Young lady, your talent contributes enormously to our comfort," Arnolde complimented her, and Irene flushed modestly.

"Aw, he's just saying that 'cause she's pretty," Grundy grumbled. That only made Irene flush with greater pleasure. Dor was not pleased, but could not isolate the cause of his reaction. The hangups of others were easier for him to perceive than his own.

"Especially when her skirt hikes up over her knees," the golem continued. Irene quickly tugged down her hem, her flush becoming less attractive.

"Actually, there are few enough rewards to a mission like this," Arnolde said. "Had I my choice, I would instantly abolish my own magic and return to my sinecure at the museum, my shame extirpated."

And there was the centaur's fundamental disturbance, Dor realized. He resented their dastardly deed that had ripped him from his contented existence and made him an exile from his kind. Dor could hardly blame him. Arnolde's agreement to travel with them to Mundania to help rescue King Trent did not mean he was satisfied with his lot; he was merely making the best of what was for him an awful situation.

"Me help he go, with big heave-ho!" Smash offered.

"But we need his magic," Irene said, verbally interposing herself to prevent further trouble. "Just as we need your strength, Smash." And she laid her hand on the ogre's ponderous arm, pacifying him. Dor found himself resenting this, too, though he understood her motive. The peace had to be kept.

They settled down for the night—and the sand gave alarm. The monsters it warned of turned out to be sand fleas—bugs so small they could hardly even be seen. Arnolde dug a vermin-repulsor spell out of his collection, and that took care of the matter. They settled down again and this time slept. Once more the nightmares were unable to reach them, since the magic horses were bound to the magic realm of Xanth and could not cross the Mundane territory intervening. Dor almost felt sympathy for the mares; they had been balked from doing their duty to trouble people's sleep for several nights now, and must be very frustrated.

They resumed their march in the morning. But as the new day wore on, the gloom of failure became more pervasive. "Something certainly appears to be amiss," Arnolde observed. "From what we understand, King Trent had to have passed this vicinity—yet the objects here deny it. Perhaps it is not entirely premature to entertain conjectures."

Smash wrinkled his hairy brow, trying to figure out whether this was another rarefied insult. "Say what's on your mind, horsetail," Grundy said with his customary diplomacy.

"We have ascertained that the Queen could not have employed her power to deceive the local objects," Arnolde said didactically.

"Not without magic," Dor agreed. "The two of them were strictly Mundane-type people here, as far as we know."

"Could they have failed to come in from the sea?"

"No!" Irene cried emotionally.

"I have queried the sea," Dor said. "It says nothing like that is in it." Irene relaxed.

"Could they have employed a completely different route? Perhaps crossed to the eastern coast of Xanth and sailed north from there to intercept another region of Mundania?"

"They didn't," Irene said firmly. "They had it all planned, to come out here. Someone had found a good trade deal, and they were following his map. I saw it, and the route passed here."

"But if you don't know—" Dor protested.

"I didn't know they were going to travel the route, then," she said. "But I did see the map when their scout brought it in, with the line on it. *Now* I know what it meant. That's all I saw, but I am absolutely certain this was the way they headed."

Dor was disinclined to argue the point further. This did seem to be the only practical route. He had told the others all he knew about King Trent's destination, and this route certainly did not conflict with that information.

"Could they have been intercepted before leaving Xanth?" Arnolde continued, evidently with an intellectual conclusion in mind. "Waylaid, perhaps?"

"My father would have turned any waylayer into a toad," she said defiantly. "Anyway, inside Xanth, my mother's illusion would have made them impossible to identify."

"Then it seems we have eliminated the likely," Arnolde said. "We are thus obliged to contemplate the unlikely."

"What do you mean?" Irene asked.

"As I intimated, it is an unlikely supposition that I entertain, quite possibly erroneous—"

"Spit it out, brownfur," Grundy said.

"My dear vociferous construct, a civilized centaur does not expectorate. And my color is appaloosa, not mere brown."

Irene was catching on to her power over the centaur, and over males in general. "Please, Arnolde," she pleaded sweetly. "It's so important to me to know anything that might help find my lost father—"

"Of course, dear child," Arnolde agreed quickly, adopting an avuncular pose. "It is simply this: perhaps King Trent did not pass this region when we suppose he did."

"It had to be within this past month," she said.

"Not necessarily. That is the extraordinary aspect of this supposition. He may have passed here a century ago."

Now Dor, Irene, and Grundy peered at the centaur intently to see whether he was joking. Smash, less interested in intellectual conjectures, idly formed sandstone by squeezing handfuls of sand until the mineral fused. His new gauntlets evidently enabled him to apply his power in ways that were beyond his natural limits before, since even ogre's flesh was marginally softer than stone. A modest sandstone castle was developing.

"You happen to sleep with your head underwater last night?" the golem inquired solicitously.

"I have, as I have clarified previously, engaged in a modicum of research into the phenomena of Mundania," Arnolde said. "I confess I know only the merest fraction of what may be available, and must be constantly alert for error, but certain conclusions are becoming more credible. Through history, certain anomalies have manifested in the relationship between continuums. There is of course the matter of linguistics—it appears that there exist multiple languages in Mundania, yet all become intelligible in Xanth. I wonder if you properly appreciate the significance of—"

Irene was growing impatient. She tapped her small foot on the ground. "How could he have passed a century ago, when he wasn't even born then?"

"It is this matter of discontinuity, as I was saying. Time seems to differ; there may be no constant ratio. There is evidence that the several Waves of human colonization of Xanth originated from widely divergent subcultures within Mundania, and, in fact, some may be anachronistic. That is to say, the last Wave of people may have originated from a period in Mundania preceding that of the prior Wave."

"Now wait!" Dor exclaimed. "I visited Xanth of eight hundred years ago, and I guess that was a kind of time travel, but that was a special case. Since there's no magic in Mundania, how could people get reversed like that? Are their times mixed up?"

"No, I believe their framework is consistent in their world. Yet if the temporal sequence were reversed with respect to ours—"

"I just want to know where my father is!" Irene snapped.

"He may be in Mundania's past—or its future," the centaur said. "We simply do not know what law governs transfer across the barrier of magic, but it seems to be governed from Xanth's side. That is, we may be able to determine into what age of Mundania we travel, whereas the access of

Mundania to Xanth is random and perhaps in some cases impossible. It is a most intriguing interface. It is as if Xanth were a boat sailing along a river; the passengers may disembark anywhere they choose, merely by picking their port, or a specific time on the triptych, so to speak, but the natives along the shores can take only that craft that happens to pass within their range. This is an inadequate analogy, I realize, that does not properly account for certain—"

"The King can be any*when* in Mundania?" Irene demanded skeptically.

"Marvelously succinct summation," Arnolde admitted.

"But he told me 'medieval,'" Dor protested.

"That does narrow it," the centaur agreed. "But it covers an extraordinary range, and if he was speaking figuratively—"

"Then how can we ever find him?" Irene demanded.

"That becomes problematical. I hasten to remind you that this is merely a theory, undocumented, perhaps fallacious. I would not have introduced it for consideration, except—"

"Except nothing else fits," Irene said. "Suppose it's right. What do we do now?"

"Well, I believe it would expedite things if we located research facilities in Mundania. Some institution where detailed records exist, archives—"

"And you're an archivist!" Dor exclaimed.

"Precisely. This should enable me to determine at what period in Mundania's history we have intruded. Since, as King Dor says, King Trent referred to a medieval period, that would provide a frame of reference."

"If we're in the wrong Mundane century," Irene said, "how do we get to him?"

"We should be required to return to Xanth and undertake a new mission to that century. As I mentioned, it seems feasible to determine the temporal locale from Xanth, and once in that aspect of Mundania, we would be fixed in it until returning to Xanth. However, this procedure is fraught with uncertainties and potential complications."

"I should think so," Dor said. "If we figured it wrong, we might get there before he did."

"Oh, I doubt that would happen, other than on the macroscopic scale, of course."

"The what?" Dor asked.

"I believe the times are consistent in particular circumstances. That is to say, within a given age, we could enter Mundania only with an elapsed period consonant with that of Xanth. Therefore—"

"We might miss by a century, but not by a day," Grundy said.

"That is the essence, golem. The particular channels appear to be fixed—"

"So let's go find the century!" Irene said, brightening. "Then all we'll need is the place."

"With appropriate research, the specific geography should also be evident."

"Then let's go find your archives," she said.

"Unfortunately, we have no knowledge of this period," Arnolde reminded her. "We are hardly likely to locate a suitable facility randomly."

"I can help there," Dor said. "It should be where there are a lot of people, right?"

"Correct, King Dor."

"Uh, better not call me King here. I'm not, really, and people might find it strange." Then Dor addressed the sand. "Which way to where most people live?"

"How should I know?" the sand asked.

"You know which direction most of them come from, and where they return."

"Oh, that. They mostly go north."

"North it is," Dor agreed.

They marched north, and in due course encountered a Mundane path that debouched into a road that became a paved highway. No such highway existed in Xanth, and Dor had to question this one closely to ascertain its nature. It seemed it served to facilitate the travel of metal and rubber vehicles that propelled themselves with some sort of magic or whatever it was that Mundanes used to accomplish such wonders. These wagons were called "cars," and they moved very rapidly.

"I saw something like that belowground," Grundy said. "The demons rode in them."

Soon the party saw a car. The thing zoomed along like a

racing dragon, belching faint smoke from its posterior. They stared after it, amazed. "Fire it send from wrong end," Smash said.

"Are you sure there's no magic in Mundania?" Grundy asked. "Even the demons didn't have firebreathers."

"I am not at all certain," Arnolde admitted. "Perhaps they merely have a different name and application for their magic. I doubt it would operate for us. Perhaps this is the reason we believe there is no magic in Mundania—it is not applicable to our needs."

"I don't want any part of that car," Irene said. "Any dragon shooting out smoke from its rear is either crazy or has one awful case of indigestion! How could it fight? Let's find our archives and get out of here."

The others agreed. This aspect of Mundania was certainly inverted. They avoided the highway, making their way along assorted paths that paralleled it. Dor continued to query the ground, and by nightfall they were approaching a city. It was a strange sort of settlement, with roads that crisscrossed to form large squares, and buildings all lined up with their fronts right on the edges of the roads, so that there was hardly room for any forest there, jammed in close together. Some were so tall it was a wonder they didn't fall over when the wind blew.

Dor's party camped at the edge of the city, under a large umbrella tree Irene grew to shelter them. The tree's canopy dipped almost to the ground, concealing them, and this seemed just as well. They were not sure how the Mundanes would react to the sight of an ogre, golem, or centaur.

"We have gone as far as we can as a group," Dor said. "There are many people here, and few trees; we can't avoid being seen any more. I think Irene and I had better go in and find a museum—"

"A library," Arnolde corrected him. "I would love to delve eternally in a Mundane museum, but the information is probably most readily accessible in a library."

"A library," Dor agreed. He knew what that was, because King Trent had many books in his library-office in Castle Roogna.

"However, that is academic, no pun intended," the centaur continued. "You can not go there without me."

"I know I'll step out of magic," Dor said. "But I won't

need to do anything special. Nothing magical. Once I find the library for you—"

"You have no certainty you can even speak their language," Arnolde said curtly. "In the magic ambience, you can; beyond it, this is problematical."

"I'm not sure we speak the same language in our own group, sometimes," Irene said with a smile. "Words like 'ambience' and 'problematical'—"

"I can speak their language," Grundy said. "That's my talent. I was made to translate."

"A magical talent," Arnolde said.

"Oooops," Grundy said, chagrined. "Won't work outside the aisle."

"But you can't just walk in to the city!" Dor said. "I'm sure they aren't used to centaurs."

"I would have to walk in to use the library," Arnolde pointed out. "Fortunately, I anticipated such an impediment, so obtained a few helpful spells from our repository. We centaurs do not normally practice inherent magic, but we do utilize particular enchantments on an *ad hoc* basis. I have found them invaluable when on field trips to the wilder regions of Xanth." He checked through his bag of spells, much the way Irene checked through her seeds. "I have with me assorted spells for invisibility, inaudibility, untouchability, and so forth. The golem and I can traverse the city unperceived."

"What about the ogre?" Dor asked. "He can't exactly merge with the local population either."

Arnolde frowned. "Him, too, I suppose," he agreed distastefully. "However, there is one attendant liability inherent in this process—"

"I won't be able to detect you either," Dor finished.

"Precisely. Some one of our number must exist openly, for these spells make the handling of books awkward; our hands would pass right through the pages. My ambience of magic should be unimpaired, of course, and we could remain with you—but you would have to do all the research unassisted."

"He'll never make it," Irene said.

"She's right," Dor said. "I'm just not much of a scholar. I'd mess it up."

"Allow me to cogitate," Arnolde said. He closed his eyes

and stroked his chin reflectively. For a worried moment Dor thought the centaur was going to be sick, then realized that he had the wrong word in mind. Cogitate actually referred to thinking.

"Perhaps I have an alternative," Arnolde said. "You could obtain the assistance of a Mundane scholar, a qualified researcher, perhaps an archivist. You could pay him one of the gold coins you have hoarded, or perhaps a diamond; I believe either would have value in any frame of Mundania."

"Uh, I guess so," Dor said doubtfully.

"I tell you, even with help, he'll foul it up," Irene said. She seemed to have forgotten her earlier compliments on Dor's performance. That was one of the little things about her—selective memory. "You're the one who should do the research, Arnolde."

"I can only, as it were, look over his shoulder," the centaur said. "It would certainly help if I could direct the manner he selects references and turns the pages, as I am a gifted reader with a fine memory. He would not have to comprehend the material. But unless I were to abort the imperceptibility spells, which I doubt very much would be wise since I have no duplicates—"

"There's a way, maybe," Grundy said. "I could step outside the magic aisle. Then he could see me and hear me, and I could tell him to turn the page, or whatever."

"And any Mundanes in the area would pop their eyeballs, looking at the living doll," Irene said. "If anyone does it, I'm the one."

"So they can pop their eyes looking up your skirt," the golem retorted, miffed.

"That may indeed be the solution," Arnolde said.

"Now wait a minute!" Irene cried.

"He means the messenger service," Dor told her gently.

"Of course," the centaur said. "Since we have ascertained that the aisle is narrow, it would be feasible to stand quite close while Dor remains well within the forward extension."

Dor considered, and it did seem to be the best course. He had somehow thought he could just go into Mundania, follow King Trent's trail by querying the terrain, and reach the King without much trouble. This temporal discontinuity, as the centaur put it, was hard to understand and harder to deal with, and the vicarious research the centaur proposed seemed fraught with hangups. But what other way was there? "We'll try it," he agreed. "In the morning."

They settled down for the night, their second in Mundania. Smash and Grundy slept instantly; Dor and Irene had more trouble, and Arnolde seemed uncomfortably wide awake. "We are approaching direct contact with Mundane civilization," the centaur said. "In a certain sense this represents the culmination of an impossible dream for me, almost justifying the personal damnation my magic talent represents. Yet I have had so many confusing intimations, I hardly know what to expect. This city could be too primitive to have a proper library. The denizens could for all we know practice cannibalism. There are so many imponderabilities."

"I don't care what they practice," Irene said. "Just so long as I find my father."

"Perhaps we should query the surroundings in the morning," Arnolde said thoughtfully, "to ascertain whether suitable facilities exist here, before we venture any farther. Certainly we do not wish to chance discovery by the Mundanes unless we have excellent reason."

"And we should ask where the best Mundane archivist is," Irene agreed.

Dor drew a word in the dirt with one finger: ONESTI. He contemplated it morosely.

"This is relevant?" the centaur inquired, glancing at the word.

"It's what King Trent told me," Dor said. "If ever I was in doubt, to proceed with honesty."

"Honesty?" Arnolde asked, his brow wrinkling at the dirt.

"I think about that a lot when I'm in doubt," Dor said. "I don't like deceiving people, even Mundanes."

Irene smiled tiredly. "Arnolde, it's the way Dor spells the word. He is the world's champion poor speller. O N E S T I: Honesty."

"ONESTI," the centaur repeated, removing his spectacles to rub his eyes. "I believe I perceive it now. A fitting signature for a King."

"King Trent's a great King," Dor agreed. "I know his advice will pull us through somehow."

Arnolde seemed almost to smile, as if finding Dor's attitude peculiar. "I will sleep on that," the centaur said. And he did, lying down on the dirt-scratched word.

In the morning, after some problems with food and natural functions in this semipublic locale, they set it up. The centaur dug out his collection of spells, each one sealed in a glassy little globe, and Dor stepped outside the aisle of magic while the spells were invoked. First the party became inaudible, then invisible; it looked as if the spot were empty. Dor gave them time to get through the unfeeling spell, then walked back onto the lot. He heard, saw, and felt nothing.

"But I can smell you," he remarked. "Arnolde has a slight equine odor, and Smash smells like a monster, and Irene is wearing perfume. Better clean yourselves up before we get into a building."

Soon the smells faded, and after a moment Irene appeared, a short distance away. "Can you see me now?"

"I see you and hear you," Dor said.

"Oh, good. I didn't know how far out the magic went. I'm still the same to me." She stepped toward him and vanished.

"You've gone again," Dor said, hastening to the spot where she had been. "Can you perceive me?"

"Hey, you're overlapping me!" she protested, appearing right up against him, so that he almost stumbled.

"Well, I can't perceive you," he said. "I mean, *now* I can, but I couldn't before. Can you see the others when you're outside the aisle?"

She looked. "They're gone! We can see and hear you all the time, but now—"

"So you'll know when I can see you by when you can't see them."

She leaned forward, and her face disappeared, reminding him of the Gorgon. Then she drew back. "I could see them then. I'm really in the enchantment, aren't I?"

"You're enchanting," he agreed.

She smiled and leaned forward to kiss him—but her face disappeared and he felt nothing.

"Now I have to go find a library and a good archivist," he said, disgruntled, as she reappeared. "If you're with me, stay away from me."

She laughed. "I'm with you. Just don't try to catch me outside the aisle." And of course that was what he should have done, if he really wanted to kiss her. And he did want to—but he didn't want to admit it.

She walked well to the side of him, staying clear of the enchantment. "No sense you getting lost."

They walked on into the city. There were many cars in the streets, all zooming rapidly to the intersections, where they screeched to stops, waited a minute with irate growls and constant ejections of smoke from their posteriors, then zoomed in packs to the next intersections. They seemed to have only two speeds: zoom and stop. There were people inside the cars, exactly the way Grundy had described with the demon vehicles, but they never got out. It was as if the people had been swallowed whole and were now being digested.

Because the cars were as large as centaurs and moved at a constant gallop when not stopped, Dor was wary of them and tried to avoid them. But it was impossible; he had to cross the road sometime. He remembered how the nefarious Gap Dragon of Xanth lurked for those foolish enough to cross the bottom of the Gap; these cars seemed all too similar. Maybe there were some that had not yet consumed people and were traveling hungry, waiting to catch someone like Dor. He saw one car stopped by the side of the street with its mouth wide open like that of a dragon; he avoided it nervously. The strangest thing about it was that its guts seemed to be all in that huge mouth—steaming tubes and tendons and a disk-shaped tongue. Oddest of all, it had no teeth. Maybe that was why it took so long to digest the people.

He came to a corner. "How do I get across?" he asked.

"You wait for a light to stop the traffic," the street informed him with a contemptuous air of dust and car fumes. "Then you run-don't-walk across before they clip you, if you're lucky. Where have you been all your life?"

"In another realm," Dor said. He saw one of the lights the street described. It hung above the intersection and wore several little visors pointing each way. All sorts of colors flashed malevolently from it, in all sorts of directions. Dor couldn't understand how it made the car stop. Maybe the lights had some kind of stun-spell, or whatever it was called here. He played it safe by asking the light to tell him when it was proper to cross.

"Now," the light said, flashing green from one face and red from another.

Dor started across. A car honked like a sea monster and squealed like a sea-monster victim, almost running over Dor's leading foot. "Not that way, idiot!" the light exclaimed, flashing an angry red. "The other way! With the green, not the red! Haven't you ever crossed a street before?"

"Never," Dor admitted. Irene had disappeared; she must have re-entered the magic aisle to consult with the others. Maybe she found it safer within the spell zone; apparently the cars were unable to threaten her there.

"Wait till I tell you, then cross the way I tell you," the light said, blinking erratically. "I don't want any blood in *my* intersection!"

Dor waited humbly. "Now," the light said. "Walk straight ahead, keeping an even pace. Fast. You don't have all day, only fifteen seconds."

"But there's a car charging me!" Dor protested.

"It will stop," the light assured him. "I shall change to red at the last possible moment and force it to scorch rubber. I get a deep pleasure from that sort of thing."

Nervously, Dor stepped out onto the street again. The car zoomed terrifyingly close, then squealed to a stop a handspan's distance from Dor's shaking body. "Shook you up that time, you damned pedestrian," the car gloated through its cloud of scorched rubber. "If it hadn't been for that blinking light, I'd a had you. You creeps shouldn't be allowed on the road."

"But how can I cross the street if I'm not allowed on the road?" Dor asked.

"That's your problem," the car huffed.

"See, I can time them perfectly," the light said with satisfaction. "I get hundreds of them each day. No one gets through *my* intersection without paying his tax in gas and rubber."

"Go blow a bulb!" the car growled at the light.

"Go soak your horn!" the light flashed back.

"Some day we cars will have a revolution and establish a new axle," the car said darkly. "We'll smash all you restrictive lights and have a genuine free-enterprise system."

"You really crack me up," the light said disdainfully. "Without me, you'd have no discipline at all."

Dor walked on. Another car zoomed up, and Dor lost his nerve and leaped out of the way. "Missed him!" the car complained. "I haven't scored in a week!"

"Get out of my intersection!" the light screamed. "You never stopped! You never burned rubber! You're supposed to waste gas for the full pause before you go through! How do you expect me to maintain a decent level of pollution here if you don't cooperate?"

"Oh, go jam your circuits!" the car roared, moving on through.

"Police! Police!" the light flashed. "That criminal car just ran the light! Rogue car! Rogue car!"

But now the other cars, perceiving that one was getting away with open defiance, hastened to do likewise. The intersection filled with snarling vehicles that crashed merrily into each other. There was the crackle of beginning fire.

Then the magic aisle moved out of the light's range, and it was silent. Dor was relieved; he didn't want to attract attention.

Irene reappeared. "You almost did it that time, Dor! Why don't you quit fooling with lights and get on to the library?"

"I'm trying to!" Dor snapped. "Where is the library?" he asked the sidewalk.

"You don't need a library, you clumsy oaf," the walk said. "You need a bodyguard."

"Just answer my question." The perversity of the inanimate seemed worse than ever, here in Mundania. Perhaps it was because the objects here had never been tamed by magic.

"Three blocks south, two east," the walk said grudgingly.

"What's a block?"

"Is this twerp real?" the walk asked rhetorically.

"Answer!" Dor snapped. And in due course he obtained the necessary definition. A block was one of the big squares formed by the crisscrossing roads. "Is there an archivist there?"

"A what?"

"A researcher, someone who knows a lot."

"Oh, sure. The best in the state. He walks here all the time. Strange old coot."

"That sidewalk sure understands you," Irene remarked smugly.

Dor was silent. Irene was safe from any remarks the sidewalk might make about her legs because she was outside the magic aisle. Dor knew Arnolde was keeping up with him, because his magic was operating. If Irene stepped within that region of magic, she would vanish. So she had the advantage and could snipe with impunity, for now.

A small group of Mundanes walked toward them, three men and two women. Their attire was strange. The men wore knots of something about their necks, almost choking them, and their shoes shone like mirrors. The women seemed to be walking on stilts. Irene continued blithely along, passing them. Dor hung back, curious about Mundane reactions to a citizen of Xanth.

The two females seemed to pay no attention, but all three males paused to look back at Irene. "Look at that creature!" one murmured. "What world is she from?"

"Whatever world it is, I want to go there!" another said. "Must be a foreign student. I haven't seen legs like that in three years."

"Her clothing is three centuries out of fashion, if it ever was *in* fashion," one of the women remarked, her nose elevated. Evidently she had after all paid attention. It was amazing what women could notice while seeming not to. Her own legs were unremarkable, though it occurred to Dor that the stilt-shoes might be responsible for deforming them.

"Men have no taste," the other woman said. "They prefer harem girls."

"Yeah . . ." the third man said with a slow smile. "I'd like to have her number."

"Over my dead body!" the second woman said.

The Mundanes went on, their strange conversation fading from Dor's hearing. Dor proceeded thoughtfully. If Irene were that different from Mundanes, what about himself? No one had reacted to him, yet he was dressed as differently from the males as Irene was from the females. He pondered that as he and Irene continued along the streets. Maybe the Mundanes had been so distracted by Irene's legs that they had skipped over Dor. That was understandable.

The library was a palatial edifice with an exceedingly strange entrance. The door went round and round without ever quite opening.

Dor stood near it, uncertain how to proceed. Mundane people passed him, not noticing him at all despite his evident difference. That was part of the magic, he realized suddenly, his contemplations finally fitting an aspect of the Mundane mystery together. He seemed to share their culture. Should he step outside the magic aisle, he would stand out as a complete foreigner, as Irene had. Fortunately, she was a pretty girl, so she could get away with it; he would not have that advantage.

At the moment, Irene was not in view; perhaps she had been more aware of the Mundane reaction, and preferred to avoid repetition. But as the Mundanes cleared the vicinity, she reappeared. "Arnolde believes that is a revolving door," she said. "There are a few obscure references to them in the texts on Mundania. Probably all you have to do is—" She saw another Mundane approaching, and hastily stepped into invisibility.

The Mundane walked to the door, put forth a hand, and pushed on a panel of the door. A chamber swung inward, and the man followed the compartment around. So simple, once Dor saw it in action!

He walked boldly up to the door and pushed through. It worked like a charm—that is, almost like a natural phenomenon of Xanth—passing him into the building. He was now in a large room in which there were many couches and tables, and the walls were lined with levels of books. This was a library, all right. Now all he needed to do was locate the excellent researcher who was supposed to be here. Maybe in the history section.

Dor walked across the room, toward a wall of books. He could check those and see if any related. It shouldn't be too hard to—

He paused, aware that people were staring at him. What was the matter?

An older woman approached him, her face formed into stern lines. "Xf ibwf b esftt-dpef ifsf," she said severely, her gaze traveling disapprovingly from his unkempt hair to his dust-scuffed sandaled feet. It seemed she disapproved of his attire.

After a moment of confusion, Dor realized he had stepped beyond the magic aisle and was now being seen without the cushion of enchantment. Arnolde had been correct; Dor could not accomplish anything by himself.

What had happened to the centaur? Dor looked back toward the door—and saw Irene beckoning him frantically. He hurried back to her, the Mundane woman following. "Xf pqfsbuf a respectable library here," the Mundane was saying. "We expect a suitable demeanor—"

Dor turned to face her. "Yes?"

The woman stopped, nonplused. "Oh—I see you are properly dressed. I must have mistaken you for someone else." She retreated, embarrassed.

Dor's clothing had not changed. Only the woman's perception of it had, thanks to the magic.

"Arnolde can't get through the spinning door," Irene said.

So that was why Dor had left the aisle! He had walked well beyond the door. Of course those small chambers could not accommodate the mass of the centaur!

"Maybe there's another door," Dor suggested. "We could walk around the building—"

Irene vanished, then reappeared. "Yes, Arnolde says the spell fuzzes the boundaries of things somewhat, so his hands pass through Mundane objects, but his whole body mass is just too much to push through a solid Mundane wall. He might make it through a window, though."

Dor went back out the rotating door, then walked around the building. In the back was a double door that opened wide enough to admit a car. Dor walked through this and past some men who were stacking crates of books. "Hey, kid, you lost?" one called.

It had not taken him long to progress from "King" to "kid"! "I am looking for the archives," Dor said nervously.

"Oh, sure. The stacks. Third door on your left."

"Thank you." Dor went to the door and opened it wide, taking his time to pass through so that the others could get clear. He smelled the centaur and ogre, faintly, so knew they were with him.

Now they were in a region of long narrow passages between shelves loaded with boxes. Dor had no idea how to proceed, and wasn't certain the centaur could fit within these passages, but in a moment Irene appeared and informed him that Arnolde was right at home here. "But it would be better to consult with a competent archivist, he says," she concluded.

"There is one here," he said. "I asked." Then another thought came. "But suppose he sics the Mundane authorities on us? He may not understand our need."

"Arnolde says academics aren't like that. If there is a good one here, his scientific curiosity—I think that's what they call magic here—will keep him interested. Check in that little office; that looks like an archivist's cubby."

Reluctantly, Dor looked. He was in luck, of what kind he was not sure. There was a middle-aged, bespectacled man poring over a pile of papers. "Excuse me, sir—would you like to do some research?" Dor asked.

The man looked up, blinking. "Of what nature?"

"Uh, it's a long story. I'm trying to find a King, and I don't know where or when he is."

The man removed his spectacles and rubbed his tired eyes. "That would seem to be something of a challenge. What is the name of the King, and of his Kingdom?"

"King Trent of Xanth."

The man stood up and squeezed out of his cubby. He was fairly small and stooped, with fading hair, and he moved slowly. He reminded Dor of Arnolde in obscure ways. He located a large old tome, took it down, dusted it off, set it on a small table, and turned the brittle pages. "That designation does not seem to be listed."

Irene appeared. "He would not be a King in Mundania."

The scholar squinted at her with mild surprise. "My dear, I can not comprehend a word you are saying."

"Uh, she's from another land," Dor said quickly. Since Irene had to stand outside the magic aisle in order to be seen and heard, the magic translation effect was not operative for her. Since Dor had been raised in the same culture, he had no trouble understanding her. It was an interesting distinction. He, Dor, could understand both the others, and both seemed to be speaking the same language, but the two could not understand each other. Magic kept coming up with new wrinkles that perplexed him.

The scholar pondered. "Oh—she is associated with a motion picture company? This is research for a historical re-creation?"

"Not exactly," Dor said. "She's King Trent's daughter."

"Oh, it is a contemporary Kingdom! I must get a more recent text."

"No, it is a medieval one," Dor said. "Uh, that is—well, King Trent is in another time, we think."

The scholar paused thoughtfully. "The Kingdom you are re-creating, of course. I believe I understand." He looked again at Irene. "Females certainly have adequate limbs in that realm."

"What's he saying?" Irene demanded.

"That you have nice legs," Dor told her with a certain mild malice.

She ignored that. "What about my father?"

"Not listed in this book. I think we'll have to try another tack."

The scholar's eyes shifted from Irene's legs to Dor's face. "This is very odd. You address her in English, and she seems to understand, but she replies in an alien tongue."

"It's complicated to explain," Dor said.

"I'd better check with Arnolde," Irene said, and vanished.

The Mundane scholar removed his spectacles and cleaned them carefully with a bit of tissue paper. He returned them to his face just in time to see Irene reappear. "Yes, that's definitely better," he murmured.

"Arnolde says we'll have to use some salient identifying trait to locate my father or mother." Irene said. "There may be a historical reference."

"Exactly what language is that?" the scholar asked, again fixing on Irene's legs. He might be old and academic, but he evidently had not forgotten what was what in female appearance.

"Xanthian, I guess," Dor said. "She says we should look for some historical reference to her parents, because of special traits they have."

"And what would these traits be?"

"Well, King Trent transforms people, and Queen Iris is mistress of illusion."

"Idiot!" Irene snapped. "Don't tell him about the magic!"

"I don't quite understand," the scholar said. "What manner of transformation, what mode of illusion?"

"Well, it doesn't work in Mundania," Dor said awkwardly.

"Surely you realize that the laws of physics are identical the world over," the scholar said. "Anything that works in the young lady's country will work elsewhere."

"Not magic," Dor said, and realized he was just confusing things more.

"How dumb can you get?" Irene demanded. "I'm checking with Arnolde." She vanished again.

This time the scholar blinked more emphatically. "Strange girl!"

"She's funny that way," Dor agreed weakly.

The scholar walked to the spot Irene had vacated. "Tubhf jmmvtjpo?" he inquired.

Oh, no! He was outside the magic aisle now, so the magic no longer made his language align with Dor's. Dor could not do anything about this; the centaur would have to move.

Irene reappeared right next to the scholar. Evidently she hadn't been paying attention, for she should have been able to see him while within the magic ambience. "Oh—you're here!" she exclaimed.

"Bnbajoh!" the scholar said. "J nvtu jorvjsf—"

Then the centaur moved. Irene vanished and the scholar became comprehensible. " . . . exactly how you perform that trick—" He paused. "Oops, you're gone again."

Irene reappeared farther down the hall. "Arnolde says we'll have to tell him," she announced. "About the magic and everything. Thanks to your bungling."

"Really, this is amazing!" the scholar said.

"Well, I'll have to tell you something you may find hard to believe," Dor said.

"At this stage, I'm inclined to believe in magic itself!"

"Yes. Xanth is a land of magic."

"In which people disappear and reappear at will? I think

I would prefer to believe that than to conclude I am losing my sight."

"Well, some do disappear. That's not Irene's talent, though."

"That's *not* the young lady's ability? Then why is she doing it?"

"She's actually stepping in and out of a magic aisle."

"A magic aisle?"

"Generated by a centaur."

The scholar smiled wanly. "I fear you have the advantage of me. You can imagine nonsense faster than I can assimilate it."

Dor saw that the scholar did not believe him. "I'll show you my own magic, if you like," he said. He pointed to the open tome on the table. "Book, speak to the man."

"Why should I bother?" the book demanded.

"Ventriloquism!" the scholar exclaimed. "I must confess you are very good at it."

"What did you call me?" the book demanded.

"Would you do that again—with your mouth closed?" the scholar asked Dor.

Dor closed his mouth. The book remained silent. "I rather thought so," the scholar said.

"Thought what, four-eyes?" the book asked.

Startled, the scholar looked down at it, then back at Dor. "But your mouth was closed, I'm sure."

"It's magic," Dor said. "I can make any inanimate object talk."

"Let's accept for the moment that this is true. You are telling me that this King you are searching for can also work magic?"

"Right. Only he can't do it in Mundania, so I guess it doesn't count."

"Because he has no magic centaur with him?"

"Yes."

"I would like to see this centaur."

"He's protected by an invisibility spell. So the Mundanes won't bother us."

"This centaur is a scholar?"

"Yes. An archivist, like yourself."

"Then he is the one to whom I should talk."

"But the spell—"

"Abate the spell! Bring your centaur scholar forth. Otherwise I can not help you."

"I don't think he'd want to do that. It would be hard to get safely out of here without that enchantment, and we have no duplicate invisibility spell."

The scholar walked back to his cubby. "Mind you, I believe in magic no more than in the revelations of a hallucination, but I am willing to help you if you meet me halfway. Desist your parlor tricks, show me your scholar, and I will work with him to fathom the information you desire. I don't care how fanciful his outward form may be, provided he has a genuine mind. The fact that you find it necessary to dazzle me with ventriloquism, a lovely costumed girl who vanishes, and a mythological narrative suggests that there is very little substance to your claim, and you are wasting my time. I ask you to produce your scholar or depart my presence."

"Uh, Arnolde," Dor said. "I know it'll be awful hard to get out of here without the spells, but maybe we could wait till night. We really need the information, and—"

Abruptly the centaur appeared, facing the scholar's cubby. The ogre and golem stood behind him. "I agree," Arnolde said.

The scholar turned about. He blinked. "These are rare costumes, I admit."

Arnolde strode forward, his barrel barely clearing the shelves on either side, extending his hand. "I certainly do not blame you for being impatient with the uninitiate," he said. "You have excellent facilities here, and I know your time is valuable."

The scholar shook the hand, seeming more reassured by Arnolde's spectacles and demeanor than confused by his form.

"What is your specialty?"

"Alien archaeology—but of course there is a great deal of routine work and overlapping of chores."

"There certainly is!" the scholar agreed. "The nuisances I have to endure here—"

The two fell into a technical dialogue that soon left Dor behind. They became more animated as they sized up each other's minds and information. There was now no doubt they were similar types.

Irene, bored, grew a cocoa plant in the hall, and shared the hot cups of liquid with Dor, Smash, and Grundy. They knew it was important that Arnolde establish a good rapport so that they could gain the scholar's cooperation and make progress on their request.

Time passed. The two scholars delved into ancient tomes, debated excruciatingly fine points, questioned Dor closely about the hints King Trent had given him in both person and vision, and finally wound down to an animated close. The Mundane scholar accepted a mug of cocoa, relaxing at last. "I believe we have it," he said. "Will I see you again, centaur?"

"Surely so, sir! I am able to travel in Mundania, am fascinated by your comprehensive history, and am presently, as it were, between positions."

"Your compatriots found your magic as intolerable in you as mine would find a similar propensity in me! I shall not be able to tell anyone what I have learned this day, lest I, too, lose my position and possibly even be institutionalized. Imagine conversing with a centaur, ogre, and tiny golem! How I should love to do a research paper on your fantastic Land of Xanth, but it would hardly be believable."

"You could write a book and call it a story," Grundy suggested. "And Arnolde could write one about Mundania."

Both scholars looked pleased. Neither had thought of such a simple expedient.

"But do you know where my father is?" Irene demanded.

"Yes, I believe we do," Arnolde said. "King Trent left a message for us, we believe."

"How could he leave a message?" she demanded.

"He left it with Dor. That, and the other hints we had, such as the fact that he was going to a medieval region, in the mountains near a black body of water. There are, my friend informs me, many places in Mundania that fit the description. So we assume it is literal; either the water itself is black, or it is called black. As it happens, there is in Mundania a large body of water called the Black Sea.

Many great rivers empty into it; great mountain ranges sur-
round it. But that is not sufficient to identify this as the
specific locale we seek; it merely makes it one possibility
among many." Arnolde smiled. "We spent a good deal of
time on geography. As it happens, there was historically a
confluence of A, B, and K people in that vicinity in medieval times—at least that is so when their names are rendered into Xanth dialect. The Avars, the Bulgars, and the
Khazars. So it does seem to fit. Everything you have told
us seems to fit."

"But that isn't enough!" Dor cried. "How can you be
sure you have the place, the time?"

"Honesty," Arnolde said. "O N E S T I." He pointed to
a spot on an open book. "This, we believe, is the unique
special hint King Trent gave you, to enable you and only
you to locate him in an emergency."

Dor looked. It was an atlas, with a map of some strange
Mundane land. On the map was a place labeled *Onesti*.

"There is only one such place in the world," Arnolde
said. "It has to be King Trent's message to you. No one else
would grasp the significance of that unique nomenclature."

Dor recalled the intensity with which King Trent had
spoken of honesty, as if there had been a separate meaning
there. He remembered how well aware the King had been
of Dor's kind of spelling. It seemed no one else spelled it
the obvious way, onesti.

"But if that's been there—that name, there in your maps
and things—for centuries—that means King Trent never
came back! We can't rescue him, because then the name
would go."

"Not necessarily," Arnolde said. "The place-name does
not depend on his presence. We should be able to rescue
him without disturbing it. At any rate, we are never certain
of the paradoxes of time. We shall simply have to go to
that location and that time, circa AD 650, and try to find
him."

"But suppose it's wrong?" Irene asked worriedly. "Suppose he isn't there?"

"Then we shall return here and do more research," Arnolde said. "I intend to visit here again anyway, and my
friend Ichabod would like to visit Xanth. There will be no
trouble about that, I assure you."

"Yes. You will be welcome here," the Mundane scholar agreed. "You have a fine and arcane mind."

"For the first time," Arnolde continued, "I look upon my exile from Centaur Isle and my assumption of an obscene talent with a certain equanimity. I have not, it seems, been excluded from my calling; my horizons have been inordinately expanded."

"And mine," Ichabod agreed. "I must confess my contemporaneous existence was becoming tiresome, though I did not recognize this until this day." Now the scholar sounded just like Arnolde. Perhaps some obscure wrinkle of fate had operated to bring these two together. Did luck or fate really operate in Mundania? Perhaps they did, when the magic aisle was present. "The prospect of researching in a completely new and mystical terrain is immensely appealing; it renovates my outlook." He paused. "Ah, would there by any chance be individuals of the female persuasion remotely resembling . . . ?" His glance flicked guiltily to Irene's legs.

"Nymphs galore," Grundy said. "A dime a dozen."

"Oh, you employ contemporaneous currency?" the scholar asked, surprised.

"Currency?" Dor asked blankly.

"A dime is a coin of small denomination here."

Dor smiled. "No, a dime is a tiny object that causes things passing over it to come to a sudden stop. When it has functioned this way twelve times, its enchantment wears out. Hence our saying—"

"How marvelous. I wonder whether one of my own dimes would perform similarly there."

"That's the idea," Grundy said. "Toss it in front of a troupe of gamboling nymphs, and grab the first one it stops. Nymphs don't have much brains, but they sure have legs." He moved farther away from Irene, who showed signs of kicking.

"Oh, I can hardly wait to commence research in Xanth!" the scholar exclaimed. "As it happens, I have a dime ready." He brought out a tiny silver coin, his gaze once again touching on Irene's limbs. "I wonder . . ."

Irene frowned. "Sometimes I wonder just how badly I really want to rescue my folks. I'll be lucky if my legs don't get blistered from all the attention." But as usual, she did not seem completely displeased. "Let's be on our way; I don't care what you do, once my father is back in Xanth."

Arnolde and Ichabod shook hands, two very similar creatures. On impulse, Dor brought out one of the gold coins he had so carefully saved from the pirate's treasure. "Please accept this, sir, as a token of our appreciation for your help." He pressed it on the scholar.

The man hefted the coin. "That's solid gold?" he exclaimed. "I believe it is a genuine Spanish doubloon! I can not accept it."

The centaur interceded. "Please do accept it, Ichabod. Dor is temporary King of Xanth; to decline would be construed as an offense to the crown."

"But the value—"

"Let's trade coins," Dor said, discovering a way through. "Your dime for my doubloon. Then it is an even exchange."

"An even exchange!" the scholar exclaimed. "In no way can this be considered—"

"Dimes are very precious in Xanth," Arnolde said. "Gold has little special value. Please acquiesce."

"Maybe a nymph would stop on a doubloon, too," Grundy suggested.

"She certainly would!" Ichabod agreed. "But not because of any magic. Women here are much attracted to wealth."

"Please," Irene put in, smiling beguilingly. Dor knew she only wanted to get moving on the search for her father, but her intercession was effective.

"In that case, I will exchange with you, with pleasure, King Dor," the scholar agreed, giving Dor his dime. "I only meant to protest that your coin was far too valuable for whatever service I might have provided, when in fact it was a pleasure providing it anyway."

"Nothing's too valuable to get my father back," Irene said. She leaned forward and kissed Ichabod on the cheek. The man froze as if he had glimpsed the Gorgon, an astonished smile on his face. It was obvious he had not been kissed by many pretty girls in his secluded lifetime.

It was now early evening. Ichabod delved into assorted cubbies and produced shrouds to conceal the bodies of the centaur and ogre. Then Arnolde and Smash walked out of the library in tandem, looking like two big workmen in togas, moving a covered crate between them. It turned out to be almost as good concealment as the invisibility spell; no one paid attention to them. They were on their way back to Xanth.

Chapter 9. Onesti's Policy

They did not go all the way back home. They trekked only to the northwest tip of Xanth, where the isthmus connected it to Mundania. Once they were back in magic territory, Irene set about replenishing her stock of seeds. Smash knocked down a jellybarrel tree, consumed the jelly, and fashioned the swollen trunk into a passable boat. Arnolde watched the terrain, making periodic forays into Mundania, just far enough to see whether it had changed. Dor accompanied him, questioning the sand. By the description of people the sand had recently seen, they were able to guess at the general place and time in Mundania.

For the change was continuous. Once a person from Xanth entered Mundania, his framework was fixed until he returned; but anyone who followed him might enter a different aspect of Mundania. This was like missing one boat and boarding the next, Arnolde explained; the person on the first boat could return, but the person on land could not catch a particular boat that had already departed. Thus King Trent had gone, they believed, to a place called "Europe," in a time called "Medieval." Dor's party had gone to a place called "America," in a time called "Modern." The shifting of places and times seemed random; probably there was a pattern to the changes that they were unable to comprehend. They simply had to locate the combination they wanted and pass through that "window" before it changed. Arnolde concluded, from their observations, that any given window lasted from five minutes to an hour, and that it was possible to hold a window open longer by having a person stand at the border; it seemed the window couldn't quite close while it was in use. Perhaps it was like the revolving door in the Mundanian library, whose turning could be temporarily stopped by a person in it—until some other person needed to use it.

On the third day it became tedious. Irene's seed collection was complete and she was restive; Smash had finished his boat and stocked it with supplies. Grundy had made himself a nest in the bow, from which he eavesdropped on the gossip of passing marine life. Arnolde and Dor walked down the beach. "What have you seen lately?" Dor inquired routinely of the same-yet-different patch of sand.

"A man in a spacesuit," the sand replied. "He had little antennae sprouting from his head, like an ant, and he could talk to his friends without making a sound."

That didn't sound like anyone Dor was looking for. Some evil Magician must have enchanted the man, perhaps trying to create a new composite-species. They turned about and returned to Xanth. This surely was not their window.

The sea changed color frequently. It had been reddish the first time they came here, and reddish when they returned, for they had been locked into that particular aspect of Mundania. But thereafter it had shifted to blue, yellow, green, and white. Now it was orange, changing to purple. When it was solid purple, they walked west again. "What have you seen lately?" Dor asked once more.

"A cavegirl swimming," the sand said. "She was sort of fat, but oooh, didn't she have—"

They walked east again, depressed. "I wish there were a more direct way to do this," Arnolde said. "I have been striving to analyze the pattern, but it has eluded me, perhaps because of insufficient data."

"I know it's not much of a life we have brought you into," Dor said. "I wish there had been some other way—"

"On the contrary, it is a fascinating life and a challenging puzzle," the centaur demurred. "It is akin to the riddles of archaeology, where one must have patience and fortune in equal measure. We merely must gather more data, whether it takes a day or a year."

"A year!" Dor cried, horrified.

"Surely it will be shorter," Arnolde said reassuringly. It was obvious that he had a far greater store of patience than Dor did.

As they re-entered Xanth, the sea turned black. "Black!" Dor exclaimed. "Could that be—?"

"It is possible," Arnolde agreed, reining his own excitement with the caution of experience. "We had better alert the remainder of our company."

"Grundy, get Smash and Irene to the boat," Dor called. "We just might be close."

"More likely another false alarm," the golem grumbled. But he scampered off to fetch the other two.

When they reached their usual spot of questioning, Dor noticed that there was a large old broad-leaved tree that hadn't been there before. This was certainly a different locale. But that in itself did not mean much; the landscape did shift with the Mundane aspects, sometimes dramatically. It was not just time but geography that changed; some aspects were flat and barren, while others were raggedly mountainous. The only thing all had in common was the beach line, with the sea to the south and the terrain to the north. Arnolde was constantly intrigued by the assorted significances of this, but Dor did not pay much attention. "What have you seen lately?" he asked the sand.

"Nothing much since the King and his moll walked by," the sand said.

"Oh." Dor turned to trek back to the magic section.

The centaur paused. "Did it say—?"

Then it sank in. Excitement raced along Dor's nerves. "King Trent and Queen Iris?"

"I suppose. They were sort of old."

"I believe we have our window at last!" Arnolde said. "Go back and alert the others; I shall hold the window open."

Dor ran back east, his heart pounding harder than warranted by the exertion. Did he dare believe? "We've found it!" he cried. "Move out now!"

They dived into the boat. Smash poled it violently forward. Then the ogre's effort diminished. Dor looked, and saw that Smash was striving hard but accomplishing little.

"Oh—we're out of the magic of Xanth, and not yet in the magic aisle," he said. "Come on—we've all got to help."

Dor and Irene leaned over the boat on either side and paddled desperately with their hands, and slowly the boat moved onward. They crawled up parallel to the centaur. "All aboard!" Dor cried, exhilarated.

Arnolde trotted out through the shallow water and climbed aboard with difficulty, rocking the boat. Some sea water slopped in. The craft was sturdy, as anything crafted by an ogre was bound to be, but still reeked of lime jelly, especially where it had been wet down.

The centaur stood in the center, facing forward; Irene sat in the front, her fair green hair trailing back in the breeze. It had faded momentarily when they were between magics, just now; perhaps that had helped give Dor the hint of the problem. It remained the easiest way to tell the state of the world around them.

Dor settled near the rear of the boat, and Smash poled vigorously from the stern. Now that they were within the magic aisle, the ogre's strength was full, and the boat was lively. The black waves coursed rapidly past.

"I wish I had known this was all we had to do to locate King Trent," Dor said. "We could have saved ourselves the trip into Modern Mundania."

"By no means," Arnolde protested, swishing his tail. "We might have discovered this window, true; but each window opens onto an entire Mundane world. We should soon have lost the trail and ourselves and been unable to rescue anyone. As it is, we know we are looking for Onesti and we know where it is; this will greatly facilitate our operation." The centaur paused. "Besides which, I am most gratified to have met Ichabod."

So their initial excursion did make sense, after all. "What sort of people do you see here?" Dor asked the water.

"Tough people with baggy clothes and swords and bows," the water said. "They're not much on the water, though; not the way the Greeks were."

"Those are probably the Bulgars," Arnolde said. "They should have passed this way in the past few decades, according to Ichabod."

"Who are the Bulgars?" Irene asked. Now that they were actually on the trail of her lost father, she was much more interested in details.

"This is complex to explain. Ichabod gave me some detail on it, but I may not have the whole story."

"If they're people my father met—and if we have to meet them, too—I want to know all about them." Her face assumed her determined look.

The boat was moving well, for the ogre's strength was formidable. The shoreline stretched ahead, curving in and out, with inlets and bays. "We do have a journey of several days ahead of us," the centaur said. "Time will doubtless weigh somewhat ponderously on our hands." He took a didactic breath and started in on his historical narrative, while the ogre scowled, uninterested, and Grundy settled down in his nest to sleep. But Dor and Irene paid close attention.

In essence it was this: about three centuries before this period, there had been a huge Mundane empire in this region, called—as Dor understood it—Roam, perhaps because it spread so far. But after a long time this empire had grown corrupt and weak. Then from the great inland mass to the east had thrust a formerly quiescent tribe, the Huns, perhaps short for Hungries because of their appetite for power, pushing other tribes before them. These tribes had overrun the Roaming Empire, destroying a large part of it. But when the Hungry chief, Attaboy, died of indigestion, they were defeated and driven partway back east, to the shore of this Black Sea, the very color of their mood. They fought among themselves for a time, as people in a black mood do, then reunited and called themselves the Bulgars. But the Buls were driven out of their new country by another savage tribe of Turks—no relation to the turkey oaks—called the Khazars. Some Buls fled north and some fled west—and this was the region the western ones had settled, here at the western edge of the Black Sea. They couldn't go any farther because another savage tribe was there, the Avars. The Avars had a huge empire in eastern Europe, but now it was declining, especially under the onslaught of the Khazars. At the moment, circa Mundane AD 650—the number referred to some Mundane religion to which none of these parties belonged—there was an uneasy balance in this region between the three powers, the Avars, Bulgars, and Khazars, with the Khazars dominant.

Somehow this was too complex for Dor to follow. All these strange tribes and happenings and numbers—the intricacies of Mundania were far more complicated than the simple magic events of Xanth! Easier to face down griffins and dragons than Avars and Khazars; at least the dragons were sensible creatures.

"But what has this to do with my father?" Irene demanded. "Which tribe did he go to trade with?"

"None of the above," the centaur said. "This is merely background. It would be too dangerous for us to deal with such savages. But we believe there is a small Kingdom, maybe a Gothic remnant, or some older indigenous people, who have retained nominal independence in the Carpathian Mountains, with a separate language and culture. They happen to be at the boundary between the Avars, Bulgars, and Khazars, protected to a degree because no one empire can make a move there without antagonizing the other two, and also protected by the roughness of the terrain. Hence the A, B, K complex King Trent referenced—a valuable clue for us. This separate region is the Kingdom of Onesti. It is ensconced in the mountains, difficult to invade, and has very little that others would want to take, which may help account for its independence. But it surely is eager for peaceful and profitable trade, and Ichabod's Mundane reference suggests that it did have a trade route that has been lost to history, which enabled the Kingdom to prosper for a century when their normal channels appeared to be blocked. That could be the trade route to Xanth that King Trent sought to establish."

"Yes, that does make sense," Irene agreed. "But suppose one of those other tribes caught my father, and that's why he never returned?"

"We shall trace him down," the centaur said reassuringly. "We have an enormous asset King Trent lacked—magic. All we need to do is go to Onesti and query the people, plants, animals, and objects. There will surely be news of him."

Irene was silent. Dor shared her concern. Now that they were on the verge of finding King Trent—how could they be certain they would find him alive? If he were dead, what then?

"Are we going to have to fight all those A's, B's, and K's?" Grundy asked. Apparently he had not been entirely asleep.

"I doubt it," Arnolde replied. "Actual states of war are rarer than they seem in historical perspective. The great majority of the time, life goes on as usual; the fishermen fish, the blacksmiths hammer iron, the farmers farm, the women bear children. Otherwise there would be constant deprivation. However, I have stocked a friendship-spell for emergency use." He patted his bag of spells.

They went on, the ogre poling indefatigably. Gradually the shoreline curved southward, and they followed it. When dusk came they pulled ashore briefly to make a fire and prepare supper; then they returned to the boat for the night, so as not to brave the Mundane threats of the darkness. There were few fish and no monsters in the Black Sea, Grundy reported; it was safe as long as a storm did not come up.

Now Arnolde expended one of his precious spells. He opened a wind capsule, orienting it carefully. The wind blew southwest, catching the small squat sail they raised for the purpose. Now the ogre could rest, while the boat coursed on toward their destination. They took turns steering it, Grundy asking the fish and water plants for directions, Dor asking the water, and Irene growing a compass plant that pointed toward the great river they wanted.

That reminded Dor of the magic compass. He brought it out and looked, hoping it would point to King Trent. But it pointed straight at Arnolde, and when Arnolde held it, it pointed to Dor. It was useless in this situation.

Sleep was not comfortable on the water, but it was possible. Dor lay down and stared at the stars, wide awake; then the stars abruptly shifted position, and he realized he had slept; *now* he was wide awake. They shifted again. Then he was wide awake again—when Grundy woke him to take his turn at the helm. He had, it seemed, been dreaming he was wide awake. That was a frustrating mode; he would almost have preferred the nightmares.

In the morning they were at the monstrous river delta— a series of bars, channels, and islands, through which the slow current coursed. Now Smash had to unship the two great oars he had made, face back, and row against the current. Still the boat moved alertly enough. Irene grew pastry plants and fed their pastry-flower fruits to the ogre so he would not suffer the attrition of hunger. Smash gulped them down entire without pausing in his efforts; Dor was almost jealous of the creature's sheer zest for food and effort.

No, he realized upon reflection. He was jealous of the attention Irene was paying Smash. For all that he, Dor, did not want to be considered the property of any girl, especially not this one, he still became resentful when Irene's attention went elsewhere. This was unreasonable, he knew; Smash needed lots of food in order to continue the enormous effort he was making. This was the big thing the ogre was contributing to their mission—his abundant strength. Yet still it gnawed at Dor; he wished *he* had enormous muscles and endless endurance, and that Irene was popping whole pies and tarts into his mouth.

Once, Dor remembered, he had been big—or at least had borrowed the body of a powerful barbarian—maybe an Avar or a Bulgar or a Khazar—and had discovered that strength did not solve all problems or bring a person automatic happiness. But at the moment, his selfish feelings didn't go along with the sensible thinking of his mind.

"Sometimes I wish I were an ogre," Grundy muttered. Suddenly Dor felt better.

All day they heaved up the river, leaving the largest channel for a smaller one, and leaving that for another and still smaller one. There were some fishermen, but they didn't look like A's, B's, or K's, and they took a look at the size and power of the ogre and left the boat alone. Arnolde had been correct; the ordinary Mundane times were pretty dull, without rampaging armies everywhere. In this respect Mundania was similar to Xanth.

Well upstream, they drew upon the shore and camped for the night. Dor told the ground to yell an alarm if anything approached—anything substantially larger than ants—and they settled down under another umbrella tree Irene grew. It was just as well, for during the night it rained.

On the third day they forged up a fast-flowing tributary stream, ascending the great Carpath range. Some places they had to portage; Smash merely picked up the entire boat, upright, balanced it on his corrugated head, steadied it with his gauntleted hamhands, and trudged up through the rapids.

"If you don't have your full strength yet," Dor commented, "you must be close to it."

"Ungh," Smash agreed, for once not having the leisure to rhyme. Ogres were the strongest creatures of Xanth, size for size—but some monsters were much larger, and others more intelligent, so ogres did not rule the jungle. Smash and his parents were the only ogres Dor had met, if he didn't count his adventure into Xanth's past, where he had known Egor the zombie ogre; they were not common creatures today. Perhaps that was just as well; if ogres were as common as dragons, who would stand against them?

At last, on the afternoon of the third day, they came to the Kingdom of Onesti, or at least its main fortress, Castle Onesti. Dor marveled that King Trent and Queen Iris, traveling alone without magic, could have been able to get here in similar time. Maybe they underestimated the arduousness of the journey. Well, it would soon be known.

Dor tried to question the stones and water of the river, but the water wasn't the same from moment to moment and so could not remember, and the stones claimed that no one had portaged up here in the past month. Obviously the King had taken another route, probably an easier one. Perhaps the King of Onesti had sent an escort, and they had ridden Mundane horses up a horse trail. Yes, that was probably it.

They drew up just in sight of the imposing castle. Huge stones formed great walls, leading up to the front entrance. There was no moat; this was a mountain fastness. "Do we knock on the door, or what?" Irene asked nervously.

"Your father told me honesty is the best policy," Dor said, masking his own uncertainty. "I assume that wasn't just a riddle to suggest where he went. We can approach openly. We can tell them we're from Xanth and are looking for King Trent. Maybe they have no connection to whatever happened—*if* anything happened. But let's not go out of our way to tell them about our magic. Just in case."

"Just in case," she agreed tightly.

They marched up to the front entrance. That seemed to be the only accessible part of the edifice anyway; the wall passed through a forest on the south to merge cleverly with the clifflike sides of the mountain to the west and north. They were at the east face, where the approach was merely steep. "No wonder no one has conquered this little Kingdom," Irene murmured.

"I agree," Arnolde said. "No siege machinery could get close, and a catapult would have to operate from the valley below. Perhaps it could be taken, but it hardly seems worth the likely cost."

Dor knocked. They waited. He knocked again. Still no response. Then Smash tapped the door with one finger, making it shudder.

Now a window creaked open in the middle of the door. A face showed behind bars. "Who are you?" the guard demanded.

"I am Dor of Xanth. I have come to see King Trent of Xanth, who, I believe, is here."

"Who?"

"King Trent, imbecile!" one of the bars snapped.

The guard's head jerked back, startled. "What?"

"You got a potato in your ear?" the bar demanded.

"Stop it," Dor mumbled at the bars. The last thing he wanted was the premature exposure of his talent! Then, quickly, louder: "We wish to see King Trent."

"Wait," the guard said. The window slammed closed.

But Smash, tired from his two days' labors, was irritable. "No wait, ingrate!" he growled, and before Dor knew what was happening, the ogre smashed one sledgehammer fist into the door. The heavy wood splintered. He punched right through, then caught the far side of the door with his thick gauntleted fingers and hauled violently back. The entire door ripped free of its bolts and hinges. He put his other hand on the little barred window and hefted the door up and over his head, while the other people ducked hastily.

"Now see what you've done, you moronic brute," Arnolde said. But somehow the centaur did not seem completely displeased. He, too, was tired and irritable from the journey, and the welcome at Castle Onesti had not been polite.

The guard stood inside, staring, as the ogre hurled the great door down the mountainside. "Take us to your leader," Dor said calmly, as if this were routine. All he could do, after all, was make the best of the situation, and poise counted for a lot. "We don't want my friend to get impatient."

The guard turned about somewhat dazedly and led the way to the interior of the castle. Other guards came charging up, attracted by the commotion, swords drawn. Smash glared at them and they hastily faded back, swords sheathed.

Soon they came to the main banquet hall, where the King of Onesti held sway. The King sat at the head of an immense wooden table piled with puddings. He stood angrily as Dor approached, his huge belly bulging out over the table. "H cdlzmc sn jmnv sgd ldzmhmf ne sghr hmsqtrhnm—" he demanded, his fat face reddening impressively.

Then Arnolde's magic aisle caught up, and the King became intelligible. ". . . before I have you all thrown in the dungeon!"

"Hello," Dor said. "I am Dor, temporary King of Xanth while King Trent is away." Of course, the Zombie Master was temporary-temporary King now, while Dor himself was away, but that was too complicated to explain at the moment. "He came here on a trading mission, I believe, less than a month ago, and has not returned. So I have come to look for him. What's the story?"

The King scowled. Suddenly Dor knew this approach had been all wrong, that King Trent had not come here, that the people of Onesti knew nothing about him. This was all a mistake.

"I am King Oary of Onesti," the King said from out of his glower, "and I never saw this King Trench of yours. Get out of my Kingdom."

Despair struck Dor—but behind him Arnolde murmured: "That person is prevaricating, I believe."

"On top of that, he's lying," Irene muttered.

"Glib fib," Smash said. He set one hamhand down on

the banquet table gently. The bowls of pudding jumped and quivered nervously.

King Oary considered the ogre. His ruddy face paled. His righteous anger dissolved into something like guilty cunning. "However, I may have news of him," he said with less bellicosity. "Join my feast, and I will query my minions."

Dor didn't like this. King Oary did not impress him favorably, and he did not feel like eating with the man. But the puddings looked good, and he did want Oary's cooperation. He nodded reluctant assent.

The servants hurried up with more chairs for Dor, Irene, and Smash. Grundy, too small for a chair, perched instead on the edge of the table. Arnolde merely stood. More puddings were brought in, together with flagons of beverage, and they all pitched in.

The pudding was thick, with fruit embedded, and surprisingly tasty. Dor soon found himself thirsty, for the pudding was highly spiced, so he drank—and found the beverage a cross between sweet beer and sharp wine from indifferent beerbarrel and winekeg trees. He hadn't realized that such trees grew in Mundania; certainly they did not grow as well. But the stuff was heady and good once he got used to it.

The others were eating as happily. They had all developed quite an appetite in the course of their trek up the mountain river, and had not paused to grow a meal of their own before approaching the castle. Smash, especially, tossed down puddings and flagons of drink with an abandon that set the castle servants gaping.

But the drink was stronger than what they were accustomed to. Dor soon found his awareness spinning pleasantly. Grundy began a little dance on the table, a routine he had picked up from a Mundane immigrant to Xanth. He called it the Drunken Sailor's Hornpipe, and it did indeed look drunken. King Oary liked it, applauding with his fat hands.

Arnolde and Irene ate more diffidently, but the centaur's mass required plenty of sustenance, and he was making good progress. Irene, it seemed, loved puddings, so she could not hold back long.

"Zmc vgn lhfgs xnt ad, ezhq czlrdk?" King Oary asked Irene pleasantly.

Oops—they were seated along the table, with the King at the end. The King was beyond the aisle of magic. But Arnolde grasped the problem quickly, and angled his body so that he now faced the King. That would extend the magic far enough.

Irene, too, caught on. "Were you addressing me, Your Majesty?" she asked demurely. Dor had to admit she was very good at putting on maidenly ways.

"Of course. What other fair damsels are in this hall?"

She colored slightly, looking about as if to spy other girls. She was getting more practiced at this sort of dissemblance. "Thank you so much, Your Majesty."

"What is your lineage?"

"Oh, I'm King Trent's daughter."

The King nodded sagely. "I'm sure you are prettier than your mother."

Did that mean something? Dor continued eating, listening, hoping Irene could get some useful information from the obese monarch. There was something odd here, but Dor did not know how to act until he had more definite information.

"Have you any news of my parents?" Irene inquired, having the wit and art to smile fetchingly at the King. Yet again Dor had to suppress his unreasoning jealousy. "I'm so worried about them." And she pouted cutely. Dor hadn't seen her use that expression before; it must be a new one.

"My henchmen are spying out information now," The King reassured her. "Soon we should have what news there is."

Arnolde glanced at Dor, a fleeting frown on his face. He still did not trust Oary.

"Tell me about Onesti," Irene said brightly. "It seems like such a *nice* little Kingdom."

"Oh, it is, it is," the King agreed, his eyes focusing on what showed of her legs. "Two fine castles and several villages, and some very pretty mountains. For centuries we have fought off the savages; two thousand years ago, this was the heartland of the battle-axe people, the Cimmerians. Then the Scyths came on their horses, driving the foot-bound Cimmerians south. Horses had not been seen in this country before; they seemed like monsters from some fantasy land."

The King paused to chew up another pudding. Monsters from a fantasy land—could that refer to Xanth? Dor wondered. Maybe some nightmares found a way out, and turned Mundane, and that was the origin of day horses. It was an intriguing speculation.

"But here at the mountains," the King resumed, wiping pudding crust from his whiskers, "the old empire held. Many hundreds of years later the Sarmatians drove out the Scyths, but did not penetrate this fastness." He belched contentedly. "Then came the Goths—but still we held the border. Then from the south came the horrible civilized Romans, and from the east the Huns—"

"Ah, the Huns," Irene agreed, as if she knew something about them.

"But still Onesti survived, here in the mountains, unconquered though beset by barbarians," the King concluded. "Of course we had to pay tribute sometimes, a necessary evil. Yet our trade is inhibited. If we interact too freely with the barbarians, there will surely be mischief. Yet we must have trade if we are to survive."

"My father came to trade," Irene said.

"Perhaps he got sidetracked by the dread Khazars, or their Magyar minions," King Oary suggested. "I have had some dealings with those; they are savage, cunning brutes, always alert for spoils. I happen to speak their language, so I know."

Dor decided he would have to do some searching on his own, questioning the objects in this vicinity. But not right now, while the King was watching. He was sure the King was hiding something.

"Have you been King of Onesti for a long time?" Irene inquired innocently.

"Not long," Oary admitted. "My nephew Omen was to be King, but he was underage, so I became regent when my brother died. Then Omen went out hunting—and did not return. We fear he strayed too far and was ambushed by the Khazars or Magyars. So I am King, until we can declare Omen officially dead. There is no hope of his survival, of course, but the old council moves very slowly on such matters."

So King Oary was in fact regent during the true King's absence—much as Dor was, in Xanth. But this King was eager to retain the throne. Had there been foul play by other than the Khazars?

Dor found his head on the table, contesting for space with a pudding. He must have gotten quite sleepy! "What's going on?" he mumbled.

"You've been drugged, you fool, that's what," the table whispered in his ear. "There's more in that rotgut than booze, I'll tell you!"

Dor reacted with shock, but somehow his head did not rise. "Drugged? Why?"

" 'Cause the Imposter King doesn't like you, that's why," the table said. "He always drugs his enemies. That's how he got rid of King Omen, and then that fake Magician King."

Magician King! It was funny, whispering with his head on the table, but fairly private. Dor's nose was almost under the pudding. "Was that King Trent?"

"That's what he called himself. But he couldn't do magic. He drank the drink, all-trusting the way they all are, the fools, and went to sleep just like you. You're all such suckers."

"Smash! Grundy!" Dor cried as loudly as he could, his head still glued to the table. "We've been betrayed! Drugged! Break out of here!"

But now many guards charged into the hall. "Remove this carrion," King Oary commanded. "Throw them in the dungeon. Don't damage the girl; she's too pretty to waste. Put the freak horse in the stable."

Smash, who had gulped huge quantities of the drugged drink, nevertheless had strength to rouse himself and fight. Dor heard the noise, but was facing the wrong way. Guards charged, and screamed, and retreated. "Give it to them, ogre!" Grundy cried, dancing on the table. "Tear them up!"

But then the violence abated. "Hey, don't slow down now!" Grundy called. "What's the matter with you?"

Dor knew what had happened. Smash had wandered outside the magic aisle, and lost his supernatural strength.

Now the flagons of drugged drink took their toll, as they would on any normal creature. "Me sleep a peep," Smash said, the last of his magic expended in the rhyme.

Dor knew this fight was lost. "Get out of here, Grundy," he said with a special effort. "Before you sleep, too. Don't let them catch you." The unconsciousness overcame Dor.

Chapter 10. Hate Love

Dor woke with a headache. He was lying on sour-smelling hay in a dark cell. As he moved, something skittered away. He suspected it was a rat; he understood they abounded in Mundania. Maybe that was a blessing; the magic creatures of the night could be horrible in Xanth.

There was the sound of muted sobbing. Dor held his breath a moment to make certain it wasn't himself.

He sat up, peering through the gloom to find some vestige of light. There was a little, which grew brighter as his eyes acclimatized; it seemed to be a candle in the distance. But there was a wall in the way; the light filtered through the cracks.

He oriented on the sobbing. It was from an adjacent chamber, separated from his own by massive stone pilings and huge wood timbers. This must be the lower region of the castle, these cells hollowed out from around the foundations. There were gaps between the supports, big enough for him to pass his arm through but not his body.

"Irene?" he asked.

"Oh, Dor!" she answered immediately, tearfully. "I thought I was alone! What has become of us?"

"We were drugged and thrown in the dungeon," he said. "King Oary must have done the same to your parents, before." He couldn't quite remember where he had gotten that notion, or how he himself had been drugged; his memory was foggy on recent details.

"But why? My father came only to trade!"

"I don't know. But I think King Oary is a usurper. Maybe he murdered the rightful King, and your folks found out. Oary knew he couldn't fool us long, so he practiced his treachery on us, too."

"What do we do now?" she demanded hysterically. "Oh, Dor, I've never felt so horrible!"

"I think it's the drug," he said. "I feel bad, too. That should wear off. If we have our magic, we may be able to get free. Do you have your bag of seeds?"

She checked. "No. Only my clothing. Do you have your gold and gems?"

Dor checked. "No. They must have searched us and taken everything they thought was valuable or dangerous. I don't have my sword either." But then his questing fingers found something small. "I do have the jar of salve, not that it's much good here. And my midnight sunstone; it fell into the jacket lining. Let me see—" He brought it out. "No, I guess not. This has no light."

"Where are the others?"

"I'll check," he said. "Floor, where are my companions?"

There was no answer. "That means we have no magic. Arnolde must be in the stable." He seemed to remember something about that, foggily.

"What about Smash and Grundy?"

"Me here," the ogre said from the opposite cell. "Head hurt. Strength gone."

Now Dor had no further doubt; the magic was gone. The ogre wasn't rhyming, and no doubt Irene's hair had lost its color. Magic had strange little bypaths and side effects, where loss was somehow more poignant than that of the major aspects. But those major ones were vital; without his magic strength, Smash could probably not break free of the dungeon.

"Grundy?" Dor called inquiringly.

There was no answer. Grundy, it seemed, had escaped capture. That was about the extent of their good fortune.

"Me got gauntlets," Smash said.

Include one more item of fortune. If the ogre should get his strength back, those gauntlets would be a big help. Probably the castle guards had not realized the gauntlets were not part of the ogre, since Smash had used them for eating. The ogreish lack of manners had paid off in this respect.

Dor's head was slowly clearing. He tried the door to his cell. It was of solid Mundane wood, worn but far too tough to break. Too tough, too, for Smash, in his present condition; the ogre tried and couldn't budge his own door. Unless the centaur came within range, none of them had any significant lever for freedom.

The doors seemed to be barred by some unreachable mechanism outside: inside, the slimy stone floor was interrupted only by a disposal sump—a small but deep hole that reeked of old excrement. Obviously no one would be released for sanitary purposes either.

Smash banged a fist against a wall. "Oww!" he exclaimed. "Now me miss centaur!"

"He does have his uses," Dor agreed. "You know, Smash, Arnolde didn't really usurp Chet's place. Chet couldn't come with us anyway, because of his injury, and Arnolde didn't want to. We pretty much forced him into it, by revealing his magic talent."

"Ungh," the ogre agreed. "Me want out of here. No like be weak."

"I think we'll have to wait for whatever King Oary plans for us," Dor said grimly. "If he planned to kill us, he wouldn't have bothered to lock us in here."

"Dor, I'm scared, really scared," Irene said. "I've never been a prisoner before."

Dor peered out through the cracks in his door. Had the flickering candle shadow moved? The guard must be coming in to eavesdrop. Naturally King Oary would want to know their secrets—and Irene just might let out their big one before she realized. He had to warn her—without the guard catching on. They just might turn this to their advantage.

He went to the wall that separated them. "It will be a good idea to plan our course of action," he said. "If they question us, tell them what they want to know. There's no point in concealing anything, since we're innocent." He managed to reach his arm through the crevice in the wall nearest her. "But we don't want them to force us into any false statements."

His hand touched something soft. It was Irene. She made a stifled "Eeek!" then grasped his hand.

"Let me review our situation," Dor said. "I am King during King Trent's absence." He squeezed her hand once. "You are King Trent's daughter." He squeezed again, once. "Arnolde the Centaur is also a Prince among his people." This time he squeezed twice.

"What are you talking about?" she demanded. "Arnolde's not—" She broke off as he squeezed several times, hard. Then she began to catch on; she was a bright enough girl. "Not with us now," she concluded, and squeezed his hand once.

"If the centaur does not return to his people on schedule, they will probably come after him with an army," Dor said, squeezing twice.

"A big army," she agreed, returning the two squeezes. "With many fine archers and spear throwers, thirsty for blood, and a big catapult to loft huge stones against the castle." She was getting into it now. They had their signals set; one squeeze for truth, two for falsehood. That way they could talk privately, even if someone were eavesdropping.

"I'm glad we're alone," he said, squeezing twice. "So we can talk freely."

"Alone," she agreed, with the double squeeze. Yes, now she knew why he was doing this. She was a smart girl, and he liked that; nymphlike proportions did not have to indicate nymphlike stupidity.

"We have no chance to break out of here ourselves," Dor said, squeezing twice. "We have no resources they don't already know about." Two.

"We don't have magical powers or anything," she agreed with an emphatic double squeeze.

"But maybe it would be better to let them *think* we have magic," Dor said, not squeezing. "That might make them treat us better."

"There is that," she agreed. "If the guards thought we could zap them through the walls, they might let us out."

"Maybe we should figure out something to fool them with," he said, this time squeezing once. "Something to distract them while the centaur army is massing. Like growing plants very fast. If they thought you could grow a tree

and burst out the ceiling and maybe make this castle collapse—"

"They would take me out of this cell and keep me away
from seeds," she said. "Then maybe I could escape and set
out some markers so the centaurs can find us more
quickly."

"Yes. But you can't just tell the Mundanes about growing things; it has to seem that they forced it out of you.
And you'll need some good excuse in case they challenge
you to grow something. You could say the time of the
month is wrong, or—"

"Or that I have to do it in a stable," she said. "That
would get me out of the heavily guarded area. By the time
they realize it's a fake, and that I can't grow anything,
I may have escaped."

"Yes." But had they set this up correctly? Would it trick
the guards into taking Irene to the stable where Arnolde
might be, or would they not bother? This business of deception was more difficult than he had thought.

Then she signaled alarm. "What about Smash? They'll
want to know how he tore off the front gate, when he can't
do a thing now."

Dor thought fast. "We have to hide from them the fact
that the ogre is strong only when he's angry. The guard at
the gate insulted Smash, so naturally he tore off the gate.
But King Oary gave him a good meal, so he wasn't really
angry despite getting drugged. Maybe we can trick a guard
into saying something mean to Smash, or depriving him of
food or water. When Smash gets hungry, he gets mean. And
he has a big appetite. If they try starving him, watch out!
He'll blow his top and tear this cellar apart!"

"Yes," she agreed. "That's really our best hope. Ill-
treatment. We don't even need to trick anybody. All we
have to do is wait. By midday tomorrow Smash will be
storming. We'll all escape over the dead bodies of the
guards who get in the way. We may not need the centaurs
at all!"

Something caught Dor's eye. He squeezed Irene's hand
to call her attention to it. The guard was quietly moving.
No doubt a hot report was going upstairs.

"You're an idiot," Irene murmured, squeezing his hand

twice. "You get these fool notions to fool our captors, and they'll never work. I don't know why I even talk to you."

"Because it's better than talking to the rats," he said without squeezing.

"Rats!" she cried, horrified. "Where?"

"I thought I saw one when I woke. Maybe I was wrong."

"No, this is the kind of place they like." She squeezed his hand, not with any signal. "Oh, Dor—we've got to get out of here!"

"They may take you out pretty soon, to verify that you can't grow plants."

She squeezed his hand warningly. "They already know." Actually, the purpose of the fake dialogue had been to convince their captors that Dor and Irene had no magic. Then if they somehow got the chance to use magic, the guards would be caught completely by surprise. In addition, they had probably guaranteed good treatment for Smash—if their ruse had been effective.

Soon a wan crack of dawn filtered in through the ceiling near what they took to be the east wall. But the angle was wrong, and Dor finally concluded that they were incarcerated against the west wall, above the cliff, with the light entering only by crude reflection; it would have been much brighter on the other side. No chance to tunnel out, even if they had the strength; what use to step off the cliff?

Guards brought Smash a huge basket of bread and a barrel of water.

"Food!" the ogre exclaimed happily, and crunched up entire loaves in single mouthfuls, as was his wont. Then, perceiving that neither Dor nor Irene had been served, he hurled several loaves through to them. Dor squeezed one through the crevice to Irene.

The water was harder to manage. No cups had been provided, but Dor's thirst abruptly intensified, perhaps in reaction to the wine of the day before. He finally borrowed and filled one of the ogre's gauntlets and jammed that through to Irene.

"Tastes like sour sweat," she complained. But she drank it, then shoved the gauntlet back. Dor drank the rest of it, agreeing with her analysis of the taste, and returned the gauntlet to Smash with due thanks. Sweat-flavored water was much better than thirst.

"Give me your hand again," Irene said.

Thinking she had more strategy to discuss, Dor passed his right arm through the crack, gnawing on a loaf held in his left. "That was a mean thing you did, getting me food," she murmured, squeezing twice.

"Well, you know I don't like you," Dor told her, returning the double squeeze. He wasn't sure this mattered to their eavesdropper, but the reversals were easy enough to do.

"I never liked you," she returned in kind. "In fact, I think I hate you."

What was she saying? The double squeeze suggested reversal, the opposite of what she said. Reverse hate? "What would I want with an ugly girl like you anyway?" he demanded.

There was a long pause. Dor stared through the crack, seeing a strand of her hair, and, as he had expected, it had lost its green tint. Then he realized he had forgotten to squeeze. Belatedly he did so, twice.

"Ugly, huh?" She squirmed about, bringing something soft into contact with his palm. "Is that ugly?"

"I'm not sure what it is," Dor said. He squeezed experimentally.

"Eeek!" she yiped, and swatted his hand.

"Ugly as sin," he said, trying to picture female anatomy so as to ascertain what he had pinched. It certainly had been interesting!

"I'll bite your hand," she threatened, in their old game.

"There are teeth there?" he inquired, surprised.

For an instant she choked, whether on mirth or anger he could not quite tell. "With my mouth, I'll bite," she clarified. But only her lips touched his fingers.

"You wouldn't dare."

She kissed his hand twice more.

"Ouch!" Dor cried.

Now she bit him, lightly, twice. He wasn't sure what mood this signified.

It was a new variant of an old game, perhaps no more, but it caused Dor to think about his relationship with Irene. He had known her since childhood. She had always been jealous of his status as Magician and had always taunted him and sicked her plants on him—yet always, too, had been the underlying knowledge that they were destined for each other. He had resisted that as violently as she—but as they grew older, the sexual element had begun to manifest, at first in supposedly innocent games and accidental exposures, then more deviously but seriously. When he had been twelve and she eleven, they had kissed for the first time with feeling, and the experience had shaken them both. Since then their quarreling had been tempered by the knowledge that each could give a new kind of joy to the other, potentially, when conditions were right. Irene's recent development of body had intensified that awareness, and their spats had had a voyeuristic element, such as when they had torn the clothes off each other in the moat. Now, when they could not be sure of their fate, and in the absence of anything else to do, this relationship had become much more important. For the moment, almost literally, all he had was Irene. Why should they quarrel in what might be their last hours?

"Yes, I definitely hate you," Irene said, nipping delicately at the tip of one of his fingers twice, as if testing it for digestibility.

"I hate you, too," Dor said, trying to squeeze but only succeeding in poking his finger into her mouth. His whole being seemed to concentrate on that hand and whatever it touched, and the caress of her lips was excruciatingly exciting.

"I wish I could never see you again," she said, hugging his hand to her bosom.

This was getting pretty serious! Yet he found that he felt the same. He never wanted to leave her. They weren't even squeezing now, playing the game of reversal with increasing intensity and comprehension. Was this merely a reaction to the fear of extinction? He could not be sure—but was unable to resist the current of emotion. "I wish I could . . . hurt you," he said, having trouble formulating a properly negative concept.

"I'd hurt you back!" She hugged his hand more tightly.

"I'd like to grab you and—" Again the problem.

"And what?" she demanded, and once more he found his hand encountering strange anatomy, or something. His inability to identify it was driving him crazy! Was it limb or torso, above or below the waist—and which did he want it to be?

"And squeeze you to pieces," he said, giving a good squeeze. That moat-scene had been nothing, compared with this.

This time she did not make any sound of protest. "I wouldn't marry you if you were the last man alive," she whispered.

She had upped the ante again! She was talking of marriage! Dor was stunned, unable to respond.

She caressed his hand intimately. "Would you?" she prompted.

Dor had not thought much about marriage, despite his involvement in Good Magician Humfrey's wedding. He somehow thought of marriage as the perquisite of old people, like his parents, and King Trent, and Humfrey. He, Dor, was only sixteen! Yet in Xanth the age of consent coincided with the age of desire. If a person thought he was old enough to marry, and wished to do so, and had a willing bride, he could make the alliance. Thus a marriage could be contracted at age twelve, or at age one hundred; Magician Humfrey had hardly seemed ready even at that extreme!

Did he want to marry? When he thought of the next few hours, perhaps his last, he wanted to, for he had known he would have to marry before his life was out. It was a requirement of Kingship, like being a Magician. But when he thought of a lifetime in Xanth, he wasn't sure. There was a lot of time, and so much could happen in a lifetime! As Humfrey had said: there were positive and negative aspects. "I don't know," he said.

"You don't know!" she flared. "Oh, I hate you!" And she bit his hand, once, and her sharp teeth cut the flesh painfully. Oh, yes, this was getting serious!

Dor tried to jerk his hand away, but she clung to it. "You oaf! You ingrate!" she exclaimed. "You *man!*" And her face pressed against his hand, moistly.

Moistly? Yes, she was crying. Perhaps there was art to it; nevertheless this unnerved Dor. If she felt that strongly, could he afford to feel less? *Did* he feel less?

Then a tidal swell of emotion flooded him. What did it

matter how much time there was, or how old he was, or where they were? He did love her.

"I—would not," he said, and tweaked her slick nose twice.

She continued crying into his hand, but now there was a gentler feeling to it. She was no longer angry with him; these were tears of joy.

It seemed they were engaged.

"Hey, Dor," a whisper came. It was from his own cell.

"Grundy!" Dor whispered back. He tried to signal Irene, but she seemed to have fallen asleep against his hand.

"Sorry I was so long," the golem said. "It took time to sleep off that knockout juice, and more time to find a good secret route here without running afoul of the rats. I talked to them—rat language seems to be much the same all over, so I didn't need the magic—but they're mean. I finally made myself a sword out of this big ol' hatpin, and after I struck a few they decided to cooperate." He brandished the weapon, a bent iron sliver; it did look deadly. Poked at a rat's eye, it would be devastating.

"Irene and I are engaged," Dor said.

The golem squinted at him to determine whether this was a joke and concluded it was not. "You are? Of all things! Why did you propose to her now?"

"I didn't," Dor confessed. "She proposed to me, I think."

"But you can't even touch her!"

"I can touch her," Dor said, remembering.

"Not where it counts."

"Yes, where it counts—I think."

The golem shrugged this off as fantasy. "Well, it won't make any difference, if we don't get out of here. I tried to talk to the animals and plants around here, but most of them I can't understand without magic. I don't think they know anything about King Trent and Queen Iris anyway. But I'm sure old King Oary's up to something. How can I spring you?"

"Get Arnolde into range," Dor said.

"That's not easy, Dor. They've got him in a stable, with a bar-lock setup like this, too heavy for me to force, and out of his reach. Crude but effective. If I could spring him, I could spring you."

"But we've got to get together," Dor whispered. "We need magic, and that's the only way."

"They aren't going to let him out," Grundy said. "They've got this fool notion that an army of warrior centaurs is marching here, and they don't want anyone to know there's a centaur in the castle."

Irene woke. "Are you talking to me, dear?" she asked.

"Dear!" Grundy chortled. "Hoo, has she lassoed you!"

"Quiet!" Dor whispered fiercely. "The guard is listening." But he wondered whether that was really his concern.

"Is that the golem?" Irene asked.

"Want to hold hands with me, dear?" Grundy called.

"Go unravel your string!" she snapped back.

"Anything but that," Grundy said, smiling mischievously. "I want to stick around and watch the nuptials. How are you going to make it through the wall?"

"Let me get at that big-mouthed imp!" Irene said. "I'll jam him down the sump headfirst."

"How did you get the poor sucker to accept the knot?" the golem persisted. "Did you scream at him, show him some forbidden flesh, and cry big green tears?"

"The sump is too good for him!" she gritted.

"If you both don't be quiet, the eavesdropping guard will learn everything," Dor warned, ravaged by worry and embarrassment.

Grundy looked at him. "Outside the magic ambience, they can't understand a word we say. How can they eavesdrop?"

Dor was stunned. "I never thought of that!" Had his entire ruse been for nothing?

"How come they fed Smash, then?" Irene demanded, forgetting her fury with the golem as she came to grips with this new question. "How come they heard about the centaur army? Seems to me you said—or did I dream that?"

"I said it, and it's true," Grundy said. "You mean *you* started that story? I overheard it when I was visiting Arnolde; then I could understand the Mundane speech."

"We started it," Dor agreed. "And we gave them the notion that Smash only has super strength when he's angry, and he gets angry when he's hungry. They brought him food very soon. So they must have understood. But how?"

"I think we're about to find out," Grundy said, fading into the shadow. "Someone's coming."

Irene finally let go of Dor's hand, and he drew it back through the wall. His arm was cramped from the hours in the awkward position, but Dor hardly regretted the experience. It was all right being engaged to Irene. He knew her well enough to know she would make a pretty good wife. She would quarrel a lot, but he was used to that, because that was the way his mother Chameleon was when she was in her smart phase. Actually, a smart woman who quarreled was not smart at all, but no one could tell her that. Irene, like her obnoxious mother, had a sense of the proprieties of the office. Queen Iris' mischief was never directed openly at the King. If Dor ever became King in fact as well as in name, Irene would never seek to undermine his power. That was perhaps a more important quality than her physical appearance. But he had to admit that she had acquired a most interesting body. Those touches she had used to tantalize him that Grundy had so acutely noted—they had been marvelously effective. Obviously she had been attempting to seduce him into acquiescence—and she had succeeded. As the Gorgon had intimated, Irene had him pretty well contained. What the Gorgon had not hinted was the fact that such captivity was quite comfortable to the captive, like a warm jacket on a cold day. Good Magician Humfrey was undoubtedly a happy man right now, despite his protestations. In fact, a man's objections to marriage were rather like Irene's objections to people looking at her legs—more show than substance.

Dor's attention was jerked back to the immediate situation by the arrival of the Mundanes. There were three guards, one carrying a crude iron bar. They stopped before Irene's cell and used the bar to pry up the wedged plank that barred it. Without that tool, evidently, the door could not be opened.

One of the guards went in and grabbed Irene. She did not resist; she knew as well as Dor did that this was the expected questioning. She would try to answer in such a way that they would take her to the stable where Arnolde was confined, if only to prove she was lying. Then she could pry up the bar on the centaur's stall, or start some devastating plant growing—

Except that she had no seeds. "Grundy!" he whispered. "Find Irene's seeds! She'll need them."

"I'll try." The golem scrambled through a crevice and was gone.

Now King Oary entered the dungeon. "Rn xnt'qd sgd Jhmf'r cztfgsdq," he said. "Vgzs hr xntq lzfhb?"

"I don't understand you," Irene said.

"His Highness King Oary asks what is your magic," one of the guards said. His speech was heavily accented, but he was intelligible.

"You know Xanth speech?" she asked, surprised. "How can that be?"

"You have no need to know," the guard said. "Just answer the question, wench."

So one of the Mundanes here spoke the language of Xanth! Dor's mind started clicking over. This explained the eavesdropping—but how could the man have learned it, however poorly? He had to have been in contact with people from Xanth.

"Go soak your snoot in the sump," Irene retorted.

Dor winced. She might be playing her role too boldly!

"The King will use force," the man warned. "Better answer, slut."

Irene looked daunted, as perhaps she was, but those insulting references to her supposed status made her angry. "You answer first, toady," she said, compromising.

The guard decided negotiation was the best course. "I met a spy from your country, tart. I am quick with languages; he taught me. Then he went back to Xanth."

"To report to my father, King Trent!" Irene exclaimed. "You promised him a trade agreement, didn't you, rogue, if he would come himself to negotiate it?"

"It is your turn to answer, hussy," the man said.

"Oh, all right, wretch. My magic is growing plants. I can make anything grow from seed to tree in moments."

Dor, peering out, could not see the man's face clearly, but was sure there was a knowing expression on it. The eavesdropper thought he knew better, but didn't want to betray his own secret snooping, so had to translate for the King. "Rgd fzud sgd khd," he said.

"H vzms sgd sqtsg!" Oary snapped.

"His Majesty suspects you are deceiving us," the guard said. "What is your real magic?"

"What does ol' fatso care? I'm not doing any magic now."

"You had magic when you came, trollop. The ogre used unnatural strength to destroy our front gate, and you all spoke our language. Now the ogre is weak and you speak your own language. What happened to the magic?"

The language! Dor cursed himself for overlooking that detail. Of course that had given away their secret! King Trent would have used an interpreter—probably this same man—and the ability of Dor's party to converse directly would have alerted cunning King Oary immediately. He had known they had operative magic and now wanted to discover the mechanism of it.

"Well, if you bring me some seeds, thug, maybe I can find out," Irene said. "I'm sure I can grow plants, if I just find the right place."

Bless her! She was still trying to get to the stable, where she really could perform.

But the Mundanes thought they knew better. "If the King says you lie, you lie, strumpet," the guard said. "Again I ask: what is your real magic? Can you speak in tongues, and cause others to do the same?"

"Of course not, villain!" she said. "Otherwise we wouldn't need you to translate to His Lowness King Pudding-belly here, would we? Plants are all I can enchant."

"Rgd vhkk mns sdkk," the guard said to the King.

"Vd rgzkk lzjd *ghl* sdkk," the King responded. "Snqstqd gdq hm eqnms ne ghl."

The other two guards grabbed Irene's arms and hauled her a few steps down the hall until they were directly in front of Dor's cell. "Prince Dor," the translator called. "You will answer our questions or see what we shall do."

Dor was silent, uncertain what to do.

"Qho nee gdq bknsgdr," the King ordered.

The two guards wrestled Irene's jacket and silver-lined fur off her body, while she struggled and cursed them roundly. Then the translator put his hand on her neckline and brutally ripped downward. The blouse tore down the front, exposing her fine bosom. Irene, shocked at this sudden physical violence, heaved with her arms, but the two men held her securely.

"Vdkk, knnj zs sgzs!" the King exclaimed admiringly. "H sgntfgs nmkx gdq kdfr vdqd fnnc!"

Dor could not understand a word of the language, but he grasped the essence readily enough. King, translator, and both guards were all gawking at Irene's revealed body. So was Dor. He had thought Irene did not match the Gorgon in general architecture, but Irene had filled out somewhat since he had last looked. He had had the chance to see during the quarrel in the moat, but there had been other distractions then. During the journey south to Centaur Isle, Irene had kept herself fairly private, and perhaps her excellent legs had led his attention away from her other attributes. Now he saw that she was no longer reaching for bodily maturity; she had achieved it.

At the same time, he was furious with the King and his henchmen for exposing Irene in this involuntary manner. He determined not to tell them anything.

"Gd khjdr gdq, xnt snkc ld," the King said. "H bzm rdd vgx! Sgqdzsdm gdq zmc gd'kk szkj."

The King was plotting something dastardly! Dor hardly dared imagine what he might do to Irene. He couldn't stand to have her hurt!

The translator stood in front of Irene and formed a fist. He drew back his arm, aiming at her belly.

"Stop!" Dor cried. "I'll tell—"

"Shut up!" Irene snapped at him. One of her knees jerked up, catching the translator in the groin. The man doubled over, and the surprised guards allowed Irene to tear herself free, leaving shreds of cloth in their hands. Bare-breasted as any nymph, she ran a few steps, stooped to pick up the door-opening bar, and whirled to apply it to Dor's door.

"Run!" Dor cried. "Don't waste time on me!"

But it was already too late. Both guards had drawn their flat swords and were closing on Irene. She turned, raising the bar defensively, determined to fight.

"No!" Dor screamed, his voice breaking. "They'll kill you!"

But now there was a new distraction. Smash, snoozing

before, had become aware of the situation. He rattled his door angrily. "Kill!" he bellowed.

Both guards and the King blanched. They believed the ogre's fantastic strength stemmed from his anger. If they hurt Irene while Smash watched—

The translator was beginning to recover from his injury; it probably had been a glancing blow. "Gdqc gdq hmsn gdq bdkk," he gasped to the other two guards. Then, to Irene: "Girl—go quickly to your cell and they won't hurt you."

Irene, realizing that she could not hope to escape the two swordsmen and knowing that the bluff of Smash's strength should not be called, edged toward her cell. The two guards followed cautiously. Smash watched, still angry, but with the sense not to protest as long as the guards were holding off. Then Irene stepped into her cell, the guards slammed the door shut and barred it, and the crisis was over.

"You should have run out of the dungeon!" Dor said with angry relief.

"I couldn't leave you," she replied. "Where would I find another like you?" Dor wasn't certain quite how to take that; was it a compliment or a deprecation?

King Oary himself seemed shaken. "Sgzs fhqk'r mns nmkx adztshetk, rgd gzr ehfgshmf rohqhs," he said. "Cnm's gtqs gdq; H ltrs ehmc z trd enq gdq." He turned about and marched out of the dungeon, followed by his henchmen. The translator, though still uncomfortable, had to remain where he thought he was just out of sight, to eavesdrop some more. The dungeon settled back into its normal gloom.

They were plotting something worse, Dor knew, but at least Irene had escaped unhurt, and the secret of their magic had been preserved, at least in part. The Mundanes knew the prisoners had magic, but still had not fathomed its mechanism. It was a temporary respite, but much better than nothing.

. "I think we'd better get out of here soon," Irene said as the Mundanes departed. "Give me your hand."

What was she contemplating this time? Dor passed his hand through the crevice.

She took it in her own and kissed it. That was nice enough, though he found himself obscurely disappointed. She had lost her jacket and blouse—

She took his wrist in her hand and had him spread his fingers. Then she put something into his hand. Dor almost exclaimed with surprise, for it was hard and cold and heavy.

It was the iron bar.

Of course! In their confusion, the guards had forgotten that Irene retained the bar she had picked up. Now Dor had this useful tool or weapon. Maybe he could lever open his door from the inside.

But a guard was in the hall, probably the translator, though there could have been a change. Dor didn't dare try the door now; he would have to wait. In fact, he could not risk prying at any other part of the cell, for the noise would alert the guard and call attention to his possession of the bar. So, for now, they had to wait—and there were things he wanted to tell Irene.

"You were awfully brave," he said. "You faced up to those thugs—"

"I was scared almost speechless," she confessed. That was surely an overstatement; she had traded gibes with the translator quite neatly. "But I knew they'd hurt you if—"

"Hurt me! It was *you* they—"

"Well, I worry about you, Dor. You wouldn't be able to manage without me."

She was teasing him—maybe. "I like your new outfit," he said. "But maybe you'd better take my jacket."

"Maybe so," she agreed. "It's cool here."

Dor removed his centaur jacket and squeezed it through the crevice. She donned it, and was quite fetching in it, though it tended to fall open in front. Or perhaps that was why he found it so fetching. At least the jacket would protect her from the cold and from the attack of instruments like swords or spears, because it was designed to resist penetration. And it wouldn't hurt to have her body concealed from the lecherous eyes of the King and his henchmen; Dor's jealousy of such things remained in force.

Grundy reappeared. "I got a seed," he said. "The bag's in the King's chamber, along with the magic sword. I knew it was safe to sneak in there, because the King was down here. But I couldn't carry the whole bag. Couldn't find the magic compass at all; they must have thrown that away. So I picked out what looked like a good seed."

"Give it here," Irene said eagerly. "Yes—this is a tangler. If I could start it and drop it in the hall—"

"But you can't," Dor said. "Not without—" He caught himself, for the eavesdropper was surely eavesdropping.

"I have an idea," Dor said. "Suppose we brought a part of you-know-who here—would it have a little magic, enough to start one seed?"

Irene considered. "A piece of hoof, maybe. I don't know. It's worth a try."

"I'm on my way," Grundy said.

"I always thought girls were supposed to be timid and sweet and to scream helplessly at the mere sight of trouble," Dor said. "But you—those guards—"

"You saw too much of Millie the Ghost. Real girls aren't like that, except when they want to be."

"You certainly aren't! But I never thought you'd risk your life like that."

"Are you disappointed?"

Dor considered. "No. You're a lot more girl—more woman than I thought. I guess I do need you. If I didn't love you before, I do now. And not because of your looks though when it comes to that—"

"Really?" she asked, sounding like an excited child.

"Well, I could be overreacting because of our imprisonment."

"I liked it better unqualified," she said.

"Oh, sure. Uh, I think you're beautiful. But—"

"Then we'd better check again after we get out of this, to see if we feel the same. No sense being hasty."

Dor was shaken. "You have doubts?"

"Well, I might meet a handsomer man—"

"Uh, yes," Dor said unhappily.

She laughed. "I'm teasing you. Girls are smarter about appearances than boys are. We go for quality rather than packaging. I have no doubt at all. I love you, Dor. I never intended to marry anyone else. But I refuse to take advantage of you when you're unsettled. Maybe when you get older you'll change your mind."

"You're younger than I am!"

"Girls mature faster. Hadn't you noticed?"

Now Dor laughed. "Just today, I noticed!"

She kissed his hand again. "Well, it's all yours, when."

When. Dor considered the ramification of that, and felt warm all over. She had a body, true—but what pleased him most was the loyalty implied. She would be with him, she would support him, whatever happened. Dor realized he needed that support; he really would foul up on his own. Irene was strong, when not jarred by an acute crisis; she had nerve he lacked. Her personality complemented his, shoring up his weakness. She was the one who had gotten them going on this rescue mission; her determination to rescue her father had never relented. With her at his side, he could indeed be King.

His reflections were interrupted by the return of the golem. "I got three hairs from his tail," he whispered. "He's very vain about his tail, like all his breed; it's his best feature. Maybe they'll be enough."

Did some magic adhere to portions of the centaur that were removed from his body? Dor brought out his midnight sunstone gem and held it close to the hairs. Almost, he thought, he saw a gleam of light, deep within the crystal. But maybe that was a reflection from the wan illumination of the cell.

"Take them in to Irene," Dor said, hardly allowing himself to hope.

Grundy did so. Irene set the seed down on the tail hairs and leaned close. "Grow," she breathed.

They were disappointed. The seed seemed to try, to swell expectantly, but could not grow. There was not enough magic.

"Maybe if I took it back to Arnolde," Grundy said.

Irene was silent, and Dor realized she was stifling her tears. She had really hoped her magic would work.

"Yes, try that," Dor told the golem. "Maybe the seed has been started. Maybe it just needs more magic now."

Grundy took the seed and the tail hairs and departed again. Dor reached through the crevice to pat Irene on the shoulder. "It was worth the try," he said.

She clutched his hand. "I need you, Dor. When I collapse, you just keep on going."

There was that complementary aspect again. She would soon recover her determination and nerve, but in the interim she needed to be steadied.

They remained that way for what seemed like a long

time, and despite the despair they both felt, Dor would not have traded it. Somehow this privation enhanced their personal liaison, making their love burn more fiercely and reach deeper. What would happen after this day he could not know, but he was certain he had been changed by this experience of emotion. His age of innocence, in a fundamental and positive sense, had passed.

Then a commotion began in the distance. The sound electrified them. Was it possible—?

Grundy burst in on them. "It worked!" he cried. "That seed started growing. The moment I got it in the magic aisle, it heaved right out of its shell. It must have been primed by your command, in that bit of magic with the tail hairs. I had to throw it down outside the stall—"

"It worked!" Irene cried jubilantly. "I always knew it would!"

"I told Arnolde where we are, just in case," Grundy continued excitedly. "That tangler will rip apart his stall!"

"But can he get through all the locked doors?" Irene asked, turning worried. Her moods were swinging back and forth now. "He can't *do* magic himself, and there's no one with him to—"

"I'm way ahead of you, doll," the golem said. "I scouted all around. He can't get through those doors, but he can get out the main gate that Smash ripped off, 'cause they haven't fixed that yet, and there's a small channel outside the castle wall, and these cells are against the wall. Unless the outside wall is over his aisle-depth—"

"And if it is?" she prompted, as if uncertain whether to go into a scream of jubilation or of despair.

"I'm sure the wall isn't," Grundy said. "It's not more than six of your paces thick, and his aisle reaches twice that far forward. But we'll soon find out, because he'll soon be on his way."

The clamor continued. "I hope Arnolde doesn't get hurt," Dor said. "King Oary took our supply of healing elixir, too."

"Probably dumped it down a sump," Grundy said. "Make all the sick maggots healthy."

"Stand by the outer wall," Irene told him. "When you can talk to it, Dor, we'll know the centaur's here."

"I'll go check on his progress," Grundy said, and scurried away again.

"That tangler should be almost full-grown now," Irene said. "I hope Arnolde has the sense to stay away from its tentacles." Then she reconsidered. "But not so far away the lack of magic kills the tree. He's got to keep it in the aisle until it does its job. Once he leaves, it will die."

"Speak to me, wall," Dor said, touching the stone. There was no response.

"What's up?" Smash inquired from the next cell.

"Grundy took a sprouted tangler seed to Arnolde," Dor explained. "We hope the centaur's on his way here."

"At length, me strength," the ogre said, comprehending.

"Hey—you rhymed!" Dor cried. "He must be here!"

"Me see," Smash said. He punched his fist through the wall near Dor.

"You've got it!" Dor said. "Go rip open your door! Then you can free Irene and me!"

The ogre tramped to the front of his cell and gleefully smashed at his front door. "Ooo, that hurt!" he grunted, shaking his gauntleted fist. The door had not given way.

"His strength is gone again!" Irene said. "Something's wrong!"

Dor cudgeled his brain. What could account for this partial recovery? "Where is the centaur now?" he asked his back wall, fearing it would not answer.

"Right outside Irene's cell," it replied. "Clinging to a narrow track above a chasm, terrified."

Dor visualized the centaur's position. "Then he can't face directly into the castle?"

"He can only turn a little," the wall agreed. "Any more and he'll fall off. Soldiers are getting ready to put arrows in his tail, too."

"So his magic aisle slants in obliquely," Dor concluded. "It covers this wall, but not the front of our cells."

"Anybody can see that, idiot," the wall agreed smugly.

Dor used his sunstone to verify the edge of the aisle. The gem flashed and darkened as it passed outside the magic. The line was only a few handspans inside Dor's wall, projecting farther into Smash's cell.

"Hey, Smash!" Dor cried. "The magic's only at this end. Bash out the outer wall to let Arnolde in."

"Right site," Smash agreed. He aimed his huge, horny, gauntleted hamfist.

"Don't hit me!" the wall cried. "I support the whole castle!" But it was too late; the fist powered through the brick and stone. "Oooo, that smarts!"

The wall turned out to be double: two sections of stone, with a filling of rubble between. Smash ripped out the loose core, then pulverized the outer barrier, gaining enthusiasm as he went. In moments bright daylight shone through the cloud of dust.

The ogre ripped out more chunks, widening the aperture. Beyond was the back of the mountain, falling awesomely away into a heavily wooded valley.

"Good to see you, brute!" Arnolde's voice came. "Clear an entrance for me before these savages attack!"

Smash leaned out. He grabbed a stone. "Duck, cluck," he warned, and hurled his missile.

There was a thud and scream as someone was knocked off the ledge. "What did you do?" Irene cried, appalled.

Then Arnolde's front end appeared in the gap in the wall. Centaur and ogre embraced joyously. "I think he knocked off an enemy," Dor said.

Irene sounded weak with relief. "Oh. I guess they're friends now."

"We need both magic and power," Dor agreed. "Each is helpless without the other. They have come to understand that."

"We have all come to understand a lot of things," she agreed, smiling obscurely.

Now Arnolde faced the front door, putting it within the aisle, and Smash marched up and kicked it off its moorings. Then he took hold of the front wall and tore it out of the floor. Debris crashed down from the ceiling. "Don't bring the whole castle down on us!" Dor warned, while Irene choked on the voluminous dust.

"Me wrastle this castle," the ogre said, unworried. He hoisted one paw to the ceiling, and the collapse abated.

There was a stray guard in the hall. The man watched the progress of the ogre a few moments in silence, then fainted.

Grundy reappeared. "Troops coming," he reported. "We'd better move."

They moved. Doors and gates were locked, but Smash smashed them clear like so much tissue. When they encountered a wall, he burst right through it. They emerged into an inner court, where flowers grew. "Grow! Grow! Grow!" Irene ordered, and the plants exploded upward and outward.

"Where is our safest retreat?" Dor asked the next wall.

"The other side of me, dolt," it replied.

Smash opened another hole and they trooped out into a section of forest. Soon they had hidden themselves well away from the castle. They were together again and free, and it felt wonderful.

They paused, catching their breaths, assessing their situation. "Everybody all right?" Dor asked around. "No serious injuries?" There seemed to be none.

"So have you reconsidered?" Irene inquired. "You know how I abhor you."

He looked at her. She was still wearing his jacket over her bare upper torso, her hair was tangled, and dirt smudged her face. She seemed preternaturally lovely. "Yes," he said. "And the answer comes out the same. I still hate you." He took her in his arms and kissed her, and she was all eager and yielding in the manner of her kind—when her kind chose to be.

"If that be hate," Arnolde remarked, "I would be interested in witnessing their love."

"The idiots are engaged to each other," Grundy explained to the others. "It seems they saw the light in the darkness, or something."

"Or something," the centaur agreed dubiously.

Chapter 11. Good Omen

"Now we have arrived," Dor said, taking charge after reluctantly disengaging from Irene. "But we have not accomplished our mission. I believe this is the place King Trent and Queen Iris came to. I think the table told me they were here, just before I passed out from King Oary's drug. But I might have dreamed that; the memory is very foggy. Have we any solid proof?"

"Apart from the henchman who speaks the language of Xanth?" Grundy asked.

"That's circumstantial," Irene said. "It only proves he had contact with the Xanth scout, not that King Trent actually came here. We have to be sure."

"My evidence is rather tenuous," Arnolde offered. "It seems that the stable hands had difficulty thinking of me as a person of intellect, and spoke more freely in my vicinity than they might otherwise have done. I declined to speak to them, in what I confess might be construed as a fit of pique—"

"Chic pique," Smash chuckled.

"And so they did not realize that the magic in your vicinity caused their language to be intelligible to you, or that you had the wit to comprehend it," Dor put in, pleased. "*We* could not communicate with them without an interpreter, so it was natural for them to assume you couldn't either. That, combined with their tending to think of you as an animal—"

"Precisely. My pique may have been fortuitous. So I found myself overhearing certain things that were perhaps not entirely my affair." He smiled. "In one case, literally. It seems one of the cooks has a continuing liaison with a scullery maid—" He broke off, grimacing. "Right beside my stall! It was instructive; they are lusty folk. At any rate, there was at one point a reference to a certain alien King who, it seems, had claimed to be able to perform magic."

"King Trent!" Dor exclaimed. "My memory was right, then, not a dream! The table did say King Trent was here!"

"I think we always knew it!" Irene agreed, glowering in memory of the betrayal associated with that table.

"The translator knew about the magic of Xanth," Dor continued. "But of course no one could do magic here in Mundania, until we discovered you, Arnolde. King Trent would have said he could do magic *in Xanth*, and the qualification got dropped in translation."

"Certainly," the centaur agreed. "It seems that King Oary somehow anticipated magic that he thought might greatly enhance his power and was very angry when that magic did not materialize. So he arrested the alien King treacherously and locked him away, hoping to coerce him into performing, or into revealing the secret of his power."

"Where?" Irene demanded. "Where is my father?"

"I regret I did not overhear more than I have told you. The alien King was not named. I do not believe the people of the stables knew his identity, or believe in his power, or know where he may be confined. They merely gossip. The apparent magic of Smash's initial display of strength, and the manner we communicated with King Oary, caused a considerable ripple of interest around the castle, and indeed in the entire Kingdom of Onesti, which accounts for the gossip about similar cases. But already this interest is waning, since both strength and communication appeared to have been illusion. It is very easy to attribute phenomena to illusion or false memory when practical explanations are lacking, and Mundanes do this often." He smiled grimly. "I daresay a new round of speculation has commenced, considering the events of the past hour. Your tangle plant, Irene, was gratifyingly impressive."

"It sure was!" Grundy agreed enthusiastically. "It was grabbing people right and left, and it ripped the stall apart. But when Arnolde left, the tangler sank down dead."

"Magic plants can't function without magic, dummy," Irene said.

"Fortunately," Arnolde agreed. "On occasion it reached for me; then I angled away from it, depriving it of magic, and it desisted. After a time it ceased to bother me."

"Even a tangler isn't totally stupid!" Irene laughed.

"At least we have more to go on," Dor said. "We can be pretty sure King Oary imprisoned King Trent and Queen Iris, and that they remain alive. Oary's experience with us must have enhanced his conviction that anyone from Xanth is hiding magic from him, since we really did have magic, then stopped showing it when he imprisoned us. He probably intended to force us to tell him the secret of magic so he could do it, too, or at least compel the rest of us to perform for him."

"King Oary strikes me as a pretty cunning old rascal," Irene said. "Wrongheaded but cunning."

"Indeed," Arnolde agreed. "From my observation, he

runs this Kingdom reasonably well, but unscrupulously. Perhaps that is what is required to maintain the precarious independence from the larger empires on three sides."

"We still need to locate King Trent," Dor said. "Arnolde, did you hear anything else that might remotely connect?"

"I am not sure, Dor. There was a reference to King Omen, Oary's predecessor who disappeared. It seems the common folk liked him and were sorry to lose him."

"He was King?" Dor asked. "I understood he was underage, so Oary was regent, and Omen never actually became King."

"I gather in contrast that he was indeed King, for about a year, before he disappeared," the centaur said. "They called him Good Omen, and believe the Kingdom of Onesti would have prospered under his guidance."

"Surely it would have," Dor agreed. He realized that King Oary might have preferred to minimize King Omen's stature in order to make his own position more secure. If the Kingdom of Onesti was well run, it could have been mostly King Omen's doing. "A trade agreement with Xanth could help both Kingdoms. Maybe King Omen was arranging that, then got deposed before King Trent arrived. King Oary's greed has cost him that chance."

"The peasants suspect that King Omen was illicitly removed," the centaur continued. "Some even choose to believe that he still lives, that King Oary imprisoned him by subterfuge and usurped power. This may of course be mere wish fulfillment—"

"And just may be the truth," Irene put in. "If King Oary deceived and imprisoned us and did the same with my parents, why not also with Good King Omen? It certainly fits his pattern."

"We are indulging in a great deal of supposition," Arnolde said warningly. "We could encounter disappointment. Yet if I may extend the rationale—it occurs to me that if King Trent and King Omen both survive, they may be confined together. We have already seen that the dungeons of Castle Onesti are not extensive. If there is another castle, and we find one confined there—"

"We find the other!" Irene finished. "And if we rescued them both, Good Omen would be King of Onesti again and

all would be well. I'd sure like to depose hoary King
Oary!"

"That was the extrapolation of my conjectures," Arnolde
agreed. "Yet I reiterate, it is highly speculative."

"It's worth a try," Dor said. "Now let's plan our strategy.
Probably only King Oary knows where King Trent and/or
King Omen are incarcerated, and he won't tell. I could
question the stones of the castle, but probably the Kings
aren't here at all, and the stones wouldn't know anything
about other places. If the local servants don't know anything about it, it probably isn't known. So the question is,
how can we get him to tell?"

"He ought to have a guilty conscience," Irene said.
"Maybe we could play on that."

"I distrust this," Dor said. "I encountered some bad people and creatures in another adventure, and I don't think
their consciences troubled them, because they simply didn't
believe they were doing anything wrong. Goblins and harpies—"

"Of course they don't have consciences," Irene snapped.
"But Oary is a person."

"Human beings can be worst of all, especially Mundanes," Dor said. "Many of them have ravaged Xanth over
the centuries, and King Oary may contemplate something
similar. I just don't have much confidence in any appeal to
his conscience."

"I perceive your point," Arnolde said. "But I think 'appeal' is not the appropriate term. A guilty conscience more
typically manifests in the perception of nocturnal specters—"

"Not many specters running around this far from
Xanth," Grundy pointed out.

"We could scare him into giving it away!" Irene exclaimed.

"Tonight," Dor decided. "We must rest and feed ourselves first—and hide from King Oary's troops."

They had no trouble avoiding the troops. It took Oary's
forces some time to organize, after the devastation Smash
had caused during the breakout, and only now, after the
long discussion, was any real activity manifesting at the
castle. Irene made vines grow, bristling with thorns; in
their natural state these had been a nuisance, but now they

were a menace. When the magic moved away, the vines died, for they had been extended far beyond their natural limits—but the tangle of thorns remained as a formidable barrier. That, coupled with the Mundanes' knowledge that the ogre lurked in the forest, kept the guards close to the castle even after they emerged. They were not eager for contact with the creature who had bashed all those holes in the massive walls.

At night, rested, Dor's party made its play. Grundy had scouted the castle, so they knew which tower contained the royal suite. King Oary was married, but slept alone; his wife couldn't stand him. He ate well and consumed much alcoholic beverage; this facilitated his sleep.

They had fashioned a platform that Smash carried to the base of the outer wall nearest the royal tower, which happened to be on the forest side. Arnolde mounted this, bringing his magic aisle within range of the King.

Irene had scouted for useful Mundane seeds and had assembled a small collection. Now she planted several climbing vines, and in the ambience of magic they assumed somewhat magical properties. They mounted wall and platform vigorously, sending their little anchor-tendrils into any solid substance they found, quickly binding the platform firmly in place. Arnolde had to keep moving his legs to avoid tendrils that swiped at his feet, until the growing stage passed that level. The plants ascended to the embrasure that marked the King's residence, then halted; the magic aisle extended more inward than upward.

Grundy used the sturdy vines to mount to that embrasure. He scrambled over, found himself a shrouded corner, and called quietly down: "I can see inside some, but I don't dare get close enough to cover the whole room."

"Talk to the plant," Irene said in her don't-be-dumb tone. She no longer used that on Dor, mute recognition of their changed situation, but obviously she retained the expertise.

"Say, yes," the golem agreed. "There's a vine that reaches inside." He paused, talking to the plant. "It says Oary's not alone. He's got a doxy in his bed."

"He would," Irene grumped. "Men like that will do anything."

It occurred to Dor that this could be the reason the translator had persisted in addressing Irene as "slut" and "strumpet." This was the type of woman King Oary normally associated with. But Dor decided not to mention this to Irene; she already had reason enough to hate Oary.

Dor climbed the vines, finding a lodging against the wall just beneath the embrasure. "Describe the room," he murmured to Grundy. "I've got to know exactly what's in it, and where."

The golem consulted with the plant. "There is this big feather bed to the right, two of your paces in from this wall. A wooden bench straight in from the embrasure, six paces, with her dress strewn on it. A wooden table to its left, one pace—and there's your sword on it, and Arnolde's bag of spells."

"Ha!" Dor exclaimed quietly. "I need that sword. Too bad it's not the variety that wields itself; I could call it right to me."

The golem continued describing the room, until Dor was satisfied he had the details properly fixed in his mind. He was able to picture it now—everything just so. "I hope my mind doesn't go blank," he called down.

"Don't you dare!" Irene snapped. "Save your fouling up for some other time. Do I have to come up there and prompt you?"

"That might help," Dor confessed. "You see, I can't make things say specific things. They only answer questions, or talk in response to my words. Usually. And the inanimate is not too bright, and sometimes perverse. So I may indeed foul it up."

"For pity's sake!" Irene took hold of the vines and began climbing. "And don't look up my skirt!" she said to Arnolde.

"I wouldn't think of it," the centaur said equably. "I prefer to view equine limbs, and never did see the merit in pink panties."

"They're not pink!" she said.

"They're not? I must be colorblind. Let me see—"

"Forget it!" She joined Dor, gave him a quick kiss, wrapped her skirt closely about her legs, and settled in for the duration. Dor had worried about the strength of the vines, with all this weight on them, but realized she would have a better notion than he how much they could hold.

"Well, start," she whispered.

"But if I talk loud enough for the things to hear me, so will King Oary."

She sighed. "You *are* a dumbell at times, dear. You don't have to talk aloud to objects; just direct your attention to them. That's the way your magic works. As for King Oary—if that snippet with him knows her trade, he won't be paying any attention to what's outside the castle."

She was right. Dor concentrated, but still couldn't quite get it together. He was used to speaking aloud to objects. "Are they really not pink?" he asked irrelevantly.

"What?"

"Your—you-knows."

She laughed. "My panties? You mean you never looked?"

Dor, embarrassed, admitted that he had not.

"You're entitled now, you know."

"But I wasn't, back when I had a chance to see."

She released her grip on the vine with one hand and reached over to tweak his cheek, in much the manner the Gorgon had. "You're something sort of rare and special, Dor. Well, you get this job done right, and I'll show you."

"Will you get on with it?" Grundy demanded from above.

"But she says not till after this job's done," Dor said.

"I was referring to the job!" the golem snapped. "*I'll* tell you what color her—"

"I will wring your rag body into a tight little knot!" Irene threatened, and the golem was silent.

Prompted by this, Dor concentrated on the magic sword on the King's table. *Groan,* he ordered it mentally.

Obediently, the sword groaned. Naturally it hammed it up. "Grooooaan!" it singsonged in an awful key.

"The doxy just sat up straight," Grundy reported gleefully as the vine rustled the news to him. "Oh, she shouldn't have done that. She's stark, bare, nude naked!"

"Skip the pornography, you little voyeur!" Irene snapped. "It's the King we want to rouse." She nudged Dor. "You know the script we worked out. 'Let me free, let me free.' "

Dor concentrated again. *Sword, I have a game for you.*

If you play your part well, you can scare the pants off bad King Oary.

"Hey, great!" the sword exclaimed. "Only they're already off him. Boy, is he fat!"

No. Don't talk to me! Talk to the King. Groan again and say, "Let me free, let me free!" The idea is you're the ghost of Good King Omen, coming back to haunt him. Can you handle that, or are you too stupid?

"I'll show you!" the sword exclaimed. It groaned again, with hideous feeling. It was definitely a ham.

"There's someone here!" the doxy screamed.

"There can't be," the King muttered. "The guards prevent anyone from getting through. They know I don't want to be disturbed when I'm conducting affairs of state."

"Affairs of state!" Irene hissed furiously.

"Affair, anyway," Dor said, trying to calm her.

"Let me free, let me free," the sword groaned enthusiastically.

"Then who's that?" the doxy demanded, hiding under the feathers.

"I am the ghooost of Goood King Ooomen," the sword answered. Dor no longer needed to prompt it.

The doxy emitted a half-stifled squeak and disappeared entirely into the feathers, according to Grundy's gleeful play-by-play report. The King clutched a feather quilt about him, causing part of the doxy to reappear, to her dismay.

"You *can't* be!" Oary retorted shakily, trying to see where the voice came from. The lone candle illuminating the room cast many wavering shadows, the plant reported, making such detection difficult.

"Coming back from the graaave to haaunt you!" the sword continued, really getting into it.

"Impossible!" But the King looked nervous, Grundy reported.

"He's a tough one," Irene murmured. "He should be terrified, and he's only worried. We're only scaring the doxy, who doesn't matter. Girls can be such foolish creatures!" Then she reconsidered. "When they want to be."

Dor nodded, worried himself. If this ruse didn't work—

"Yoooou killed me," the sword said.

"I did not!" Oary shouted. "I only locked you up until I figured out what to do with you. I never killed you."

The doxy's face reappeared, replacing the rounder portion of her that had showed before. "You locked up Good Omen?" she asked, surprised.

"I had to, or I never would have gotten the throne," the King said absently. "I thought he would foul up as King, but he didn't, so there was no way to remove him legitimately." As he talked, he hoisted his porcine torso from the bed, wrapped the quilt about it, and stalked the voice he heard. "But I didn't kill him. I am too cautious for that. It is too hard to undo a killing, if anything goes wrong. So this can't be his ghost."

"Then whose ghost is it?" the doxy demanded.

"No ghost at all," the King said. "There's no one there." He picked up the sword. "Just this sword I took from the Xanth Prince. I thought it was magic, but it isn't. I tried it out, and there's nothing remarkable about it except a fine edge."

"That's not true!" the sword cried. "Unhand me, varlet!"

Unnerved at last, the King hurled it out the embrasure. "The thing talks!" he cried.

"Well, that's one way to recover my weapon," Dor murmured.

"Try for my bag of seeds," Irene suggested. "I can do a lot with genuine magic plants."

Grundy had located the seeds, carelessly thrown in a corner; no doubt Oary had been disappointed when he discovered the bag did not contain treasure, though he should have been satisfied with the gold and diamonds Dor had carried. Greed knew no restraint! "You can't get rid of me that way," the seedbag said as Dor mentally prompted it. "My ghost will haunt you forever."

"I tell you, I didn't kill you!" Oary said, looking for the new voice that sounded seedy. "You're just making that up."

"Well, I might as well be dead," the seedbag said. "Locked up here alone—it's awful."

"What do you mean, alone?" Oary demanded. "The Xanth King is in the next cell, and the sharp-tongued Xanth Queen in the third. They wanted to know what had happened to you, and wouldn't deal with me, so now they know."

Irene's free hand clutched Dor's shoulder. "Confirmation!" she whispered, thrilled.

Dor was equally gratified. The talking objects had hardly terrorized Oary, but they had evoked his confession nevertheless. Dor continued to concentrate. *But you're way out in nowhere,* he thought to the bag.

"But we're way out in nowhere," the bag dutifully repeated. Dor was getting better at this as he went. He had never before used his talent in quite this way; it was a new aspect.

"Nowhere?" The King pounced on the bag and shook it. "You're in the Ocna dungeon! The second biggest castle of the Kingdom! Plenty of company there! I'd be proud to be in that dungeon myself! Out, you ungrateful bag!" And he hurled it out the embrasure.

"What?" the doxy demanded. She had evidently heard only the last few words.

"Out, you ungrateful bag," the table repeated helpfully. "That's what he said."

"Well, I never!" the doxy said, flushing wrathfully.

"Don't tell *me* you never!" the feather quilt she had retained said. "I was right here when you—"

The doxy slapped the quilt, silencing it, then wrapped it about her and stalked out. "Help!" the quilt cried. "I'm being kidnapped by a monster!" Then it was beyond the magic aisle and said no more.

"Guards!" the King bellowed. "Search the premises! Report anything remarkable."

There was a scream from the hall, and the sound of someone being slapped. "He said premises, not mistresses!" the doxy's voice cried.

There was a guttural laugh. "But we do have something remarkable to report."

"He's seen it before!" she retorted. Her footfalls moved on away.

Guards charged into the room. Quickly they ascertained that no one except the King was in the tower. Then they spied the tip of the vine that had grown into the embrasure. They investigated it—while Dor and Irene scrambled down the wall. Grundy leaped from above them, dropping to the centaur's back. "Take off!" he cried.

Arnolde in turn launched himself from the platform, landing with heavy impact on the dark ground and galloping off. The platform was shoved violently by the back thrust of his hooves, so that the vines holding it in place were wrenched from the wall. Suddenly Irene was falling, her support gone, while Dor dangled tenuously from his vine, his grip slipping.

But Smash the Ogre was there below. He snatched Irene out of the air and whirled her around, absorbing the shock of her fall. Her skirt flew out and up—and now at last Dor saw her panties. They were green. Then Smash deposited her gently on the ground while Dor slid down as quickly as he could, weak with relief. "I'm glad you were there!" Dor gasped.

"Me glad centaur was still near," Smash said. "He out of range now."

Which meant that the ogre's magic strength was gone again. Irene had fallen in those few seconds that the rear extension of the aisle remained. Now Smash's nonrhyming showed that the Mundane environment had closed in.

"Someone's out there!" King Oary cried from the embrasure. "After him!" But the guards had no good light for the purpose, and seemed loath to pursue a magic enemy in the moonlight.

"You sword," Smash said, pressing it into Dor's hand. "You seeds," he said to Irene, giving her the bag he had rescued.

"Thanks oodles, Smash," she said. "Now let's get away from here."

But as they moved out, a small gate opened in the castle wall and troops poured forth bearing torches. "Oary must have caught on that it was our magic," Dor said as they scrambled away.

Soon they caught up to the centaur, who had stopped as soon as he realized what was happening. Dor felt no different as they re-entered the magic aisle, but Smash's panting alleviated; his strength had returned.

Quickly Dor summarized their situation. "We're together; we have our magic things, except for Arnolde's spells, and we know King Trent, Queen Iris, and King

Omen are alive in Castle Ocna. Oary's troops are on our trail. We had better hurry on to rescue the three, before the troops catch us. But we don't know the way."

"Every plant and rock must know the way to Ocna," Grundy said. "We can ask as we go along."

The guards were spreading out and combing through the forest. Whatever virtues King Oary lacked, he evidently compelled obedience when he really wanted it. Dor's party had to retreat before them. But there were two problems: this section of forest was small, so that they could not remain concealed long; and they were being herded the wrong way. For it turned out that Ocna was half a day's walk northwest of Onesti, while this forest was southeast. They were actually moving toward the village settlement, where the peasants who served the castle dwelt. That village would, in the course of centuries, expand into the town of Onesti, whose designation on the map had given them the hint where to find King Trent. They didn't want to interfere with that!

"We've got to get on a path," Irene said. "We'll never make it to Ocna tonight traveling cross-country. But the soldiers will be patrolling the paths."

"Maybe there's a magic seed for this," Grundy suggested.

"Maybe," Irene agreed. "Another tangler would do—except I don't have one. I do have a cherry seed—"

"The kind that grows cherry bombs? That would do it!"

"No," Arnolde said.

"What's the matter, horsetail?" the golem demanded nastily. "You'd rather get your rump riddled with arrows than throw a few cherries at the enemy?"

"Setting aside the ethical and aesthetic considerations—which process I find objectionable—there remain practical ones," the centaur said. "First, we don't want a pitched battle; we do want to elude these people, if possible, leaving them here in a fruitless search while we proceed unchallenged to Ocna. If we fight them, we shall be tied down indefinitely, until their superior numbers overwhelm us."

"There is that," Dor agreed. Centaurs did have fine minds.

"Second, we must keep moving if we are to reach Ocna

before dawn. A half-day's march for seasoned travelers by day, familiar with the route, will be twice that for us at night. A cherry tree can't travel; it must be rooted in soil. And since it is magic—"

"We'd have to stay with it," Irene finished. "It'd die the moment we left. Anything magic will be no good away from the magic aisle."

"However," the centaur said after a moment, "it might be possible to grow a plant that would distract them, even if it were dead. Especially if it were dead."

"Cherry bombs won't work," Grundy said. "They don't exist in Mundania. They wouldn't explode outside the aisle."

"Oh, I don't know," Irene said defensively. "Once they are mature and ready to detonate, it seems to me they should be able to explode anywhere. I'd be willing to try them, certainly."

"Possibly so," the centaur said. "However, I was thinking of resurrection fern, whose impact would extend beyond the demise of the plant itself."

"I do have some," Irene said. "But I don't see how it can stop soldiers."

"Primitives tend to be superstitious," the centaur explained. "Especially, I understand, Mundanes, who profess not to belive in ghosts."

"That's ridiculous!" Dor protested. "Only a fool would not believe in ghosts. Some of my best friends are—"

"I'm not certain all Mundanes are fools," Arnolde said in his cautious way. "But these particular ones may be. So if they encountered resurrection fern—"

"It could be quite something, for people who didn't know about it," Irene agreed.

"And surely these Mundanes don't," Arnolde said. "I admit it is a bit of a dastardly deed, but our situation is desperate."

"Dastardly deed," Dor said. "Are you sure that counterspell we used with the salve worked?"

The centaur smiled. "Certainly I'm sure! We do not *have* to do such a deed, but we certainly can if we choose to."

Irene dug out the seed. "I can grow it, but you'll have to coordinate it. The wrong suggestion can ruin it."

"These primitives are bound to have suffered lost relatives," the centaur said. "They will have repressed urgings. All we shall have to do is establish pseudo-identities."

"I never talked with resurrection fern," Grundy complained. "What's so special about it? What's this business about lost relatives?"

"Let's find a place on a road," Arnolde said. "We want to intercept the Mundanes, but have easy travel to Ocna. They will pursue us when they penetrate the deception."

"Right," Irene agreed. "I'll need time to get the fern established so it can include all of us."

"Include us all in *what?*" the golem demanded.

"Resurrection fern has the peculiar property of—" the centaur began.

"Near here!" Smash called, pointing. Ogres had excellent night vision.

Sure enough, they had found a path, a rut worn by the tread of peasants' feet and horses' hooves.

"Do you go to Ocna?" Dor asked the path.

"No. I merely show the way," it answered.

"Which way is it?"

"That way," the section of path to their west said. "But you'll have trouble traveling there tonight."

"Why?"

"Because there is something wrong with me. I feel numb, everywhere but here. Maybe there's been a bad storm that washed me out."

"Could the path be aware of itself beyond the region of magic?" Irene asked Dor.

"I'm not sure. I don't think so—but then, it does know it goes to Ocna, so maybe it does have some awareness. I'm not used to dealing with things that straddle magic and nonmagic; I don't know all the rules."

"I believe it is reasonably safe to assume the path is animate only within the aisle," Arnolde said. "In any event, this is probably as good a place for our purpose as any. The soldiers are surely using this path, and will circle around here. It is better to meet them in a manner of our choosing than to risk an accidental encounter. Let us begin our preparations."

"Right," Irene said. "Now the fern will grow in the

dark, but needs light to activate its magic. The soldiers will have torches, so it should be all right."

"I have the sunstone," Dor reminded her. "That can trigger the fern, if necessary. Or we could clear out some trees to let the moonlight in."

"Good enough," she agreed. She planted several seeds. "Grow."

"But what does it *do?*" Grundy asked plaintively.

"Well, it relates to the psychology of the ignorant spectator," Arnolde explained. "Anyone who comprehends its properties soon penetrates the illusion. That is why I feel it will be more effective against Mundanes than against citizens of Xanth. Thus we should be able to deceive them and nullify the pursuit without violence, a distinct advantage. All we have to do is respond appropriately to their overtures, keeping our own expectations out of it."

"What expectations?" the golem demanded, frustrated.

Dor took a hand. "You see, resurrection fern makes figures seem like—"

"Refrain!" Smash whispered thunderingly. "Mundane!" Ogres' hearing was also excellent.

They waited by the growing fern. In a moment three Onesti soldiers came into view, their torches flashing between the trees, casting monstrous shadows. They were peering to either side, alert for their quarry.

Then the three spied the five. The soldiers halted, staring, just within the magic aisle. "Grandfather!" one exclaimed, aghast, staring at Smash.

The ogre knew what to do. He roared and made a threatening gesture with one hamfist. The soldier dropped his torch and fled in terror.

One of the remaining soldiers was looking at Irene. "You live!" he gasped. "The fever spared you after all!"

Irene shook her head sadly. "No, friend. I died."

"But I *see* you!" the man cried, in an agony of doubtful hope. "I hear you! Now we can marry—"

"I am dead, love," she said with mournful firmness. "I return only to warn you not to support the usurper."

"But you never cared for politics," the soldier said, bewildered. "You did not even like my profession—"

"I still don't," Irene said. "But at least you worked for Good King Omen. Death has given me pause for thought.

Now you work for his betrayer. I will never respect you, even from the grave, if you work for the bad King who seeks to send Good King Omen to his grave."

"I'll renounce King Oary!" the soldier cried eagerly. "I don't like him anyway. I thought Good Omen dead!"

"He lives," Irene said. "He is in the dungeon at Castle Ocna."

"I'll tell everyone! Only return to me!"

"I can not return, love," she said. "I am resurrected only for this moment, only to tell you why I can not rest in peace. I am dead; King Omen lives. Go help the living." She moved back to hide behind the centaur, disappearing from the soldier's view.

"Beautiful," Arnolde whispered.

"I feel unclean," she muttered.

The third man focused on Grundy. "My baby son—returned from the Khazars!" he exclaimed. "I knew they could not hold you long!"

The golem had finally caught on to the nature of resurrection fern: it resurrected the memories of important figures in the viewers' lives. "Only my spirit escaped," he said. "I had to warn you. The Khazars are coming! They will besiege Onesti, slay the men, rape the women, and carry the children away into bondage, as they did me. Warn the King! Fetch all troops into the castle! Barricade the access roads! Don't let more families be ravaged. Don't let my sacrifice be in vain! Fight to the last—"

Dor nudged the golem with his foot. "Don't overdo it," he murmured. "Mundanes are ignorant; they aren't necessarily stupid."

"Let's move out," Irene whispered. "This should hold them for a while."

They moved out cautiously. The two soldiers remained by the fern, absorbed by their thoughts. Before rounding a curve in the path, Dor glanced back—and saw a giant, pretty spider, of the kind that ranged about rather than forming a web. The decorations on its body resembled a greenish face, and it had eight eyes of different sizes.

"Jumper!" he exclaimed—then stifled himself. Jumper had died of old age years ago. He had been Dor's closest friend, when the two had seemed to be the same size within the historical tapestry of Castle Roogna, but their worlds were different. The spider's descendants remained by the tapestry, and Dor could talk to them if he arranged for translation, but it wasn't the same. They seemed like interlopers, taking the place of his marvelous friend. Now he saw Jumper himself.

But of course it was only a resurrection, not the real friend. As Dor reminded himself of that, the image reduced to the standing soldier. How Dor wished it could have been genuine! This new separation, albeit from a phantom, was painfully poignant.

"So the fern resurrects precious memories," Grundy said as they got clear. "The person looking sees what is deepest-etched in his experience. He really should know better."

"Oh, what do you know about it?" Irene said irritably. "It's an awful thing to do to a person, even a Mundane."

"You looked back, too?" Dor asked.

"I saw my father. I know he isn't dead, but I saw him." She sounded choked. "What a torment it would have been if that were all I would ever see of him."

"We'll soon find him," Dor said encouragingly. This, too, he found he liked about her—her human feeling and loyalty to her father, who had always been a large figure in Dor's own life.

She flashed him a grateful smile in the moonlight. Dor understood her mood; his vision of his long-gone friend had wrenched his emotion. How much worse had it been for the Mundanes, who lacked knowledge of the mechanism? It was indeed a dastardly thing they had done; perhaps the violence of ogre and sword would have been gentler.

Soon, however, they heard the commotion of pursuit. The resurrection fern had perished, or at least had become inactive after the magic aisle left it; there would be no more visions there. The stories of the three affected soldiers would spread alarm, but there would also be many who still followed their orders to capture Dor's party.

They stepped from the path, hiding in the brush—and the troops rushed on past. A snatch of their dialogue flung out: ". . . Khazars coming . . ." It seemed the golem's information had been taken to heart!

"I think they've forgotten us," Irene said as they stepped back on the path. "The resurrections gave them other things to think about. Now they aren't even looking for us. So maybe we can travel to Ocna safely."

"It was a good move we made, strategically," Dor said. "A dirty one, perhaps, and I wouldn't want to do it again, but effective."

"First we must pass Castle Onesti," Arnolde reminded them.

They got past Onesti by following the directions the path gave. There was a detour around that castle, for peasants had fields to attend to, wood to fetch, and hunting to do well beyond the castle, and the immediate environs were forbidding.

This path angled down below the clifflike western face of the peak the castle stood on, wending its way curvaceously through pastures and forest and slope. Several parties of soldiers passed them, but were easily avoided. It seemed these people took the Khazars seriously!

Beyond the castle the way grew more difficult. This was truly mountainous country, and there was a high pass between the two redoubts. Dor and the others were not yet fully rested from their arduous climb to Onesti of a day or so ago; now the stiffness of muscles was aggravated. But the path assured them there was no better route. Perhaps that was its conceit—but they had no ready alternative. So they hauled themselves up and up, until near midnight they came to the highest pass. It was a narrow gap between jags.

It was guarded by a select detachment of soldiers. They could not conveniently circle around it, and knew the soldiers would not let them through unchallenged.

"What now?" Irene asked, too tired even to be properly irritable.

"Maybe I can distract them," Dor said. "If I succeed, the rest of you hurry through the pass."

They worked their way as close to the pass as they could without being discovered. Arnolde oriented himself so that the magic aisle was where they needed it. Then Dor concentrated, causing the objects to break into speech.

"Ready, Khazars?" an outcropping of rock cried.

"Ready!" came a chorused response from several loose rocks.

"Sneak up close before firing your arrows," the outcropping directed. "We want to get them all on the first volley."

"Save some for our boulder!" the upper face of the cleft called. "We have a perfect drop here!"

The Onesti soldiers, at first uneasy, abruptly vacated the cleft, glancing nervously up at the crags. It seemed impossible for anyone to have a boulder up there, but the voice had certainly been convincing. They charged the rocks, swords drawn. "Move out!" Dor cried.

Arnolde and Grundy charged for the pass. Smash and Irene hesitated. "Go on!" Dor snapped. "Get through before the magic ends!"

"But what about you?" Irene asked.

Dor concentrated. "Retreat, men!" the outcropping cried. "They're on to us!" There was the sound of scrambling from the rocks.

"I'm not going without you!" Irene said.

"I've got to keep them distracted until the rest of you safely clear the pass!" Dor cried, exasperated.

"You can't keep on after—"

Then the voices stopped. The magic aisle had passed.

"After Arnolde gets out of range," she finished lamely.

The soldiers, baffled by the disappearance of the enemy, were turning about. In a moment they would spy the two; the moonlight remained too bright for effective concealment in the open.

"I grew a pineapple while we waited," Irene said. "I hate to use it on people, even Mundanes, but they'll kill us if—"

"How can a magic pineapple operate outside the aisle?" he demanded, knowing this argument was foolish, but afraid if they moved that the soldiers would spy them.

She looked chagrined. "For once you're right! If cherry bombs are uncertain, so is this!"

Smash was standing in the cleft. "Run!" he cried.

But the soldiers were closing in. Dor knew they couldn't make it through in time. He drew his sword. Without its magic, it felt heavy and clumsy, but it was the best weapon he had. He would be overwhelmed, of course, but he would die fighting. It wasn't the end he would have chosen, had he a reasonable choice, but it was better than nothing. "Run to Smash," he said. "I'll block them off."

"You come, too!" she insisted. "I love you!"

"Now she tells me," he muttered, watching the soldiers close in.

Irene threw the pineapple at them. "Maybe it'll scare them," she said.

"It can't. They don't know what—"

The pineapple exploded, sending yellow juice everywhere. "It detonated!" Dor exclaimed, amazed.

"Come *on!*" Arnolde called, appearing behind the ogre. Suddenly it made sense; the centaur had turned about and come back when they hadn't followed. That had returned the magic to the vicinity, just in time.

They ran to the cleft. The Mundanes were pawing at their eyes, blinded by pineapple juice. There was no trouble.

"You were so busy trying to be heroes, you forgot common sense," Arnolde reproved them. "All you needed to do was follow me while the Mundanes' backs were turned. They would never have known of our passage."

"I never was strong on common sense," Dor admitted.

"That's for sure," Irene agreed. "That juice won't hold them forever. We'll have to move far and fast."

They did just that, their fatigue dissipated by the excitement. Now the path led downhill, facilitating progress somewhat. But it was treacherous in the darkness at this speed, for the mountain crags and trees shadowed it, and it curved and dropped without fair warning. Soon the soldiers were in pursuit.

But Dor used his talent, making the path call out warnings of hazards, so that they could proceed more rapidly than other strangers might. His midnight sunstone helped, too, casting just enough light to make pitfalls almost visible. But he knew they couldn't remain on the path long, because the soldiers were more familiar with it, and had their torches, and would surely catch up. They would have to pull off and hide—and that might not be enough, this time. There was too little room for concealment, and the soldiers would be too wary.

Then disaster loomed. "The bridge is out!" the path warned.

"What bridge?" Dor panted.

"The wooden bridge across the cut, dummy!"

"What happened to it?"

"The Onesti soldiers destroyed it when they heard the Khazars were coming."

So Dor's party had brought this mischief on itself! "Can we cross the cut some other way?"

"See for yourself. Here it is."

They halted hastily. There, shrouded by darkness and fog, was a gap in the mountain—a fissure four times the full reach of a man, extending from the clifflike face of the peak above down to the deep valley below, shrouded in nocturnal fog. Here the moonlight blazed down, as if eager to show the full extent of the hazard.

"A young, vigorous centaur could hurdle that," Arnolde said. "It is out of the question for me."

"If we had the rope—" Irene said. But of course Chet had that, wherever he was now.

Ascent of the peak seemed virtually impossible, and there was no telling what lay beneath the fog. The bridge had been the only practical crossing—and only fragments of that remained. This had become a formidable natural barrier—surely one reason the Khazars had been unable to conquer this tiny Kingdom. Any bridge the enemy built could readily be hacked out or fired.

But now the torches of the garrison of the upper pass were approaching. That was the other pincer of this trap. A few men could guard that pass, preventing retreat. The slope was steep here, offering little haven above or below the path. If the soldiers didn't get them, nature would.

"The salve," Irene said. "See the fog—we've got to use the salve!"

"But the curse—we've lost the counterspell!" Dor protested. "We'll have to do some dastardly deed!"

"Those soldiers will do some dastardly deed to *us* if we don't get away from here fast," she pointed out.

Dor looked at her, standing in the moonlight, wearing his jacket, her fine-formed legs braced against the mountain. He thought of the soldiers doing a dastardly deed to her, as they had started to do in the dungeon. "We'll use the salve," he decided.

They scrambled down the steep slope to reach the level of the mist. They had to cling to trees and saplings, lest they slide into the cleft involuntarily.

Dor felt in his pocket for the jar—and found the dime he had obtained from Ichabod in Modern Mundania. He had forgotten that; it must have slipped into another crevice of his pocket and been overlooked. It was of course of no use now. He fumbled farther and found the jar.

Quickly they applied the salve to their feet. The supply was getting low; this was just about the last time they would be able to use it. Then they stepped cautiously out onto the fog.

"Stay close to Arnolde," Dor warned. "And in line. Anyone who goes outside the magic aisle will fall through."

Now the soldiers reached the cut. They were furious when they discovered no victims there. But almost immediately they spied the fugitives. "Cnvm adknv!" one cried. "Sgdx'qd nm sgd bkntc." Then he did a double take.

For a moment the soldiers stared. "Sgdx can't do that!" one protested as the rear of the magic aisle swung around to intersect him.

But their leader found the answer. "They're sorcerers! Spies sent by the Khazars. Shoot them down!"

Numbly responsive to orders, the soldiers nocked arrows to their bowstrings. "Run!" Dor cried. "But stay with Arnolde!"

"This time I'll bring up the rear, just to be sure," the centaur said. "Lead the way, the rest of you."

It made sense. The main part of the magic aisle was ahead of the centaur, and this way Arnolde could angle his body to keep them all within it. Dor and Irene and Smash charged forward as the first volley of arrows came at them. Grundy rode the centaur; it was the best way to keep him out from underfoot. They crossed the fog-filled cut, coming to the dense forest at the far side.

"Aaahh!" Arnolde screamed.

Dor paused to look back. An arrow had struck the centaur in the rump. Arnolde was crippled, trying to move forward on three legs.

Smash was leading the way. He reached out to grab the branch of a tree that projected through the fog. He ripped that branch out of its trunk and hurled it uphill and across the cut toward the soldiers. His aim was good; the soldiers screamed and flung themselves flat as the heavy branch landed on them, and one almost fell into the chasm.

Then Smash charged back across the cloud. He ducked down, grabbed the centaur by one foreleg and one hindleg, and hefted him to shoulder height. "Oh, I say!" Arnolde exclaimed, amazed despite his pain.

But within the ambience of magic, there was no strength to match that of the ogre. Smash carried Arnolde to the slope and set him down carefully where the ground rose out of the fog. This place was sheltered from the view of the soldiers; there would be no more shooting.

"But the arrow," the centaur said bravely. "We must get it out!"

Smash grabbed the protruding shaft and yanked. Arnolde screamed again—but suddenly the arrow was out. It had not been deeply embedded, or the head would have broken off.

"Yes, that was the appropriate way to do it," the centaur said—and fainted.

Irene was already sprouting a seed. They had lost their healing elixir with Arnolde's bag of spells, but some plants had curative properties. She grew a balm plant and used its substance on the wound. "This won't cure it all the way," she said. "But it will deaden the pain and start the healing process. He should be able to walk."

Smash paced nervously. "Yet—Chet," he said. "Mundane, the pain—"

Dor caught on to the ogre's concern. "We don't know that a Mundane wound will always become infected the way Chet's did. That was probably Chet's bad luck. Also, he was bitten by a wyvern, so there might have been poison, while Arnolde was struck by an arrow. This is a different situation—I think." Still, the coincidence of a second centaur getting wounded bothered Dor. Could it be part of the salve's curse? The centaurs had had to use twice as much salve, since they had four feet, and perhaps that made them more susceptible to the curse.

Arnolde soon woke and agreed that the agony of the wound was much abated. That was a relief, for at least two reasons. Nevertheless, Dor decided to camp there for the remainder of the night. Their chance of approaching Castle Ocna secretly was gone anyway, and the recovery of their friend was more important. After all, the centaur's aisle of magic was essential to their welfare in Mundania.

Chapter 12. Midnight Sun

At midday, weary but hopeful, they reached Castle Ocna. This was less imposing than Castle Onesti, but still formidable. The outer wall was far too high for them to scale. "Me bash to trash," Smash offered confidently.

"No," Dor said. "That would alert the whole castle and bring a hundred arrows down on us." He glanced at Arnolde, who seemed to be doing all right; no infection was in evidence. But they wanted no more arrows! "We'll wait until night and operate quietly. They'll be expecting our attack, but won't know exactly what form it will take. If we can bring the magic aisle to cover King Trent, he'll be able to take it from there."

"But we don't know where in the castle he is," Irene protested anxiously.

"That's my job," Grundy said. "I'll sneak in and scout about and let you know by nightfall. Then we'll wrap this up without trouble."

It seemed like a good idea. The others settled themselves for a meal and a rest, while the golem insinuated his way into the castle. Arnolde, perhaps more greatly weakened by his injury than he showed, slept. Smash always conked out when he had nothing physical to do. Dor and Irene were awake and alone again.

It occurred to Dor that bringing the magic aisle to bear on King Trent might not necessarily solve the problem. King Trent could change the jailor to a slug—but the cell would still be locked. Queen Iris might make a griffin seem to appear—but that would not unlock the cells. More thinking needed to be done.

They lay on the slope, in the concealment of one of the huge ancestral oaks, and the world was deceptively peaceful. "Do you really think it will work?" Irene asked worriedly. "The closer I get, the more I fear something dreadful will happen."

Dor decided he couldn't afford to agree with her. "We have fought our way here," he said. "It can't go for nothing."

"We have had no omens of success—" She paused. "Or *have* we? Omen—King Omen—can he have anything to do with it?"

"Anything is possible with magic. And we have brought magic to this Kingdom."

She shook her head. "I swing back and forth, full of hope and doubt. You just keep going on, never suffering the pangs of uncertainty, and you do generally get there. We'll make a good match."

No uncertainty? He was made of uncertainty! But again, he didn't want to undermine what little confidence Irene was grasping for. "We have to succeed. Otherwise I would be King. You wouldn't want that."

She rolled over, fetching up next to him, shedding leaves and grass. She grabbed him by the ears and kissed him. "I'd settle for that, Dor."

He looked at her, startled. She was disheveled and lovely. She had always been the aggressor in their relationship, first in quarreling, more recently in romance. Did he really want it that way?

He grabbed her and pulled her back down to him, kissing her savagely. At first she was rigid with surprise; then she melted. She returned his kiss and his embrace, becoming something very special and exciting.

It would have been easy to go on from there. But a note of caution sounded in Dor's mind. In the course of assorted adventures he had come to appreciate the value of timing, and this was not the proper time for what offered. "First we rescue your father," he murmured in her ear.

That brought her up short. "Yes, of course. So nice of you to remind me."

Dor suspected he had misplayed it, but as usual, all he could do was bull on. "Now we can sleep, so as to be ready for tonight."

"Whatever you say," she agreed. But she did not release him. "Dear."

Dor considered, and realized he was comfortable as he was. A strand of Irene's green-tinted hair fell across his face, smelling pleasantly of girl. Her breathing was soft against him. He felt that he could not ask for a better mode of relaxation.

But she was waiting for something. Finally he decided what it was. "Dear," he said.

She nodded, and closed her eyes. Yes, he was learning! He lay still, and soon he slept.

"Now aren't we cozy!" Grundy remarked.

Dor and Irene woke with a joint start. "We were just sleeping together," she said.

"And you admit it!" the golem exclaimed.

"Well, we are engaged, you know. We can do what we like together."

Dor realized that she was teasing the golem, so he stayed out of it. What did it matter what other people thought? What passed between himself and the girl he loved was their own business.

"I'll have to tell your father," Grundy said, nettled.

Suddenly Dor had pause to reconsider. This was the daughter of the King!

"I'll tell him myself, you wad of string and clay!" Irene snapped. "Did you find him?"

"Maybe I shouldn't tell a bad girl like you."

"Maybe I should grow a large flytrap plant and feed you to it," Irene replied.

That fazed the golem. "I found them all. In three cells, the way the three of you were, one in each cell. Queen Iris, King Trent, and King Omen."

Irene sat up abruptly, disengaging from Dor. "Are they all right?"

Grundy frowned. "The men are. They have been through privation before. The Queen is not pleased with her situation."

"She wouldn't be," Irene agreed. "But are they all right physically? They haven't been starved, or anything?"

"Well, they were a bit close-mouthed about that," the golem said. "But the Queen seems to have lost weight. She was getting fat anyway, so that's all right, but I guess she hasn't been fed much. And I saw a crust of bread she left,

It was moldy. The flies are pretty thick in there, too; must be a lot of maggots around."

Irene got angry. "They have no right to treat royalty like that!"

"Something else I picked up," Grundy said. "The guard who feeds them—it seems he eats what he wants first, and gives them the leavings. Sometimes he spits on it, or rubs dirt in it, just to aggravate them. They have to eat the stuff anyway, or starve. Once he even urinated in their drinking water, right where they could see him, to be sure they knew what they were drinking. He doesn't speak, he just shows his contempt by his actions."

"I have heard of this technique," Arnolde said. "It is the process of degradation. If you can destroy a person's pride, you can do with him what you will. Pride is the backbone of the spirit. Probably King Oary is trying to get King Omen to sign a document of abdication, just in case there is ever any challenge to King Oary's legitimacy."

"Why is he keeping the others alive, then?" Dor asked, appalled by both the method and the rationale. Mundanes played politics in an ugly fashion.

"Well, we have seen how he operates. If he lets the three spend time together and become friends, then he can use the others as leverage against King Omen. Remember how you told me he was going to torture Irene to make you talk?"

"He's going to torture my parents?" Irene demanded, aghast.

"I dislike formulating this notion, but it is a prospect."

Irene was silent, smoldering. Dor decided, regretfully, to tackle the problem of freeing the prisoners. "I hoped King Trent could use his power to break out, but I'm not sure how transformation of people can unlock doors. If we can figure out a way—"

"Elementary," Arnolde said. "The King can transform the Queen to a mouse. She runs out through a crevice. Then he transforms her back, and she opens the cells from the outside. If there are guards, he can transform her to a deadly monster to dispatch them."

So simple! Why hadn't he, Dor, thought of that?

Irene shifted gears, in the manner of her sex, becoming instantly practical. "Who is in the cell closet to the wall?"

"The Queen." The golem frowned. "You know, I think she's the only one the magic aisle can reach. The wall's pretty thick in that region."

"So my father probably can't transform anyone," Irene said.

Trouble! Dor considered, trying to come up with an alternate suggestion. "The Queen does have powerful magic. It should be possible for her to free them by means of illusion. She can make them see the cells as empty, or containing dead prisoners, so that the guards open the gates. Then she can generate a monster to scare them away."

"There are problems," Arnolde said. "The aisle, as you know, is narrow. The illusion will not operate outside it. Since two cells are beyond—"

"The Queen's illusion will have very limited play," Dor concluded. "We had better warn her about that. She should be able to manage, if she has time to prepare."

"I'm on my way," Grundy said. "I don't know how this expedition would function without me!"

"There isn't one of us we can do without," Dor said. "We've already seen that. When we get separated, we're all in trouble."

As the night closed, they moved to the castle, trying to reach the spot nearest the Queen's cell as described by the golem. Again there was no moat, just a glacis, so that they had to mount a kind of stone hill leading up to the wall. Dor could appreciate how thick that wall might be, set on a base this massive.

Castle Ocna was alert, fearing the invasion of the Khazars; torches flickered in the turrets and along the walls. But Dor's party was not using the established paths and remained unobserved. People who lived in castles tended to be insulated from events outside, and to forget the potential importance of the exterior environment. It occurred to Dor that this also applied to the whole land of Xanth; few of its inhabitants knew anything about Mundania, or cared to learn. Trade between the realms, hitherto a matter of erratic chance, should be established, if only to facilitate a more cosmopolitan awareness. King Oary was evidently not much interested in trade, to the detriment of his Kingdom; he regarded the Xanth visitors as a threat to his throne. As indeed they were—since he was a usurper.

"Now we can't plan exactly how this will work," Dor said in a final review. "I hope the Queen will be able to make an illusion that will cause the guards to release her, and then she can free the others."

"She'd love to vamp a guard," Irene said. "She'll make herself look like the winsomest wench in all Mundania. Then when he comes close, she'll turn into a dragon and scare him to death. Serve him right."

Dor chuckled. "I think I know how that works."

She whirled on him in mock fury. "You haven't begun to see how it works!" But she couldn't hold her frown. She kissed him instead.

"The lady appears to have given fair warning," Arnolde remarked. "You won't see the dragon until you are securely married."

"He knows that," Irene said smugly. "But men never learn. Each one thinks he's different."

Arnolde set himself against the wall, changing his orientation by small degrees so that the aisle swung through the castle. "Grundy will have to report whether we intercept the Queen," he said. "I can not perceive the use of the aisle."

"If anything goes wrong," Irene said, "Smash will have to go into action, and I'll grow some plant to mess them up."

They waited. The centaur completed a sweep through the castle without event. He swept back, still accomplishing nothing. "I begin to fear we are, after all, beyond range," he said.

Smash put one cauliflower ear to the wall. "Go down for crown."

"Of course!" Dor agreed. "They are in the dungeon! Below ground level. Aim down."

With difficulty, Arnolde bent his forelegs, leaving his hindlegs extended, tilting his body down. He commenced another sweep. This was quite awkward for him, because of the position and his injury. Smash joined him, lifting him up and setting him down at a new angle, making the sweep easier.

"But if they are too far inside for the aisle to reach—" Irene murmured tensely.

"Grundy will let us know," Dor said, trying to prevent

her from becoming hysterically nervous. He knew this was the most trying time for her—this period when they would either make contact or fail. "We may catch Queen Iris, then sweep on past, and it will take a while for the golem to relay the news."

"That could be it," she agreed, moving into the circle of his arm. He turned to kiss her and found her lips eager to meet his own. Once she had declared her love, she made absolutely no secret of it. Dor realized that even if their mission failed, even if they perished here in Mundania, it was privately worth it for him in this sense. He had discovered love, and it was a universe whose reaches, pitfalls, and potential rewards were more vast than all of Mundania. He held the kiss for a long time.

"Is this how you behave when unchaperoned?" a woman's voice demanded sharply.

Dor and Irene broke with a start. There beside them stood the Queen. "Mother!" Irene cried, half in relief, half in chagrin.

"Shamefully embracing in public!" Queen Iris continued, frowning. She had always been the guardian of other people's morals. "This must come to the attention of—"

The Queen vanished. Arnolde, turning as well as he could to face her image, had thereby shifted the magic aisle away from Iris' cell, so that the Queen's magic was interrupted. She could no longer project her illusion-image.

"Beg pardon," the centaur said. He shifted back.

Queen Iris reappeared. Before she could speak again, Irene did so. "That's nothing, Mother. This afternoon Dor and I slept together."

"You disreputable girl!" Iris exclaimed, aghast.

Dor bit his tongue. He had never really liked Queen Iris and could hardly have thought of a better way to prick her bubble.

The centaur tried to reassure her. "Your Majesty, we all slept. It—"

"You, too?" Iris demanded, her gaze surveying them with an amazing chill. "And the ogre?"

"We're a very close group," Irene said. "I love them all."

This was going too far. "You misunderstand," Dor said. "We only—"

Irene tromped his toe, cutting him off. She wanted to

continue baiting her mother. But Queen Iris, no fool, had caught on. "They only saw up your skirt, of course. How many times have I cautioned you about that? You have absolutely no sense of—"

"We bring the King?" Smash inquired.

"The King!" Iris exclaimed. "By all means! You must march in and free us all."

"But the noise—" Dor protested. "If we alert the soldiers—"

"You forget my power," Queen Iris informed him. "I can give your party the illusion of absence. No one will hear you or see you, no matter what you do."

Such a simple solution! The Queen's illusion would be more than enough to free them all. "Break in the wall, Smash," Dor called. "We can rescue King Trent ourselves!"

With a grunt of glee, the ogre advanced on the wall. Then he disappeared. So did the centaur. Dor found himself embracing nothing. He could neither see nor feel Irene, and heard nothing either—but there was resistance where he knew her to be. Experimentally he shoved.

Something shoved him back. It was like the force of inertia when he swung around a corner at a run, a force with no seeming origin. Irene was there, all right! This spell differed from the one the centaur had used; it made the people within it undetectable to each other as well as to outsiders. He hoped that didn't lead to trouble.

A gap appeared in the wall. Chunks of stone fell out, silently. The ogre was at work.

Dor kept his arm around the nothingness beside him, and it moved with him. Curious about the extent of the illusion, he moved his hand. Portions of the nothingness were more resilient than others. Then he found himself stumbling; a less resilient portion had given him another shove. Then something helped steady him; the nothingness was evidently sorry. He wrapped his arms about it and drew it in close for a kiss, but it didn't feel right. He concluded he was kissing the back of her head. He grabbed a hank of nothingness and gave it a friendly tug.

Then Irene appeared, laughing. "Oh, am I going to get even for that!" Then she realized she could perceive him in the moonlight. She wrapped the jacket about her torso—it had fallen open during their invisible encounter—and drew him forward. "We're getting left be—" She vanished and silenced.

They had re-entered the aisle. Dor kept hold of her nothing-hand and followed the other nothings into the hole in the wall.

For a moment they all became visible. Arnolde was ahead, negotiating a pile of rubble; Smash had broken through to the lower level, but the path he made was hardly smooth. The centaur, realizing that the aisle had shifted away from the Queen, hastily corrected his orientation. They all vanished again.

Castle personnel appeared, gaping at the rubble, unable to fathom its cause. One stepped into the passage—and vanished. That created another stir. As yet the Mundanes did not seem to associate this oddity with an invasion.

The ogre's tunnel progressed apace. Soon enough it broke into the Queen's cell, then into King Trent's and finally King Omen's. At that point the parties became visible again. There was ambient light, courtesy of the Queen's illusion. Dor was uncertain at what point illusion became reality, since light was light however it was generated, but he had learned not to worry unduly about such distinctions.

Irene lurched forward and flung herself into King Trent's arms. "Oh, daddy!" she cried with tears of joy.

Now Dor experienced what he knew to be his most unreasonable surge of jealousy yet. After all, why should she not love her father? He glanced about—and saw Queen Iris watching her husband and daughter with what appeared to be identical emotion. She, too, was jealous—and unable to express it.

For the first time in his life, Dor felt complete sympathy with the Queen. This was one shame he shared with her.

The King set Irene down and looked about. Suddenly it was incumbent on Dor to make introductions and explanations. He hurried up. "Uh, we've come to rescue you, King Trent. This is Arnolde the Centaur—he's the one who made the magic aisle—that's his talent—and this is Smash the Ogre, and Irene—"

King Trent looked regal even in rags. "I believe I know that last," he said gravely.

"Uh, yes," Dor agreed, flustered, knowing he was really fouling it up. "I—uh—"

"Do you know what he did, father?" Irene asked King Trent, indicating Dor.

"I did not!" Dor exclaimed. Teasing the Queen was one thing; teasing the King was another.

"Anyway, Dor and I are—" Irene's voice broke off as she spied the third prisoner.

He was a stunningly handsome young man who radiated charisma, though he, too, was dressed in rags. "King Omen," King Trent said with his customary gravity. "My daughter Irene."

For the first time Dor saw Irene girlishly flustered. King Omen strode forward, picked up her limp hand, and brought it to his lips. "Ravishing," he murmured.

Irene tittered. Dor felt a new surge of jealousy. Obviously the girl, so ardent toward Dor a moment ago, was now smitten by the handsome Mundane King. She was, after all, fifteen years old; constancy was not her nature. Yet it hurt to be so suddenly forgotten.

Dor turned his eyes away—and met the gaze of the Queen. Again there was a flash of understanding.

"Now we have business to accomplish," King Trent said. "My friend King Omen must be restored to his throne. To make that secure, we must separate the loyal citizens of Onesti from the disloyal."

Dor forced his mind to focus on this problem. "How can anyone in this castle be loyal? They kept their King prisoner in the dungeon."

"By no means," King Omen said resonantly. "Few were aware of my presence. We were brought in manacled and hooded, and the only one who sees us is a mute eunuch who is absolutely loyal to Oary the Usurper. No doubt the castle personnel were told we were Khazar prisoners of war."

"So only the mute knew your identity?" Dor asked, remembering Grundy's description of the man's activities. But the golem sometimes exaggerated for effect. "At least he brought you food."

"Food!" the Queen cried. "That slop! Irene, grow us a pie tree! We haven't had a decent meal since this happened."

Irene wrenched her eyes off King Omen long enough to dig out and sprout a seed. Quickly the plant grew, leafing out in the illusion of daylight and developing big circular buds that burst into assorted fruit pies.

King Omen was amazed. "It's magic!" he exclaimed. "What an ability!"

Irene flushed, pleased. "It's my talent. Everyone in Xanth does magic."

"But I understood no magic would work here in the real world. How is it possible now?"

Evidently Dor's introduction of Arnolde had not been sufficient for one who was completely unused to magic. "That's the centaur's talent," he explained. "He's a full Magician. He brings magic with him in an aisle. In that aisle, everyone's talent works. That's why we were able to come here."

King Omen faced King Trent as they bit into their pies. "I apologize, sir, for my nagging doubt about your abilities. I have never believed in magic, despite the considerable lore of our superstitious peasants. Now I have seen the proof. Your lovely wife and lovely daughter have marvelous talents."

Irene flushed again, inordinately thrilled.

"King Omen is really a fine young man," Queen Iris remarked to no one in general.

Dor felt cold. The Queen's favor was not lightly gained; she had extremely strict and selfish notions of propriety, and these were focused largely on her daughter. Queen Iris had evidently concluded that King Omen was a suitable match for Irene. Of course the final opinion was King Trent's; if he decided on King Omen, Dor was lost. But King Trent had always supported Dor before.

Suddenly a huge fat man burst upon them. His eyes rounded with amazement as he spied the visitors in the dungeon and the pie tree. Then he drew his sword. He charged upon King Omen.

Irene screamed as the man passed near her father. Then the Mundane turned into a purple toad, his sword clattering to the floor. King Trent had transformed him.

"Who was that?" Dor asked, his startlement subsiding raggedly.

"The mute eunuch guard," King Omen said, picking up the fallen sword. "We bear him no love." He considered the toad speculatively. It was covered with green warts. "Yes, your magic is impressive! Will he remain that way?"

"Until I transform him again," King Trent said. "Or until he leaves the region of magic. Then, I believe, he will slowly revert to his normal state. But that process may take months and be uncomfortable and awkward, if someone does not take him for a monster and kill him before it is complete."

"A fitting punishment," King Omen said. "Let him begin it." He urged the toad on out of the magic aisle by pricking it with the point of the sword.

"Now let's consider prospects," King Trent said. "We have achieved a significant breakthrough here, regaining our magic. But very soon the usurper's picked private troops, comprised largely of Avar mercenaries, will lay siege to us here, and we have no magic that will stop a flight of arrows. We are certain that the general populace will rally gladly to King Omen, once they realize he is alive; but most of the people are outside the castles, and we are in danger of being wiped out before that realization prevails. We must plan our strategy carefully."

"I must advise you that the magic associated with me is in a fairly narrow aisle," Arnolde said. "It extends perhaps fifteen paces forward, and half that distance back, but only two to either side. Therefore the Queen's illusion will be limited to that ambience, and any person outside it will be immune."

"But a lot can be done within the aisle," Dor said. "When Irene and I lagged outside the aisle, we reappeared—but the rest of you remained invisible to us. We weren't immune to the illusion, just outside it. So the Queen can keep us all from the perception of the Mundanes. That's a considerable asset."

"True," the centaur agreed. "But now that they know about our magic, we can not prevent them from firing their arrows into this region in a saturation pattern that is bound to wipe us out. I have already had experience with this tactic." He rubbed his flank ruefully. The healing had continued nicely, but he still walked slightly stiffly.

"We must take cover, of course," King Trent agreed. "There is now plenty of rubble to shield us from arrows.

But we can not afford to remain confined here. The problem will be the elimination of the enemy forces."

"Maybe we can lure them in here and ambush them," King Omen suggested. "We now have two swords, and I am impressed with the ogre's strength."

"No good," Grundy said. He had reappeared during their feast on the pies and now took a small pie for himself. "The Avar commander is a tough, experienced son of a buzzard who knows you have magic. He is heating a cauldron of oil. Soon he'll pour it down the dungeon steps. Anyone hiding here, with or without magic, will be fried in oil."

"Impossible to fill this chamber with oil," Queen Iris said. "It would all leak out."

"But it will cover the whole floor first," Grundy said. "You'll all get hotfeet."

Dor looked down at his sandals nervously. He did not like the notion of splashing through a puddle of boiling oil.

Trent considered. "And an ambush waits outside the dungeon?"

"Sure thing," Grundy agreed. "You don't think they let you sit here and gorge on pies just because they like you, do you?"

"Turn us all into birds, father," Irene suggested. "We'll fly out before they know it."

"Two problems, daughter," King Trent said. "You will have trouble when you fly outside the magic aisle. I'm not sure how you will function, but probably poorly, as you won't be able to change back, yet the magic will be gone. Also, I can not transform myself."

"Oh—I forgot." She was chagrined, since the rescue of her father had been her whole purpose.

"We have to get you safely out of here, sir," Dor said. "The Land of Xanth needs you."

"I have every present intention of returning," King Trent said with a smile. "I am now merely pondering mechanisms. I can deal with the Avars readily enough, provided I can get close enough to them with my magic power intact. That means I shall have to remain with Magician Arnolde."

"And with me," Queen Iris said. "To keep you invisible. And the ogre, to open doors."

"And me," Irene said loyally.

"You I want safely out of the way," her father said.

There was a bubbling noise. "The oil!" Grundy cried. "We've got to move!"

Smash went into action. He started bashing out a new channel.

They became invisible. But Dor had a mental picture of where each person was; King Trent, Arnolde, and the Queen were near the ogre, ready to follow in his new tunnel and avoid the spilling oil. But Irene and the golem were on the far side of the chamber. The oil was already flowing between them and the ogre. They would be trapped—and as the centaur moved away, they would become visible and vulnerable, even if they avoided the oil.

Dor ran across to pick up a fragment of rubble. He tossed it into the flowing oil. He grabbed more chunks and tossed them, forming a dam. But it wasn't enough; he wasn't sure Irene could make it through.

Then the pieces started flying into place at double the rate he was throwing them. Someone else was helping. Dor could not tell who, or communicate directly; he simply continued tossing stones, damming off the hot oil. Soon it formed a reluctant pool. Dor filled in the crevices of the dam with sand, and the way was clear. The oil ploy had been abated, and Irene could cross to safety.

Now a troop of guards charged down the steps, swords drawn. They wore heavy boots, evidently to protect them from the oil they thought would be distracting their quarry. It should have been a neat double trap. They didn't know the quarry had departed.

Still, the Avars could use their bows to fire arrows up the new tunnel, doing much harm. Dor leaped across to guard the tunnel entrance, trusting that the others had by now safely passed through it. An invisible guardian could hold them off long enough, perhaps.

Then he saw his own arms. The magic aisle had left him vulnerable!

The soldiers spied him in the torchlight. They whirled to attack him.

Another sword flashed beside him. King Omen! *He* was the other person who had helped dam the hot oil!

No words were exchanged. They both knew what had to

be done; they had to guard this entrance from intrusion by the enemy until King Trent could handle his task.

The ogre's new passage was too narrow to allow them to fight effectively while standing inside, and the dungeon chamber was too broad; soldiers could stand against the far wall, out of sword range, and fire their arrows down the length of the tunnel. So Dor and Omen moved out into the chamber, standing back to back near the wilting pie tree, and dominated the entire chamber with their two swords. Dor hoped King Omen knew how to use his weapon.

The Avars, no cowards, came at them enthusiastically. They were of a wild Turk nomad tribe, according to Arnolde's secondhand information, dissatisfied with their more settled recent ways, and these mercenaries were the wildest of the bunch. Their swords were long, single-edged, and curved, made for vigorous slashing, in contrast with Dor's straight double-edged sword. Here in the somewhat confined region of the dungeon, the advantage lay with the defenders. Omen cut great arcs with his curved blade, keeping the ruffians at bay, and Dor stabbed and cut, severing an Avar's hand before the soldiers learned respect. Dor's sword was not magic now; he had to do it all himself. But he had been taught the rudiments of swordplay, and these now served him well.

Several bats shot out of the tunnel and flew over the heads of the Avars, who mostly ignored them. One bat, as if resentful of this neglect, hovered in the face of the Avar leader, who sliced at it with his sword. The bat gave up and angled out of the chamber.

But swordplay was tiring business, and Dor was not in shape for it. His arm soon felt leaden. Omen, too, was in a poor way, because of his long imprisonment. The Avars, aware of this, pressed in harder; they knew they would soon have the victory.

One charged Dor, blade swinging down irresistibly. Dor tried to step aside and counter, but slipped on blood or oil and lost his footing; the blade sliced into his left hip. Dor fell helplessly headlong. "Omen!" he cried. "Flee into the tunnel! I can no longer guard your back!"

"Xnt zqd gtqs!" Omen exclaimed, whirling.

The Avars, seeing their chance, charged. Omen's blade flashed in another circle, for the moment daunting them, while Dor fought off the pain of his wound and floundered for his lost sword. His questing fingers only encountered something mushy; a spoiled chocolate pie from the dead pie tree.

Two Avars stepped in, one countering King Omen while the other ducked low to slice at Omen's legs. Dor hefted the pie and smashed it into the Avar's face. It was a perfect shot; the man dropped to his knees, pawing at his mud-filled eyes, while the stink of rotten pie filled the chamber.

King Omen, granted this reprieve, dispatched the remaining Avar. But already another was charging, and Dor had no other pie within reach. Omen hurled his sword at the bold enemy, skewering him, then bent to take hold of Dor and haul him back to the tunnel.

"This is crazy!" Dor cried. Despite the peril of their situation, he noticed that Omen, too, had been wounded; a slash on his left shoulder was dripping bright blood, and it was mixing with the gore from Dor's own wound. "Save yourself!"

Then the Avars were closing for the final assault, knowing they faced two unarmed and injured men, taking time to aim their cuts. Even if Omen got them to the tunnel, he would be doomed. He had been a fool to try to save Dor—but Dor found himself rather liking the man.

Suddenly a dragon shot out of the tunnel, wings unfurling as it entered the dungeon chamber. It snorted fire and hovered in the air, raising gleaming talons, seeking prey. The Avars fell back, amazed and terrified. One made a desperate slash at the monster—and the sword passed right through the dragon's wing without resistance or damage.

Illusion, of course! The magic had returned, and now the Queen was fighting in her spectacular fashion. But the moment the Avars realized that the dragon had no substance—

It worked the opposite way. The Avar, discovering that he could not even touch the dragon, screamed and fled the chamber. He was far more afraid of a spiritual menace than of a physical one.

King Omen, too, stared at the dragon. "Where did that come from?" he demanded. "I don't believe in dragons!"

Dor smiled. "It's an illusion," he explained. They were

able to converse again, because of the ambience of magic. "Queen Iris is quite an artist in her fashion; she can generate completely credible images, with smell and sound and sometimes touch. No one in all the history of Xanth has ever been able to do it better."

The dragon spun to face them. "Why, thank you, Dor," it said, dissolving into a wash of color that drifted after the departing Avars.

Now Irene appeared, as the Avars scrambled to escape the dragon. "Oh, you're hurt!" she cried. Dor wasn't sure whether she was addressing him or Omen.

"King Omen saved my life," he said.

"You were the only one with sense enough to dam off the oil to save the girl," Omen replied. "Could I do less than help?"

"Thanks," Dor said, finding himself liking this bold young King more than ever. Rival he might be, but he was a good man.

They shook hands. Dor didn't know whether this was a Mundane custom, but King Trent had evidently explained Xanth ways. "Now our blood has mingled; we are blood brothers," Omen said gravely.

Irene and Iris were tearing up lengths of cloth from somewhere, fashioning bandages. Irene got to Omen first, leaving Dor for her mother. "I suspect I underestimated you, Dor," the Queen murmured as she worked efficiently on his wound, cleaning and bandaging it after applying some of the plant healing extract. "But then, I also underestimated your father."

"My father?" Dor asked, bewildered.

"That was a long time ago, before I met Trent," she said. "None of your business now. But he did have mettle in the crunch, and so do you."

Dor appreciated her compliment, but regretted that her modification of attitude had come too late. Irene had focused on King Omen. He tried to stop himself from glancing across to where Irene was working on the Mundane King, but could not help himself.

The Queen caught the glance. "You love her," she said. "You did not before, but you do now. That's nice."

Was she taunting him? "But you endorse King Omen," Dor said, his emotion warring within himself.

"No. Omen is a fine young man, but not right for Irene, nor she for him. I support your suit, Dor; I always did."

"But you said—"

She smiled sadly. "Never in her life did my daughter do what I wished her to. Sometimes subtlety is necessary."

Dor stared at her. He tried to speak, but the thoughts stumbled over themselves before reaching his tongue. Instead, he leaned forward and kissed her on the cheek.

"Let's get you on your feet," the Queen said, helping him up. Dor found that he could stand, though he felt dizzy; the wound was not as critical as it had seemed, and already was magically healing.

King Trent appeared. "You did good work, men. Thanks to your diversion, I was able to get close to the majority of the Avar soldiers. I turned them into bats."

So that was the origin of the bats Dor had seen! One bat had tried to warn the remaining Avars, without success.

"But the Avars are not the only enemies," King Omen said. "We need to weed out the other collaborators, lest assassins remain among us."

"Magic will help there," King Trent said. "Iris and Dor will see to it."

"We will?" Dor asked, surprised.

"Of course," the Queen said. "Can you walk?"

"I don't know," Dor said. His feelings about Irene's mother had just been severely shaken up, and it would take some time for them to settle into a new pattern. He stepped forward experimentally, and she gripped his arm and steadied him. He half wished it were Irene lending him support.

The Avars, however, had discovered that the dragon did not follow beyond the dungeon. They were not yet aware that their backup contingent had been eliminated. Now they charged back into the chamber.

"They're catching on to the illusion," Grundy said. "We'd better get out of here."

True enough. The Avars were stopping just outside the magic aisle and nocking arrows to strings. They had found the way to fight magic.

Smash went back into action. He ripped a boulder out of the foundation and hurled it at the Avars. His strength existed only within the aisle, but the boulder, once hurled, was just as effective beyond it as the arrows were within it. The troops dived out of the way.

The party moved back up the tunnel, Dor limping. Dragons flew ahead and behind, a ferocious honor guard.

In due course they reached the main hall of Castle Ocna. A number of the castle personnel were there, huddled nervously at one end. The Avars had spread out and used other routes, and now were ranged all around the hall. The castle staff were afraid of the Avars, and did not yet know King Omen lived. Thus the castle remained in King Oary's power despite King Omen's release.

"The ogre and I will guard King Omen," King Trent said. "Irene, grow a cherry tree; you and the golem will be in charge of defensive artillery. Magician Centaur, if you please, stand in the center of the hall and turn rapidly in place several times as soon as I give the signal. Iris and Dor, your powers reach farther than mine; you will rout out the lurking Avars."

"You see, I know how my husband's mind works," Queen Iris murmured. "He's a genius at tactics."

"But the Avars are beyond the magic aisle!" Dor protested. "And they know about your illusions. They're pretty smart, in their fashion. We can't fool them much longer."

"We don't need to," Iris said. "All you have to do is have any stones in the magic aisle call out the position of any lurking Avars. The rest of us will take it from there."

"Ready, Irene?" Trent inquired.

Irene's tree had grown rapidly, and now had a number of bright red cherries ripening. "Ready, father," she said grimly.

Dor was glad King Trent was a good tactician, for he, Dor, had only the haziest notion what was developing. When Arnolde turned, it might bring some Avars within the magic aisle, but most would remain outside. How could those others be nullified before they used their bows?

"Now it gets nervy," King Trent said. "Be ready, ogre. King Omen, it's your show."

King Omen mounted a dais in the center of the hall. He was pale from loss of blood, and carried his left arm awkwardly, but still radiated an aura of Kingliness. Irene picked several of the ripe cherries, giving some to Grundy, who stood beside a pile of them. Smash lifted a solid wooden post to his shoulder.

Arnolde, in response to Trent's signal, began turning himself about in place. Dor concentrated, willing the stones in the hall to cry out if any Avars were hiding near them. Queen Iris fashioned an illusion of extraordinary grandeur; the dais became a solid gold pedestal, and King Omen was clothed in splended royal robes, with a halo of light about his body.

"Hearken to me, minions of Castle Ocna and loyal citizens of the Kingdom of Onesti," the King declaimed, and his voice resonated throughout the chamber. "I am King Omen, your rightful monarch, betrayed and imprisoned by the usurper Oary. Now my friends from the magic Land of Xanth have freed me, and I call upon you to renounce Oary and resume your rightful homage to me."

"Mknn jko!" the Avar leader cried in his own language. "Ujqqv jko fqyp!"

An arrow flew toward King Omen. Smash batted it out of the air with his stake. "Oww!" the arrow complained. Dor's talent was operating too effectively. "I was only doing my duty."

As Arnolde turned, the magic aisle rotated, reaching to the farthest extent of the hall. "Here's an Avar!" a stone cried as the magic engaged it. "He shot that arrow!"

"Shut up, you invisible tattletale!" the Avar snapped, striking at what he assumed was there.

Now a winged dragon launched toward the Avar, belching forth fire. "You, too, you fake monster!" the man cried. He drew his sword and slashed at the dragon.

Irene threw a cherry. It struck the floor at the Avar's feet and exploded. The man was knocked back against the wall, stunned and soaked with red cherry juice.

Arnolde had hesitated, facing the action. Now he resumed his turning. Another stone cried out: "There's one behind me!" The dragon, flying in the moving aisle, sent out another column of flame, rich and red. This time Irene timed her throw to coincide, and the cherry bomb detonated as the dragon's apparent flame struck. That made the dragon seem real, Dor realized.

"All of you—shoot your cttqyu!" the Avar leader called as the magic aisle passed by him. "Vjg oqpuvgtu ctg lwuv knnwukqpu!" But his men hesitated, for two of their number had been stunned by something that was more than illusion. The cherry bombs did indeed detonate outside the ambience of magic; maybe there were, after all, such things in Mundania.

Arnolde continued to turn, and the stones continued to betray the Avars. The lofted cherries commanded respect among the Avars that King Omen did not. The ogre's bat prevented their arrows from scoring, and the Queen's illusions kept them confused. For the flying dragon became a giant armored man with a flashing sword, and the man became a pouncing sphinx, and the sphinx became a swarm of green wasps. Thunder sounded about the dais, the illusion of sound, punctuating King Omen's speech. Soon all the remaining Avars had been cowed or nullified.

"Now the enemy troops are gone," King Omen said, his size increased subtly by illusion. "Loyal citizens of the Kingdom of Onesti need have no fear. Come before me; renew your allegiance." Stars and streamers floated down around him.

Hesitantly, the castle personnel came forward. "They're afraid of the images," Grundy said.

The Queen nodded. Abruptly the monsters vanished, and the hall became a region of pastel lighting and gentle music—at least within the rotating aisle. Heartened, the people stepped up more boldly. "Is it really you, Your Majesty Good Omen?" an old retainer asked. "We thought you dead, and when the monsters came—"

"Hold!" a strident voice called from the archway nearest the castle's main entrance.

All turned. There stood King Oary, just within the aisle. Dor realized the man must have ridden to Castle Ocna by another route, avoiding the path with the bridge out. Oary had figured out where Dor's party was heading, had known it meant trouble, and hastened to deal with the situation before it got out of control. Oary had cunning and courage.

"There is the usurper!" King Omen cried. "Take him captive!"

But Oary was backed by another contingent of Avar mercenaries, brought with him from the other castle. The ordinary servitors could not readily approach him. He stood just at the fringe of the magic aisle, so that his words were translated; he had ascertained its limit. He could step out of it at any moment.

"Fools!" Oary cried, his voice resounding throughout the hall. "You are being deluded by illusion. Throng to me and destroy these alien intruders."

"Alien intruders!" King Omen cried, outraged. The stars exploded around him, and gloriously indignant music swelled in the background. "You, who drugged me and threw me into the dungeon and usurped my throne—you dare call me this?"

The people of the castle hesitated, looking from one King to another, uncertain where their loyalty should lie. Each King was imposing; Oary had taken time to garb himself in full regalia, his royal cloak, crown, and sword rendering his fat body elegant. King Omen was enhanced by Queen Iris' magic to similar splendor. It was obviously hard for the ordinary people to choose between them, on the basis of appearance.

"I call you nothing," Oary roared, with the sincerity of conviction that only a total scoundrel could generate. "You do not even exist. You died at the hands of Khazar assassins. You—"

The stars around Omen became blinding, and now they hissed, sputtered, and roared with the sound of the firmament being torn asunder. The noise drowned out Oary's words.

"Nay, let the villain speak," King Omen said. "It was ever our way to let each person present his case."

"He'll destroy you," Queen Iris warned. "I don't trust him. Don't give him a chance."

"It is Omen's choice," King Trent said gently.

With that, the illusion stopped. Not in the slightest way did Queen Iris ever oppose her will to King Trent's—at least in public. There was only the Mundane court, silent and drab, with its huddled servants facing the knot of Avars.

"You are no more than an illusion," Oary continued boldly, grasping his opportunity. "We have seen how the aliens can fashion monsters and voices from nothing; who doubts they can fashion the likeness of our revered former King?"

Queen Iris looked pained. "Master stroke!" she breathed. "I knew we shouldn't have let that cockatrice talk!"

Indeed, the castle personnel were swayed. They stared at King Omen as if trying to fathom the illusion. The very facility of Queen Iris' illusions now worked against King Omen. Who could tell reality from image?

"If King Omen somehow returned from the dead," King Oary continued, "I would be the first to welcome him home. But woe betide us all if we proffer loyalty to a false image!"

King Omen stood stunned by the very audacity of Oary's ploy. In their contest of words, the usurper had plainly scored a critical point.

"Destroy the impersonator!" Oary cried, seizing the moment. The people started toward King Omen.

Now King Omen found his voice. "How can you destroy an illusion?" he demanded. "If I am but a construct of air, I will laugh at your efforts."

The people paused, confused again. But once more Oary rushed into the gap. "Of course there's a man there! He merely *looks* like King Omen. He's an imposter, sent here to incite you to rebellion against your real King. Then the ogre can rule in my stead."

The people shuddered. They did not want to be ruled by an ogre.

"Imposter?" King Omen exclaimed. "Dor, lend me your sword!" For in the confusion Dor had recovered his sword, while King Omen had lost his.

"That will settle nothing," King Trent said. "The better swordsman is not necessarily the rightful King."

"Oh, yes, he is!" Omen cried. "Only the royalty of Onesti are trained to fine expertise with the sword. No peasant imposter could match Oary. But I am a better swordsman than the usurper, so can prove myself no imposter."

"Not so," Oary protested. "Well I know that is an enchanted sword your henchman has given you. No one can beat that, for it makes any duffer skilled."

The man had learned a lot in a hurry! It had never occurred to Dor that King Oary would be so agile in debate. Evidently his head was not filled with pudding.

Omen glanced at the sword, startled. "Dor did not evince

any particular skill with it," he said with unconscious disparagement of Dor's technique.

"It is nevertheless true," King Trent said. "Dor was outside the magic aisle when he used it."

"That's right," Dor agreed reluctantly. "In the aisle, with that sword, anyone could beat anyone. Also, the Queen's illusion could make King Trent look like you, King Omen—and he is probably a better swordsman than you are." Dor wondered just after he said it whether he had made that comparison because he smarted from Omen's disparagement of his own skill. Yet King Trent was the finest swordsman in Xanth, so his point was valid.

"You fools!" Queen Iris expostulated. "Victory in your grasp, and you squander it away on technicalities!"

"It's a matter of honesty," Dor said. "O N E S T I."

King Omen laughed, able to grasp the spelling pun within the centaur's range. "Yes, I understand. Well, I will fight Oary outside the magic aisle."

"Where your wound will weaken you, and you will have the disadvantage of using a straight sword when you are trained to a curved one," Queen Iris said. "If those aren't enough, the imposter's Avars will put an arrow in your back. Don't be even more of a fool than you need to be. Oary's trying to maneuver you into a position where his treachery can prevail. I tell you, I know the type."

Dor was silent. The Queen knew the type because she *was* the type. That made her a good adviser in a situation like this.

"But how can I prove my identity?" King Omen asked somewhat plaintively.

"Let the castle personnel come to you and touch you and talk with you," King Trent suggested. "Surely many of them know you well. They will be able to tell whether you are an imposter."

Oary tried to protest, but the suggestion made too much sense to the castle personnel. King Trent's ability to maneuver had foiled Oary's stratagems. Non-Avar guards appeared, reaching for their weapons, and they were more numerous than the Avars. It seemed that news of this confrontation had spread, and the true Onesti loyalists were converging.

Seeing himself losing position, Oary grudgingly agreed.

"I will join the line myself!" he declared. "After all, I should be the first to welcome King Omen back, should he actually return, since it is in his stead I hold the throne of Onesti."

Queen Iris scowled, but King Trent gestured her to silence. It was as if this were a game of moves and countermoves, with limiting rules. Oary was now going along with King Trent's move, and had to be accommodated until he made an open break. Dor noted the process; at such time as he himself had to be King for keeps, this might guide him.

"Come, King," King Trent said, taking Omen by the arm. "Let us all set aside our weapons and form a receiving line." Gently he took the magic sword and passed it over to Queen Iris, who set it carefully on the floor.

Oary had to divest himself of his own weapon, honoring this new move. His Avars grumbled but stayed back. Smash the Ogre moved nearer them, retaining his post. This encouraged them to keep the peace.

The line formed, the palace personnel coming eagerly forward to verify the person of King Omen. The first was an old man, slow to move but given the lead because of the respect of the others.

"Hello, Borywog!" King Omen said, grasping the man's frail arm. "Remember what a torment I was when a child, and you my tutor? Worse than my father was! You thought you'd never teach me to spell! Remember when I wrote the name of our Kingdom as HONESTY?"

"My Lord, my Lord!" the old man cried, falling to his knees. "Never did I tell that abomination to a soul! It has to be you, Your Majesty!"

The others proceeded through the line. King Omen knew them all. The case was becoming conclusive. King Trent stood behind him, smiling benignly.

Suddenly one of the men in the line drew a dagger and lunged at Omen. But before the treacherous strike scored, the man became a large brown rat, who scurried away, terrified. A palace cat bounded eagerly after it. "I promised to stand bodyguard," King Trent said mildly. "I have had a certain experience in such matters."

Then Oary was at the head of the line. "Why, it *is* Omen!" he exclaimed in seeming amazement. "Avars, sheathe your weapons; our proper King has returned from the dead. What a miracle!"

King Omen, expecting another act of treachery, stood open-mouthed. Again King Trent stepped in. "So nice to have your confirmation, King Oary. We always knew you had the best interests of the Kingdom of Onesti at heart. It is best to resolve these things with the appearance of amicability, if possible. Dor, why don't you conduct King Oary to a more private place and work out the details?"

Now Dor was amazed. He stood unspeaking. Grundy appeared, tapping Dor on the leg. "Take him into an anteroom," the golem whispered. "I'll get the others."

Dor composed himself. "Of course," he said with superficial equilibrium. "King Oary, shall we adjourn to an anteroom for a private discussion?"

"By all means," Oary said, the soul of amicability. He seemed to understand the rules of this game better than Dor did.

They walked sedately to the anteroom, while King Omen continued to greet old friends and the Avars fidgeted in their isolated mass. Without Oary to command them, the Avars were ineffective; they didn't even speak the local language.

Dor's thoughts were spinning. Why had Oary welcomed Omen, after trying to deny him and have him assassinated? Why did he pretend not to know where Omen had been? And why did King Trent, himself a victim of Oary's treachery and cruelty, go along with this? Why, finally, had King Trent turned the matter over to Dor, who was incompetent to understand the situation, let alone deal with it?

Irene, Smash, and Arnolde joined them in the anteroom. Oary seemed unperturbed. "Shall we speak plainly?" the Mundane inquired.

"Sure," Irene retorted, drawing her jacket close about her. "I think you stink!"

"Do you folk comprehend the situation?" Oary asked blithely.

"No," Dor said. "I don't know why King Trent didn't turn you into a worm and step on you."

"King Trent is an experienced monarch," Oary said. "He deals with realities, rather than emotions. He goes for

the most profitable combination, rather than simple vengeance. Here is reality: I have one troop of Avars here who
could certainly create trouble. I have more at the other castle. It would take a minor civil war to dislodge those mercenaries, whose captains are loyal to me—and that would
weaken the Kingdom of Onesti at a time when the Khazar
menace is growing. It would be much better to avoid that
nuisance and keep the Kingdom strong. Therefore King
Omen must seek accommodation with me—for the good of
Onesti."

"Why not just—" Irene started, but broke off.

"You are unable to say it," Oary said. "That is the symp-
tom of your weakness, which you will have to eliminate if
you hope to make as effective a Queen as your mother.
Why not just kill me and be done with it? Because your
kind lacks the gumption to do what is necessary."

"Yeah?" Grundy demanded. "Why didn't you kill King
Omen, then?"

Oary sighed. "I should have, I suppose. I really should
have. But I liked the young fool. No one's perfect."

"But you tried to have him killed just now," Dor said.

"A desperate measure," Oary said. "I can't say I'm
really sorry it failed. The move came too late; it should
have been done at the outset, so that Omen never had opportunity to give proof of his identity. Then the game
would have been mine. But that is the measure of my own
inadequacy. I didn't want to retain my crown enough."

Dor's emotions were mixing. He knew Oary to be an
unscrupulous rascal, but the man's candor and cleverness
and admission of civilized weakness made it hard to dislike
him totally. "And now we have to deal with you," Dor said.
"But I don't see how we can trust you."

"Of course you can't trust me!" Oary agreed. "Had
I the option, I would have you right back in the dungeon,
and your horse-man would be touring the Avar empire as a
circus freak."

"Now see here!" Arnolde said.

"If we can't kill him, and can't trust him, what can we
do with him?" Dor asked the others.

"Throw him in the same cell he threw King Omen,"
Irene said. "Have a sadistic mute eunuch feed him."

"Smash destroyed those cells," Grundy reminded her.

"Anyway, they aren't safe. One of his secret henchmen might let him out."

"But we've got to come up with a solution for King Omen!" Dor said. "I don't know why this was put in my hands, but—"

"Because you will one day be King of Xanth," Oary said. "You must learn to make the hard decisions, right or wrong. Had I had more experience before attaining power, I would have acted to avoid my present predicament. Had Omen had it, he would never have lost his throne. You have to learn by doing. Your King Trent is one competent individual; it was my misfortune to misjudge him, since I thought his talk about magic indicated a deranged mind. Usually only ignorant peasants really believe in sorcery. By the time you are King, you will know how to handle the office."

This made brutal sense. "I wish I *could* trust you," Dor said. "You'd make an excellent practical tutor in the realities of governing."

"*This* is your practical tutoring," Oary said.

"There are two customary solutions, historically," Arnolde said. "One is mutilation—the criminal is blinded or deprived of his extremities, so he can do no further harm—"

"No!" Dor said, and Irene agreed. "We are not barbarians."

"You are not professional either," Oary said. "Still you balk at expedient methods."

"The other is banishment," the centaur continued. "People of your species without magical talents used to be banished from Xanth, just as people of my species *with* such talents are banished. It is a fairly effective device."

"But he could gather an army and come back," Dor protested. "King Trent did, way back when he was banished—"

"But he did not conquer Xanth. The situation had changed, and he was invited back. Perhaps in twenty years the situation will be changed in Onesti, and Oary will be needed again. At any rate, there are precautions. A selective, restricted banishment should prevent betrayal while keeping him out of local mischief. It would be advisable not to call it banishment, of course. That would suggest there was something untoward about the transfer of power, instead of an amicable return of a temporarily lost King.

He could be assigned as envoy or ambassador to some strategic territory—"

"The Khazars!" Grundy cried.

"Hey, I don't want to go there!" Oary protested. "Those are rough people! It would take all my wit just to survive."

"Precisely," the centaur said. "Oary would be something of a circus freak in that society, tolerated but hardly taken seriously. It would be his difficult job to maintain liaison and improve relations with that empire, and of course to advise Onesti when any invasion was contemplated. If he did a good enough job for a long enough period, he might at length be pardoned and allowed to retire in Onesti. If not—"

"But the Khazars are bound to invade Onesti sooner or later," Oary said. "How could I prevent—"

"I seem to remember that at this period the Nordic Magyars were nominally part of the Khazar empire," Arnolde said. "They remained, however, a discrete culture. Oary might be sent to the Magyar court—"

"Where he would probably foment rebellion against the Khazars!" Dor said. "Just to keep the action away from Onesti. It would take constant cunning and vigilance—"

"What a dastardly deed!" Irene exclaimed gleefully.

Surprised, they all exchanged glances. "A dastardly deed . . ." Dor repeated.

"We were cursed to do it," Irene said. "Before the moon got full—and it's very nearly full now. Let's go tell the others how Ambassador Oary is going to the Magyars."

"Purely in the interest of serving the Kingdom I love so well, to promote the interests of my good friend and restored liege, King Omen," Oary said philosophically. "It could have been worse. I thought you'd flay me and turn me loose to beg naked in the village."

"Or feed you to the ogre," Grundy said. "But we're soft-headed, and you're too clever to waste."

They trooped out. "Oary has graciously consented to be your ambassador to the Magyar court of the Khazar empire," Dor told King Omen, who had finally completed the receiving line. "He wants only what is best for the Kingdom of Onesti."

"Excellent," King Omen said. He had evidently been

briefed in the interim. "And who will be Xanth's ambassador to Onesti?"

"Arnolde Centaur," King Trent said promptly. "We realize that his enforced absence from his home in Centaur Isle is a personal sacrifice for him, but it is evident we need a certain amount of magic here, and he is uniquely qualified. He can escort specially talented Xanth citizens, such as my daughter, when trade missions occur."

Arnolde nodded, and Dor saw how King Trent was facilitating things for the centaur, too. Arnolde had no future at Centaur Isle anyway; this put a different and far more positive face on it. Naturally Arnolde would not spend all his time here; he would have time to visit his friend Ichabod in the other aspect of Mundania, too. In fact, he would be able to do all the research he craved. There was indeed an art to governance, and King Trent was demonstrating it.

"Ah, your daughter," King Omen said. "You told me about her, during our long days of confinement, but I took it for the fond imaginings of a parent. Now I think it would be proper to seal the alliance of our two Kingdoms by a symbolic personal merger."

Dor's heart sank. King Omen certainly wasn't reticent! He moved boldly to obtain what he wanted—as a King should. Dor doubted that he himself would ever be that type of person. The irony was that he could not oppose King Omen in this; he liked the man and owed him his life, and Irene liked him, too, and was probably thrilled at the notion. The alliance did seem to make sense, politically and personally. If there were benefits to being in line for the Kingship, there were also liabilities; Dor had to give way to what was best. But he hated this.

King Trent turned to Irene. "How do you feel about it? You do understand the significance."

"Oh, I understand," Irene agreed, flushing becomingly. "It makes a lot of sense. And I'm flattered. But there are two or three little points. I'm young—"

"Time takes care of that," King Omen said. It was evident that her youth did not repel him, any more than the youthfulness of the doxy had repelled King Oary. "In fact, women age so quickly, here in Onesti, that it is best to catch them as young as possible, while they remain attractive."

Irene paused, as if tracking down an implication. In Xanth, women remained attractive a long time, with the aid of minor magic. "And I would have trouble adjusting to a life with no magic—" she continued after a moment.

"A Queen does not need magic!" King Omen said persuasively. "She has power. She has authority over the entire kitchen staff."

Irene paused again. "That much," she murmured. It was evident that men dominated the society of Onesti, while in Xanth the sexes were fairly even, except for the rule about who could be King.

Dor thought of living the rest of his life in Mundania, unable to utilize his own magic or participate in the magic of others. The notion appalled him. He doubted Irene could stand it long either.

"And I'm in love with another man," Irene finished.

"But the girl's love has nothing to do with it!" King Omen protested. "This is a matter of state." His eyes traveled along the length of her legs.

King Trent considered. "We conduct such matters differently in Xanth, but of course compromise is essential in international relations. If you really desire my daughter—"

"Father!" Irene said warningly.

"Now don't embarrass your father," Queen Iris said. Irene reacted with a rebellious frown that she quickly concealed. It was the old syndrome; if her mother pushed something, Irene did the opposite. Dor's secret ally had struck again. Bless the Queen!

King Trent's gaze passed across them all, finishing with the Queen, who made the slightest nod. "However," he continued, "I understand that in some societies there is a certain premium on the, shall we say, pristine state—"

"Virginity," Irene said clearly.

"But we never—" Dor started, just before she stomped on his toe."

King Omen had caught the motion. "Ah, I did not realize it was you she loved, blood brother! You came all the way here at great personal risk to help restore my throne; I can not—"

"Yet a liaison would certainly be appropriate," King Trent mused.

"Father!" Irene repeated sharply. Queen Iris smiled

somewhat smugly in her daughter's direction. It was strange, Dor reflected, how the very mannerisms that had annoyed him in the past now pleased him. Irene would never go with King Omen now.

"Yet there is that matter of pristinity," King Omen said. "A Queen must be above—"

"Do you by chance have a sister, King Omen?" King Trent inquired. Dor recognized the tone; Trent already knew the answer to his question. "Dor might—"

"*What?*" Irene screeched.

"No, no sister," Omen said, evidently disgruntled.

"Unfortunate. Perhaps, then, a symbolic gesture," King Trent said. "If Prince Dor, here, is taking something of value to King Omen, or perhaps has already compromised the value—"

"Yes," Irene said.

"Shame!" Queen Iris said, glaring at Dor with only the tiniest quirk of humor twitching at one lip.

"But—" Dor said, unwilling to confess falsely.

"Then some token of recompense might be in order," King Trent concluded. "We might call it a gift, to preserve appearance—"

"The midnight sunstone!" Dor exclaimed. After all, it was just about midnight now. Without waiting for King Trent to take the matter further, Dor drew it from his pocket. "King Omen, as a sincere token of amity between the Kingdom of Xanth and the Kingdom of Onesti and of my appreciation for the manner you saved my life, allow me to present you with this rarest of gems. Note that it shines in the presence of magic—but turns dull in the absence of magic. Thus you will always know when magic is near." He gave the gem to King Omen, who stepped out of the magic aisle, then back in, fascinated by the manner the gem faded and flashed again.

"Oh, yes," King Omen agreed. "I shall have this set in my crown, the most precious of all my treasures!"

But now Irene was angry. "I will not be bought for a gem!" she exclaimed.

"But—" Dor said helplessly, stepping toward her. Right when he thought things had fallen into place, they were falling out again.

"Stay away from me, you slaver!" she flared, retreating.

"I think I am well off," King Omen murmured, smiling.

Dor did not want to chase her. It was undignified and hardly suited to the occasion. Also, he could not move rapidly; his fresh wound inhibited him. Yet he was in a sense on stage; he could not let her walk out on him now.

Then he remembered the dime. He had a use for it after all! He clutched it out of his pocket and threw it at her moving feet.

Irene came to an abrupt stop, windmilling her arms and almost falling. "What—" she demanded.

Then Dor caught up to her and took her in his arms.

"The dime!" she expostulated. "You made me stop on a dime! That's cheating!"

Dor kissed her—and found an amazingly warm response.

But even amidst the kiss, he realized that Arnolde was facing in another direction. Irene had been outside the magic aisle when she stalled on the dime. "But—" he began, his knees feeling weak.

She bit lightly on his ear. "Did the Gorgon let go of Magician Humfrey?" she asked.

Dor laughed, somewhat nervously. "Never."

"Another dastardly deed performed in the light of the midnight sunstone," Grundy said. And Dor had to hold Irene delightfully tight to prevent her from kicking the golem.

About the Author

Piers Anthony is the name of a hopelessly Mundane character who has difficulty taking About-the-Author notes seriously. He was born in England, moved to Spain, had his sixth birthday aboard the ship that brought him and the former King Edward VIII of England to the New World, and took three years to get through first grade because he couldn't learn to read. Naturally he grew up to be a writer whose interest was in islands, peninsulas, Kings and illiteracy. His early problems in math still manifest in his tendency to crowd five or six novels into a trilogy. He now lives in the backwoods of Florida with his brown-eyed wife, blue-eyed daughters, and brown-eyed horses and dogs. The old railroad tracks that cut through the hill in sight of their house bear a suspicious resemblance to the Gap Chasm; the drooping live oaks with their Spanish Moss are reminiscent of tangle trees, and if the local sugar sand isn't very sweet, at least it is excellent for miring vehicles. The Land of Xanth is real for those who understand it. Those who don't believe in it are relegated to Mundania: it serves them right.

Piers Anthony lost count of his novels when they approached the number of his years of age. His first was written in 1956 and was never published. His second, *Chthon*, was published in 1967. Now he turns them out at the rate of about three a year. The first Xanth revelation, *A Spell for Chameleon*, won the August Derleth Fantasy Award for best novel of 1977. But the real success of Xanth is indicated by the fact that it has generated more fan mail than any other series by this author, from people ranging in age from nine to (censored). Xanth is spreading; a tangle tree was recently spotted in Colorado, and night mares have ranged even farther out.

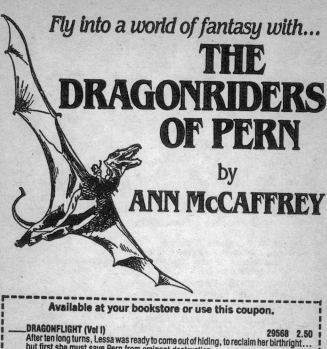